# HANNAH ALEXANDER

# Double Blind

Steeple
Hill®

Published by Steeple Hill Books™

STEEPLE HILL BOOKS

Steeple
Hill®

ISBN-13: 978-0-373-78573-5
ISBN-10:     0-373-78573-9

DOUBLE BLIND

## Acknowledgments

We are always grateful to our editor, Joan Marlow Golan, and her wonderful staff and colleagues, Krista Stroever, Emily Rodmell, Lee Quarfoot, Megan Lorius, Maureen Stead, Amy Jones and Diane Mosher, for untiring editorial support, marketing and encouragement.

Thanks to our agent, Karen Solem, for great direction and wisdom.

Thanks, again, to Mom, Lorene Cook, for going far beyond the high calling of motherhood to help us in every sort of situation imaginable, whether it be reading, editing, publicity, cooking or catsitting. We love you.

Thanks to Vera Overall, Mother, who always encourages us and shows her pride in her son.

Thanks to Barbara Warren of the Blue Mountain Editorial Service for spotting problems before they become a part of the book.

Thanks to Jerry and Mary Lou Baugher for their love and hospitality, whose experience serving in a Navajo school was a great benefit.

Our deepest debt is to our Lord, who allows us to keep working at playing.

# ☙ Chapter One ❧

Curved, white wolf fangs gleamed against the blackness of Sheila Metcalf's closed eyelids. She winced, eyes opening wide as a clipboard slipped from her fingers for the second time in less than an hour. It clattered onto the tile floor of the private patient room of Hideaway Hospital. As the sound reverberated into the hallway, her neck and shoulder muscles knotted with anxiety.

She glanced at the bed, where her patient, Mrs. Mann, remained asleep. At least the commotion had not disturbed her. Sheila only wished *she* didn't feel so disturbed this morning...so unsettled, with an old, haunting, long-suppressed nightmare threatening, more than once, to follow her into her waking hours.

"Hey, girl, what's up?" Jill Cooper, slender, dark haired and attractive, strode into the room at her usual brisk pace. She rescued the clipboard from the floor, glanced at it, then gave Sheila a look of concern. "Something wrong?"

"Sorry," Sheila said. "I'm fumble fingers this morning for some reason."

"Time for a break." Jill's voice was filled with the concern so evident in her gentle blue eyes. With her typical economy of movement, she set the clipboard on the nursing desk, then turned again to Sheila. "Why are you a fumble fingers?"

"I'm just distracted. I promise I'm not usually like this."

"Think I don't know that?" As nurse director of Hideaway Hospital, Jill had every right to question a substitute nurse's bumbling mistakes, but her concern was warm and personal.

Sheila tried to smile, and knew the result was more of a grimace. She and Jill had known each other since Sheila had fled here to Hideaway with her father twenty-four years ago. The older sister of one of Sheila's best friends in school, Jill understood what it was like to live with specters from the past.

Jill took a step closer. "So what's the distraction?" she asked softly. "Want to talk about it?"

Sheila thought about the shadows of memories that never quite materialized, questions that had returned to nag at her after all these years. The fangs. The terror.

"Relax," Jill said. "We don't eat nurses for breakfast."

Sheila forced a smile. The confessions could wait until later. "Dr. Jackson tells me differently."

Jill chuckled. "Call her Karah Lee, and don't listen to a thing she says. I picked on her a little when she first arrived, and she'll never let me live it down." Jill's blue eyes turned serious again. "What is it?"

"Just stuff. I'll get it figured out, don't worry."

"All the same, I think you need some downtime. A few minutes to regroup." Jill reached into the pocket of her scrub top and pulled out a stethoscope. "Besides, Preston Black is in the building." She said the words with one eyebrow raised, a half grin on her face. "He wants to talk to you."

Sheila ran the tip of her tongue along her teeth to keep herself from saying anything. Preston didn't understand the word *no*.

Jill held up her hands, correctly reading Sheila's expression, her blue eyes twinkling. "Don't blame me. I didn't tell him you were working today, he just saw your Jeep in the lot. He's placing a bid for the upcoming construction on the hospital, and he's come to talk to our new comptroller, Doris Batson." Jill winked. "You'd better keep your hands on that man. Doris is one of my best friends from high school, and I can tell you from personal experience that she's a hunk magnet. Half the men in the hospital are already drooling over her."

Sheila gave a pointed glance toward Mrs. Mann, in the bed across the room. Though the casual atmosphere here was a relief from the tension in her old job, Sheila hoped the staff didn't make a habit of discussing personal issues in front of the patients.

"Mrs. Mann isn't wearing her hearing aids," Jill assured Sheila. "I keep trying to get her to put them in her ears, but she refuses. Says they garble everybody's voices."

As Jill stepped to the patient's bed, she glanced over her shoulder at Sheila and jerked her head toward the door. "Out. Now. That's a direct order. Even if you don't talk to Preston, you need a break."

"Where is he?"

"Front office, chatting to Blaze Farmer last I saw him. I'll see you in the break room in a few minutes, and you can tell me all the juicy details, including this strange desire you suddenly seem to have to go to Arizona."

Sheila's eyes narrowed. "Preston can't keep his mouth shut."

"Actually, I think it was Blaze who blabbed for all to hear, and you know what good buds Preston and Blaze are. Was it supposed to be a secret?"

"Not necessarily, but it wasn't something I wanted to be discussed by everyone in the break room, either."

Jill pointed her thumb toward the hallway. "Out. We'll talk about it later. Try to grab a cruller before Karah Lee and Blaze eat them all."

Sheila sighed. Jill laughed. Mrs. Mann grunted, and Jill leaned over the bed, pressing her fingers to the elderly lady's wrist.

"How are you feeling this morning, my dear?" she shouted.

Mrs. Mann gave Jill a look of complete trust. Sheila recognized the expression, because she'd been the recipient of that kind of trust from her patients many times. She had to keep reminding herself she was a good nurse.

A good nurse. Yes. She was.

When Clark Memorial Hospital in Branson lost federal funding last month, there had been some major layoffs. Though Sheila had worked there for five years, she still lacked enough seniority to save her job.

Amazing how losing a position, even when it wasn't personal, certainly *felt* personal. With the population growth in this region of the state, the labor market was wide-open…except for registered nurses, it seemed. She'd discovered, when she went looking for a job, that there were a lot of mature nurses retiring to Branson to work part-time. She couldn't find a job. Now she was per diem at three regional hospitals, and until she could get back on her feet financially, she'd moved in with her father on the farm a mile from Hideaway.

Shaking her head, Sheila stepped quietly from Mrs. Mann's

room into the wide hallway. It would be easily expected for anyone to ask why on earth a thirty-four-year-old woman would find it necessary to get back on her feet. But it would be more pertinent to ask why she'd been so inept at choosing a husband in the first place. Ryan's irresponsible money management had been apparent to her long before his untimely death, but his romantic affairs had not. She couldn't forgive herself for having such blind trust in him through ten years of marriage.

In an effort to escape her bad memories, she'd recently reverted to her maiden name. The change wouldn't keep the creditors at bay, but she no longer wanted to be identified with the man who had betrayed her in so many ways.

Still, she'd rather be dealing with the difficulties caused by a faithless husband than the situation that had arisen this past weekend.

Every time Sheila closed her eyes, the imprint of black letters announcing the deaths of two of her childhood friends superimposed on her lids. The names had stirred only dim memories when she'd first read the letter two days ago but the impact of the deaths, the call of a time long past, had grown more and more disturbing during this morning's work.

The familiar sounds of distant laughter, coughing and the moan of an elderly lady with dementia down the hallway, all helped Sheila focus a little more on her current job, but not completely. The past kept intruding on her thoughts—especially the loss that she had never reconciled in her heart or in her life.

The resurfacing memories scraped raw her nerves and set her heart beating double-time. Those recent deaths were tragedy enough, but she'd been forced to admit to herself this morning that they had been only the catalyst for a deeper horror that had haunted her for twenty-four years.

She walked toward the early May sunlight streaking through the blinds at the end of the hallway. Why had the past suddenly become so relevant to her again after all this time?

Her father hadn't intended for her to see the obituary announcement for Tad and Wendy Hunt. Maybe Dad had the right idea. And maybe Sheila shouldn't have been such a snoop—even though the letter had suggested that she might be able to step into the breach created in the clinic by the sudden rash of deaths at the school. Tad and Wendy weren't the only ones who had died.

"Hey, stranger," came a warm, deep voice. Preston Black stepped from the stairwell into that May sunshine at the end of the hall. His tall frame and broad shoulders cast a great deal of shadow along the hallway…the way his presence cast conflicting shadows over her thoughts.

She watched him stroll toward her. "Preston, we agreed not to—"

"You were the one who decided not to see me. I didn't actually agree to anything, but I promise to back off. I won't argue with you—"

"This isn't about the fight." She resisted the urge to take a step backward as he came toward her. "Okay, maybe it is about the fight, in a way, because I do not appreciate your telling a teenager, who in turn has told the whole hospital, about the subject of our fight."

"Don't call Blaze Farmer a teenager within his hearing. I didn't tell him about any fight—and it wasn't a fight, it was a strong disagreement—"

"Which is a fight, and you must have told him, because Jill just mentioned it to me."

He grinned at her. "I didn't think it was a secret that you wanted to go to Arizona, and we never actually fought, Sheila. Fighting connotes yelling, and—"

Sheila couldn't prevent a smile of irony. "We're doing it again. We can't seem to say three words to each other without arguing."

"Discussing. Let's just call it that. Healthy discussion is good for the soul."

"We've *fought* since Saturday," she said, "which is *not* good for *my* soul." It was why she'd wanted some space from him, because she did not want him to influence her decision; he had too much effect on her already.

"Sorry," he said. "Could we just take a short walk? You're due a break, aren't you?"

"I'm supposed to save Karah Lee and Blaze from the crullers."

"I beat you to it." Preston patted his belly…his tight, muscled stomach. The phrase "washboard abs" must have been coined with him in mind. The man had the physique of someone who worked out every day, but he never stepped foot in a gym. He simply enjoyed working outdoors, hiking, building his own cabin. For the fun of it, no less; his prior career had been as a CPA and financial advisor. He'd been good at that, too.

Sheila couldn't help appreciating the results of those outdoor activities, both in his musculature, and in the beautiful log cabin in the woods on which he'd completed the finishing touches barely a month ago.

He tugged on her elbow with the entreating look that always weakened her defenses. "If I start another argument with you, I'll let you drive my Jeep all the way out to Arizona. In fact, I'll drive you, myself—*if* you go."

She led the way to the nearest exit, suppressing a smile that would betray her thoughts. Preston knew her well. How easy it would be to capitulate right now. "Just the Jeep, please."

He gave an exaggerated sigh.

In spite of her misgivings about the subject and their relationship at the moment, she laughed, needing to allow herself the pleasure of his company for a little while. It was his presence that had helped her banish the past back to where it belonged—both the recent history with her late husband, and the distant, more disturbing history that was the true origin of this sense of loss that seldom left her in peace.

He pushed the door open and stepped into sunshine, then escorted her out, his attention on her even more focused than usual. With Preston, she couldn't help herself; not only did he make her heart pound, he made her laugh, and made her think more deeply about her faith—because he asked so many questions that challenged her beliefs.

And yet, this time she had to draw the line. Shielding her eyes from the morning light, she looked up into Preston's calm, gray-blue eyes, framed by brown-black waves of hair that were due a cut.

She had to face the fact that if she left him here, there was Doris Batson, the new comptroller, a beautiful woman, as accomplished as he in the intricacies of finance, who might be waiting in the wings for him. But Preston would have to make his own decisions about that.

"I promise to miss you," she said, then saw the sudden flash of pain in those eyes.

His jaw muscles flexed as he obviously resisted the urge to restart the argument. "Then it's definite."

She nodded. She hadn't realized it until this moment, but she was going to Arizona. Twin Mesas' Christian boarding school desperately needed help, and she wanted to help it.

It was also the place that held the secrets of her past. Others might be able to put the past behind them and move forward, but she felt stranded there, still searching for her mother. And now there were more children at that school, who had lost not only a mother, but a father, as well.

She knew it was illogical to think that she might have something in common with those children after twenty-four years...but what if she did? What if she could help them in some way? She couldn't bear thinking about other children facing the same night terrors she was now facing.

She also could not endure the nightmares much longer. It was time to find some answers, once and for all, so she could move on with her life.

## ❧ Chapter Two ❧

Preston Black had never wanted so badly to break a promise. This was one argument he needed to have with Sheila, and she refused to argue. Why hadn't he been able to make her use that characteristic logic of hers?

She and her father had fled from Arizona for a good reason. They hadn't been back since, and now, when there suddenly seemed to be some unexplained epidemic of deaths at Sheila's former school, she had no business tempting fate—particularly since one of the deceased had worked in the very clinic where Sheila would be working if she returned.

Wasn't it enough that Sheila's mother, who'd also been a nurse, had died at that same school?

But he didn't say any of this. He even resisted reminding Sheila that she wasn't a missionary, and if she returned to the mission school for a few weeks, she would fall even further behind in paying off her late husband's debts. Besides, she wasn't trained in testing patients for the plague…or any of the other diseases that were endemic to that area of the country.

He gazed down into her feminine face with the gamine features, hazel eyes, firm chin. Like other important women in his life, she had a stout heart. His sister had combated threats from a stalker for years. His mother continued to battle a wicked mental illness with a brave spirit that had been bruised and wounded again and again, but never broken.

That was why Preston had recognized Sheila's courage when he'd seen it…and fallen in love with her. Now, sure, he admired her spirit, but she wasn't being reasonable about this. Why not?

He reached up to brush several strands of her thick, dark brown hair from her shoulder and to look at those lush lips, usually so quick to smile. At this moment, they seemed as weighted with sadness as her eyes.

"This is what you feel you have to do?" he asked.

Her eyes narrowed slightly. He could tell she was expecting him to continue to protest.

"I'm keeping my promise," he said. "I meant it. I have no right to tell you what you can and cannot do." They'd made no promises to each other about their relationship—or rather, at this point, nonrelationship.

He was learning to use that word more often. *Relationship.*

She gave a soft sigh and reached up to touch his chin, gently. "Yes, Preston, I feel I need to do this."

He braced himself. "Are you doing it to get away from me?"

The soft touch became a sharp tap on his shoulder, and the tender glance disappeared. "I told you the reasons. You don't seem to listen."

He raised his hands. "Okay, that's fine, I realize this isn't all about me, but I just don't think you've been completely forth-coming. If even part of the reason you're doing this is to escape me, there are many safer ways than hauling yourself alone across country to a desolate—"

She raised a hand. "Finish that sentence, and you'll be forking over your Jeep for my trip."

"Sorry." He forced a smile. "Of course, my Jeep has air-conditioning, and yours doesn't. You probably should use mine."

"Who needs air-conditioning? It's barely May."

"You know how hot it gets out there in the summer? May becomes June becomes July, and you don't know how long you'll be there."

She slid a folded sheet of paper from the pocket of her tiger-print scrubs, her slender hands graceful as she unfolded and scanned the letter.

Preston studied her face as she read. He knew the contents of the letter, of course. She'd shown it to him Saturday after she found it on her father's desk in his home office.

Buster Metcalf was an agricultural engineer who had moved with his family to the Navajo reservation in Arizona when Sheila was five. Five years later, when Sheila was ten, her mother had died suddenly, mysteriously. And that was all Preston had learned in the year he had known Sheila. He'd marveled at the lack of information he'd been able to get out of her about Evelyn Metcalf.

Sheila looked up and caught him watching her. "What?"

"Since we're not arguing now, I'm just asking a question for the sake of information, but I don't want you to bite my head off."

Her eyes narrowed once more.

"Honestly," he said, holding up his palms. "I'm just curious. How close were you to the victims of that fire?"

"Those victims have names. Tad and Wendy Hunt."

"Right. It's just that I've heard you speak in glowing terms about your other friends, but Tad and Wendy never came up." Though Sheila's father had kept in touch with some old friends from the reservation from time to time, Sheila hadn't seen anyone from her past in all these years, but now that the school's clinic suddenly needed emergency staffing, she was ready to drop everything and hurry to be of help?

Granted, selflessness was a part of her character, but Preston thought that she was also responsible to a fault. And right now, her own life was in such flux, she couldn't afford the time or the emotional energy.

"I had a lot of friends." She returned her attention to the letter.

Besides Tad and Wendy Hunt, who had returned to their alma mater to work and serve after college, someone else had died—Bob Jaffrey, the principal of the school. He had contracted and succumbed to an aggressive illness only days before the fire that took the other lives.

Sheila looked up at Preston again. "Canaan needs help in the worst way, not only because he had to step into Bob's shoes, but there's no one to take Wendy's place as office assistant. I'm free."

Preston had heard enough about Sheila's treasured memories of her friend Canaan York to provide enough misgivings about her trip back to the school all by themselves.

"I thought Canaan was the school's doctor," he said. "Why is he suddenly filling in as principal? Can't a teacher do it?"

"Good question. I'll ask when I get there."

Preston tamped down his frustration. "Have you even checked to see if they'll accept you?"

"I called and spoke with Johnny Jacobs yesterday evening."

Preston nearly groaned out loud. Johnny Jacobs was Canaan's grandfather, the man who owned the school.

Preston could no more help his strong distrust of this situation than he could help his growing madness over this bullheaded woman to whom he'd had the questionable pleasure of giving his heart.

How, for instance, did Johnny Jacobs found a religious school, pay the staff himself and not give in to the temptation to direct the curriculum with his personal biases about God? He did accept donations for the school, as well, but what kind of overseers kept track of his actions? He could be one of those control freaks with his own religion, a cultist.

How could Preston stand by and watch the woman he loved involve herself in this situation?

And yet, far from influencing her, he knew if he said any more about it now, he would only lose what little favor he had left with her.

He felt more than helpless. More than frustrated.

Sometimes she just didn't make sense to him.

"It was home for five years. I can't ignore it," she said, looking up at Preston.

"I don't understand why anyone would have sent your father the news, anyway. He isn't a doctor. After all these years—"

"But Mom was a nurse, and she worked with the kids. She knew everyone."

Preston stared at her, and he knew the puzzlement he felt was plain in his expression.

She closed her eyes, and he heard her soft intake of breath.

He waited, staring at the dark fan of her eyelashes against her pale skin, then felt his heart squeeze, falling head over heels once again as she opened her eyes and looked up at him.

"What?" he asked softly.

"I think Johnny Jacobs always suspected that my mother's death wasn't from natural causes."

"Did he ever say that?"

"He would never have said anything like that to me."

"But after all this time—"

"I can't tell for sure, but when I spoke with him, I got the impression that he suspects…I don't know…something odd about these recent deaths. Maybe I'm jumping to conclusions, but I had the impression that he feels Mom's death and these recent ones might be connected somehow."

Preston held his tongue between his teeth. Even more reason for her to *not* go out there!

She read his expression once again. "Yes, I know my mother's death was a long time—"

"And no reason to suspect that—"

"But if Johnny feels there's a connection—"

"You don't know that for a fact."

"Not in so many words."

What Preston thought was that Johnny Jacobs was eager to get Sheila out there because she was willing to be cheap labor. Had the man given any thought to her safety?

"There's no reason to think I might be in danger," she said.

"Except that Wendy Hunt worked in the clinic, your mother was the school nurse and now you're going out there to work in that same clinic."

As she gazed into his eyes, his heart contracted again. "You'll think this is crazy, I'm sure, but I can't help thinking this could be God's timing."

*Oh, great, she's pulling out the big guns. Who could argue with God?* Of course, Preston had promised not to argue. But it couldn't hurt to gather as many facts as possible about this endeavor. "So am I to understand that the reason Mr. Johnny Jacobs contacted your father about these deaths was to find out if you would go out there?"

She hesitated. "He knew I was in the medical profession now. Apparently he called Dad a week ago to see if I could go out. Dad just never told me."

Preston took the letter from her hands and looked at it. There was something in Sheila's past that she held back, even at those times when she seemed to share everything else in her heart. He'd realized Saturday that she was drawn to return to the place that had her history, where she'd been robbed of her mother....

Yes, she was going to help her old friends and she loved working with children, but she needed to solve a mystery in her life.

"Let me go with you," Preston said.

She gave him a look of infinite tenderness, then took the letter from him and shook her head. "Nope."

"You think I'll only be in the way."

She hesitated, then gave him a quick kiss on the cheek. "I know you will." She looked at her watch, then refolded the letter and slid it back into her pocket. "I'm on my way to Arizona."

As she turned to leave, he reached for her and caught her hand. In the year he'd known her, in all the time they'd spent together, he had never told her of the depth of his commitment to her. She didn't want to hear it. Even now, he could see the wariness in her eyes.

"I...want you to know that I... My Jeep is yours if you need it."

She smiled and squeezed his hand, then pulled away and went back into the hospital. The words he longed to say remained unspoken.

## ❧ *Chapter Three* ❧

On Friday the thirteenth of May, the blue canopy of Northern Arizona sky shimmered with the sun's rays, baking clumps of sage and meager stands of white-gold bunchgrass. The few clouds that nestled against rims of distant mesas did nothing to ease the punishing heat.

In spite of dry, hot air rushing in through window and vent, sweat gathered and dripped from every pore of Sheila Metcalf's body. Where had all this heat come from? It was only the middle of May.

She couldn't remember when she'd felt this alone or frightened. She missed Preston. She missed seeing the way his blue-gray eyes contrasted vividly against his tanned face. This separation would be good for both of them, but that knowledge didn't keep her from wanting to be with him.

Her father hadn't been too crazy about her return to this place, either. Together, he and Preston had mounted a united front for the first time since they'd met, but she hadn't allowed them enough time to complete their mission. After making the decision to come, she'd taken two days to handle her arrangements and pack, and then she was off before either man could catch his breath.

Now she stared at the shimmering mirage on the deserted blacktop road ahead of her, driving ever nearer to the setting of her childhood nightmares. What on earth had she done? She wasn't prone to making impetuous decisions. Why start now?

What kind of phantom was she chasing, alone, in the heart of the Navajo reservation? Dad had implied she might encounter the same danger her mother had met twenty-four years ago, but that brief comment had been all she'd been able to get out of him, the cranky old widower.

Actually, Dad wasn't old at all. He was fifty-eight. And he only got cranky when she tried to talk to him about Mom, or when anyone tried to set him up with a woman.

Though Sheila couldn't remember her mother very well— the shadowy images in her mind took clearer form only when she looked at old photographs—she never forgot the love that filled her whenever she thought of Mom. She always carried with her an impression of happiness at the memory of the small Navajo school she'd attended while Mom and Dad had worked in the area—Dad helping the farmers and shepherds, Mom treating children and families.

Mom had been Sheila's inspiration to pursue a medical career. Right now she couldn't help wondering if she'd have been better suited to Dad's specialty—agriculture.

All during this hot drive—why hadn't she taken Preston up on his offer to let her use his Jeep?—Sheila had journeyed as deeply into her memories as she could, frustrated by Dad's unwillingness to communicate with her about Mom. With every mile she drew closer to the school, the tension in her body was increasing, the images from the nightmare arising more frequently, and more horribly.

At the school, Sheila would be conducting the children's year-end physicals, drawing blood, as well as operating the clinic lab, keeping a close watch over the students who boarded at the school. When the term ended, she would be testing families coming to collect their children for the summer break. In a mission school such as Twin Mesas, families were encouraged to take advantage of the medical care. Sheila would truly be following in Evelyn Metcalf's footsteps.

Johnny Jacobs and his grandson, Canaan York, remained concerned about the cause of the former principal's death, she knew. It was a natural concern, of course, considering the responsibility on their shoulders not only for the health and safety of the children, but for all the families of the student body. According to Johnny, Bob Jaffrey's family had refused to allow an autopsy.

Sheila squinted into the sun's glare as she rounded a curve, and, for perhaps the tenth time today, questioned her decision. But after two long, painful years, dealing with the loss of her husband, and his betrayals, she felt she was at least finally making an effort to sort some sense out of the first part of her life—even if it meant returning to the scene of her childhood terrors to find answers to some difficult questions.

A movement far ahead on the right side of the road drew her gaze and broke her concentration. Whatever it was disappeared in the white glare of the sun. She fidgeted in her seat, stretching taut muscles, willing away the anxiety that had persisted throughout this trip. It was a frequent condition lately, something she couldn't blame on the letter from the school, or even on her turbulent attraction to Preston.

Her digestion had started acting up about a week after Ryan's death and the discovery of his unfaithfulness. Within three months, she'd lost so much weight she had to punch extra holes in her belt to hold up her jeans—a need she would have rejoiced about at any other time of her life.

Many mornings she'd awakened with a stiff neck and a headache from troubling dreams she couldn't remember—at least not until the past few days.

The shock of Ryan's death, and the gradual discovery of his affairs during their marriage had chipped away at her self-confidence and her faith in life. For the first year of widowhood, she'd often battled against a wavering faith in God.

Why her? After losing her mother at such a young age, why had she been forced to endure yet another tragic loss?

Dad had instilled strong Christian convictions within her. Sometimes she even questioned whether that set of standards was at the root of her troubles. Although Twin Mesas held many good memories for her, it was also where all her worst memories had been made—and it was a Christian school, where strict Christian values were taught and upheld.

Though Sheila had never renounced her faith entirely, she had rebelled against many of its strictures—most notably the one about believers marrying within their faith.

And look where it had landed her. Never again.

What hurt the most was that she had been the last to know about Ryan's affairs. His final fling had been with the woman who was killed in the auto accident with him, Theresa Donohue, the fourth-grade math teacher whose classroom had been just down the hall from Ryan's. But not one of Sheila's friends had told her, though she'd discovered later that several of them had been aware of Ryan's extramarital activities.

The movement on the desert, closer this time but still several hundred feet ahead, caught Sheila's attention once again. The sun's glare continued to blur the figure, but when she looked away she could see it dimly in her peripheral vision, the same way her nightmares caught her sometimes when she woke up in the mornings. The figure was too small to be a horse. A sheep, perhaps? Or a large dog?

She kept her attention on the road and allowed the approaching animal to develop along the side of her vision. It drew nearer, and she recognized the shape. A German shepherd.

Or a wolf.

She flexed her damp hands, wiping first one then the other on her jeans, blinking several times. It could have been anything but canine, and she'd be okay. But she'd rather see a nest of rattlesnakes in the middle of the road than the shape of a dog.

Suddenly, the animal disappeared, and a cloud of dust rose where it had been. She glanced that way, but saw nothing. Strange.

The steering wheel jerked in her hand. The right front tire of the Jeep sank into the soft shoulder of the road, and Sheila realized she'd allowed her focus to drift too far. She pulled the steering wheel to the left. A loud *pop-thunk* startled her.

She caught her breath, fighting the wheel, but the deep sand would not relinquish its hold. The Jeep coasted a hundred feet down the road and then came to a stop.

She'd blown a tire.

"Great driving, Metcalf," she muttered to herself. "Now look what you've done."

Glancing again across the broad slope of the desert horizon, she found herself wishing that a blown tire was her only problem.

Canaan York slowed his silver-blue Plymouth Voyager to ease the impact of a deep pothole that stretched across the dirt road. He scanned the broad plain of desert surrounding the solitary mountain of White Cone. Tanya Swift's family lived about two hundred yards ahead. Their small frame home, painted clover-green with dark spruce shutters, was a mansion compared to the other houses in this section of the Navajo reservation.

When Canaan reached the house, he stopped, frowning. Maybe the little runaway hadn't come back home.

A cloud of trailing dust rolled past the van and drifted in through the open windows, depositing a layer of grit over everything. Canaan blinked and tugged down on the bill of his baseball cap.

He glanced in the rearview mirror to make sure no dust streaked his face. He knew that, aside from the light tone of his skin, his long, somber face and dark brown hair and eyes identified him as Native American. Navajo. The People. But he was also well aware that the white half of his heritage continued to instill distrust in a few Navajo.

Unfortunately, Tanya's family belonged to that few, depending on the circumstances. And now this had to happen. He could only hope Tom and Linda Swift had already left for their thrice-yearly tour of the Southwest to sell their crafts. If they were here, he would most likely get an earful on his inability to control the students at the school…one lecture among many he'd received from several sources since stepping into the breach two weeks ago and inheriting a job for which he'd never asked—nor trained.

He wondered, as he'd often done lately, why his grandfather had been so adamant that no one else at the school could do the job.

A movement caught his attention from a window beside the kitchen door. He studied the low-slung house for a moment. With an intuition developed over years of working with people, he knew Tanya was there. The empty driveway told him she was alone.

He climbed from the van and walked toward the house.

Twelve-year-old Tanya opened the door before he had a chance to knock. Her large, slanted, exotic eyes were filled with defiant apprehension.

"Hi, Canaan." Her gaze darted past him. "You alone?"

He nodded. She reminded him of a half-grown lamb, inquisitive and always landing herself into trouble.

She relaxed visibly and stepped aside. "I know what you're thinking, and I know what you're going to say."

He ducked slightly at the threshold, taking slow steps, allowing his eyes to adjust to the dimness of the unlit house.

"You've learned the art of mind reading on your long walk home?" he asked.

"You know I didn't—"

"Walk all that way?" In the gloom, Canaan found a yellow-and-red-patterned kitchen chair and sank into it. "How often do I have to talk to you about hitchhiking?"

Tanya took two mincing steps toward him, the delicate lines of her young face sliding into a grin of mischief. "Who said I hitchhiked? Maybe I turned into *Yenaldlooshi* and raced the wind home."

Canaan studied her expression to see if she was teasing. She wasn't. He willed away the chill that slid over his skin. For a year, he had battled this superstition at the school, but it had persisted, even grown, the way a piñon sapling grew in the heat of the Arizona sun during a year of good rain. The children had recently begun to blame Navajo spirit entities for everything from unfinished homework to illness to lost track races.

He would have another talk with Betsy Two Horses. Giving her permission to teach a couple of informal classes on the ancient Navajo customs did not include filling the kids' heads with terrifying myths.

"Maybe you raced like the wind to escape *Yenaldlooshi*," he suggested to Tanya, and continued to watch her expression carefully.

She pivoted away, but not before he saw the fear in her eyes.

He sighed. "Tanya, who tells you there is a skinwalker at the school?"

She shrugged, refusing to look at him, which revealed the extent of her fear and clued him to the reaction she expected from him. She wanted him to deny the possibility of any kind of evil beings.

If Wendy Hunt were still alive, she would've been the one to come and get Tanya. She would've reassured the girl that there were no evil animal beings, only evil people. Canaan sure missed Wendy's influence right now. Wendy also would have had an additional advantage as the mother of Tanya's friend April.

Or rather, Tanya's former friend.

Canaan couldn't give any reassurances to Tanya. "Why would this skinwalker still be at the school and not here? Wouldn't he have followed you home, if he's after you?"

"He doesn't know the way." She was still serious; no teasing here. "I left after sunrise this morning, so he couldn't follow me." She believed what she was saying.

"But he can follow your tracks tonight, and your parents are gone," Canaan reminded her. "What if he knows you, and knows where you live?"

Tanya stepped to the long window that overlooked a cactus-and-rock garden. With a stiffened spine, she stared out across the plain, her chin raised defiantly.

"Come back with me now, Tanya, and you'll be safer."

"You can't protect me from everything."

"I didn't say I could, but do you really want to stay alone here?"

Her chin lowered a fraction. A tremor shook her. "I don't want to stay at that school. He's there, Canaan."

"Who, exactly, is he?"

Tanya jerked around, dark eyes wide.

"Have you forgotten that my great-grandfather was a *hataalii*, a medicine man?" Canaan asked.

She shook her head. "I haven't forgotten. That's why I trust you."

"I know of the spirits we have always feared," he said. "The only way to fight this evil is with a more powerful spirit. You're safer from the skinwalker at the school than you are here."

Tanya's eyes narrowed in disbelief.

"This skinwalker you fear," he said slowly, "what animal form does he take?"

Tanya stared at him and did not answer.

He hazarded a guess, hoping he was wrong. "The wolf?"

A quick intake of breath.

"I know about your fear." The wolf was one of the most terrifying characters in Navajo lore, a destroyer. Canaan felt another chill of foreboding. "My Christian grandfather taught me special prayers to keep the Navajo werewolf away when I was afraid. He taught me when I was very young, and I still remember."

Some of the tension eased from Tanya's face. "You mean Johnny Jacobs?"

Canaan nodded.

"How much do you remember of these prayers?" she asked.

"All of them, but it isn't the words alone that protect us. It's where we keep our hearts and minds."

Tanya hesitated. "What…what about that woman?"

"What woman?"

"The one who's coming. The *biligaana* who's going to be there today. The white doctor."

"You mean Sheila Metcalf. She has nothing to do with any skinwalker, and she isn't a doctor, she's a nurse."

The girl pressed her lips together, obviously refusing to hear his words.

"Sheila lived here with us for five years." His voice was sharper than he intended. "She and I grew up together. I knew her."

Tanya searched his expression. "You…you knew her?"

"Yes. She was a good friend. She was also a good friend to the Hunts."

"She's white. Look what happened to Mr. and Mrs. Hunt."

"I'm half white, my grandfather, the school's owner, is not Navajo, but that hasn't stopped your father from sending you to our school." Tanya's father was a selective bigot, but his bigotry would overtake his daughter, too, if Canaan allowed it. Sheila's arrival might be good for the children, if they would respond sensibly.

He stepped toward the door. "You coming with me?"

Tanya's jaw slackened. "You're leaving? Now?"

"I have work to do at the school."

Tanya paused, then nodded her head. "Okay. I'll come. But you teach me that prayer before it gets dark tonight. Okay?"

Canaan bowed mockingly. "Yes, boss."

## ❦ Chapter Four ❦

Sheila tightened the final lug nut on the wheel, tested to make sure all was secure, then released the jack, glad she hadn't taken Preston up on his offer of his Jeep. With her own vehicle, she knew where everything was and had been able to change the tire in ten minutes.

After heaving the equipment into the back, she cast a wary glance across the desert for at least the twentieth time. All that moved was the undulating air above the ground, dancing in the unseasonably hot weather. A green line of cottonwood trees to the south told her there was a stream of water nearby. To the west, the plain seemed to stretch all the way to the foot of the towering Twin Mesas, at least two miles away.

She glanced back down the road and saw a sizable boulder a couple hundred feet away that she must have struck with the tire when she allowed the vehicle to wander so far off the road.

"Dumb, dumb," she muttered to herself.

It wasn't until she was again behind the wheel, pulling onto the road, that she realized her heart had been racing, her hands sweating, and her breath doing double time all the while she was outside the Jeep.

She drove barely a half mile, checking the rearview mirror several times, when she saw the sign for Twin Mesas School and turned off Route 77 onto a gravel road.

Piñon and juniper trees bordered each side of the road for a mile leading to the school. The campus was set in the middle of what appeared to be a flat plain, but she knew that hidden hollows and rocky arroyos mottled the topography.

The trees along the road cast little shade. She'd forgotten how sparse shade could be out here. Everything looked hot and dusty.

As she approached, Sheila's gaze darted back and forth across the road, searching for another phantom, even as she scolded herself for allowing her imagination to run wild. No more specters materialized, of course. By the time she reached the school building, she also reached the conclusion that the heat had affected her. An overactive imagination didn't help, nor did the headache that pressed along the back of her skull.

She loosened her death grip on the steering wheel and studied the place. Simple, large adobe buildings with rounded corners formed a courtyard around a playground partially shaded by piñon trees. A small garden of rocks and petrified wood ringed the first building, a pattern that repeated all through the courtyard. It would have looked peaceful to her, if not for the apprehension that she couldn't shake.

Sheila didn't recognize this place.

During her last phone call with Johnny Jacobs, he had mentioned that most of the buildings were new. He'd also asked her if she was sure she wanted to come.

She would bet her Jeep that Dad had called Johnny and tried to get him to talk her out of coming. Johnny hadn't admitted to it when she'd asked him, but she'd heard hesitation in his voice.

Though Johnny lived in Tucson now, he'd always kept a close watch on all his holdings, and was particularly concerned about Twin Mesas, so much so that a year ago he'd sent his grandson, Dr. Canaan York, to keep a watchful medical eye on the children and their families. And now Canaan was interim principal. Why couldn't Johnny have come to help out for the remainder of the school year? He had a background in education, whereas Canaan did not.

Canaan. Gentle, always laughing, smaller than the other boys his age when he was growing up. He'd been called pipsqueak, although Sheila had never called him that, of course. She had known how deeply that taunt had wounded him, but he'd never let on to anyone else how much it had hurt.

Sheila parked the Jeep by a split log railing at the first rock garden with a spindly olive tree in the middle, barely big enough to cast a shadow, much less provide shade. She turned off the motor and sat for a full minute, studying the landscape.

Occasional breezes whipped the sunbaked sand into vague, ghostly forms that darted between the buildings. If not for the sign beside the road, and the view of Twin Mesas from where she sat, she might have decided that her map had been misleading.

The thought barely developed, though, before three little boys shot out of the door of the building in front of her. Giggling and talking, they glanced her way, then ran toward the playground in the center of the circle of buildings.

Sheila released the steering wheel. Well, it looked like a school, anyway.

She shoved open the door of the Jeep and got out. She glanced at the boys, now climbing the wrong side of a slide.

The door they had exited swung open again, and a man strode out, a handsome man, Navajo. He didn't look quite fifty. His black hair, close-cropped, grew thick enough to look good so short. Though not much taller than Sheila's five foot five, his powerfully built body gave him the appearance of height. Doc Cottonwood.

He glanced at Sheila briefly, looked away, then jerked to a stop and stared at her. She stared back, attempting to moisten her suddenly dry mouth.

He walked toward her.

She suddenly felt like a schoolgirl again, with a huge crush on her favorite teacher.

He stopped before he reached the Jeep; his dark, inquisitive eyes searched her face, penetrating her protective exterior like a drill through soft wood.

"Sheila."

She caught her breath.

A smile lifted the corners of his lips. "Little Sheila."

"Hello, Doc."

With a sudden burst of laughter, he sprang toward her, arms outstretched. She managed a weak smile just before he grabbed her up in a bear hug and swung her around.

"Been expecting you!" he exclaimed as her feet touched ground again. "Took you long enough. Canaan's been talking about you coming for days. You two will have a lot to catch up on."

She couldn't keep from staring at him. He was still here after all these years, as handsome as she remembered. His dark brows and strong, bulldog chin still gave him that iron-stern expression with which he'd controlled even the most rebellious boys in gym class.

She dragged her gaze from his and gestured around at the buildings. "It's all changed."

He grinned, a brief flash of white teeth against red-brown skin. "Good thing," he said, his attention never leaving her face. "Those old buildings nearly crumbled around us before Johnny made the right decision. He should've taken down all the shacks along the back road, but he couldn't bring himself to do it. How about me? Have I changed?"

Sheila stood back to get a good look at his strong, still-young physique, which showed well in a pair of gray shorts and a snug red knit shirt. For her benefit, he even flexed a couple of muscles.

She grinned. "Not at all." Gone was her schoolgirl crush, of course, but his charisma couldn't be denied.

"Neither have you." He leaned forward and chucked her under the chin.

Some things never changed.

She held out her dirty hands, motioning at her smudged white T-shirt and scruffy jeans. "Is there a place where I can clean up before meeting anyone else? I had a blowout a few minutes ago, and—"

He held up his hand. "Never fear, your apartment is ready for you. Give me the damaged tire and I'll have it repaired in our auto shop on campus."

Without another word, Doc got into the passenger side of the Jeep and gestured to Sheila. "Come on, I'll show you where you're staying."

Sheila hesitated. She'd been instructed to report to Canaan York at the principal's office as soon as she arrived.

"Canaan had to leave for a couple of hours," Doc said,

reading her expression—something he'd always done well. "One of the kids decided she wanted her mommy, and he had to go drag her back."

Sheila glanced at him. There was that sharp way of speaking that Doc sometimes had that could hurt a sensitive child. As a track coach, he inspired either great loyalty or fearful respect. Either way, it got the job done. Even Sheila had won a race as a child, and had discovered, while in training, that Doc Cottonwood reserved his sharpest words for his favorite students.

She followed Doc's instructions and drove the Jeep across the school grounds to the far side of the open courtyard.

When they reached the two-story building that Doc said housed the staff, he led the way to one of the ground-floor apartments. He opened the door and held it for her to enter.

"It's small but efficient," he said. "One bedroom, one bath, but count yourself lucky. A lot of the teachers have to share a bathroom."

The interior smelled of the dry wind of the surrounding plain, flavored by sunbaked cedars and piñons. The walls were the color of kiln-dried clay.

"April Hunt just finished cleaning the place," Doc said. "She cleans the offices and some of the apartments and classrooms for money that she blows on clothes on the mall trip once a month."

Sheila turned to him. "April? Was she related to—"

"Tad and Wendy, yep. Their daughter." He sobered, heavy brows lowering as he shook his head. "They had three kids, Steve, Jamey and April. Awful tragedy."

Sheila nodded, feeling again the shock of the news. "Tad and Wendy were friends of mine when I lived here."

The dark gaze snapped back to her. "Probably brought back memories for you."

She spread her hands. How was she supposed to answer him? "The Hunt children are staying at the school?"

He gave his customary, curt single nod. "They're still reeling from the blow, of course. Their clan would take them in, but the kids want to be here. So they'll be staying at least until school is out. They're living in one of the small old cottages at the edge of the campus."

"Wasn't it one of those cottages where Tad and Wendy died?" Sheila asked.

Doc nodded. "Johnny didn't tear down all the buildings when he rebuilt the place. Unfortunately, it was one of the old shacks that burned."

"What caused the fire?" Sheila asked. "I gathered Johnny didn't know."

"No idea yet." He waved his hand around the living room. "What do you think? The apartments were the latest addition, built last summer."

Sheila took the hint and allowed him to change the subject. She walked across a slate floor and reached out and touched the soft, plush love seat upholstered in shades of terra-cotta. The kitchen, separated from the living room by a breakfast bar, continued the desert decor.

"It's beautiful," she said. "It looks as if Johnny called in a professional decorator."

Doc cleared his throat. "That would be me."

She looked at him in surprise. "No way."

His eyes glinted with pride. "Cheap labor."

"You did this?" She shook her head as she admired the taste and style, took in the modern kitchen appliances. "I'd never have dreamed it."

"You didn't know your tough old track coach had a touch

of the artist in him, did you?" He walked into the kitchen and opened the window over the sink. "Since I stayed on through the summer last year, I had to do something to earn my keep between sessions with the track team."

"How did the summer sessions pay off with the team?"

"Trophies in every category."

"Congratulations. I know that isn't unusual for you, though," she said.

He nodded his acceptance of her approval. "Let's bring in your things, and then I'll get that tire taken care of for you."

He strode out ahead of her toward the Jeep.

She hesitated, glancing around the apartment, then through the window out across the plain. The gap was breached. After an agonizing time of alternating dread and expectancy, she had arrived.

This was the last place on earth she wanted to be.


Canaan and Tanya were about a half mile from the turn to the school when Tanya gasped and reached across the seat to grab his sleeve.

"Canaan, look!"

She leaned forward, lips parted. She slapped her hand against the windshield in the direction of a white-and-blood-red mound of fur at the right side of the road ahead of them.

Canaan stepped on the brake. A dog.

Tanya grabbed his arm again, her short nails digging into his flesh as the van rolled to a stop.

"It's Moonlight!" Her voice rose to a screeching crescendo. "It's our Moonlight!" She clawed at the latch, scrambling to get out.

"Tanya, wait." Canaan shoved the gearshift into Park and reached for the girl's arm. "A wounded animal is dangerous."

"She's not hurt, she's dead! Look at the blood." Tanya's face crumpled. She jerked away from Canaan and jumped out onto the pavement.

Before he could get out of the van, she'd reached the dog and dropped to her knees. Sobs shook her body. With dismay, Canaan recognized Moonlight, the white animal that had wandered onto the school grounds a week or so ago and been adopted by the children, who had attempted to keep it a secret from the adults—no pets were allowed on school property.

The big dog's eyes stared, sightless. But she hadn't been dead long; Canaan caught a whiff of the faint coppery odor of blood and saw that flies had not yet begun to gather.

He bent down, took Tanya by the shoulders and pulled her to her feet. She whirled around and buried her face in his stomach.

"The wolf killed her, Canaan!" Her voice was muffled against his T-shirt. "He was jealous of her and he killed her."

Canaan held her, feeling more and more uneasy at the way Tanya spoke about the wolf. "Moonlight has obviously been hit by a car, Tanya. You can see that." And since he could see no black tire marks on the pavement, it looked as if whoever hit her didn't even try to stop. In fact, it looked as if someone might have intentionally swerved onto the soft sand shoulder to reach the dog. Anger warmed Canaan's face.

Tanya raised her head, her stare accusing. Sniffing hard, she stepped away from him, as if she resented his logic.

Canaan turned and followed her back to the van. He would have to break the news to the other children as soon as they reached the school. They would be as devastated as Tanya.

What a bad scene for Sheila to witness when she arrived here. Especially in light of the difficulties she'd had here just before she and her father moved away. Maybe the whole thing could be handled before she arrived.

"You should keep the wolf talk to yourself, Tanya," he warned. "Others, especially the older people, won't want to hear it."

"But why not?"

"Because some of the old ways still linger. Our people don't talk about the wolf to others, because they believe anyone could be the wolf."

Tanya shot him a look of alarm.

He smiled. "I'm not trying to scare you, I'm just trying to let you know how others might react."

"But you're right, it could be anyone," she whispered, her wide-eyed gaze aiming toward the school. "And I don't know who."

## Chapter Five

Sheila and Doc Cottonwood set her two suitcases in the bedroom just as the crunch of tires on gravel reached them from outside.

"That must be Canaan and Tanya now," Doc said, leading the way back out the door. "Might as well start meeting the kids. Tanya's probably going to be your first challenge."

"Why is that?"

"She likes her way. She's a drama queen. Her parents spoil her when they're with her, and she's good friends with the Hunt children, so she's annoyingly emotional right now."

In spite of the abrasiveness of his words, Sheila thought she picked up on some concern in his voice. "Is she having a lot of trouble with Tad and Wendy's deaths?"

He nodded as he led the way back out of the apartment. "You'll see what I mean when you meet her."

Sheila took the sidewalk, curious about what Canaan York would look like all grown-up.

She recognized him immediately, of course. As a child, he'd been small for his age. Now, as he climbed from the van he'd parked beside her Jeep, he straightened to a height well over six feet, long and lean, dressed in jeans and a gray T-shirt…and a green baseball cap.

He'd always worn a baseball cap.

His skin was well tanned, bare arms muscled, his eyes dark, watchful. He met Sheila's gaze for a bare second before the young girl, Tanya, exploded from the passenger side of the van.

"It's Moonlight, Doc! She's dead!" The girl had long black hair and strong features that would one day lead to beauty. She was possibly in her early teens, with the developing contours of a woman. Tears streaked her cheeks as she flung herself into Doc's arms. "She's out on the highway. We've got to go get her!"

Sheila saw Doc's expression harden, and his arms went rigid in the act of encircling Tanya. He raised his gaze to meet Canaan's.

Canaan nodded as he walked toward them, his sober face pained as he flicked a quick glance at Sheila, then looked back at Doc. "Looks like someone hit her with a car. We'll take the pickup out and load her."

"No need. I'll take care of it," Doc said.

Canaan's attention shifted again. "Hello, Sheila." He took her hand and squeezed it. His hand engulfed hers. "I'm sorry this has happened on your first day."

Sheila didn't speak, didn't return the pressure of Canaan's hand. She stood perfectly still. That dog in the desert…

No. She hadn't lost her mind.

But a whisper of foreboding settled on her.

Doc released Tanya and turned to Sheila, brows lowering with obvious puzzlement at her silence.

"Wh-what color was it?" Sheila asked Canaan. "What kind of...dog?"

"She was just a big white mutt," Canaan said.

"Kind of like a German shepherd?" Sheila asked.

"So did you see the dog?" Canaan asked.

"Well, I thought I saw something in the desert as I drove in, but I didn't see anything on the road." She thought again about the blowout...and the big rock on the shoulder of the road. "I had some trouble with my Jeep, hit a rock or something, but—" She hesitated, then shook her head. "The animal I saw was out in the desert, not under the wheel of my car."

Tanya turned narrowed eyes toward her in accusation.

Sheila shook her head, still thinking about that rock. It was white, shining in the sunlight. The dog had been white.

Canaan glanced toward the front of Sheila's Jeep. Instinctively, she looked, as well. All she saw was the dent that had been there for several years. No blood, nothing to indicate impact with the hapless animal.

Tanya glared at Sheila. "You just got here, didn't you?"

Sheila nodded.

"Moonlight was a fresh kill." The words coming from the girl held an ominous quality. "I think you killed her."

Sheila shook her head. Surely she'd have seen some evidence...would have seen the dog, if she'd hit it. But she'd been too busy fighting her steering wheel, then changing the tire in record time. The noise she'd heard couldn't have been the sound of the tire hitting an animal...could it?

But she hadn't actually walked down the road to make sure that what she had taken to be a big rock was, indeed, a rock and not the lifeless form of a dog. It hadn't even occurred to her at the time. Why should it?

Tanya's small fists flexed, her jaw jutting out as she gnashed her teeth. "It's what we can expect from a *biligaana!*"

"Hold it right there." Doc put a hand on Tanya's shoulder. "Enough of this. You know better."

Tanya jerked free of Doc's hand. "But look at her! She acts guilty."

"Stop it, Tanya," Canaan said. "Quit while you're ahead and go to your dorm."

The girl stared at Canaan, rebellion in every line of her face, anger dark in her eyes. She turned to Doc, as if for help.

"You heard Canaan," he said, then turned to Sheila. "Of course, you wouldn't have—"

"How do you know?" Tanya demanded.

"Okay, that does it." Canaan stepped forward, took Tanya by the shoulders and aimed her in the direction of the dormitories. "You need a lesson in the value of silence."

"I'll take her." Doc moved quickly. "She can help me take the tire to the shop and dispose of the dog. That'll take some of the pepper out of her today."

With a shrug, Canaan stepped aside. "Sure, but what about tomorrow? And the next day?"

Doc nodded grimly. "I'll let you worry about that. You're the principal now."

Sheila braced herself once more. This was quickly developing into the horrible experience she had feared, though not for reasons she ever imagined.

* * *

Canaan listened to Doc's footsteps echo around the curve of adobe buildings and mingle with Tanya's low, urgent voice as she did her best to convince her mentor of who knew what.

And then Canaan turned to look at Sheila, who was also watching Doc and Tanya, her eyes troubled, confusion in every line of her face.

He hadn't expected to remember her so well—hadn't known that twenty-four years could seem like mere days in his memory. Yes, she was an adult now, but she was still Sheila…and he could still read her.

He hated to treat his old friend, whom he'd once loved like a sister, like a crime suspect, but he needed to know what was going on. And something was definitely going on.

"What do you mean, you didn't see her?" he asked gently.

His question dragged her attention away from Doc and Tanya. "What?"

"You obviously saw the dog, and you haven't out and out denied hitting her. Do you think it's possible you hit her? Maybe didn't see her in the road because of the glare?"

"I…uh…I told you I saw something." Her face had grown pale. "Just not on the road."

"I didn't see any skid marks on the pavement," he said, trying hard to keep any accusation out of his voice. "But I did see tire tracks in the sandy shoulder. I thought it looked as if someone went to extra lengths to make sure the animal was dead."

That brought some color back to Sheila's face. The bright sunlight also exposed tiny lines of worry around her eyes and accentuated the downward turn of her lips, making him further regret this line of questioning. He knew she would never intentionally run down an animal, but he needed to know what did happen, especially now.

She looked away and took a slow, deep breath. "Right. Guess I've not made myself clear, but do you mind if we continue this grilling inside? It's been a long, hot trip from Missouri." Without waiting for a reply, she stepped back into the apartment, stood by the door until he stepped in, then closed it. "Have a seat. I want something to drink. You?"

He shook his head and sat on the love seat. She was stalling, bumbling around in the small kitchen, searching for glasses, testing the tap.

He watched every nervous move, his concern deepening. "There's cold water in the fridge," he said at last.

She ignored him and filled her glass with tap water.

"It's not an option." He continued watching her, remembering her occasional stubbornness when they were children. "It's the only drinking water you have. It's brought in once a week. That's never changed."

With a sigh, Sheila emptied the glass into the sink, set it on the counter and strolled back into the living room, obviously trying hard to look unflustered. "Guess my memory isn't what it used to be."

He waited and watched as she sat across from him in a straight-backed chair. Wasn't she going to explain about the dog? This was the friend he'd loved when they were children, a champion with a tender heart. How many times had he thought about calling her in Missouri, just to see how she was doing? But he never had. How many times, driving east during his medical training, had he considered stopping in Hideaway to look her up? Especially when his own marriage had gone so wrong, and he'd found himself longing for simpler times.

"The Sheila I knew would never have purposely hit a dog," he said, hoping to reassure her.

She grew still, her glance stabbing at him quickly before sliding away again. "The Sheila I *know* wouldn't, either," she snapped.

It disappointed him that she had taken his statement wrong.

"I'm sorry, Sheila, I'm just having trouble understanding everything that's happened this—"

"Join the club," she snapped. Immediately, she looked chagrined, staring down at her hands, strands of her dark, windblown hair falling across her face. She opened her mouth as if to say something, then closed it again, sighed.

"I don't know about you folks out here," she said, "but a suspect is innocent until—"

"We folks out here care about our animals as much as you hillbillies back in Missouri," Canaan said. He'd intended for that to sound like his old, teasing sarcasm, but for some reason it came out a little more sharply than he'd expected. Her irritation with him, when he was only trying to get to the truth, was not helpful.

Sheila's mouth snapped shut and her eyes narrowed at him.

Oops. He knew that look. It'd been a while, but it still wasn't a look he'd wanted to invoke from her.

"And you're in charge here?" she muttered.

He grimaced. "For lack of a better leader." Granddad had warned him that there would be days his mouth would get him into trouble. This was one of them. Backpedal, fast. "Sorry, Sheila, that was uncalled for."

"You bet it was. You got something against Missourians?"

"Nope."

"Fine. I've got nothing against the Navajo, and most of the

time I don't even hold it against men for being men, but I'm not about to let one manhandle me. The Canaan York I knew would never have tried."

Okay, this wasn't the Sheila he'd known as a child. Where had this hard streak of bitterness come from? "People change, then, don't they?" he said softly.

"Yeah, they do. You didn't used to have this chip on your shoulder."

He wondered if his eyes might bug out of his head. *He* had a chip? "You're adept at changing the subject."

"Did you come here to talk to me about my new job, or just harass me about a dog?"

"Neither." He hesitated. His recent suspicions were affecting his manners. "I'm the welcoming committee."

She grimaced. For a moment, they stared at each other, then Canaan realized the ugly irony of those words. He grimaced. "I tried to give it a personal touch."

Sheila raised a dark brow. "I'll consider myself welcomed." Her voice dripped sarcasm in every word. "This isn't exactly what I expected." Though her tone suggested that it might have been what she'd feared.

"I'll try to do better."

She nodded, then her shoulders dropped slightly. "Canaan, I'm very, very sorry about the kids' dog. I don't know what happened, and I don't know what I can do about it now." She clasped her hands and looked down at them pensively. "The trip must have taken more out of me than I expected it to. I thought I was up to this, but maybe not."

Canaan waited.

She continued to stare at her hands. She said no more.

From the Navajo side of his ancestry, Canaan had learned

to be comfortable with long stretches of silence during conversation. Busy, useless chatter bothered him. Sheila, obviously, would not inflict that annoyance on him. She used to be quite a talker. Until her mother's death.

When she finally raised her head, he saw tears in her eyes.

He suppressed a groan. What now? Two crying females in one day. He was not ready for more tears.

"Sheila, I'm sorry. I shouldn't have said—"

"Oh, stop it." She dashed the tears away with an impatient swipe of her fingers. "Please get a different welcoming committee next time."

He stood up. Time for a quick and merciful departure. "Why don't you take a rest, and I'll let you know when dinner's ready in the cafeteria."

"That's an improvement. Why couldn't you have said that when you first got here?" She stood and walked him to the door. She even managed a tentative smile, a well-remembered smile. With the quick jolt of recognition also came the memory of the sense of loss he'd felt for so many long weeks after she'd left.

He returned her smile. "See you in an hour or so."

"Right. Thanks for the warning."

The scent of death…it has haunted me for weeks. Even as I stand in the bright sunlight and watch the life that teems in the children at this great school, I catch that scent. The spirit of the wolf is rumored to enjoy death, and when that spirit comes over me, I catch that passion.

But when that spirit does come over me, I am no longer myself. I am the wolf. My voice changes, my back bows. I walk less upright. The skins I use to cover myself fit me as if they are my own fur. These fools who say there is no other spirit but the precious Lord they serve at this school…they understand so little of the true realm of power.

Let them keep believing there is no such power. The children know. The adults never believe them. And when an adult happens on the truth, I see to it—the spirit of the wolf sees to it—that this adult is silenced forever, no matter the loss to me.

I miss my hogan today, where the smoke of the cedar fire engulfs me like a magical caress. The winds of change drive the heat of the sun through this school and bring a growing threat to me. I must be ever more vigilant, not only to the task before me, but to detection. That would ruin all I have worked for in my life—and the deaths of others would be in vain. As always, though I work with others who also crave the wealth and power we have labored for all these years, I am alone. No one else truly understands the soul-searing power of the spirit of the wolf.

## ❖ Chapter Six ❖

Preston Black sat on the deck of Graham and Willow Vaughn's log lodge on the shore of Table Rock Lake, listening to his giggling nieces, Lucy and Brittany, at play by the water. He'd never have dreamed he would love babysitting so much, but those two little charmers captured his heart the first time he met them last year.

A movement caught his attention from across the lake. Blaze Farmer was paddling a canoe from the boys' ranch on the other shore, about a quarter mile away. Preston knew it was Blaze because it was time to exercise the horses, and also because Blaze was the only Hideaway citizen with skin the color of espresso.

When Preston's sister and brother-in-law had left him in charge of the place for two days, he had *not* agreed to do all the chores, keep the horses watered and exercised, the chickens fed and eggs collected. Blaze was in charge of that, for which Preston was deeply grateful. Keeping up with a nine- and six-year-old was enough to keep him occupied.

He appreciated that occupation right now. It couldn't have come at a better time. He'd been able to do little besides worry about Sheila and brood about their situation. He'd searched the Web countless times for the diseases endemic to the Southwest. That had been a mistake. Squirrels in the Grand Canyon carried fleas that carried the plague. Although anthrax had not been mentioned as a concern at the school at this point, he'd discovered that this nasty little killer could be found in the wool of sheep, which were raised on Navajoland.

He'd harassed nearly every medical person in Hideaway, including Graham and Willow, with questions about hantavirus. This, of course, was fruitless, because hantavirus was not endemic to Missouri, and those who worked in the Ozarks focused on Ozark illnesses.

Hantavirus was the deadly virus that most often occurred in the southwestern part of the country. Deer mice were carriers of this strain of hemorrhagic fever. The droppings from these mice spread the disease through the air.

Though Sheila had assured Preston before she left that the buildings at the school were new and closely monitored for rodents, he knew all the monitoring in the world couldn't catch everything.

But his real fear wasn't over the diseases in the area. Yes, the principal had died from the effects of a microogranism, but Sheila's mother had not, and neither had the Hunts. Preston couldn't help connecting the deaths of Sheila's mother and Wendy—both of whom worked in the school clinic. He might be stretching it a bit, but he couldn't shake his worry.

The canoe was almost to the lake's halfway point—a distance of about six hundred feet—and Blaze waved. As Preston waved back, the cell phone chirped from his pocket. He pulled it out and checked the number. Sheila. At last.

He flipped open the phone, eager to hear her voice, yet determined not to let on how badly he missed her, or how much he worried. "Are you there yet?"

"I'm here." She sounded tired…and something more.

Sheila Metcalf was an eternally upbeat person who tended to lift the spirits of others—without irritating. Many perky people got on Preston's nerves, but for as long as he had known Sheila, her presence had soothed him. Their relationship hadn't always been comfortable, but being in her company was like a good day of fishing on James River.

"What's wrong?" he asked.

The barest of hesitations alerted him further. "It's been a long drive," she said. "It's hot, and I'm tired."

"What happened?"

"What makes you think—"

"Did you find any sick people?"

"I just got here—how am I supposed to have done that?" The fatigue in her voice had quickly turned to irritation, not a usual response from her.

"Did you have trouble on the road?" he asked.

No reply. Which meant she'd had trouble on the road.

"Did the Jeep break down?" he asked. "I knew you should have taken mine."

The continued silence disturbed him. He watched as Blaze moored the canoe to the small dock about a hundred feet down the gentle slope of hill from the house.

Lucy and Brittany ran to greet their good friend. Brittany hurled herself into his big, strong arms while Lucy hung back, suddenly shy. Lucy adored Blaze Farmer; she had informed Preston that she was going to marry Blaze when she grew up. Preston had a feeling Lucy might have some competition.

The handsome young college student could have an active social life if he weren't so busy, completing three years of study in two years, helping out at the boys' ranch that he called home, working part-time at the hospital for his foster mother, Dr. Cheyenne Gideon, taking care of most of the animals in town—Blaze intended to become Hideaway's first full-time veterinarian.

Just watching the kid work made Preston tired.

"There was something in the desert." Sheila's voice was shaky as it reached Preston over the receiver.

His full attention snapped back to her. "Something like what?"

"It looked like an animal running toward the road, maybe a dog. A German shepherd. I saw it as I drove, and then it just seemed to disappear in a puff of smoke."

Preston waited, tamping down on his alarm while the thought of rabies crossed his mind. He was losing it.

"It drew too much of my attention," she said. "Next thing I knew, I was off the road. I heard a pop-thud. I had a blowout from hitting a rock, had to change the tire, but if I hit a dog during all that mess, I'd have surely known it."

He frowned. "What?"

She sighed. "There was a dog found dead on the side of the road near where I had the blowout, and it seems I'm now being blamed for hitting it. Some kind of school pet, I guess."

"Why does everybody seem to think you hit this dog?"

"I think it's because they want to believe it."

He really didn't like the sound of her voice. He hadn't liked this journey from the beginning, but telling her that right now wouldn't help. "So why are you suddenly doubting yourself?" he asked gently. "You'd have known if you hit a dog. In fact, you'd have jumped to the dog's aid, tried to resuscitate it and barring that, you'd have hauled the poor creature into your Jeep and taken it for help."

There was a sigh, and then silence.

"Sheila?"

"Thanks. I needed to hear that. It's just so…so upsetting to be suddenly accused of this…this awful thing barely minutes after arriving here."

"Bad omen, huh?"

There was a short silence, then a sniffle.

He really, really didn't like this. He stood up, ready to pack immediately and fly to Arizona. Sheila always had both feet solidly planted on the ground…and now she was talking about disappearing dogs, and crying because she thought people didn't like her?

"Are you feeling okay?" he asked. "You're not sick, are you? Because you don't sound like yourself."

"Don't you start, too."

"I'm not starting anything, I just think—"

"I'm fine, okay? It's just that when Canaan and Tanya—she's one of the students at the school—when they arrived…" Sheila sighed. "Anyway, it wasn't pretty, and I'm tired, and I know this will all blow over, but I'm not feeling the best about things right now."

"I could come out—"

"And do what?" Snappy again. "Preston, we've already discussed this. I'm doing what I need to do. I'm just running into some…bumps along the way. Literally."

He wanted to be there, but it would do no good to dwell on his frustration, or on hers. "I understand," he said instead. And he did understand. "Just keep in mind that I'm only a phone call away."

"I know." Voice soft again, she sounded defeated. And frightened. "Thanks. That helps, it really does. I think I'm going to take a short nap. Maybe everything will look better after I've rested."

"You said Canaan York was your friend from childhood."

"We were the best of friends, and if circumstances hadn't been as they are, it would have been great to see him."

Preston had never been jealous before. Of course, he'd never been this in love before, either. "It seems to me that such a close friend would have given you the benefit of the doubt." Already, he disliked this Canaan York. To be honest, he'd felt a chill toward the guy from the moment Sheila began talking about him in such glowing terms before leaving Missouri. A man had his limits.

"Yes, well, people change," she said.

Preston could have told her that. In fact, he remembered telling her that very thing, which she hadn't exactly appreciated at the time.

"Besides, as acting principal, he has to get to the bottom of things, and I was the obvious suspect."

"He accused you of hitting the dog?" he asked. The jerk.

She groaned. "Let's say he seems to have some concern about my presence here, and the dog tragedy didn't help." Again, the weariness.

"Just remember my thoughts are with you," Preston said.

She was silent.

"Sheila?"

"Yes, I know, your thoughts are with me, but I think what I need right now is something more powerful than mere thoughts, Preston."

Her words caught him unprepared. He knew what she meant. She was a prayerful person. He was not. And that was *her* issue with *him*. No matter how many times they'd argued, discussed, challenged and questioned each other, their differing views about faith had formed a wall between them. No matter how many ways they came at it, the problem was still there…and seemed to be growing.

"I'll be here if you need me," he said.

"Yes. I know. Thanks, Preston. I'll talk to you soon."

He said a simple goodbye before disconnecting. He wanted to tell her a lot more, to reassure her, but he didn't see how he could do that. He didn't know what she was dealing with out there, and she was intentionally keeping several states between them.

How he hated being on standby.

And yet, Sheila had led him to believe that, right now, it was this or nothing. He couldn't bear nothing.

Canaan stepped through the large room he'd occupied far too much in the past few weeks—the principal's office. When he was a student here, it was the one place all the children dreaded to go. That hadn't changed for him. In fact, he'd learned that the principal hated disciplining the child more than the child hated to be disciplined.

Or, at least, this principal hated it. He was not principal material. When his grandfather had asked him to fill this position on an emergency basis, the teachers and other staff had promised to help him with the load. Now he was afraid to ask for help. Whom could he trust?

He entered the clinic, where he'd spent many nights lately, often falling asleep at the desk in the corner. Sinking into the well-used chair, he turned his attention to the bank of file cabinets, where patient records dating back to the founding of the school thirty years ago were waiting for him to study.

And study them he must, as soon as he found time.

People in these parts, including the staff, believed Canaan's grandfather, Johnny Jacobs, to be a wealthy man. After all, he'd spared no expense on the new buildings last year, especially the clinic, which was, in truth, a very modern medical station, with excellent technical capabilities. The equipment had all been donated by Arizona hospitals, but Johnny made sure that everything was in good working order.

What few people knew was that Granddad had sunk his whole fortune in Twin Mesas and three other mission schools around the state, with just enough generated income to meet the payroll at each school. He also accepted donations from several benefactors who had supported his goals for educating Navajo children from the start. He kept careful records, which he shared with the other contributors.

It was the principal's job at each school to make an annual report. Bob Jaffrey had done the preliminary work for Twin Mesas this year, but it was up to Canaan to complete it. He looked at a stack of files piled on a corner of the desk and sighed—yet another task he didn't feel capable of performing.

Canaan loved and respected his grandfather. He would do anything to help him and this school. The problem was that Canaan had almost reached his limit.

When he'd first discovered Sheila was coming, he'd been hopeful. Hard on the heels of that hope, he'd recalled the trouble Sheila had endured here at the time of her mother's death. He would never forget the haunted child she'd become before her father took her away. No one had seen her pain as Canaan had.

Because of this knowledge, he'd argued with his grandfather about this choice. He'd also argued with Doc Cottonwood, who thought Sheila's arrival would be reason for celebration.

Johnny Jacobs was not a man easily swayed, or he'd have given up on his dreams for his Navajo friends years ago. He was sold on Sheila's qualifications, and Canaan hadn't been able to talk him out of her coming.

After all, as Granddad had emphasized, Sheila was grown now: her traumatic experiences were long behind her. He believed she could handle returning, and that she was familiar enough with their ways that she would be an excellent fit with the schoolchildren she would be helping.

Judging by today, however, Canaan had even more doubts that she'd be able to carry out what needed doing—the blood testing, the physicals. He knew she could perform the tasks, but would she be able to win over the sometimes skeptical children and staff?

Tanya's reaction concerned him. And Tanya wouldn't be the only one to resist Sheila's presence.

He would have to wait and see.

## ✤ Chapter Seven ✤

Preston shoved his cell phone into the front pocket of his shirt as Blaze walked up the hill toward the house, with a child holding on to each hand. Brittany chortled with laughter at something he had just said; Lucy chuckled with less abandon...though not with less enjoyment. Blaze knew enough animal jokes and stories to keep the girls entertained all day, and he seemed to be having as much fun as they were.

Several of the staff at the Hideaway Hospital had tried to convince Blaze that he had a future in pediatrics. His favorite comment was that he preferred piglets to kidlets, though judging by his behavior with Lucy and Brittany, he would be hard-pressed to charm a baby pig with any more tenderness.

"What's up?" Blaze stepped up onto the deck, eyeing the glass Preston held in his hand. "That your famous Preston Black iced coffee? Got any more?"

Preston jerked his head toward the kitchen door behind

him. "Help yourself. There's coffee and ice in the kitchen. You know where the glasses are."

Blaze grimaced and shook his head. "Nah. It doesn't taste the same if I have to make it myself. Yours are always the best."

"Who'd ever suspect the great, hardworking Blaze Farmer would be too lazy to make his own drink?" Preston quipped.

"Ask Cook. He'll tell you how my cooking skills have dropped off since I started college. I can peel taters and haul groceries from the store, but once I start to work around the stove, the boys at the ranch suddenly discover they've got to be somewhere else for supper."

"I guess it's a good thing Fawn Morrison can cook, then," Preston teased, and was rewarded by a warm, if clueless, smile. Blaze and Fawn—both students at College of the Ozarks—had been best friends since Fawn's arrival in Hideaway two years ago. Nearly the whole population of the town knew they were sweet on each other, except for the two of them.

"She's got Bertie's black walnut waffles down to a fine art," Blaze said. "And she's about to improve on the recipe. I get the rundown on every ingredient change she makes, and I get to sample the results."

Preston didn't pursue the subject. Those two kids would pick up on the obvious one day. Until then, let their friendship continue to develop; it was the best way to build a long-lasting marriage. But then, Preston hadn't ever been married, so what would he know?

Blaze frowned at him. "You got something on your mind today?"

Preston glanced toward the door. "Why don't I make you my special iced cappuccino."

"Why don't I take the girls horseback riding as soon as they wash all the lake mud off their arms and legs," Blaze said, giving the girls a pointed look.

Before Preston could respond, Lucy and Brittany were racing into the house, arguing over who would be first at the sink.

With a smile, Preston jerked his head toward the door, and led the way inside to make Blaze's favorite coffee drink.

Blaze followed. "Sheila get to Arizona yet?"

Preston nodded.

"She doing okay?"

Preston placed ice in the blender and started adding coffee, cream, spices. "Not sure."

"That don't sound good."

Preston gave his young friend a glance. Blaze had arrived in Hideaway as a fifteen-year-old kid with dreadlocks, an undeserved reputation as an arsonist…and a broken heart. His father, a divorced veterinarian, had raised Blaze well until the day of his death.

That was when life for poor Blaze—whose given name was Gavin—went swiftly downhill. According to the local grapevine, Blaze's mother had no maternal instincts, and consequently, the boy had ended up at the boys' ranch across the lake. Dane and Cheyenne Gideon loved him like a son and were obviously proud of his scholastic accomplishments.

Blaze was very literate, but he had a tendency toward slang, perhaps used in an effort to fit into his surroundings.

Preston set the completed coffee drink on the counter. "One Preston Black Special, just for you."

"You still thinking about a road trip?" Blaze asked.

"Thinking will do me no good. She doesn't want me there."

Blaze waited, his coffee-dark eyes watchful as he sipped his drink.

Preston had never been one to make friends easily. It didn't take a genius to figure out the reason: no child with a mentally ill mother dared to invite friends over after school. And so he was therefore surprised by his developing friendship with this kid. Blaze had a special talent for sliding beneath a person's defenses.

Preston also reminded himself that Blaze had a reputation for matchmaking, earned since his arrival in Hideaway, and the kid was proud of it.

"Since when did Sheila start telling you where you could and couldn't go?" Blaze asked.

Preston gave Blaze a mock glare. "I'm for sure not going down *that* road, pal. I want to stay friends with her, not alienate her completely."

Blaze took a long, slow drink of the Preston Special. "Seems to me it can't get much worse than it already is…unless she up and renews her friendship with that man in Arizona. You got any guarantee against her doing that?"

"There are never any guarantees about anything when it comes to women," Preston said. "You should know that by now."

Blaze shook his head. "Not me. I'm just a poor student, trying to figure out how to make his own way in the world." He set his glass down. "Of course, even busy as I am, seems I'd have time to take a trip to Arizona, if anyone were to ask me to ride shotgun."

The girls ran back into the room, ready to go riding with Blaze. Preston grinned at them. "Don't be too hard on the horse."

"We won't, Uncle Preston," Lucy said, gazing up at Blaze with complete adoration.

Blaze winked at her, then opened the door to usher the girls outside. He looked back over his shoulder at Preston. "We could call it a mission trip, you know. From what Sheila said, they could use some more medical help out there to check the kids."

"Aren't you forgetting something?" Preston asked. "I'm not medical."

"Clinics always need willing aides, and you're a whiz with numbers and finances. Mission schools always need a lot of that, too. If the place doesn't need your brain, it could probably use your brawn, fixin' things, hammerin' nails, you know, things like that."

Preston nodded as Blaze walked out the door with the girls. Blaze always tended to slice to the heart of a matter. Sheila wanted space, and she was candid about the reason why.

Neither Preston nor Sheila could deny the attraction between them—a powerful draw that often left common sense and thoughtful consideration in the dust. Though they remained chaste, their attraction still influenced their ability to make good decisions.

At least, that was what Sheila said. Preston knew she had good reasons to go to Arizona—even more compelling reasons than Blaze's—but Preston couldn't help feeling that one of her unspoken motives was to get away from him so it would be easier to break things off with him for good.

Until now, he'd been comfortable respecting her wishes. But after talking with Blaze, that didn't seem like such a good option, after all. Sheila had spoken of Canaan York with a great deal of affection, which Preston found impossible to ignore. Did she hold some kind of hope of renewing her childhood friendship with the man?

What if the unthinkable happened? Sheila and Canaan had been good friends once—and he was the grandson of the owner of Twin Mesas School, as well as a physician, and most likely a Christian. Buster Metcalf, Sheila's father, had mentioned, too, that Canaan was no longer married.

Preston wasn't the kind of man to panic, but neither did he want to just sit on his thumbs here in Missouri and risk losing the only woman who had ever made him see the possible merits of a lasting marriage.

He knew Blaze had a passion for medicine of any kind, be it animal or human. Trauma junkie that he was, the kid could make a great pediatrician or a great E.R. doc, if he wanted. And he'd made it obvious he would love to take a trip to Arizona.

With some creative reasoning, Preston and Blaze might be able to drive to Arizona and call the drive a mission trip. For sure, it would be that for Blaze.

Preston's first priority was Sheila's safety. The Navajo reservation didn't seem to him to be a safe place at the moment, and the more he thought about Blaze's words, the more convinced he became that sitting here waiting for Sheila to call wasn't necessarily the best thing for her.

Sheila wouldn't buy this thinking, of course, and she would resent his interference. No matter what Sheila said, though, one thing was obvious—Canaan York needed more help just to see that the kids and their families received the usual medical screening before school let out for the summer. Blaze could help get it done in half the time, and Preston did know how to do paperwork.

Wouldn't that be worth a little emotional risk for her, in the long run?

A black shadow-image with long, pointed ears and sharp, blood-smeared fangs raced across the darkness after Sheila.

Her mouth opened in a mute scream. Her body tensed, then jerked, bringing her wide-awake. She lay still for a moment, body stiff, as awareness of the dream slipped away and relief flooded her.

She gazed around the shaded room, grown darker with the dying sun. Perspiration filmed her skin, soaking her hair and clothes, even the bedspread.

A warm, dry breeze blew through the open window beside the bed, pushing past the lapis lazuli curtains. The tang of cedar was pleasant, but it stirred the dead ashes of the dream, evoking once more the monster that kept stalking her into her waking hours—a familiar specter that had impelled her here in the first place.

"Sheila?"

At the sound of her name, she had no trouble imagining the voice of that monster, calling to her from beyond the divide between sleep and consciousness.

"Are you in there?" he asked.

She felt a wash of relief and relaxed. It was Canaan's muffled voice, reaching her from outside the apartment door. She blinked and sat up, swinging her legs over the side of the bed.

Canaan knocked.

"Coming," Sheila called, her voice barely more than a croak. She closed her eyes and swallowed, willing her heart to slow. The day's events had mingled with her nightmares, making it all more real and more frightening.

"Are you okay, Sheila?"

"Yes, I'm coming, keep your cap on." Great. She was in no mood to exchange small talk in the school cafeteria with new faces and with old acquaintances who had lived only in her memories for the past twenty-four years, and her reunion with Canaan wasn't turning out to be as comfortable as she'd hoped it would be. So much for old friendships. After the incident with the dog, even Doc Cottonwood might no longer be so welcoming. She had prepared herself for this, though. She'd known it might not be easy to come back here; this could be a challenging exercise in patience—and fortitude.

She opened the door, still fingering the hair out of her face. It didn't surprise her to see that Canaan had on a different ball cap than the one he'd worn this afternoon.

Sheila tried to force a smile that she couldn't quite get to materialize. "Hi. Guess I fell asleep."

"I'm glad you decided to take a nap. Are we on speaking terms again?"

"I hope so, because I wanted to ask you about your ball cap collection. How many do you have now?"

He grinned. "I've whittled them down over the years, but I still have about fifty."

"You had more than that when I lived here."

He removed the one on his head to reveal shiny black hair, cut above his ears. Shorter than Preston's.

And why was she comparing the two men, all of a sudden? "I also wanted to ask you about the beautiful works of art." She gestured toward two wood carvings on the coffee table. One was a life-size head of a bighorn sheep; the other was a startlingly beautiful replica of the famed Rainbow Bridge stone arch on Lake Powell.

"The initials on the bottoms of these are *CY*." She picked up the carving of Rainbow Bridge. "Anyone you know?"

"Sounds familiar," he said.

She sighed. Canaan York had always been willing to shoulder responsibility when anything went wrong, and always reluctant to take credit—like for the beautiful results of his creativity.

"So you followed in your mother's sculpturing footsteps," she said. "Is she still creating her fascinating works?"

He nodded, obviously proud of his mother. "Her name is known in some circles all across the country."

"I think these are just as beautiful. I'm honored you used them to decorate my apartment."

She replaced the carving on the coffee table, aware of Canaan's flush of pleasure and his effort to suppress it.

"Thanks. Are you hungry?"

"Not too much." Sheila glanced at her watch. "Look, I'm sorry, but I'm really not up to this right now. Why don't you—"

"You need to eat." His deep voice suddenly became firm. "Besides, you should start meeting some of the staff. You don't want them to think that you think you're too good to eat with them, do you?"

Sheila grimaced. Her head ached. But she did need to start meeting the staff, and she didn't want to do it all alone.

"You aren't my boss until I start work," she said. "But I guess I can force myself to eat."

Canaan gave her a smile, erasing the serious expression that seemed to be permanently attached to the adult Canaan York. "Hope you still like mutton stew."

Sheila made a face, and Canaan chuckled.

"It's a special treat for the others. They're also serving chicken fried steak for those with *biligaana* tastes."

"Good."

"By the way, Betsy Two Horses is still in the cafeteria. She's head cook now. She and your mother were once pretty good friends, weren't they?"

"Yes, they were." It would be good to see Betsy again. Not that she and Sheila would have time to talk with a dinner crowd around, but just to see her again... Sheila reached up and fingered the turquoise-and-gold cross at her throat.

Seeing Betsy would bring so many of her memories crashing back. But the time had come to face them—and there was no turning back now.

## Chapter Eight

Canaan sat on the sleeper sofa in Sheila's small apartment, listening to the splash of water in the bathroom as Sheila got ready to go to dinner. She obviously was reluctant to join him for tonight's meal. He wasn't exactly ecstatic about it, either. He would have enjoyed sharing a meal with her without the prying eyes of the whole student body and faculty on them. How he would love to sit down with her and catch up on the past years.

Sheila joined him, and they stepped out into the darkening, cooler air of evening.

"I had forgotten how suddenly night falls here," she said. "In Missouri, the sunset hangs on forever."

"I remember," he said.

She looked up at him. "You were in Missouri?"

"When I had rotations, I drove through a couple of times. I discovered that, in the Ozarks, the sun seems to spread out into the heavier, moister atmosphere there, and then, just before it starts its plunge past the horizon, it lingers in the line of forest."

"Sounds as if you enjoyed it."

"I did."

"I wish you'd tried to contact Dad or me on your way through. We could have put you up for the night."

"It just never seemed to be the right time." Especially since she had been married then. Canaan doubted her husband would have understood an old male friend simply stopping by to spend the night.

He couldn't help noticing as they walked that Sheila was studying every line of every building, every plant. It must be disconcerting to find a once-familiar home changed so completely.

All of the old school buildings were gone, and it seemed to take her a few moments to realize that the cafeteria, just ahead and to their right, was set in exactly the same position as the old one.

"The new cafeteria's prettier," Canaan said, and was rewarded by a fleeting look of surprise. Amazing he could still, at times, read her mind.

Piñon and olive trees, thriving in this climate, surrounded the cafeteria. Canaan had considered planting cactus, as well, but he couldn't risk harm to children playing in the area.

"It seems as if some calm, gentle spirit has encompassed the school," Sheila said.

He warmed at her words of praise. "Thank you."

"Don't tell me you did the landscaping," she said.

He nodded. "Doc said I needed a deeper tan."

"That sounds like something he would say." Warm affection filled her words. Sheila had once been one of Doc Cotton-wood's favorite young students; when he had taken her under his wing, it had helped establish her as just another student, and not a *biligaana*. Her friendship, in turn, had encouraged Canaan to face up to the bullies who'd picked on him.

"I enjoyed the gardening," Canaan said.

"More than you enjoy medicine?" she asked.

"No, but I like it more than being principal. Besides, the physical activity did me good."

She glanced up at him, and he thought he caught a brief gleam of approval as her gaze rested on the breadth of his shoulders, and again he relished that approval. Having been the smallest in his class, he had despaired as a child of ever growing. His growth spurt had hit in his senior year of high school. Perhaps it was this feeling of isolation for so long in his childhood that had kept him hitting the books when other classmates were more active in sports.

"Once the trees have matured," Sheila said, "this whole place will look like an oasis from the road."

"That's the plan." He hesitated. Though it would be great to bask in her kind words—particularly after the uncomfortable circumstances accompanying her arrival—he couldn't linger there. "Were you looking for an oasis when you decided to come here?"

"Nope." Clipped. Almost sharp, and the tone relayed *Back off* clearly enough for most people.

"So why did you come?" He wasn't most people.

"Because I'm between permanent jobs at the moment. And no, I wasn't fired from my previous position. The hospital where I worked lost federal funding and had to cut back on staffing."

"A loss of federal funding would shut down most hospitals."

"It probably will this one, as well, eventually, but it's still limping along right now."

"What was the infraction?"

"One of the doctors refused to accept a patient being transferred from a smaller hospital. The patient died in transit to the other hospital in town." She looked up at him. "Do I have to undergo another employment interview? Your grandfather already asked me these questions."

"I'm just curious," Canaan assured her. "So you suddenly decided, after all these years, that you'd like to work for room and board and paltry pay in the isolation of this school?"

She didn't reply.

"It's been a bad homecoming for you," Canaan said. "I'm sorry I'm not making it any easier."

"You sure aren't."

He glanced at her, appreciating the profile of the grown-up Sheila. She looked a lot like her mother, though her hair was darker; her mother had been blond. Evelyn Metcalf had been a beautiful woman—at least, from the viewpoint of a ten-year-old boy who didn't know very much about women. Sheila had inherited those looks.

It appeared that she'd also inherited a strong strain of her father's dynamic personality. Although that strength seemed to have left her earlier today.

"I think you've had a difficult couple of years," he said.

She didn't look at him, but slowed her steps to match his. "You've been talking to your grandfather."

"Of course. I was sorry to hear about the death of your husband."

She nodded but said nothing.

Canaan wanted to ask why she'd resumed using her maiden name, but that was pushing it too far. Maybe after dinner.

"I gather you're not thrilled about my presence here," she said.

"I am, in a way."

Amusement came and went in her expression. "A very small way."

"Fishing for compliments?" he asked.

She chuckled suddenly, and he couldn't help smiling. When they were kids, any time Canaan became frustrated and bemoaned his size, she'd poke him in the ribs and say, "Catch a big one, York, but you'll have to clean it yourself." Since Canaan wasn't a fisherman, she'd had to explain the fishing reference she'd learned from her father.

"We're not talking about how I feel right now," Canaan said. "We're talking about your true mission here."

She scowled at him. She even had a pretty scowl.

"Don't get me wrong," he said. "If I weren't in the position I'm in, I wouldn't be asking any questions, I'd just be happy to see you, no matter why you came."

"That wasn't the impression I got."

He spread his hands. "Things aren't as I'd like them to be."

"What did your grandfather tell you about me?"

"Not enough for me to form an opinion, only that you'd had a rough two years, you needed a break for a few weeks and that you were the best nurse in the county."

She glanced at him.

He shrugged. "Direct quote from your father, I think."

"Are you still open to discussion about the dog this afternoon?"

"To be honest, though I was upset about Moonlight, something else about your behavior concerned me."

"Because I didn't realize I'd hit her?"

Canaan shook his head, not sure, exactly, why he had even admitted that much. "Because you probably didn't hit her."

Her steps slowed further. "You really think that?"

He nodded.

"You could have fooled me."

"You didn't defend yourself, Sheila. Tanya jumped to conclusions because of that."

"I had the impression that she didn't need much encouragement. It's been a long time since I've been called a *biligaana* with such vehemence." She shrugged. "Hillbilly, yes, but not *biligaana*."

"That's another thing," he said. "The words I used in an attempt at a joke, you interpreted as hostility."

As a group of children marched past them on the sidewalk, Canaan called greetings to them, then returned his attention to Sheila. "You weren't yourself today."

"You don't know me as an adult, so you can't say that."

"Okay, sorry. I meant to say that the Sheila I once knew would never have allowed anyone to unfairly accuse her."

"Well, this Sheila couldn't help second-guessing what she saw. Did you ever think that there might have been two dogs on the road today? The dog I saw in the desert distracted me at the wrong time, and the dog alongside the road—perhaps a buddy— got under the wheel of the tire as I veered from the road."

"So now you're trying to work out a scenario in your mind that you can accept. The Sheila I knew would never try so hard to place herself in the wrong."

"That makes the third time you've mentioned the Sheila you knew. Mind telling me a little more about this other me?"

No difficulty there. He'd given it a lot of thought since his last conversation with his grandfather. "The Sheila I remember best is the one I knew when her mother was alive."

She looked away. This interested him, since he could have

sworn Sheila had returned to Twin Mesas, at least in part, to discover more about Evelyn Metcalf, her death and her life here. He had no idea what her father had told her, but Canaan wasn't going to pass along old hurtful gossip about Evelyn.

Although there hadn't been much. The People did not make a habit of speaking ill of the dead, because they rarely spoke of the dead at all.

"Don't you and your father discuss your mother?" he asked.

"We're talking about young Sheila right now."

He nodded. Fair enough. "She laughed a lot, she spoke her mind and she despised bullies. She wasn't afraid to face down the biggest kid on the playground if he was picking on the pip-squeak."

Canaan saw her wince at the name he'd been called so often.

"No one would call you that now," she said.

"Sometimes I wonder if I grew so tall just to prove those bullies wrong."

She smiled at him. "Or maybe to prove me right? That you were the best guy at Twin Mesas."

He tentatively returned the smile. "I sure missed that after you left."

Her smile was a fleeting thing, and once again she stared at the ground, looking pensive.

"I often wondered if the real Sheila ever resurfaced," he said. "By the time you and your dad left here, your heart had gone into hiding. You never cried for her."

She looked at him, obviously startled. "I cried."

"For your mother? I know you cried about leaving here, and about leaving me. You never mentioned your mother's name, never talked about her."

"My father never mentioned her."

A troop of little girls pranced across the sandy playground from the dormitories. Their dorm mother, a plump woman with short black hair and olive-toned skin, waved to Canaan. He waved back as the group filed through the cafeteria entrance.

"You remember the day of my mother's death that well?" Sheila asked.

"It isn't something I'm ever likely to forget, the day Granddad carried you in from that desert, dehydrated and nearly catatonic." He could still close his eyes and see his grandfather's gaunt face and tortured eyes as he carried her, surrounded by teachers and dorm parents from the school.

"It was the day I lost my best friend," he said softly. "You were never the same."

He watched her close her eyes, and he knew he'd scored an unintentional hit. Sheila Metcalf had come back to Twin Mesas to find what she'd lost as a child.

Why did he suspect that the tragedy of Evelyn's death could somehow be connected to the recent tragedies that had taken place here at the school? Could it be because Wendy Hunt had called him just before the fire, telling him she had found something disturbing, and that he needed to see it?

Evelyn Metcalf had done the same long ago. Canaan had been in the cafeteria, slouched over his food, under orders from his dorm room father to eat it all before leaving. Canaan's smallness had seldom been a bonus for him, but at that time no one had seen him. He'd overheard Evelyn whisper something to Betsy behind the counter. "I need to talk to you later," she'd said. "I found something in the medical records that I can't figure out."

Moments later, Canaan had seen a teacher, Kai Begay, get up from his table in the faculty section, behind a partition.

Later, Evelyn had been found dead. Canaan had always wondered if anyone else had heard the exchange.

If it had been just his child's imagination that made him suspect something sinister had happened, then why was he so anxious now that danger may have lain in wait all these years?

## ❧ *Chapter Nine* ❧

Sheila felt sick all of a sudden—and in over her head. She had lost all her curiosity about her mother, though she was sure that would return. But now, everything seemed to be happening too quickly.

"So, I think we've exposed everything about Sheila that we can tonight," she said drily, hesitating at the cafeteria door. "Why don't we learn a little about Dr. Canaan York?" Anything to delay the inevitable plunge.

To her relief, he took the hint and ceased further probing. He also didn't open the door. "I'm not a good principal."

"Most doctors I know wouldn't make good principals, but this position is temporary, isn't it?"

He nodded. "If I can make it three more weeks."

"I understand this has been your first year at the school clinic."

He looked at her. "I'm sure Granddad managed to tell you

everything about my life since you left. He has a tendency to…um…boast a little more than I'd like him to."

"Oh, yeah, you mean the way he has of saying, 'My grandson, the doctor,' every other sentence?"

Canaan chuckled.

"He told me you joined a clinic practice in Ganado as soon as you'd completed your residency."

"That's right," Canaan said. "Many of the Twin Mesas' graduates went to college in Ganado, so I knew many of my patients already."

"Sort of like built-in job security," she said.

Canaan hesitated. How he wished he'd been able to have built-in marriage security so easily. "You know how hard it can be for The People to trust outsiders, or even strangers in our tribe."

"Your grandfather said a large percentage of Twin Mesas' graduates go on to college."

"Yes, Granddad's proud of that." Canaan hesitated. "I am, too."

Sheila glanced up at the change in his voice. "You don't sound too sure of that."

He shook his head. "Some of the graduates didn't make it to college. Two didn't even live to graduate. They had such high hopes for the future, but they died before they could realize their dreams."

"How?"

"Accidents."

"What kind of accidents?"

"One from heatstroke. He was found out in the desert two years ago. He should have known better. He grew up in this desert."

"And the other?" Sheila asked.

"Car wreck down in Gallup last year. Hit by a drunk."

"So the deaths were unrelated."

He grimaced.

She wondered if he realized how poorly he hid his thoughts. He'd never been good at keeping his emotions off his face. "So you came here after you became so concerned about the deaths."

He didn't return her look. "After Grandad asked me to."

"He wanted you here to keep an eye on things," she guessed.

He glanced through the glass doors into the cafeteria. "And that didn't work, either. Three died under my watch."

"And the Hunts were also former students," she said.

"All three were former students. Bob Jaffrey was, as well."

"You're desperate to find out what's going on."

He nodded.

"Tell you what, I'll keep a close eye on your work next week, and give you a critique on Friday."

"Just what I need," he said dryly. "Another critic."

"I've heard there's been quite a turnover of principals in the past few years," she said.

"Seems that way."

"I'm not getting myself into the middle of a mess, am I?" she asked. "You know, student pranks, stuff like that?"

"No pranks. Nothing we can't handle."

"But there is something."

He turned to look at her for a long moment as his hand went to the cafeteria door. He grasped the handle, then stood still. "Do you remember when we were kids, we used to try to help Granddad's neighbor herd his sheep?"

"And we spooked them every time."

"Right. The kids remind me of those spooked animals."

"How?"

He opened his mouth, then closed it again, shaking his head. "I'm afraid you'll see what I mean when you start talking to them." He pulled open the door. "If you do, will you tell me?"

"I'll add it to my critique."

Sheila took a deep breath and preceded Canaan into the noisy cafeteria. The huge room, as modern and clean as the exterior of the building, had been designed with children in mind. Bulletin boards held beautiful drawings and collages. She wondered if Canaan had a hand in the inspiration for some of the masterpieces.

The aromas were the same as they had been nearly a lifetime ago. Sheila knew if she closed her eyes, the smell of yeasty rolls and bubbling stew would draw her back to the days when Betsy Two Horses had stood at the serving line, teasing and laughing with the hungry children.

Recognition and remembered affection warmed Sheila as she caught sight of the Navajo woman. Funny how she could remember Betsy and Canaan and the ruggedness of the land surrounding the school so very well, but she could barely remember her mother's image.

No, not funny, but certainly sad.

From across the length of the large cafeteria, Betsy didn't look more than fifty, though she must be past seventy. Tendrils of her hair, still as black as Sheila remembered, had escaped the ponytail that emphasized her thin, angular face. As she reached up to push the strands back, her dark eyes met Sheila's.

For a moment, Betsy stared. Her thick, dark brows gave her

a glowering appearance, until a gleam of recognition lightened the woman's expression.

Canaan touched Sheila's arm and led her forward, past the chattering kids holding their trays and the dorm parents who monitored to make sure their charges behaved while the principal was in the room.

"Well, Betsy?" Canaan said. "You told me you'd recognize her."

Betsy looked at Canaan, then at Sheila. In the light, the deep lines of her face belied the youthful blackness of her hair, but the warmth in those eyes welcomed as it had so long ago.

"I knew her," Betsy said, then directed her gaze to Sheila. "Did you think I wouldn't?"

"It's been a long time," Sheila said.

Betsy studied Sheila more closely. "You've always looked like Evelyn." She explained to Canaan, "Sheila's mother."

"I know," Canaan said dryly. "I was here, too, remember?"

Before they could talk further, a group—Sheila guessed they were teachers—entered the cafeteria, talking and laughing as energetically as students…until they saw Sheila.

Silence descended, amusement disappeared and the expressions on various faces ranged from curiosity to resentment.

For the first time, Sheila became aware of the paleness of her skin. It felt strange. She couldn't remember ever feeling out of place at this school when she was a little girl. Always, when she'd been here, she had belonged.

Canaan touched her arm and addressed the new arrivals. "Come and meet Sheila Metcalf, the nurse Johnny Jacobs has hired to help me in the clinic. She and I attended school together here when we were children, which means she's one of us."

Sheila felt only slightly relieved when a few of the expressions lightened. One heavyset woman who had passed them earlier with a group of children stepped forward and picked up her tray, interest sharpening her delicate features.

"I hear you're going to examine my kids," she said, selecting her silverware. "I have first- and second-grade girls."

"This is Jane Witherbe," Canaan told Sheila, putting an arm on the woman's shoulder. "She's been a teacher and dorm mother here for a lot of years."

Jane nodded, dark eyes friendly, and the smile revealed she was older than she first appeared. "I remember you, Sheila. My first year here was—" the smile disappeared "—it was the year you left."

"You'll like her kids," Canaan said smoothly. "They're well behaved."

Another of the women spoke up. "They're all good kids. They mind their teachers and dorm parents."

One of the men snorted, his expression still grim, his gaze most unwelcoming as he studied Sheila's face. "That's because they're all *Dineh*."

Sheila knew that word. It was what the Navajo called themselves. It meant *The People*. The man looked familiar, and for a moment Sheila held his dark gaze. She remembered his name without having to be told. Kai Begay. He'd been a teacher-parent when Sheila had lived here. But he hadn't been unfriendly then, had he?

"Sheila was with us for several years, Kai," Canaan said. "You should remember her, since you were here at the time her parents came. Her mother was our nurse, and her father helped the local farmers to utilize their land more efficiently."

Kai Begay's chin came up as he met Canaan's gaze and held

it for a moment. Canaan returned the look. Kai cleared his throat and looked away.

Something relaxed inside Sheila. Canaan might not feel as if he would make a good principal, but he was obviously making an effort to retain control of the staff, no matter how unpopular that might make him.

Betsy Two Horses returned her attention to the steam table in front of her.

As the talk increased and the tension eased, Sheila pushed her tray along the counter.

Betsy gave her a quick once-over. "You're starving yourself," she said, her voice brusque as always, but her eyes still warm.

"I've actually gained some weight," Sheila told her.

"Well, gain some more." Betsy held up a ladle of stew. "Mutton." Her dark eyes gleamed with the barest touch of humor. "Your favorite."

Sheila nodded and enjoyed the look of surprise on Betsy's face. She'd never developed a taste for the stew as a child, and she'd been teased about it a few times. But who was to say her tastes hadn't changed in twenty-four years?

When Canaan turned with his tray toward a far table, Sheila glanced at Betsy wistfully. When the glass door opened and more people entered, Sheila turned away and wove between the tables to where Canaan waited. Later. She and her old friend would have time to become reacquainted soon.

In spite of what she'd told Canaan, Sheila had no appetite. In fact, she hadn't felt hungry all week. Now, as she glanced into the bowl of thick stew, nausea bubbled in her stomach. The reaction of the dorm parents, especially Kai Begay, concerned her. It didn't help that she felt as if time had shifted, as if she were a child again.

Canaan held her chair out for her.

He sat down after she did. He bowed his head, said a brief prayer softly, as if to himself, then tore off a corner of his bread and dipped it in his stew.

"Fry bread?" Sheila asked. "I didn't see that."

He chewed, swallowed. "You were so busy watching Betsy, you pushed your tray right past it. She was always good with us kids, wasn't she?"

Sheila nodded, fingering the cross at her throat. "She gave me this." She glanced toward the serving line, where Betsy was greeting incoming diners with a quick word or nod.

"That necklace?" Canaan bent forward and examined it more closely. "Did she make it?"

"No, her husband made it for her a few years before he died. She gave it to me after my mother died."

"It's skillfully made. Do you wear it often?"

Sheila nodded. "Almost all the time when I was growing up. Every time I touched it, I could remember that someone loved me enough to give me something that meant a lot to her. She told me that she had worn it constantly after her husband's death, until her fear of life went away and she no longer felt alone."

"Do you still feel alone?"

She gave him a wry look. "I'm thirty-four years old, I have plenty of friends in Hideaway, my father is whole and healthy and Preston…" She smiled.

"Yes? Preston…?"

"A good friend."

"Is that a euphemism for a person of consequence in your life?" Canaan asked.

"Let's just say my life is full and very interesting at the moment."

"Because of Preston?"

Though Canaan watched her intently, she didn't elaborate. Best not to get into a discussion about other difficulties in her life right now.

Obviously curbing his curiosity, Canaan gestured toward the teachers and dorm parents who were making their way to a long table set apart from the children. "Most of the staff are warmhearted, good people. There will always be a *certain* percentage of people who have trouble accepting newcomers, no matter who they are, or what color."

"I'm no newcomer to Kai Begay," Sheila reminded him. "He knew me when I was a child, and I don't remember any resentment from him then. I don't remember the problem being so prevalent here before."

"You were a child then."

"Children can sense things, and I would have sensed that brand of prejudice."

"But Kai is not antagonistic with children," Canaan said. "He loves them, which is why he's remained here all these years. This is his life."

"Did he treat my parents the way he's treating me now?"

Canaan pulled off a section of his fry bread and set it on her plate. He drizzled honey from a plastic container on the table on the other piece. "Kai has always been outspoken, but he loves the children."

Sheila watched him take a big bite of the bread. "You didn't answer my question, and you're just repeating yourself. Does he pass his prejudice along to the children?"

Canaan chewed and swallowed, chewed and swallowed, giving her a disgruntled look. "You never broke that habit, did you?"

"Of what?"

"Asking me a question as soon as I put food in my mouth."

"You're doing better, though. Now, at least, you don't talk with your mouth full."

Canaan gave his sweetened bread a loving look, then set it back onto his plate. "Kai eats with the kids and spends a lot of his free time with them. What do you think?"

"It's a shame he feels the way he does. The children need to learn to get along with people of every race if they're to function in the world outside the reservation."

Canaan nodded, picking up his bread again. "You're right. Absolutely. Now let me eat."

Sheila sighed and picked up her fork, faking an appetite, though she didn't expect to fool Canaan. He seemed to remember a lot of things about her, and his memories intrigued her.

## ❧ Chapter Ten ❧

Canaan watched Sheila play with her fork, studying those long, slender fingers, remembering how those strong hands had done physical battle for him once upon a time.

She shouldn't be here rescuing him now. As a child, she'd acquired some bruises and a couple of cuts on the playground while standing between him and the bullies. This time, worse things could happen.

She stopped fiddling with the fork and looked up at him. "Why are you frowning?"

"Was I frowning?" He took a bite of the fry bread.

"I doubt Kai's the only one on the reservation who feels the way he does," Sheila said, picking up on their previous conversation as if nothing had interrupted it.

Canaan shrugged.

"I'm just curious about who's being taught to resent those

with different skin," she said. "Do all the kids have this resent-ment toward whites?"

Dropping the bread again, Canaan sighed and leaned back. "Of course not, but I can see both sides. I've been involved in arguments concerning both sides. Bigotry is a waste, and I ob-viously hate it more than most, but some of Kai's opinions are valid."

"For instance?"

He sighed and leaned forward again, resting his elbows on the table and lowering his voice. This was the Sheila he remem-bered, but the grown-up Sheila in argument mode might prove to be a little more daunting than his young friend of days gone by.

"Don't look at me like that," he said. "I'm not condoning verbal abuse or prejudice. But the elders hate to see their long-held customs die away to nothing."

"You'd be amazed how often I hear that in Branson. It isn't just here on the reservation, Canaan. Nothing stays the same. Time changes everyone."

"I bet you don't hear anyone complain about the dying language of America in Branson."

"You don't get out much, do you?" Sheila asked. "Branson is all about tourism, and tourism, in its way, is a kind of subtle corruption of the country, with a constant influx of people from other cultures, with other languages."

"I'm not talking about just a dying language, but a dying heritage that our people have honored throughout our history," Canaan said. "The children in this school don't speak the language of the *Dineh* anymore. The old ones tell them the old stories, which are considered fairy tales by many of the children."

"Is Kai teaching them?"

"He tries. So do Jane and Betsy, and even my grandfather when he comes to the school, though he's white. The children feel it's pointless to learn a useless language or outmoded customs. They don't honor the things their parents honored."

"If their parents honored the language, wouldn't they have spoken it at home?" Sheila asked. "The kids would have learned it there."

Canaan shook his head, frustrated. "You're not getting it, Sheila. More and more of our young people are leaving the reservation and never coming back—never giving anything back to the heritage that made them who they are. I don't think that was Granddad's intention when he established the reservation schools."

"What's changed?" she asked. "Your people have always been either stuck here on this reservation, struggling to make a living, or forced to leave their home and family traditions and join the white society."

"In this area, especially, resentment is building over the problem."

She set down her fork and returned his frown. "Why now? It's been that way since long before I lived here. Besides, the Navajo nation is the largest and wealthiest Native American nation in the country."

He shook his head, glad she'd at least kept her voice down as she revealed her ignorance so blatantly. He'd have thought Sheila, of all people, would understand. "That tells you how the others fare."

Sheila stirred her coffee and glanced around the room. Canaan followed her gaze and caught several curious stares, some friendly, one brooding—Kai's.

"As far as wealth is concerned," Canaan continued, "the money doesn't trickle down far enough—our people are as capable of greed and dishonesty as anyone else, especially since many of our ancient ways, which dealt harshly with greed, have been forgotten. We are never allowed to forget that many of us still must depend on the charity of the American government to survive."

He felt her attention on him, and he realized he sounded obsessed. "It isn't the same as providing for ourselves," he said softly.

"But the Navajo are developing their resources."

"That's often my argument when the subject comes up. Unfortunately, others are not so optimistic. The problem isn't recent. Much of it stems from the way our people were treated in the past."

"The broken treaties?"

"Not that far past. I'm talking about the earlier mission schools, where kids were punished for speaking their native tongue."

"I remember Dad talking about those schools, but he was indignant about them."

"Then your father might be more sympathetic to our situation than you seem to be." Canaan realized that had come out too sharply.

She ignored his slip. "How does this antiwhite attitude differ from those early mission schools? Bigotry is bigotry, no matter what side you're on."

"There might be a little more to it than that," Canaan said, then shook his head and shot a quick glance toward Kai.

"He dislikes me, personally?" Sheila asked.

Canaan grimaced. "He doesn't even know you now."

"He remembers my parents."

Canaan remembered overhearing Kai use some very strong words about Evelyn. Sheila didn't need to know about those things spoken in the heat of anger.

"Did my father fight with him over something?" Sheila pressed. "Daddy has always had a quick temper, but it's been a long time since—"

"No, Kai and your father got along okay."

Sheila's hazel eyes—which had always seemed capable of seeing more than she was meant to see—narrowed with interest. "My mother, then."

Canaan brushed away a memory. "She and Kai had their differences of opinion from time to time, but that's not quite it, either." He leaned forward and lowered his voice. "Kai's still guided by some of the beliefs with which he was raised. He knows your arrival will stir memories of your time here as a child and of your mother's death. Her name is sure to come up." That much was true, anyway.

"You bet it is."

"Did you ever notice, when you were a child, that the Navajo avoid speaking the names of the dead?"

"Yes, I think I remember. But I never knew why."

"It's because of a fear that the spirit of the dead will overhear, and think it's a call to return. Of course, it is believed that any lingering spirit is always evil."

"I thought the spirit was believed to linger for only four days after death," she said. "Not twenty-four years."

"Well, your mother's death is still a mystery. We had no peace about her passing."

"You can't possibly be saying you think my mother's ghost is still hanging around the school, seeking revenge on someone."

"Of course not, but I can't deny that others might be entertaining those concerns. Your presence here will bring back her memory. Who knows what kind of trouble that could stir up."

Sheila sat back in her chair with a sigh.

Canaan knew she might find out more about her past if she dug deeply enough, but at what cost? He'd told Granddad this was a bad idea.

Canaan finished his stew, then glanced at Sheila's untouched tray and felt immediately contrite. "Here I am depressing you."

Sheila grimaced. "If you meant to put me on a guilt trip, that was a good send-off."

"Why should you feel guilty?"

"I'm white. Isn't it understood in this country that white Americans must pay for all the nasty acts of their ancestors?"

Canaan leaned closer. "Unfortunately, your…whiteness might have been part of Tanya's problem this afternoon."

"You don't say," Sheila drawled.

"But that wasn't all."

"Back to the dog again? I promise to talk to Doc as soon as I see him—"

"Yes, I think Moonlight's death upset her most of all. She'll get over it. She's a loving, forgiving child, and I know she's curious about you, even though she's struggling with ingrained family prejudice." He took his fork and speared a chunk of mutton from Sheila's untouched bowl of stew.

Typically, most people under a great deal of pressure lose their appetites, but he seemed to have an iron stomach.

"Mind telling me again how you came to have that blowout on the road?" he asked.

Her eyes narrowed. "The story hasn't changed, Canaan."

"You're talking about a dog disappearing in a puff of smoke, which distracted you and caused you to run off the road and hit a rock. Or you're considering the possibility that there might have been two dogs."

She nodded, wincing at his tone. "Crazy as it sounds."

"What about the sun's glare?" he asked. "That glare was bad today. What if the dog you saw was a reflection? Moonlight could have been to the right of your Jeep, but her reflection in the window could have doubled, making you think you saw her to your left."

"Or what if I'm lying to you? Or what if this is another dream I'm having, and I'll wake up with you pounding on my door, insisting it's dinnertime."

He sighed. "It doesn't hurt to consider other possibilities."

"Any more up your sleeve?"

"I heard a report from a delivery guy, Charlie, who comes through here twice a week."

She groaned. "Oh, great, you're really serious about this. So tell me what the delivery guy saw."

"He said he saw a tan-colored Jeep weaving all over the road before stopping at the side of the road."

Her gaze sharpened. "Did he see the *dog?*"

"He didn't mention it, and he was coming from the other direction, possibly too far away." He hesitated. Stared down into the stew. Hesitated some more.

"What is it?" she asked.

"Do you drink?" He had to ask for the sake of thoroughness.

She blinked, obviously irritated now. "All the time. I drink water, milk, lemonade—"

"Were you drinking liquor this afternoon?"

She glared at him. "Did you smell any on my breath?"

He winced inwardly, hating this conversation. "I'm not trying to accuse you of anything, and I'm not trying to give you a hard time, but Charlie did—"

"Yes, I know, Charlie saw me weaving all over the road like a drunk." She glanced around, then leaned closer. "Why couldn't the jerk have come to see if I was okay, instead of tattling to my boss and causing me more trouble?" she asked more softly.

"I didn't ask him that."

"No, Canaan, I was not drunk this afternoon—you didn't smell anything on my breath. Did I act drunk when you talked to me? And no, I don't do—" She broke off, obviously aware that her rising voice had attracted the attention of several of the diners around them. "I don't do drugs. Feel free to do an alcohol or drug test on me anytime, but I'd better see everybody else taking the same test. You have no reason to accuse me—"

"Would you please keep your voice down?"

She closed her mouth again.

"Look, I didn't ask to be interim principal, and I know I'm not doing a very good job of this, but give me a break, will you? I'm doing the best I can."

"Well, I could have done without this lovely dinner tonight." To his surprise, her voice softened, and he recognized a dry humor deep in her eyes. "My driving skills may be in question, but there's no reason to suspect me of anything else. Fortunately for this school and for my career as a nurse here, my job does not include driving. Are you this nosy all the time? With everybody?"

"I'm not being—"

"Oh, yeah, I remember now." Her voice dropped a few decibels. "You always were curious about everybody else's business."

"I was concerned." He tried to scowl at her, but somehow he couldn't put his heart into it. He was remembering an incident when they were kids on the playground, fighting over a ball. She had won the argument; he had given in first. Then she gave him the ball. She wasn't afraid of a fight. In fact, she seemed to love a good one. But she never held resentment. She forgave easily.

Two more people entered the cafeteria, and Canaan glanced toward the door. "Here come Doc and Tanya."

"Right. I guess I'd better get ready for round two," Sheila muttered. "Tell me what grade Tanya is in."

Canaan watched Tanya for a moment, saw the nervous darting of her gaze, the tightness of her arms folded over her chest, the way her black hair fell into her face. "She's in seventh grade, but for some reason she had trouble in school last year and has been taking the remedial reading class. She's twelve going on eighteen, and very bright."

As Doc went through the serving line, Tanya's gaze reached Canaan. She nibbled her lower lip when she saw Sheila beside him. Instead of picking up a tray, she left Doc and wove her way around the tables to Canaan and Sheila.

She stopped beside Canaan, her brown arms still crossed, an expressive, dark brow lifted as if in summons.

"You promised."

"There's time yet," Canaan said. "There's no reason to be impolite."

"It's dark, Canaan, and you promised to…" She glanced at

Sheila, stuck her chin out, and continued, "…to exorcise the dorm."

Sheila audibly swallowed a gasp.

Canaan avoided looking at her. She must think he was a madman.

## ❧ Chapter Eleven ❧

Sheila was dreaming. That had to be it. Her earlier suggestion that she would soon wake to hear Canaan announcing dinner was the most likely reason for all this craziness.

Exorcisms? Accusations that Sheila was drunk this afternoon? If this wasn't a dream, she was going to sock somebody soon. Preferably Canaan.

Canaan's voice registered. "Tanya, I did not say I would exorcise the dorm, I told you I would teach you the prayers I learned as a child to keep away the spirits that are frightening you."

"Spirits?" Sheila echoed. Definitely a dream.

Tanya shot a glance her way, her expression noticeably lacking in rancor, given her reaction to Sheila earlier. There was room for only fear in the girl's eyes.

When Doc reached the table, Canaan picked up his tray and

stood. "Excuse us for a few minutes, Doc. Tanya and I are going to her dorm for a little bit."

"Fine, stay as long as you need. Going to bless the rooms? The buildings could probably all use a good blessing. Need me to come? I know where Bob kept the anointing oil."

"No, we won't be long."

Doc's plastic tray clattered on the table as he set it where Canaan's had been and took his seat. His gaze rested warmly on Sheila, and his hand reached out to cover hers with a reassuring pat. Then, like Canaan, he bowed his head, but he did not pray aloud.

Seconds later, sensing Sheila's attention, he looked up at her. "You look sick. If you're going to throw up, don't do it on me."

"Exorcism?"

Understanding dawned in his black eyes. "The prayers? That's no exorcism, whatever Tanya calls it. It's just Canaan's way of easing the minds of the kids who've told each other too many scary stories." He picked up his coffee cup and took a long swallow, then winced, making a face at the apparent heat. "Tanya's got an active imagination."

"So the kids believe Canaan's some kind of ghost-buster?"

Doc put his cup down. "Don't believe in ghosts, huh?"

Sheila didn't want to go there. "Why do the children believe in them?"

"Because they're kids." He paused, glancing around at the other diners. "Didn't you believe in monsters when you were a child?"

She thought of the nightmares that still came to her, remembering her irrational fear of dogs, then nodded. "I was assured countless times that no monsters existed."

"Who told you that?"

"My father. My Sunday school teachers."

He shrugged. "Did you believe them?"

"I tried, but it was hard for me, since I knew my mother had been taken by a monster."

Doc watched her in silence for a moment. "A monster didn't get your mother."

"Then tell me what it was."

His motions slowed, and he caught Sheila's gaze. "Maybe you don't need to talk about all this right now. There's plenty of time to discuss the details of your mother's death." He picked up his fry bread and glanced at Sheila's plate. "Aren't you going to eat Betsy's bread? She made it because she knew you were coming. She remembered how much you loved it."

"I'm sorry." Sheila glanced at her plate of uneaten food. "I'm trying to come to terms with some things."

"Tanya's trying, too," Doc said. "That's all the exorcism is about. Canaan's helping her."

Sheila raised her spoon and dipped it in the stew. So this wasn't a dream. She'd never seen anyone go to such lengths to reassure children that there were no monsters beneath the beds, but she'd never seen a twelve-year-old as afraid as Tanya appeared when she walked into the cafeteria.

Doc glanced thoughtfully toward the door, then back at Sheila. "Sometimes, though," he said softly, "there *are* monsters."

The words chilled Sheila. She watched Doc eating his stew with obvious enjoyment, as if he hadn't just said what he had. She wanted to ask him to elaborate, but then he would.

She thought about Tanya's reaction to the dog today, and wondered how much of the girl's hostility had been the simple response to her fear.

The dog. "Doc, I'm so sorry about what happened today. I would never intentionally harm—"

"Of course you wouldn't." Doc picked up his knife and fork and cut his meat. "Tanya overreacted this afternoon, but as I told you, she's emotional right now. She's over it. Now let it rest, Sheila."

His voice was gentle, firm and kind. Sheila tried to do as he said. "Thank you." She took a sip of milk and forced down another bite of stew.

What was it about Tanya that puzzled her? Why was it she seemed to feel a thread of connection, some sense of empathy, with a stranger? Perhaps fear was more of a bonding agent than she'd realized.

Canaan felt Tanya's accusing look as they walked through the darkness.

"You forgot," Tanya accused.

"I did not forget."

"But it's nighttime! You know what happens then."

They stepped onto the sidewalk that led to Tanya's dorm, three buildings away. Silence hovered over the school as if that silence, itself, had a spirit. It seemed everyone on campus was in the cafeteria. The place felt eerily deserted.

Tanya scampered closer to Canaan's side.

"Relax," Canaan said. "The Navajo werewolf waits until dark to begin preparations for his work, preparations that take time. You'll be safe for another hour yet."

"How do you know so much about the Navajo werewolf?"

"My Navajo grandfather told me."

"What kind of preparations?" she asked, her voice breathless.

Canaan didn't want to terrorize her, but neither did he want her to relax her guard when he also felt there was a threat. "Oh, things like putting on his costume, constructing his dry paintings on the hogan floor and invoking his spirits. That can take a long time." He didn't dare tell her that someone with a lot of practice—years of practice—might be doing these dry paintings in much less time.

Tanya's breath caught audibly. He knew she was straining her ears for mockery in his voice, but she wouldn't detect any.

"Where does he prepare?" she asked.

"Come on, Tanya, everyone knows he lives in a haunted hogan somewhere in Piñon Valley."

Tanya clutched his arm. "Why are you talking like this? Are you making fun of me?"

"Have I ever made fun of you?"

Her clutch tightened. "No."

"Have I ever made fun of anyone at this school?"

No answer, but he felt the brush of her hair against his arm as she shook her head.

"You're wondering why I take this as seriously as you do?"

"Uh-huh. The dorm parents don't. They won't even let me talk about the wolf. Jane gives me demerits when I do."

"That's because of a long-held belief by our ancestors that to talk about something or someone is to call attention to ourselves. You talk about the wolf, you call its attention to you, and that just places you in danger. Same as talking about the dead."

"Then why are you talking about it?"

"Because I believe differently."

"Why?"

"I believe in the power of Christ to protect me. You need to know that you aren't alone. You also need to realize that this is no game."

Tanya walked beside him a few more steps, holding tightly to his arm with both hands. "April says the new nurse could be a Navajo werewolf."

"She's not even Navajo. That doesn't make sense. And Nurse Metcalf just got here today."

"But she killed Moonlight. Isn't that a sign?"

"You accused her of killing Moonlight, but you have no proof that she did. You know how the dog liked to hang around the highway. I'm surprised she didn't get hit before now."

"Some dogs have special powers, you know."

"They do not. Who's been filling your head full of these myths?"

Tanya shrugged. "Maybe Moonlight was protected until a wolf got to her." Tanya hesitated for a moment. "The white woman."

Canaan stopped walking. "If you keep up this kind of talk, I'll turn right around and go back to the cafeteria. That's how rumors get started." He pulled from her grasp and turned.

"No, Canaan! Please!" Tanya grabbed his arm again. "I'm just telling you what April told me."

"April couldn't have been the one to tell you Nurse Metcalf killed Moonlight, because you never saw April from the time we found the dog to the time you so rudely made that accusation."

"No, but April hates whites, and she'd been talking about a white wolf coming to the school, and this afternoon it seemed like she was right. Ever since her parents died, she's talked like that."

Canaan started walking again. "She didn't hear that kind of talk from her parents."

"No."

"I sure hope it wasn't from any of the teachers."

Tanya was silent.

"You're one of her friends," Canaan prodded. "You know where she's getting these silly ideas."

"Are you sure they're silly?"

"Tanya." He stopped again.

"Okay! I'll tell you. Her brother Steve." She tried to tug him forward.

Canaan took a deep breath, rubbing his neck as he willed away the tension. He was tempted to accuse Tanya of lying, or march her right over to the cafeteria, where Steve was one of the workers, and let Tanya accuse the seventeen-year-old to his face.

After the death of his parents, the boy had pretty much taken over the parenting of his younger brother and sister, Jamey and April. Steve was hardworking, dependable and a loving brother. Though obviously devastated by the tragedy, he was otherwise logical and well-adjusted.

Canaan decided he could leave this battle to another day. Besides, if Tanya was right about the intolerance of the Hunt children, they wouldn't listen to someone who was half-white.

"Don't talk to them about this," Tanya begged. "They know I'm here with you. They'll blame me for telling you."

"Any other instructions before we get on with this?"

Tanya shook her head.

"Good. I want you to stop listening to Steve and April. Every time you trash the white people with your words, you not only sound ignorant, you insult half of my ancestors. I don't like it. Whites have nothing to do with the activities of our tribal monsters—we have enough imagination to do that all by ourselves."

Tanya stepped close to him, her fear evident on her face,

which was illuminated by a security light on the dorm build-ing. "Okay, I'm sorry. Please, Canaan, come on. It's dark."

He didn't move. He wanted more information. "Where did April and Steve get the idea that a white person could be a Navajo werewolf?"

"I don't know...they didn't say. They were afraid to say."

"Betsy wouldn't have told them that, would she?" Canaan didn't relish trying to reprimand someone as old and authori-tative as Betsy Two Horses. She was Granddad's age.

"I don't know. Please, Canaan."

"Why have you become so frightened of the wolf all of a sudden these past few weeks? Steve and April don't have such a strong influence on you, do they?"

Tanya squirmed, glancing toward the door. "Please, I'm scared." He could feel her hands shaking as she held his arm. "The more I try to think about it, the more it scares me."

Canaan finally relented. He would get no more information out of her by terrifying her. "Okay, let's go."

She nearly pulled him forward as she peered toward the shadows of the buildings and bushes.

"Tanya, have you seen one?"

Her breath caught audibly. "I can't tell you."

"Why not?"

"I...I just can't. It's dangerous to speak about it."

"Or maybe you don't want to talk about it because there's nothing you can tell me for sure. You're just afraid there *might* be something out there, and you don't want to be alone, in case there is."

"He's out there." Her voice was a trembling whisper, and she sounded very certain about what she said.

Those whispered words chilled him.

They reached the double front doors of the dorm, and he pulled the right door open.

Tanya hesitated, peering into the gloom.

"Go ahead, it's safe," he assured her.

"You first."

He went in.

She followed cautiously, reaching for the light switch inside the doorway. "How will your prayers fight this wolf?"

"You can battle the spirit of evil only with good. All good in my life comes from the Holy Spirit of God, not from myself, or magic words or ancient rituals and symbols. From God alone."

"B-but I'm not a Christian. I don't know if I believe—"

"What do you believe? Do you believe in the old ways, like Betsy?"

"She says that the old words protect her."

"We've talked about this. You've learned about Jesus in Sunday school. Nothing we do will protect us from a force more powerful than we are. We are dependent on the power of God."

Tanya glanced out the window, and Canaan could almost read her mind. It was too long after dark. The wolf had had time to prepare his sand painting and complete his rituals. He could be coming.

"What can we do now?" She glanced from window to door.

"We use weapons of the light. Human souls need to be filled with light, or darkness will fill them." He reached his hand to her and waited until she took it. "Repeat after me."

"What are you going to say?"

"I'm going to quote some verses from Ephesians and pray for God's goodness to fill our souls and bless these rooms."

"Will it work if I'm not a Christian?"

Canaan didn't want to terrify her into a faith in Christ. He didn't believe that would be faith at all. "I am protected. I'll pray for your protection and for the protection of this school. But you have learned that God has His own will, and we don't always know what that is."

"So you're saying this might not work?"

"I'm saying that if we ask God for His protection against the evil in this place and if we put ourselves under His protection, the evil cannot harm us."

"But…my father says Christ will steal my spirit, that it will never be mine again. If that's what you—"

"Your father can't be too afraid of that, or he wouldn't be sending you to this school. He knows what we teach and believe."

"He doesn't like the Navajo schools in town, and we live too far away. Please don't force me to be a Christian."

"No one can ever force you," Canaan said. "I'll pray for your protection. But will you please promise me that the next time the wolf visits you, you'll tell me?"

She stared hard at the darkness pressing in through the window. "But he'll hurt me if I tell."

"The wolf?"

Tanya nodded, closing her eyes. "He'll bury me alive in the sand on the desert." Her voice rose and fell in a breaking whisper. "He'll kill my family, the way he killed the parents of my friends. He has power."

Canaan took her hands in his and held them tightly, and he felt her trembling. "Did Steve or April tell you this?"

"No."

"Who told you?"

"I just know."

"How do you know?"

Tanya squeezed Canaan's hands. "The wolf is coming. He'll be here soon. It's starting again. Hurry, Canaan, chase him away!"

## ✤ Chapter Twelve ✤

Preston slid his cell phone earpiece over his ear and spoke Sheila's name. It automatically dialed her cell phone, which began to ring as he opened his dresser drawer and pulled out socks and briefs. He expected to reach her voice mail. He intended to leave a simple message of encouragement and love.

To his surprise, he heard children talking and laughing in the background just before she spoke.

"Preston? Sorry, I meant to turn this thing off when I came to dinner. What's up?"

"Nothing much." Except he was pulling his duffel from the cedar-lined closet of his roomy master bedroom, which he had built a few months ago, thinking about a future with Sheila. "I was just worried about how you sounded when we spoke earlier. If you can't talk right now, that's okay. I just wanted to know how you were doing."

There was a hesitation. "Too early to tell." It sounded as if she'd cupped her hand over her mouth to muffle her reply from other ears. "But if you're asking if I want you to ride out here on your silver stallion and save me, the answer is—"

"Okay, fine, I don't need my nose rubbed in it." And he didn't need to hear her tell him to stay in Missouri, because then he might have to lie, and he was a horrible liar. "And my stallion is gunmetal, not silver."

"Whatever." There was the hint of a smile in her voice.

"How's Canaan?" he asked, unable to resist. "Things better?"

"Um, I'll have to get back with you on that, too."

"You do that."

Sorry he'd asked—sorry he'd even thought about it—he found himself wishing he *was* the lying type. He could have attended church with Sheila, said all the right things, quoted all the right passages of scripture. That was what a lot of the business people in the area did, attending church on Sunday and placing a cross or a fish symbol on their signs and business cards so that during the rest of the week they could gather green little sheaves from their clueless customers and clients.

He pulled some jeans from hangers, grabbed some summer shirts and stuffed the duffel.

"Are you going to tell me why you really called?" Sheila asked.

"Blaze wants to know if there are any more openings for cheap labor in the clinic out there."

"I haven't even seen the clinic yet. I had hoped Canaan would show it to me tonight, but he's busy with another project right now."

Preston frowned. Was that a thread of perplexity in her voice? She was seldom perplexed. "Well, anyway, I know you're probably hungry." There. That was a lie, because he knew she wouldn't be hungry. She always lost her appetite when stressed. "Keep in touch with me, please? I want to make sure you're doing okay."

There was a pause, and he braced himself. There'd been times in the past when he could have sworn she was a mind reader, and he didn't want to argue with her tonight about whether or not he and Blaze should join her.

"I'll call," was all she said. "Thanks, Preston. I'll talk to you soon."

"Yes," he said. "We'll talk soon." Very soon.

After they disconnected, he tossed his shave kit on top of the clothes, added a few other items, then realized the contents were spilling out of the duffel. Time to stop dancing around the idea of this road trip and make the decision. Should he pull his suitcase from the walk-in closet?

The note of dejection he'd heard in her voice just before the disconnect was enough to make his decision for him.

Always, when growing up, Preston had been independent. He'd had to be, especially when his mother had a bad episode, with a younger sister needing someone to provide solid guidance and a father too preoccupied with his wife's needs to be there for anyone else. When Preston went away to college for the first time, he'd called home barely three weeks later to discover that, once again, his sister, Willow, was alone, their mother back in the hospital.

Against all advice, he became a college dropout. He postponed returning for a year, then graduated summa cum laude in an accelerated program, and never regretted giving up that year for his sister.

He had a feeling he might regret tonight's decision, but he couldn't let Sheila stay out in that distant place alone, feeling she had no friends. As soon as Willow and Graham returned home, Preston was leaving for Arizona. Today was Blaze's last day of school commitments for the summer. If, for some reason, Blaze couldn't go, Preston would go by himself.

Sheila watched grumpy Kai Begay pick up his tray and walk toward the trash cans, his long black ponytail trailing down his back. He glanced over his shoulder at her one last time before putting away his utensils. He would not meet her gaze, but she got the message well enough.

A warm hand rested gently on her arm. She looked up to find Doc watching her.

He squeezed her arm and let go. "You going to tell me why you came all the way out here for a job?"

"I thought you knew. I'm between jobs. I learned about the Hunts' deaths and Canaan's need for help in the clinic."

Doc watched her with a look she knew well. He was the eternal skeptic. "You can tell everyone else that story if you want. But tell me why you're really here."

She hesitated, unprepared to go into detail.

"And what's happened to you?" he asked, before she could form an acceptable reply. "I didn't expect you to be the giggly little girl you used to be, but I also didn't expect this." He gestured to her face.

"Thanks a lot, Doc. I didn't realize I looked so bad."

"You didn't inherit those dark circles from your parents. And do you always bite your fingernails to the quick?"

She looked down at her hands, uncomfortable but not surprised by his sharp eye. "It makes sense to keep them short because of the work I do. Have you been talking to Canaan or Johnny Jacobs?"

"Johnny? No. I didn't have to. You can make at least five times as much money nursing in Missouri as you can here, and I know your mother was an excellent nurse. You're so much like her, I don't doubt you're good, so you would have no trouble getting a job closer to Missouri. The reason most teachers come to this school is because they feel called by God, or they feel at home in a Navajo environment. I don't think this is an assignment from God, and you can't be feeling comfortable here. What's your story?"

She nudged her tray across the table and rested her elbows on the edge. "What happened to my mother?"

He sighed and nodded. "That's what I thought."

"You're a smart man, but even you don't know everything." She gave him a grin to take the edge from her blunt words. "I came to help Canaan, but I think I have a right to know what truly happened to my mom, and no one's ever given me a straight answer."

Doc pushed his tray back and set his coffee cup down. "We can clear up the mystery very quickly. She died of insulin shock."

She felt a surge of disappointment. He couldn't possibly have fallen for that line, could he? "That was one theory of many, and not at all a proven fact. Why do you support that particular theory?"

"The autopsy. We knew she was diabetic. When the examiner discovered there was no other cause of death, the answer became obvious to me, though no one else seemed willing to accept it."

Sheila shook her head. If the answer had been that simple, Dad would have explained it years ago.

"She'd overexerted on a walk out in the desert," Doc said. "Didn't carry any of her usual hard candy with her and couldn't get back to the school in time. Johnny didn't find her for hours."

"But I was with her."

"You remember that?"

"No, but I've been told by my father, by Johnny, even by Canaan, that I was found out in the desert, lying beside my mother's body, nearly incoherent in the heat. I could never tell my father anything when he tried to find out what I was doing there, and I know there are questions in his mind, as well."

Doc waited, watching his plate.

Sheila leaned forward. "Is it possible my mother's death was intentional?"

Doc sat very still for another moment. "In what way?"

"Did she kill herself?"

He looked at her. "Why would you ask that?"

"I'm not sure, except for some…I don't know, some vague memories I have about that time."

"What do you remember?"

Sheila couldn't tell him that. Until arriving here, she'd remembered nothing. Now she was catching brief glimpses of time past that wouldn't completely materialize. "I seem to recall she was very unhappy sometimes. Did anyone here say anything to you about her after Dad and I left?"

He spread his hands "All I heard were silly guesses by the uninformed."

"For instance?"

He didn't look at her. "Nothing important."

"It might be to me. Why don't you let me decide for myself what I do and do not need to know."

He frowned. "It wouldn't do any good. Rumors aren't fact, but they can hurt."

How did she tell this man who was now a stranger that she couldn't be hurt any more than she already had been? She'd had nightmares about this place, and since discovering that her marriage was a farce, she needed some answers on which to build the rest of her life.

"I think I have a right to know what people are saying about my mother," she said, "if for no other reason than to be prepared in case I hear it from someone else."

His midnight-black gaze scanned the cafeteria—perhaps studying the faces of those who might have told him something about Evelyn Metcalf?

Sheila followed his line of vision and caught him and Betsy Two Horses exchanging a quick glance. Then his gaze traveled to the older teenager who'd been helping Betsy behind the counter, washing dishes, serving food, stirring pots on the stove. Sheila had overheard the kid's name. Steve Hunt. He would be Tad and Wendy's son, then?

"Okay, I'll tell you one thing," Doc said at last, surprising her. "Some said she died because she played with the powers of bad spirits."

"Bad spirits?"

He sighed, looking at Sheila sadly. "You see, this is why I don't think you need to hear these things, but you're right, at least you need to be prepared in case the rumors start again. Some say that Evelyn dabbled in Navajo witchcraft."

He could have backhanded her and caused less shock, but she didn't let it show. She hoped.

"As I said, I'm sure it's only rumor."

Sheila couldn't tell if he meant the words. In fact, he suddenly seemed unable to maintain eye contact with her. She studied his face, the strong jawline, the raven-black eyes. "I'm sure you don't want to tell me who would say this," she told him.

He shook his head.

"What would make anyone suspect such a thing?"

He looked at her, a deep well of sadness in his eyes. "Ignorant superstition," he said. "It's typical. Anyone who behaves strangely is a suspect around here. Your mother liked to take long, solitary walks in the desert. She promoted healthy eating, and raised her own little garden of organic produce before it became popular in this region of the country. She stirred up trouble in the cafeteria when she didn't think the food was wholesome enough and she reprimanded the dorm parents for high-sugar snacks in the dorms."

"The reprobate." Sheila's sarcasm held an unfortunately caustic note.

Doc gave her a sharp look. "It doesn't help when whites come barreling onto the reservation, preaching about what we do wrong. A gentler approach would have been a lot more effective."

Okay, now he was making it personal. First Canaan, now Doc. It was enough for one day. She was less prepared for this than she had realized. Slowly, with precision, she gathered her utensils onto her tray. "I'll take that under advisement. Would you please give my apologies to Canaan when he returns?"

"Leaving so soon?" It was Doc's turn for sarcasm.

"I just realized I need some time tonight to brush up on my spells and potions." She stood with her tray.

Doc laughed, his deep voice echoing through the cafeteria. Before she could walk away, he placed a hand on her arm. "Will you be okay?"

"Thanks for your concern, but I'm not ten years old anymore. I'll be fine."

She hadn't felt this shaken since first discovering the truth about her late husband's infidelities. How could it get any worse?

* * *

The night descends to total darkness, until no trace of sun lingers on the western horizon. I stand on a deserted hilltop, bare shoulders gleaming from the little light left in the heavens. It will be a black night. The slivered moon barely pricks the darkness. I've always liked it that way.

The whipping, cold wind matches the void deep in my heart. She is back.

She is my enemy.

Why has she returned? The question has echoed in my thoughts many times since word arrived of her coming.

I turn away from the jagged horizon of the Twin Mesas and bend to enter the doorway of the death hogan. The flickering shadows of an interior fire bring calm to me. The secrets held within this room—the knowledge those secrets will someday bring—will make everything worthwhile, but they are purchased at such a steep price. My calling is to keep those secrets, to make sure they are not lost and aren't exposed before their time comes.

I must be willing to do whatever it takes to protect those secrets. Sheila threatens them, but she might also hold answers to some of my questions.

It has been so long. Could she possibly still be carrying those answers? After all this time, can she help? Or will she be more of a threat?

Such confusion. Her arrival has put us both in danger. From each other. I must master this fear of her if I am to survive. But how much does she know?

I reach for my fur cape, shivering as it settles over my naked shoulders. Stepping to the doorway and gazing wistfully in the direction of the school, I utter a sigh that comes from a deep well of ancient longing. Someone will meet me tonight and tomorrow night. I'm never alone during the school year. I'm always busy.

Summers drag by in spurts and starts. But the school year is ripe with possibilities.

The cycle will soon be complete, and my work here will no longer be necessary. If I can only hold Sheila off until it is finished.

## Chapter Thirteen

Early Saturday morning Betsy Two Horses scraped the last dollop of thick, five-grain cereal into the steam pan. She cleaned the wooden spoon with her finger, then licked her finger. Mmm, just right. This was another of her specialties. With honey and milk, hot biscuits and fruit, this breakfast would remind everyone about how much they would miss Betsy Two Horses all summer. Nobody cooked like Betsy.

She set out a large tub of butter in a bowl of ice. Pots clattered at the huge, stainless-steel sink, where her young assistants scrubbed.

"Be careful back there!" she called over her shoulder. "We don't want to break anything this close to the end of the year. Bad luck."

The clock above the dining room entrance read six o'clock. Betsy frowned. The girl would be here soon. Sheila. Not a girl now. Betsy would have to remember that.

Last night, Sheila's hazel eyes had been filled with questions that had been left unanswered all these years. No, more than just questions. They'd held a hunger in them, a deep-rooted need to know. And Betsy was so very afraid Sheila's need might lead her to the wrong place.

Sheila looked much younger than her thirty-four years, though lines had drawn smudges between her finely shaped brows, and around her eyes. She still wore that necklace Betsy had given her all those years ago—a necklace she had given specifically to comfort a hurting little girl whose mother had just died.

Betsy wiped at a spot of spilled cereal on the stainless-steel table. What worried her most about Sheila was that thread of tension that had come and gone in her face last night. Betsy knew what first-day nerves looked like, and that didn't look like Sheila's problem. This had looked much deeper—more like an old pain that still festered.

The glass door opened, scattering Betsy's thoughts like water on a hot grill. She looked up at the slender figure stepping briskly through the door. Fresh scrubbed, neatly dressed in jeans and blouse, Sheila looked wide-awake. She looked too awake. Her gaze darted around the empty cafeteria before reaching Betsy. Her full lips, bare of makeup, pursed, then turned up in a hesitant smile as she approached Betsy at the serving table.

"Morning, Betsy. I see you have help today. It's a good thing. The others are going to hit you full force in just a few minutes."

"How would you know?"

"I saw them congregating in front of the dorms to say grace, same as they used to." The girl's light, lilting voice held a waver—again of tension—that made her seem young and vulnerable.

Betsy grunted, filling a bowl to the top with cereal and a heap of butter. She set it on Sheila's tray, added two biscuits and some sliced oranges. "Today's nothing. Wait until Monday, then you'll see a crowd. Now, I want to see every bit of this gone when you bring this tray back." She pushed the tray toward Sheila. "Better get in a habit of a good breakfast. You won't handle all those kids next week without some food."

Sheila slid her tray toward the coffeepot, hesitated, turned back. Betsy met Sheila's eyes and smiled.

"Thank you," Sheila said.

Betsy grunted again and turned to watch Steve Hunt pull another pan of biscuits from the oven.

"Betsy," Sheila said.

Betsy's head came up. She straightened her spine, met and held Sheila's gaze with difficulty.

"Do you remember when I used to come and help you in the mornings with breakfast?" Sheila placed her tray back on the counter for a moment.

"Couldn't forget. You made more mess..." Betsy caught herself. She sometimes forgot how her rough tongue could hurt a person's feelings.

"Oh, I know I wasn't much help," Sheila continued, that soft voice drawing away Betsy's unease, "but I still remember how you made me feel as if I were helping, letting me work the toasters, dish out the butter and jam. Remember how I always loved to work the dishwasher? I think I got pretty good at it. I know I sure felt important when the kids saw me working back there with you."

Betsy nodded. How could she forget that little kid with the big eyes and a broad grin that promised so much mischief? She really had been helpful in the kitchen when she wasn't spilling something. And she was bright besides. Evelyn, proud mother, had often bragged of her daughter's good grades.

Until the grades fell. And the wide grin faded. Evelyn had problems of her own about then, which had left her little time to spend with her daughter.

Betsy picked up a serving spoon and stirred the cereal. Too many memories.

"Did you miss me, Betsy?" Sheila asked.

"Yup." Betsy's gaze focused on the turquoise cross, wrapped in a casing of delicately worked gold.

Sheila reached up and touched the cross, watching Betsy. "You do remember."

Betsy replaced the spoon and wiped her hands on her apron. "Of course I do. I'm not senile yet. A person doesn't just forget five years out of her life." She looked at Sheila, felt a rush of compassion for the little girl she had been. "How... What did you and your father do when you moved to Missouri?" She remembered the change in the atmosphere in the kitchen before Evelyn's death.

"Daddy got a loan and bought a farm about a mile from a little village called Hideaway, on the shore of Table Rock Lake. Not a big farm, but enough for some cattle, a few chickens."

Betsy wondered if the horror had stopped for them there. She glanced at Sheila, and thought not. Sheila's outgoing personality had been buried under a cloud of gloom after losing her mother. Or had that, too, begun earlier? Betsy couldn't remember, hadn't wanted to remember.

"Is he still on the farm?" Betsy asked.

"Yes, he's still there." Sheila looked down at her tray, her thoughts seemingly elsewhere.

Betsy shook her head, turning away. It was there again, that lurking darkness that had surrounded the girl before. Betsy sensed it.

Sheila looked back up. She glanced around, and lowered her voice. "Betsy? Can you tell me what happened when Mom died? There are so many things I need to—"

Betsy caught her breath. "Not now. Not yet. Get settled. Get to know the kids and find out what they need. You have a lot of work to do between now and the end of school."

A delicate pink stained Sheila's cheeks. She nodded. "Okay, but soon?"

The door opened again, and several young children filed inside. "Yes, we will talk. Now I have to get to work. Hungry people are coming. Eat that cereal before it cools." Betsy turned to call her helpers.

The early arrivals, second- and third-grade girls, talked and giggled, lifting the pressing gloom of this early morning's silence as they approached the stack of trays. Most of the children went home over the weekend; the ones who stayed lived so far away their parents couldn't pick them up and take them home every Friday.

Betsy saw Sheila glancing at them as she took her place at a table in the far corner of the dining room.

As Betsy served and kept an eye on the diners, the first little girls, with their dorm mother, Jane, sat down at a table next to Sheila's. One of the bolder ones reached across and tugged at Sheila's sleeve.

Sheila looked around. The little girl giggled. Betsy saw a transformation in Sheila's expression, as if the child had chased away, for a time, a bad spirit. With an affectionate smile, Sheila spoke to the child, and the girl giggled again. Maybe this place would be good for Sheila.

"Morning, Betsy."

Startled, Betsy glanced up to see Tanya Swift, droopy-eyed and pale, reach for two slices of wheat toast.

Betsy pushed the butter forward. "Late night last night?"

Tanya shook her head. "Didn't sleep too well."

An eruption of laughter reached them from out in the dining room. Tanya glanced over her shoulder. She frowned when she saw Sheila entertaining the children with funny faces.

"I see you've already met her."

Tanya grimaced, nodded.

Laughter around Sheila once more. Betsy grunted. The younger ones would accept a white nurse more easily than the older ones would. But by the looks of Tanya, Sheila hadn't won this one. Not yet. She would. Betsy watched as Tanya glanced with curiosity at Sheila's antics, and a smile almost crossed the girl's mouth before she caught herself.

Kai came in with three of his students, and Betsy turned her attention to the man. She liked Kai. He came from up near Black Mountain, where she'd lived for the first fifteen years of her life—where Doc Cottonwood had also grown up. Kai could tell stories about some of the people all three of them knew. She liked his stories, almost as much as Doc and the kids did. But Kai hated whites.

No, hated was too strong. Over the years he'd shown more of the distrust that many of their people carried for whites. He didn't appreciate Sheila's arrival, Betsy could tell, and it was because he remembered. He'd been the one most outspoken against Sheila returning and had made his opinion known. Kai better watch his mouth this time.

He approached the serving line with his tray and glanced

up at Betsy. The wrinkles around his dark eyes stretched with surprise at the cold look of warning she shot him.

"What's wrong with you?" he asked, his voice still gruff with sleep.

She plopped a serving spoonful of cereal in a bowl and slid it across the counter to him. She jerked her head in Sheila's direction and waited until Kai looked that way.

"Leave her alone," Betsy said.

"I will. I'll leave her as alone as I can."

"You know what I mean. You knew her, too. Her parents raised her here. She went to school with our children, played with our children. She isn't going to hurt anyone."

Kai picked up his tray. "She's not a kid anymore. What if she turns out like her mother?" Without waiting for an answer, he led his boys to the far side of the dining area from where Sheila sat.

"He's right."

Betsy jerked her head around to find her helper, Steve Hunt, watching Sheila from behind the counter. His dark, slightly slanted eyes narrowed when Sheila's voice could be heard joking with the others.

"What are you talking about?" Betsy put her hands on her hips and turned to glare up at the young man, her chin pointed at his chest. "Don't tell me you've been listening to Kai, too."

"I don't have to listen to Kai. Can't you see it, Betsy? She took a job that should've gone to one of our people. Jobs are scarce here on the reservation, anyway."

"So are Navajo nurses willing to come back here and help. They want to go out into the white world, where the pay and benefits are better."

"If it's better there, why did she come here?" He turned his sullen gaze on Sheila once again. "She doesn't belong here."

A burst of laughter reached them, and Betsy saw Sheila helping one little third-grade girl balance a spoon on her nose, to the nearly unbearable delight of the other children.

"She was raised here," Betsy said, turning to see Canaan York enter the cafeteria, then stand grinning at Sheila's antics.

"Her mother died here," Steve said.

"What do you know of that? You weren't even born yet."

"I heard stories about her, bad stories."

"Who told you those stories?" Betsy demanded. "Kai?"

"No, not Kai." Steve looked down. "Other kids."

Betsy would have to watch this one, as well. With his parents gone, he had no one to keep him in line, and he was in the prime years of his life for a little troublemaking.

She could feel it in the air. Something was going to happen soon.

## Chapter Fourteen

Canaan took a tray and slid it along the stainless-steel serving counter toward Betsy Two Horses and Steve Hunt. He couldn't keep his gaze from wandering back over his shoulder to Sheila. This was the Sheila he remembered so well from childhood, always giggling with the other little girls, playing mischievous tricks, though never anything cruel. She'd learned that balancing act right here…or at least, in the old cafeteria. Tad Hunt had taught it to her, if Canaan remembered it right.

Canaan thanked Betsy for his cereal, poured himself a cup of coffee and carried his tray to Sheila's table. Two little girls who had left their seats to get closer to Sheila now scurried back to their places at a word from their dorm mother.

"You used to get into trouble every other morning for that balancing spoon act," Canaan told Sheila as he took the empty chair across the table from her. He nodded at the uneaten food on her tray. "And that was why. You got so busy playing you forgot to eat."

"Yes, Mother." Sheila made a face at him, but she poured honey over her cereal and picked up her spoon. "I forgot I knew how to do that until just a few minutes ago. Funny the things you forget about your childhood, until you return to it."

Canaan noticed she still didn't take a bite of her food. "What's wrong, don't you like Betsy's five-grain cereal? You'd better be careful not to hurt her feelings. Looks like she gave you an extra helping."

With the laughter gone from Sheila's eyes, the dark smudges beneath them appeared more prominent against the pale white skin of her face. She tipped a few drops of her milk over the cereal and took a bite.

Canaan watched this silent stranger. Only a moment before he could have sworn his old friend Sheila had peered across the table at him with those wide eyes, grinning with some secret thought of mischief. But this dark-smudged gaze held nothing, as if it had gone purposely blank. He glanced toward the kitchen, and found Betsy and Steve watching them in silence.

Canaan leaned forward. "Sheila?"

She looked up.

"You left before I returned from the dorms last night. Doc said you were tired. I hope you slept well."

"Fine." She dropped her spoon onto the table and stopped all pretense of eating. "Daddy raised me in a Baptist church, all strict and by the book. I thought I'd learned everything there was to know about the Bible until I went to college, and then I made friends with people from different denominations. I went to lots of different churches with lots of different friends, but I never saw a single exorcism take place in any of those churches."

"You won't see an exorcism here, either," Canaan said, "but if you'd come with us last night, you'd have seen some pretty heavy prayer going on."

Sheila leaned closer. "Why is Tanya so scared?"

He shrugged.

"She ran away yesterday, didn't she? That means she's pretty frightened."

Canaan nodded. If it was obvious to Sheila, it must be obvious to everyone, which was what bothered him.

"What is there to fear here at the school?" Sheila asked.

"Nothing for real, I hope." *Not yet.*

"You hope? What could there be?"

"If I knew, don't you think I'd be doing something about it?"

"Last night you said there was something frightening the kids, but you couldn't explain it."

He looked around and saw that most of the kids had finished their breakfasts and left. "The grades seem to have dropped since I arrived here. Two of the dorm parents have reported children waking up in the middle of the night screaming from nightmares."

"The same children every time? Could they be having problems at home?"

"These were children who stay at the school through the weekends because their homes are so far away."

"Have these children suggested anything that might be causing the dreams?" Sheila asked.

"They're afraid to talk."

"What else?"

"The older children seemed restless in class. They've become harder to control, which keeps me busy in the principal's office, which is why you're here."

"Something is bothering the children, but none of them will tell you what's wrong. Is that because they're afraid of you? We were always afraid of the principal."

"But we weren't afraid of the nurse," he said.

"That's because she was my mother."

"No, it's because the nurse isn't the disciplinarian, the principal is. Think about it, Sheila. I only took over as interim principal two weeks ago. Before that, I was the clinic doctor. Wendy Hunt was my office assistant. The kids would have told one of us."

"Wendy wasn't a nurse, was she?"

"No, she just helped out with files and some procedures, took vitals for me, that kind of thing. I taught her how to run the equipment, even how to draw blood."

"What did Tad do?"

"He taught and helped coach the track team."

"Doctors can instill fear in a child," Sheila said. "They order painful procedures."

"Then maybe you can reach them in a way I couldn't," Canaan said.

"The children with nightmares never described them?" Sheila asked.

He shook his head.

"And the dorm parents don't have any idea what's going on?"

"No."

"What about the teachers?"

"Nothing, just complaints of bad behavior."

"Interesting that there would be a problem like this in a Christian school," Sheila remarked.

"It isn't so strange when you think about the ancient

conflict between good and evil. Where goodness flourishes, evil will search for an opportunity to destroy it. How can we expect anything different?"

"I thought you said you were hoping they had nothing to fear."

"Not a physical presence. Evil is always around, but when it takes a physical form it becomes a physical and spiritual battleground."

She studied him silently for a moment, and like the child he'd once been, he wanted to squirm with the discomfort of her scrutiny. There was something...personal about it.

"You take your faith seriously, don't you?" she said at last.

This surprised him. "You don't?"

"Of course I do, but it's just...I don't know...nice to see a man who isn't afraid to defer to the Almighty."

"You were married, weren't you?"

"For ten years."

"Was it a good marriage?"

She grimaced. "Getting a little personal, aren't you?"

"I tend to do that. It's the doctor in me."

"No, it's the Canaan in you. You always asked a lot of questions, even when they weren't appropriate. I remember when you asked one of our teachers why she had dark roots in her blond hair."

"Oh, yeah, Mrs. Reilly. She didn't last the year. Nice change of subject."

Sheila's gaze roved around the room, settled for a few seconds on Betsy's bowed head at the sink, then returned to Canaan. "My husband wasn't exactly what I would call a devoted Christian."

"Are you saying he wasn't a believer?"

She hesitated, nodded. "I met him at a singles class at church. Turns out he was just cruising for chicks."

He smiled. "It's been a long time since I've heard that phrase."

"I was obviously not very discerning, or I'd have realized before the wedding that he didn't share my faith. Love does make people blind."

"Granddad said you were widowed."

"Two years ago," she said. "How about you? No wife? Your grandfather told me you've been too busy to find someone after your divorce."

Good old Granddad. "He's getting desperate. He even signed me up for an online dating service, but he was very specific. He's looking for a Navajo woman who intends to stay in Navajoland."

Sheila chuckled. Her laughter was infectious, as it had always been, feminine and lilting. Canaan felt a smile catch at his lips despite the reason for her amusement.

"Come on, Canaan, a handsome guy like you probably has to fight the women away."

He willed his face not to flush—an unfortunate carryover from his pip-squeak days. "I've never fought a woman away."

"No, if I know you—which, of course, I don't anymore— you probably never even noticed when a woman was interested in you."

"I think I would notice."

She shook her head, still smiling.

"Want a tour of the school?" His turn to change the subject.

"What I'd like is an orientation of the clinic."

"I've got one errand to run, then I'll have some time to show you around."

"Will it take long? I think I'll take a walk on the trail that leads toward Piñon Valley."

Canaan nodded and stood. "You should have just enough time. And you want to do it alone, right? You used to do that all the time."

Sheila blinked, obviously surprised. "I did?"

"Sure, don't you remember?"

"There are a lot of things I don't remember."

"Then a walk might do you some good." He picked up his tray and left her to make her own way into the desert, where he hoped, for her sake, she might uncover some happy memories for once.

## ∼ Chapter Fifteen ∼

Sheila watched Canaan's retreating figure—tall, confident, at ease in his own skin, even if he wasn't at peace with the situation here at the school.

His comment baffled her. Why couldn't she remember simple things like solitary walks in the desert?

There was a lot she did remember—such as racing through the desert with the other children, laughing, teasing, playing tag, getting dirt and sand in her shoes. Not too far from here were some hills painted by the colors of the windblown sand, just as beautiful as the hills of the Painted Desert, down on I-40.

Sheila and Canaan had once explored them without their parents' permission. Later, Canaan's conscience betrayed them. He confessed, and they were both restricted from playing together for a week.

She smiled at the memory as she deposited her eating

utensils in a plastic bin, waved goodbye to Betsy and stepped outside into the bright morning sunlight. Not all her memories of this place were unpleasant. In fact, most were very good.

The cotton-dry breeze had warmed with the sun, and Sheila raised her face to the sky and breathed deeply the scent of dusty, sunbaked sage. From the sidewalk beside the cafeteria, she saw a small, lone figure walking several yards out in the desert, away from the school. The breeze was stiffer out there in the open, and it picked up eddies of dust and swirled them in the air, like old phantoms trying to come to life.

The figure turned, and Sheila recognized Tanya's heart-shaped face and dark brows. The girl's long black hair whipped across her neck, and she pushed it out of her eyes as she stared at the school.

Sheila stepped off the sidewalk and walked toward her, and saw the girl stiffen. For a moment, it looked as if she might turn and run like a frightened kitten. But her slender shoulders straightened and her firm chin raised a bit higher.

Smiling to herself, Sheila slowed her steps. Tanya was a beautiful girl and obviously very skittish right now. The last thing Sheila wanted to do was make her more afraid.

Tanya had shown a surreptitious interest in Sheila this morning at breakfast, when Sheila was playing with the younger children. There had been a wistfulness in her expression that Sheila had inferred as a desire to belong. In the short time Sheila had been here, she hadn't seen Tanya interacting with any of the other kids her age.

Tanya nibbled her lower lip as Sheila approached her.

"Hello, Tanya. I don't think we were properly introduced yesterday. I'm—"

"I know who you are," she said. "You're the new nurse. I'm supposed to apologize. Canaan says I have a temper that will get me into trouble someday."

Sheila stopped a few feet away. "I knew you were upset."

"Moonlight was a good dog."

"I'm sure she was, and no animal deserves to die that way. I'm sorry it happened."

Tanya's eyes filled with quick tears. She turned her head and swiped at them.

"You must have loved her," Sheila said.

Tanya shrugged and kicked at an anthill.

"Maybe you can get a puppy."

"We aren't supposed to have pets in the dorms."

"No, I suppose that would be a bit much. Speaking of the dorms, did Canaan take care of the problem in yours last night?"

Tanya gave a sharp gasp, residue of tears glistening on her face.

Sheila hurriedly said, "I'm not making fun of you. I sure wouldn't ridicule you for your fears. Everyone has them."

"Not everybody. Canaan's not afraid of anything. Neither are Betsy Two Horses or Doc Cottonwood or Steve Hunt."

Sheila decided not to remark on that. Though she had been told that Tanya was friends with the Hunt children, Sheila hadn't had the opportunity to see her with them. All she had seen of Steve was a glare or two shot at her from behind the kitchen counter.

"What about you?" Tanya asked.

"You mean do I ever get scared? Of course."

Tanya shoved her hands into the pockets of her jeans and kicked at some pebbles on the ground. "You're supposed to outgrow stuff like that."

"Maybe so, but I didn't. I think a lot of people are scared of something, but they cover it up once they reach a certain age because they're expected to outgrow their fears."

Tanya studied her with eyes that glowed dark amber in the sun. "I didn't want to hear that."

Sheila suppressed another smile and stepped along the faint trail that wound along a ridge into the desert. "Want to walk with me a little way?" She didn't wait for Tanya's reply, but immediately set off and heard soft footsteps behind her.

"You play like a kid," Tanya said.

Sheila nodded. In the cafeteria, she wasn't behaving the way Tanya obviously expected an adult to behave. "Is there a problem with my having fun?"

"No, but I'm just saying if you play like a kid, maybe you've never grown up. That's why stuff still scares you."

"I see what you mean," Sheila said, trying, and failing, to match Tanya's serious tone.

"Doc and Canaan like you."

Sheila's footsteps slowed as she tried to keep up with Tanya's train of thought. The girl seemed younger than twelve.

"They don't know me anymore," Sheila said. "I was younger than you are now when I left here."

"But they still like you."

"Yes, and I like them, but that doesn't mean they know me."

Tanya was walking beside Sheila now. "What kinds of things are you afraid of?"

Sheila glanced to her side to see Tanya watching her, stepping over the terrain like a sure-footed antelope, never stumbling, focus intent. "Oh, things like my loved ones getting sick or dying," Sheila said. "Death scares me the same way it does everybody else."

"Canaan says Christians don't have to be afraid of death, because they're going to heaven."

"That's true, and I'm not saying it's right for us to fear. I don't know of very many people who are perfect Christians, though. Not very many people want to die."

Tanya nodded. "I'm not a Christian. My father says to do that I'll have to let somebody else take over my spirit, and he doesn't want me to let the God of the *biligaana*—" She caught herself and looked at Sheila.

"That's scary, too, isn't it?" Sheila said. "Letting someone else, even God, take over your spirit."

"Nobody has the right to control me."

"Some might say that the Creator has every right to control His creation. When we allow Him to guide us, we're wise in acknowledging His role in the universe."

Tanya shrugged. "What else are you afraid of? You weren't afraid to drive out here all by yourself alone."

"I'm not afraid of driving."

"Were you afraid to leave your family?"

"No. I was sad to leave my father and my friends back home in Missouri, but I knew I'd be going back soon."

"Don't you have kids?"

"No. If I had children, I wouldn't have come—" She stopped herself, wishing she could take back those words. Tanya's parents left her at home when they traveled.

"Oh." Tanya walked a few paces in silence, then said, "I have friends whose parents died. Jamey and April Hunt's parents died this spring when their house burned down, and my best friend, over in Ganado, lost her mother when she was only five."

Sheila slowed her steps and raised her hands to shield her eyes from the sun. "What's your best friend's name?"

"Donna. She's a lot older than me, but she's still my best friend now, and she's my cousin. She's going to have a baby in a couple of months."

"How old is Donna?"

"Eighteen. She and her dad lived next door to us until she got married and moved. Now she weaves rugs at Hubbell Trading Post."

"She's going to have a baby?"

"Yes, but it's not what everybody thinks. She got pregnant right after she got married, not before."

"You said you were friends with April and Jamey Hunt."

"Yes, April used to be a friend of mine," Tanya said, then she fell silent.

Sheila glanced at the child again, and finally recognized the expression she had noted earlier in Tanya's eyes. Loneliness. It explained why she had so readily agreed to this walk, and to talk about things one wouldn't expect her to talk about with a strange *biligaana*.

Loneliness was an emotion Sheila understood well. She had wondered several times whether that loneliness might have motivated her to continue her relationship with Preston.

Yet, she knew better. She simply liked Preston. Yes, she loved him, but having given herself hours and hours on the road on her drive here to brood about it, she realized that she and Preston were compatible. They liked the same things, they spoke the same language and even though he did not claim to be a believer, he had been raised by believers, he had grown up knowing the Bible. If not for that one big problem between them, she knew a marriage with him could be very good.

She glanced back toward the school and thought about Canaan. At one time, they, too, had been very compatible.

"April's been different lately," Tanya said.

"You're not friends with April anymore?" Sheila asked.

A shrug. "I like her brother better. Jamey's not bossy and doesn't say mean things."

"She's probably been hurting quite a bit since her parents died."

A nod.

"Does she ever talk about her parents' deaths?"

A shake of the head. "But lately she's been acting weird."

"How?"

"Mean. She picks even more on her younger brother, Jamey."

"It's hard to lose your parents."

Tanya looked up at her. "Jamey lost his parents, too. I lose mine all the time when they go on trips to their craft shows."

Sheila nodded.

"I miss them so much. I don't even want to think about how I'd feel if they didn't come back."

"It's hard," Sheila said. "My mother died when I was ten."

"When you were here?"

Sheila nodded.

"How did she die?"

Sheila caught a whiff of an old, familiar scent that drifted to her on an air current, but she couldn't quite place it. "I never found out."

Tanya stopped walking. "Your mother was the school nurse. I've heard Jane talking about it."

"That's right." Sheila glanced over the horizon to find a thin plume of smoke rising into the clear sky. That scent…

"April and Jamey's mother worked in the clinic," Tanya said.

Sheila glanced at her, drawn by the suddenly hushed voice. "Yes."

"And now you're here." Dark eyes widened.

Sheila could tell Tanya had connected the incidents with her mother and Wendy. "Nothing's happened to me."

"But it might."

"Things are always happening to people, but just because something happened to my mother when we lived here doesn't mean it'll be the same in my case. Canaan runs the clinic now, and nothing's happened to him. There have been countless health professionals at the clinic in the days since my mother's death, and I've heard nothing about their fate."

Tanya frowned. Her footsteps slowed as she glanced toward the horizon. "You smell that?"

Sheila nodded, slowing with her. "Some kind of wood smoke."

"Cedar." The word was whispered, and Tanya stopped walking.

"What does that signify?"

Tanya glanced back toward the school. "I've got to get to the dorm. I...I want to put some things away in my chest." She pivoted, and her steps quickened as she followed the trail back. She didn't wait for Sheila to follow.

## ❧ Chapter Sixteen ❧

The duffel bag hit the backseat of Preston's Jeep at the same time a whoop of joy reverberated through the cab.

"Free!" Blaze hopped into the passenger seat. Denim short pants, inexpertly hemmed, revealed black legs that bulged with muscles. A pale blue T-shirt emphasized his strong arms and broad chest.

Reportedly, the young man's most striking physical characteristic was his eyes. Preston had overheard, often enough, the women of Hideaway remark on the beauty of those eyes. But then women tended to romanticize, and Preston did not. He knew from experience that kindness lay behind those dark eyes and friendly features. Blaze Farmer had a mature grasp of human nature despite his age.

"I'm gonna miss that place," Blaze said.

Preston slid into the driver's seat and closed the door. "What place?"

Blaze gestured across the lake toward the boys' ranch that had been his home since a little before his sixteenth birthday. Now, at nineteen, he had just completed the equivalent of six semesters at College of the Ozarks. The kid was smart, and he was a hard worker.

"We'll be back soon," Preston assured him.

"With Sheila, right?"

"That remains to be seen. At any rate, I want to see that she's okay."

"We'll need to stop somewhere on the way and take some chocolate as a peace offering."

Preston scowled at him as he pulled out into the street in front of the general store. "I'm not fighting with her. Why would I need to make peace?"

"You'll be fighting when we get there, trust me. Are you going to drive back out to the farm and say goodbye to the girls?"

"I already said goodbye. Their parents are happily home, and all is well in their world. Why would I be fighting with Sheila?"

Blaze gave him a look that said, *I can't believe you're that dense.*

Preston relented. "I know she *says* she doesn't want me there, but remember you're the one who talked me into this in the first place."

"Still don't hurt to have a peace offering. Even if you're not fighting, peace offerings are good insurance."

"Fine. I'm sure we'll find a good place for chocolate on the way."

"And flowers."

"Don't get carried away."

"Purple daisies and dark chocolate, the darker the better."

Preston grimaced at the winding road ahead. He'd

thought he knew Sheila pretty well. After all, they'd met more than a year ago. Blaze had worked with her only a few times at the hospital. "How do you know so much about her?"

"I listen," Blaze said. "Women talk all the time when they're working. Any man who listens is a wise man."

As they left the town of Hideaway far behind, Preston decided he might just swallow some pride and discover what else this cocky nineteen-year-old could tell him about romance.

Sheila stood on the desert trail long after Tanya had run between the buildings and out of sight. The school didn't resemble anything in her memories, except for the tailing of small shacks that stretched out from the main campus—the only remnant of the old school. Even so, she felt a strange sense that she had stood in this place before.

The scent of smoke reached her again, and she closed her eyes. It was such a familiar aroma, one that threaded through many of her early memories. As a child, she had often caught that scent on the wind during track practice after school. She had known about local superstitions, how the fragrance of a certain incense indicated the presence of a skinwalker in the area—a Navajo witch who dressed in the skins of a particular animal.

The kids had told scary skinwalker stories late at night, and she remembered countless nightmares about the Navajo werewolf—the most frightening of skinwalkers—a witch covered in wolf skin. She wondered if those stories had been the basis for her fear of dogs. It didn't seem quite reasonable, but her fears weren't reasonable, either.

There was a significance about that particular scent....

Tingles of one hidden memory snaked through her mind.

That smoke…incense…a hazy, smoke-filled hogan with log beams above her…and sharp pain.

"No," Sheila whispered, willing away that memory even as it developed. She wasn't ready to remember yet.

*Take this slowly.* She glanced again toward the school and caught sight of Canaan's lanky frame walking between buildings. He had obviously completed his errand. The orientation could begin.

Without looking back, she returned to campus.

Preston filled the Jeep with gasoline in Aurora, Missouri, where Blaze insisted on taking the helm. Though Preston protested, he was glad the kid had the driving skills and sense of direction to get them safely to Sheila. It meant Preston didn't have to carry the burden of the trip while worrying about Sheila's circumstances.

"I'm not sure where a person would be able to find purple daisies in Arizona," Preston said as Blaze settled behind the wheel.

"Yellow Pages would work," Blaze said, glancing at him. "They even have those in Indian country, you know."

"Native American. Maybe we could find a florist in Albuquerque."

"Native American?" Blaze snorted. "That would make me African-American. Excuse me, I'm American and I'm me. The long descriptive stuff just don't work for me."

"Well, would you mind not even introducing the subject when we get there? Don't start pushing hot buttons at this school," Preston warned. "We're trying to get on Sheila's good side, not alienate her or the powers that be at this place."

Blaze looked at his watch. "How long before we're there?"

"With any luck," Preston said, "we should be pulling into the school by tomorrow evening."

"Then be prepared for worship service tomorrow evening. I know you don't like it, but you'll be expected to do it."

"I know how to go through the motions," Preston said.

Blaze gave him a glare.

"Watch the road."

Blaze returned his attention to Highway 39. "Sheila deserves more than just the motions."

"I can't help that."

"Neither can she. You can have all the right motions and all the right words, but if the most important thing doesn't come from your heart, it won't work." He braked gently for a curve.

"She knows how I feel. I'm not trying to fool her. I wouldn't dare try. She's too smart, and she has a lot of insight."

Blaze gradually increased the speed, though Preston noticed that he stayed a bit below the limit along this lush, curving stretch of road. "So you think she's smart and has a lot of insight, but that she's just duped?"

"What do you mean?"

"You don't believe in God, and you know she does. I might not know much, but it seems to me that's a big thing to disagree on. If you don't believe, then you've gotta think she's a dupe for believing."

"I've never said I didn't believe."

"In Christ?"

"In God."

"So you don't believe in the Son of God, but you believe in God."

Preston opened the atlas to the state of Arizona. "I know Him, all right. I'm just not on speaking terms with Him."

"So you believe that Jesus—"

"Could we drop the subject? I know the drill, Blaze. I've been over and over this with Sheila, and we're at an impasse. I don't believe God is there for me. He might be there for every superpious Christian who has never suffered or lost anything in life, but He hasn't been there for me or my family. Judging by what Sheila's gone through for the past couple of years—except, of course, for the good fortune of meeting and falling in love with me—I can't see that Christianity offers much."

"So the bit about everlasting life and heaven and all that soared right over your head in Sunday school, right?"

"If I want to argue about God, I'll have every opportunity for that as soon as I see Sheila again. Mind if I take a break from it until then?"

"You could practice on me. Meanwhile, you might want to think about that guy she's with in Arizona. I heard he's some kind of missionary or something. You've got some major competition, if you ask—"

"Just watch the road, would you?" Preston leaned his seat back and placed the open atlas over his face. "Wake me when we get there."

"Amarillo tonight?"

"Tucumcari. I want to get there tomorrow, not sometime next week. Now drive, and leave me in peace."

He heard Blaze chuckle softly to himself. This was going to be a long road trip if the kid thought he was going to get Preston Black saved before they reached Twin Mesas.

Canaan completed Sheila's orientation of the huge clinic at the bank of filing cabinets lined up against the wall. The snarl of misfiled and often incomplete medical records was his biggest challenge, yet also his best hope in figuring out what might be going on with the kids.

She gave a soft whistle. "Your grandfather sure didn't spare any expense on this place."

Canaan pulled an office chair from the desk and gestured for her to sit down, then pulled a handful of manila folders from the top drawer. "I saw you talking with Tanya. Has she come down from her high horse with you?"

With a smile, Sheila took the folders from him. "I had forgotten that phrase. Yes, I think Tanya's fine with me. What are these?"

"They're medical records on the Hunts and Bob Jaffrey. Also on Teddy Whitehorse and Jim Begay."

"Begay? A relative of Kai's?"

Canaan shrugged. "The name Begay is as common here as Smith or Jones in the rest of the country. Teddy and Jim were the students I mentioned to you last night. They died in separate incidents before they started college."

"You still think there's some kind of significance to all these deaths?"

Canaan nodded as he pulled another chair over. He sat down, then leaned forward, elbows on his knees. "You came out here to find out what happened to your mother. I'll help you in any way I can, Sheila. I want to know, too. I also want to find out what happened to all these people, and what's disturbing the children now."

Sheila's clear, straightforward gaze met his. He thought he saw apprehension in her eyes, but she had never been one to avoid what she feared. Her tendency was to face down her fears, no matter what it might cost her—and that tendency had earned her a few bruises when she lived here.

"You were there for me when we were children," he said softly. "I'm here for you now."

"You didn't want me here."

He shook his head. "I didn't. Still don't feel completely comfortable with you here."

"Why not?"

He wasn't sure how to answer that question.

"Because you think I could be in danger," she said.

He grimaced. "There are some things we have to take seriously in our lives. Not often, and I don't mean we should live as if we're afraid of the world, but sometimes there really is danger."

She leaned forward, and he found himself withdrawing from her nearness. Her presence affected him at a deeper level than it ever had before, and he was not comfortable with his response to her.

"You don't think the fire was an accident?" she asked.

"I'm not sure what to think, but I can't let it go. I'd like for you to read through these files today, and then if you would get started on some others I've flagged as soon as possible—"

"Show me which ones and I'll do it today. I'm just glad to have the chance to do something proactive for once."

He got up and pulled out the file drawer where he had earmarked some other records that had concerned him. Part of him was uncomfortable that he once more required her assistance— Sheila to the rescue. But another part felt a powerful rush of relief that she was working beside him. He didn't want to try to analyze the myriad reasons for these feelings. Right now, he didn't care. Whether by divine intervention or a malevolent hand, she was here. He would do all he could to see to her safety, and he would also utilize her skills, knowledge and memories to help him unravel the elusive mystery that hung over this school.

## ∝ *Chapter Seventeen* ∝

Embers of wood collapse onto themselves as I rouse from my Sunday-morning trance. I rise to my knees in the middle of the hogan, the cedar smoke burning my throat and nostrils. The peyote button has left my tongue furred with its bitter, clinging aftertaste. Or is that, also, the smoke? I can't tell.

The vision still teases my inner eyes with wisps of knowledge, distorting my human sight. The spirit seldom answers my call, even with the enticement of peyote, but it sprang at me full force this time, its message plain. She must be brought here again.

The dream wavers and fades, and my sight clears. Much as I court the power, its intensity frightens me. I've never liked being controlled.

A strong breeze whispers through the open doorway, stirring the embers again, filling the hogan with thick smoke. I bend low and stumble out the door into the brisk morning air.

Spirit of the wolf. The wolf is the true power, my witchcraft the only witchcraft—much more powerful than any other. But others might discover the truth soon, in spite of the power. I must do what I've done before to stop this discovery, or the truth could destroy my power for all time. It could destroy everything.

I raise my face to the wind, exulting in its caress. A sliver of moon, hanging amid a smattering of stars, hooks one bright star in its curve, much the way a wolf's claw catches prey.

I smile. It's the way I will catch the enemy who would destroy what I'm doing. This is the opportunity I've been waiting for.

In the Sunday-morning gray light, just before dawn, Tanya Swift's eyes flew open. She gasped in terror and sprang up in bed. Her heart throbbed, blood pounding through her head, drowning out the nightmare howl of the wolf.

He was here, at this school. She knew it, but she couldn't understand how. It felt as if pieces of time had been taken from her memory, and she couldn't find them. They'd been stolen from her.

No one would understand. No one would listen to her, not even Canaan. All he did was pray, and how could his prayers control the wolf?

She did remember being afraid. The past few days she'd had flashing thoughts of a dark room, of smoke that had the scent she'd caught yesterday when she was walking with Sheila Metcalf. Could those be part of the bad dream? But she also remembered the pain, and that was no dream.

As if in answer to her memory, the pain began again, this time thrusting low in her belly, shooting needles through her body. She bent over double and gritted her teeth to keep from crying out. This was worse than monthly cramps.

The light grew outside, and Tanya knew it was time to move. The wolf would be hiding now, and she had to get away. If she waited, someone would stop her again, as Canaan did Friday.

She slipped out from beneath her blanket, groping in the darkness for the clothes and shoes she'd stashed beneath her bed. Her dorm mother and other dorm mates were watching her more closely now that she'd already sneaked out once, so she didn't want to make noise. She would pull her clothes on outside.

Susan, in the next bed, turned over, rustling the covers and yawning.

Tanya stopped breathing. Don't wake her up!

Silence settled again, and Tanya crept barefoot into the hallway, her bundle of clothes and shoes clutched to her chest.

A movement startled her and she froze.

The dorm mother had stepped out in the hall, on her way to the bathroom.

Tanya took a deep, silent breath, and went the other way, into the big general room. Two other hallways branched off from there, with other bedrooms down each hall, where people were sleeping. Maybe they were even waking up now. It was a good thing she'd soaped the hinges of the front door yesterday.

It didn't make a sound when Tanya pulled it open and stepped outside.

*Dear Jesus, protect me,* she prayed. *Fill me with—*

The wind flew up, grabbing at her. It felt like fingers of the spirits plucking at her, but she pulled the door shut behind her. She would not let a simple wind chase her back inside.

*Dear Jesus, keep me safe. Help me to not be afraid—*

The bush beside her rustled as another puff of wind whistled through it. Like an invisible monster, the wind attacked her from around the side of the dorm, from across the playground.

*Dear Jesus, just help me!* She dressed quickly and pulled on her shoes on the front step. A sharp breeze wrapped her hair around her face, blinding her and catching at her clothes. She tied her hair in a knot at her neck, squatted to tie her shoes and stared around the gray, empty school yard.

Taking a deep breath for courage, she stepped onto the road and walked toward the highway.

Sunday-morning sunshine streamed in through Sheila's bedroom window as she tied back her hair and pulled on her jogging shorts. It was early yet, just past seven o'clock; there should be plenty of time for a good run and a shower before church.

She needed the exercise. Canaan had worked her hard in the clinic yesterday, but despite a crick in her neck and a sore back from poring over countless medical records, there had been few results. By the time they heard the children marching toward the cafeteria, they realized they'd missed lunch and that it was dinnertime.

They had returned to the clinic after dinner for another few hours. Canaan had not become more garrulous as an adult. He was comfortable with silence and didn't need a constant flow of conversation.

Sheila was filling a water bottle when someone knocked on her front door. She opened it up to find Canaan, standing there in jeans and a fresh, red T-shirt, face unshaven, hand raised to knock again.

"I'm glad you're up and dressed," he said. "I've got a problem." Without waiting for an invitation, he stepped inside and pulled off his red baseball cap to reveal a disheveled mass of shiny black hair. "When you talked with Tanya yesterday, did she say anything to you about her plans for today?"

"Plans? No, we didn't get around to that. What—"

"She's gone again. Her dorm mother called me earlier."

"Couldn't she be out walking in the desert?"

"I've already searched the whole campus, the cafeteria, the trails around the school."

"You think she's run away again? But why?"

"I doubt the reason has changed since Friday." His voice cracked, and he looked tired. He'd probably stayed at the clinic long after she'd left late last night. "She's spooked. She can't have gotten far, because she's afraid to travel at night, and she was in bed last night."

Sheila groaned. "Maybe she went home."

"I don't think she'd go there again. Did she talk much yesterday?"

"Yes. After her less than warm welcome Friday, that seemed odd to me."

"I'm not surprised. She craves adult attention. She gets lonely for her family when they're gone. What did she talk about?"

"She apologized—sort of—for being angry with me Friday, but she was still upset about the dog's death."

"What else?"

"What struck me was what she didn't talk about," Sheila said. "She didn't talk about what frightened her so badly. She talked about her friends, and—"

"Which friends?"

"The Hunt children and her cousin Donna, who's expecting a baby."

"Donna."

"According to Tanya, she's married and she works at Hubbell Trading Post, weaving blankets."

"Sounds like a good place to start." He jammed on his hat and pivoted back toward the door.

"Hold on," Sheila said, grabbing her water bottle. "I'm coming with you."

Tanya was fast. She knew it. She could run faster than the wind of a storm. But she couldn't run faster than the wolf.

He would find her again if she stayed at the school, and she didn't want to live if he found her.

Had his spirit found her already? This awful pain clawed at her as if a devil had forced his way inside her. The pain grew through her body until there wasn't a place she didn't hurt.

The pain grew stronger as she walked. She had come only about eight miles north of the school on Route 77 when the cramps in her stomach grew so bad she had to rest.

Her clothes clung to her skin with the sweat that dripped from her, even though the sun hadn't yet warmed the air. Her face felt hot, and her ears rang, echoing through her head so loudly she barely heard the cry of a hawk overhead.

She stepped off the road, stopped to steady herself against the dizziness and climbed down toward a gully below a bridge. No curious motorists would be able to stare at her there, or call and report her to the Navajo Tribal Police. Sometimes tourists driving through the reservation decided they must watch out for the children, as if the *Dineh* didn't know how to take care of their own.

She stripped off her sweat-soaked red jacket, then felt it catch on a piñon stump and jerk from her fingers. But it didn't matter. She would rest for a while, just a little while, then go on.

The pain sharpened. Something was wrong. She'd never felt this bad before. Her legs grew weaker. She had to lie down. She needed to reach the shadows below the bridge before—

Sudden moisture warmed her inner thighs. She looked down to find red the color of her jacket spreading down toward her knees. The warmth quickly became pain again, shooting up her back, stabbing into her belly, and down her legs. Her knees lost their strength.

She stumbled into a stand of grass. Her legs refused to work. She fell forward, hitting her forehead against the hard-packed dirt as the pain continued to spread, mingling with the heat.

This was what happened when you tried to run from the wolf.

## ❧ Chapter Eighteen ❧

Sheila winced as the Plymouth Voyager hit another pothole in the road. She could see why they met very little traffic, even though the soothing desert colors of terra-cotta, sand, turquoise sky and piñon green created a magical backdrop of scenery.

No phantoms stalked her from the roadside today, but she remained alert, nevertheless, as Canaan drove north toward Hubbell Trading Post. He drove slowly enough for them to scan both sides of the road, far out into the desert. Sheila wielded a pair of binoculars that he had pulled from the glove compartment. Every so often, she studied the surrounding plain to the east.

"Have you contacted her parents yet?" she asked.

He shook his head. "I have their schedule in my office."

"Wouldn't they be more likely to know where she would be? They might have a number for Donna."

"I've already called the trading post to alert them, in case

Tanya shows up. If we don't find her this morning, I'll be forced to call her parents, but I hate to overreact and alarm them unnecessarily."

"Where are they now?"

"They should be in Phoenix, if they followed the schedule. They travel three times during the year to craft fairs across the country, and each trip takes about a month."

"Three months," Sheila murmured. "Without Tanya?"

"She goes with them on their summer trip, but they don't want to take her out of school. She has always seemed to be happy at the school before."

"If I were in Tanya's place, I might have a lot of fears, too, if my parents abandoned me so often."

He gave her a sharp glance. "They come back as often as they can, and I've tried to spend extra time with her this year. I know dorm parents and doctors aren't good substitutes for parents, but we try. She's not abandoned."

"I realize that, but I'm saying that she might feel abandoned, even if she isn't."

Canaan sighed. "Consider the alternatives. The Swifts make their living with their blankets and jewelry. The area where they live is already too populated with goats and sheep, so they can't have a herd." With a nod of his head, he indicated the open land. "There are few jobs on the reservation. And Tom and Linda Swift are too proud to accept assistance. Besides, they are true artists, and they do well."

"I'm glad about that, but Tanya suffers for it."

Canaan glowered at her.

"I'm sorry, I don't mean to sound judgmental."

"Could've fooled me."

She returned the glower. "I lost my mother when I was ten

years old, and then my father moved with me to a placed filled with strangers. Hideaway is a wonderful town, but I lost all my friends, my security, my foundation, within a few months. It was a struggle to connect with new people, and I believe it influenced my choices as an adult."

"You mean your choice of a husband?"

She shot him another look of annoyance. "We're talking about Tanya here."

"It sounds like we're talking about you. Don't let the bitterness of your choices influence your judgment with this child of the Navajo. We have our own set of problems, and they don't always correlate with others outside the reservation."

"But I can't help wondering how Tanya must feel."

"I realize that. I feel for her, too, but unlike you, she sees her parents when they're home, and she knows the dorm parents, teachers and the other kids. The school isn't new to her. Something besides homesickness is troubling her now. Don't confuse your issues with hers. You're two different people."

"Ah, yes, this haunting menace that has to be exorcised from the—" Sheila caught sight of a movement out in the desert, and raised her binoculars to study it. The movement turned out to be a couple of shepherd dogs playing together.

She lowered the binoculars.

"You were saying?" Canaan prompted.

She looked at him, noting the scruffy shadow of beard growth on his normally clean-shaven face. "Maybe you're right. Who am I to suggest ways to help Tanya? I'm not in her situation. No way for me to identify with her." Sheila glanced toward the field again, pulled the binoculars to her eyes and studied the shepherd dogs for several seconds.

"You see something suspicious?" Canaan asked.

"Until now, I haven't been able to remember a time when I wasn't afraid of dogs." She lowered the binoculars and looked at him. "Until now."

His black eyebrows rose above the line of his ball cap. "Really?"

She nodded. "Now I remember."

"You're afraid of dogs?"

"You don't remember how terrified I was of dogs? What kind of best friend were you?"

"But you loved dogs," Canaan said. "Are you sure you're not hallucinating?"

"After we moved to Hideaway, we never had a dog, even though Dad could have used one on the farm."

"Maybe your dad was being overprotective."

She shook her head.

"I can remember a time when dogs didn't scare you."

She glanced toward the shepherds and again had a spontaneous recollection. "Do you remember the two puppies we rescued from the side of the road one Saturday?"

"I sure do," he said. "We were about eight."

"You named them Amy and Bluebird," she said, surprised by the clarity of this memory. She looked at Canaan. Something about being with him seemed to trigger that kind of clarity of thought at times.

"All the kids laughed at the names," he said.

"But they still liked the puppies, even though we got into trouble sneaking them into the buildings at night."

"So at age eight," Canaan said, "you obviously were not afraid of dogs."

"Maybe that's just because they were helpless puppies. Someone had dumped them, left them to die."

"We raised them at the school," Canaan said. "And they grew almost as tall as we were, but you were never afraid of them."

Canaan was right. Sheila remembered playing with them, running and wrestling, laughing, and never once being frightened by either dog. The memory was so vivid.

"So what changed?" Canaan asked softly.

"Maybe that's something I need to find out."

Canaan drove in silence for a few moments, and Sheila stared out at the open plain. As if a spigot had been turned on, more memories rushed into her mind, happy ones about the good times.

"I remember you tutored me in science and math," she said.

"And you're a nurse now, so it obviously helped."

"In exchange for the tutoring, I provided the muscle." She glanced across the cab in time to see Canaan grimace, and knew she hadn't chosen the most comforting memory on which to focus. "You obviously no longer have need for that," she offered. "I remember how we found the puppies," she said softly.

"What do you mean?"

"You knew they were there. No one had seen them, because they were out of view. You just knew."

He shrugged, eyes narrowed as he continued to study the landscape. "I heard a whimper. I know the sound of distress." He glanced at her. "I also know the look. I've seen it in your eyes several times, and I don't think you're just homesick."

"Watch the road, and don't change the subject. It's a special gift you have."

"Changing the subject?"

"Empathy."

Canaan shrugged. "I'd hope both of us would tend to have some empathy, considering the professions we chose."

"Well, when you think about it, that might be counterproductive. It's hard to be objective when you identify too much with your patients."

"I know. I've always had to struggle with that."

"Maybe it's because you experienced so much rejection because you were half white, half Navajo."

"I was always too sensitive."

"And you're not now?"

He shot her a wry smile. "Maybe I am."

"I especially remember your sensitivity to others," Sheila said. "You always seemed to be tuned in to others' feelings. I remember you cried for people."

Canaan groaned. "I didn't cry that much. Have a heart, Sheila. A grown man doesn't like to be reminded of stuff like that."

Brief memories flashed through Sheila's mind of a much-younger Canaan—bending over one of the puppies, crying because it had been abandoned; Canaan crying when a little boy fell from the swing set and broke his arm; Canaan crying for Sheila about something…but this memory didn't focus.

"Why do I remember you crying for me?" she asked.

"You were leaving."

"No, before we left. It was… I think you were sorry because I was hurt…or my feelings were hurt."

He looked at her. "Do you remember getting into trouble the year before you left?"

"What kind of trouble?"

His brow furrowed as he returned his attention to the road. "It seems to me you were talking too much in class."

"The only teacher I can remember ever reprimanding me was Doc."

Canaan's brow cleared. "That's right. It was him. He wouldn't let you attend one of the track meets with the rest of the team." He looked at her. "Remember now?"

The slow emergence of another memory disturbed her. "I was telling stories to the other kids, and he didn't like them. They were about…" She glanced at Canaan.

"The wolf," he said.

The words struck her with a blast of recognition. "You remember?"

A muscle clenched in his jaw as he hesitated. "Not totally."

"So you're just guessing?"

He shook his head. "Not totally."

"Canaan."

"I don't remember much, only that you were having nightmares, and then on Friday I discovered that Tanya has been terrified of the Navajo werewolf."

"That's what she's afraid of?"

He nodded.

More memories assaulted Sheila, the harsh ones that had frightened her so badly yesterday, of smoky darkness and a bitter taste in her mouth, and fear of a lurking presence, just out of view, and sharp pain. With the memories came a tightening of her neck and shoulder muscles.

"You didn't tell me," she said.

"You didn't need to hear about that."

"Then this thing with Moonlight had a lot more significance for all of us than we realized."

"Tanya did more than realize it. I think she's taken it so much to heart that it's why she's run away again."

Sheila raised the binoculars to her eyes, her mind skittering away from the memories for a moment. She focused the lenses on someone out on the rolling hills ahead and to the left of the road, but as they drew closer it turned out to be a brightly dressed shepherd with a flock of sheep and goats.

"When we were kids, I remember thinking that you laughed too much," Canaan said when Sheila lowered the binoculars. "You always seemed happy, and it made you popular with the other kids. I don't think they ever thought as much about your being white as they did about my being half white. Maybe I was just a little jealous of sharing your friendship." He glanced at her. "It wasn't until you stopped laughing that I missed the sound of it."

"When was that?"

"A few months before you left."

She looked at him.

"That was when you got into trouble for talking about the wolf."

Sheila remembered then. He was right. The wolf dreams and fear of dogs hadn't come until after her ninth birthday. "My mother gave me a book about dog breeds for my ninth birthday."

"Which means you developed your fear of dogs after that."

"What would I have known about the Navajo werewolf?"

"He is the embodiment of witchcraft," Canaan said.

"But I was just a little kid. Where would I have heard about it?"

"Haven't you ever sat around a campfire and told ghost stories?"

Sheila shook her head. "Not that I remember. So you're saying we probably heard stories from our friends, and I believed them?"

He sighed, obviously frustrated. "I think there's more to it than that, Sheila."

"For instance?"

"That's what I've been trying to find out."

"Do you think Betsy Two Horses might tell us something?"

Canaan looked at her. "I've considered that, but what if she's part of the problem? I think my grandfather wanted me to take Bob's place because he knows he can trust me. At this point, I don't know who else to trust."

"You trust me."

"You aren't from here. You aren't the one who's causing the problem. I asked Betsy to share some old customs with the kids. Now I'm not so sure that was a good idea. I meant for her to teach practical facts like how our ancestors built homes and cooked and hunted. I think she might have been teaching about the old spirits."

"Do you really think Betsy would terrify Tanya with stories about the Navajo werewolf?" Sheila asked.

He shook his head.

"Me, neither." Sheila thought of Tanya, alone out there somewhere. Afraid. Running from...from the same thing Sheila had feared as a child? The same monster that still haunted her through her dreams?

Canaan slowed at a rough spot on a bridge. The piñon trees grew thickly here. He didn't resume speed right away, but searched the shadows and the crevices in the ground. No Tanya.

Canaan slowed the van again when they reached the intersection with state Route 264. He pulled alongside the road and made a U-turn.

"Where are we going?" Sheila protested. "What about Ganado?"

"Tanya couldn't have come this far this morning, and I know she wouldn't have left the school during the night."

"Maybe she hitched a ride as she did last time."

"If we don't find her, we'll go on to Ganado."

They had backtracked almost four miles when Sheila saw a splash of red in one of the low branches of a piñon tree on the hard-packed bank of an arroyo. As they drove over the bridge that crossed it, she turned to get a closer look.

"Stop."

Canaan pulled to the side of the road. Sheila had her seat belt unbuckled and was jumping out as the van came to a stop. It was a red jacket, like the one she'd seen Tanya wearing yesterday morning. As she reached down and untangled it from the tree, her gaze wandered farther down the bank.

There lay Tanya in the bright sun, her right arm over her head.

## Chapter Nineteen

Canaan saw Tanya's body on the ground, saw the blood along her inner thighs and felt sick.

"Canaan!" Sheila scrambled down the bank ahead of him.

Canaan reached behind the front seat for the small doctor's bag he always carried with him and rushed down the hillside.

"Airway's clear and she's breathing," Sheila called over her shoulder.

Canaan reached them as Sheila felt Tanya's carotid artery for a pulse. "Rhythm's fast, but there. She's too warm. Dehydration, no doubt."

Again, Canaan looked at the blood. So much of it.

Sheila looked up at him. "Could she be pregnant? This looks like a miscarriage."

"No way, not Tanya. There's got to be another—"

"The last time I saw this much blood, the woman was having a miscarriage."

He knelt at the girl's other side. "Let's get her taken care of before we try to diagnose her." He took Tanya's hands and squeezed them. "Tanya, can you hear me?"

Tanya's long, black lashes fluttered, then her eyes opened wide, and she looked up into Canaan's face with a flash of terror. "The wolf, Canaan!"

"What about him? Did someone hurt you?"

Her face crumpled. She moaned hoarsely, in pain, pressing her hands into her abdomen. "He caught me."

"You were attacked?" Canaan exclaimed.

"No."

Canaan bit back a groan of frustration. "Then when did he catch you?"

Tanya shook her head. "I don't know."

"Then he couldn't have caught you, or you would know. What really happened? Why are you bleeding?"

Tanya struggled to sit up, but Canaan pressed her back. "Don't move until we know how badly you're hurt."

"I didn't get hurt when I fell."

"You mean you just started to bleed?"

She nodded. "I was so weak. Please, Canaan, pray at him. Chase him away."

Sheila brushed long strands of black hair from Tanya's face and neck. "It's okay, honey, he can't get to you through us."

"But he did." Tears filled Tanya's eyes. "He already did."

Canaan noted the tears with relief. She wasn't too dehydrated for them. "We'll talk about this later. First, we need to take care of what's happening now."

"But he did this to me." Tanya touched her abdomen, and her hand trailed farther down to touch the blood. "This is what happens when…" Her eyes drooped shut and her head lolled sideways in another faint.

Canaan picked her up and turned to carry her up the side of the arroyo.

Sheila followed. "I'll drive."

"I'll drive, you sit with her in the back. We'll take her to Keams Canyon. It's the closest hospital. Did you bring your cell phone?"

"It's in my pocket."

"Call the school." He gave her Doc's number. He would also have to call Tanya's parents, but he didn't want to do that until he knew what was going on with Tanya. He dreaded that call.

Preston and Blaze didn't pull onto I-40 until nine o'clock Sunday morning, after spending the night at a dilapidated roadside motel on the western edge of Amarillo, Texas. Preston was not in a good mood.

"If we start itching today, we'll know why," Blaze said. "The bite of a bedbug is intensely pruritic."

"English on this trip," Preston said. "Stop showing off."

"That means if we've been bitten by bedbugs, the itching'll be awful."

"The sheets were clean, Blaze."

"Doesn't matter. If bedbugs were in our mattresses, the bugs could have reached us. They're tiny."

"You know, I haven't had breakfast yet," Preston reminded him. "I don't have your cast-iron stomach, and now I'm going to see bugs crawling around on my eggs."

"I'm sorry."

"I couldn't sleep last night, and I don't need to be reminded about bedbugs. We'd have stayed at a better place if we could have found one, but since our navigator got us lost in Oklahoma City—"

"How was I supposed to know about the roadwork?" Blaze asked. "They didn't have good signs. You could've stopped and asked for directions, but no, what you really wanted was to make a good reason to miss evening worship at the school. You know we're not gonna make it until Monday now."

"So it's a good thing we didn't tell Sheila we were coming."

"In spite of bedbugs, I slept like a baby," Blaze said. "Want me to drive?"

"After breakfast."

"I could use a cruller."

"You could use a few salads. Didn't anybody ever tell you all that unhealthy food will turn to fat someday?"

"Cheyenne tells me that all the time, but it hasn't happened yet. I'm still a growing boy."

Preston wished he'd been able to find a cup of coffee somewhere at the motel before leaving. Blaze's chatter was the next best thing to wake him. If only he would turn the volume down.

"You're worried about Sheila," Blaze said.

Preston didn't see any reason to deny the truth, but he didn't see any reason to acknowledge it, either.

"Did you try praying for her?"

Preston nodded.

"Really?"

"Don't act so surprised. And don't talk so loud until after I've had coffee." Preston didn't think God would answer any of his prayers. Even so, when he'd awakened in the early-morning hours, after sleeping for perhaps fifteen minutes, he had immediately thought of Sheila and said a silent prayer for her safety. It had been much like those he'd prayed as a child for his mother to get well.

Mom never got well. And now Preston couldn't help feeling that Sheila was in danger, and it was up to him, not God, to protect her.

Sheila sank down beside Tanya's bed in the Emergency Department of the hospital at Keams Canyon. The girl had awakened in the van long enough to swallow some water. Then she had remained weak and listless for the remainder of the trip. Now, with blood tests taken and an exam complete, Canaan had gone to make his dreaded call to Tanya's parents.

Sheila checked the IV line to make sure the saline drip was running fast enough. Tanya was dehydrated, though not dangerously so.

When she turned back, she found Tanya had opened her eyes, and was watching her.

"How are you feeling, honey?" Sheila asked, automatically touching Tanya's forehead with the backs of her fingers—not an official medical procedure, but something she had long ago realized patients appreciated—the human touch.

Tanya licked her lips. "Not as bad. Where are we?"

"We're at the hospital at Keams Canyon."

Tanya sucked in her breath and tried to sit up. "Why?"

Sheila reached for her and gently eased her back down. "Relax, it's okay. We had to find out what was wrong with you. Don't you remember? We found you unconscious, lying below the road."

Tanya squinted as she peered around the room at the stainless-steel cabinet, the privacy curtain and the tray table beside the bed. "White man's medicine can't help. He'll know."

Sheila shook away a chill. "Who will know?"

Tanya glanced toward the curtain. "Don't say anything in front of them."

"But, Tanya, the medicine can help. They're going to take care of you."

Tanya shook her head and sat up. "No, they aren't. This will just make it all worse. When he finds out—"

"Listen to me." Sheila reached for Tanya's hand, and was reassured by the girl's firm grip. "What happened to you has happened to a lot of…women, and a wolf didn't do it."

"You don't understand. You don't know." Tanya looked around the room again. "Is it still daylight?"

"Of course. It's not even noon on Sunday. You haven't been out that long. Tanya, did you sleep at all last night?"

"I couldn't sleep. I don't think Canaan's prayers are protecting the dormitory, so I have to stay awake and make sure nobody comes in."

No wonder she'd slept all the way here.

Tanya looked up at Sheila, then down at the turquoise cross Sheila wore around her neck. "Betsy says turquoise can be used as a medicine against bad magic."

Sheila reached up and touched the cross. The stone was warm from resting against her skin. "She told you that?"

Tanya nodded. "Do you wear it to scare him away?"

Sheila decided not to pretend she didn't know exactly who Tanya was talking about, or how frightening that wolf was, but she wondered…did Betsy think this pretty stone would have power against a ruthless enemy twenty-four years ago?

"No, I wear it to remind myself of God's love when I have trouble remembering."

"Maybe it protects you," Tanya said.

Sheila hesitated. "Tanya, the test results aren't back yet, but—"

"I know what happened to me. The wolf cast a spell."

"No, honey, it wasn't a spell."

"Yes, it was. He did it because I tried to run away. I prayed Canaan's prayer, and this is what happened." She raised the crisp, white sheet that covered her and looked down. She looked back up at Sheila, surprise obvious. "It's gone. The blood's gone."

"You were in and out of consciousness. We cleaned you up." Sheila touched Tanya's bare, brown arm. "Honey, I know you've been told the facts of life."

Tanya frowned. "I know all that. But this wasn't just cramps, I know. I've had cramps, and they don't hurt like—"

"It could have been more this time."

"More? You mean there's more?"

Sheila hesitated, then leaned closer and lowered her voice. "Are there any boys you like at school, or back home at White Cone?"

"Why?"

"I know the boys in your classes probably joke about sex, and I know—"

"That doesn't have anything to do with me."

"Honey, have you missed any periods? Is it possible you were—"

A gasp. "You think I'm pregnant!"

Sheila hesitated, searching for the right words. "Judging by the condition you were in when we found you, it appears you could have been pregnant, but—"

"You're wrong. You don't know me at all."

"I know I don't, and Canaan—"

"He thinks I'm pregnant?"

"He's waiting for the results of the test, which shouldn't take long."

"Good." Tanya pulled the sheet up around her neck. "Then you'll see I'm not pregnant. This hospital can't help me."

"Tanya, you know how we got you all cleaned up, and you don't remember it?"

Tanya raised her eyebrows and waited.

"When I was a child, a little younger than you, I was afraid of the wolf, just as you are."

Tanya looked skeptical.

"I lived here for five years, and my mother died at the school. I'm just beginning to discover things I had forgotten, especially about the wolf. There are still places in my memory that seem blank. Do you have anything like that? Times you can't remember?"

Tanya scrutinized her, eyes narrowed in thought, as if she might be weighing Sheila's words to decide if she was telling the truth.

"You remember the smoke you smelled yesterday when we were talking?" Sheila asked.

Tanya nodded. "Cedar."

"It frightened you, and you ran back to the school. Why?"

"It's his warning."

"What kind of warning?"

"That he's nearby."

"Have you seen him?"

Tanya looked away, then shook her head. "I remember some things." Her voice came softly, almost a whisper. "They were just things, like fire in a hogan, and a chant."

"Do you remember words in the chant?" Sheila asked.

Tanya shook her head. "I remember the snout of a wolf, but that could have been in my dreams. I don't know."

"I understand." Sheila felt sick. She wanted to be able to tell Tanya she would be okay, that they would protect her. And they might be able to if only they knew who was hurting Tanya.

"Honey, you're a very beautiful young girl, and physically mature for your age—"

Tanya jerked away, glaring at Sheila. "You think I've been sleeping around."

"No, I don't. I think you honestly don't know what's happened to you because you don't remember."

"I never did anything like that." Tanya's eyes filled with tears. She turned away, her shoulders hunched, body curling into the fetal position. "I'd remember that," she said, her voice muffled by the pillow and blanket.

"No, that's just the point, Tanya. You might not have remembered a thing."

"I'd remember something about it. Just wait until the test results. Then you'll see that's not what this is."

"Canaan called Doc, and he's coming to see you."

"I don't want him to come here. I don't want him to know about all this, until you have the results of the tests to prove that I'm not pregnant."

"Honey, even if he knows there was a pregnancy, he'll also know that you are innocent. We may need his help to find the person who's doing this."

## ❧ Chapter Twenty ❧

Canaan turned from his contemplation of a cloudless sky to see Sheila enter the tiny hospital waiting room. The dark circles beneath her eyes were more prominent than when she'd arrived at the school on Friday. He knew he had not improved her situation. Why had he even gone to her apartment this morning? He should have handled this on his own, without involving her.

She didn't come back to Arizona to reclaim her role as his personal hero, and he didn't need one. It had surprised him yesterday when they had fallen so naturally into the familiar repartee that they'd had as children. It had also encouraged him, though he didn't want to look too closely at why.

She hugged herself and shivered. "Twelve years old." She closed her eyes, wincing as if in pain. "How could this happen? It's a nightmare. It's so…" She walked to a window to stare out at the nearby canyon walls that seemed to loom over the hospital. "It's so wrong."

Canaan joined her at the window. "You're convinced it was a miscarriage, but don't jump to conclusions. The test results should be back shortly, and then we'll know for sure what we're dealing with."

She looked up at him. "Don't go into denial on me, Canaan."

"I'm not in denial about anything. There were no injuries, no one attacked her. To hemorrhage like that... I know it appears to be a miscarriage, but I know Tanya and her family. This is so alien to her nature, that—"

"Pardon me, but you have no idea what kind of nature a young girl might have when she feels alone and needs to feel loved and wanted."

He felt his teeth grinding with exasperation as she once again criticized the ways of people whom she didn't even attempt to understand.

"Sorry," she said. "I'm not trying to imply that her parents did anything wrong. What I'm saying is that—"

"I know what you're trying to say, but the way you say it is an insult."

"That's not my intention. I'm simply speaking from...experience, Canaan."

He blinked.

"It wasn't my mother's fault she died, and my father did all he knew to do, but I felt abandoned anyway. And I acted out. All I'm saying is that Tanya's experience might be somewhat the same. She might do as I did and look for attention in the wrong places, not because she's a bad girl, but because she desperately needs to feel loved. Don't automatically label her as a bad girl if you find out this is a miscarriage."

"I wouldn't do that."

"It certainly sounded to me as if you would. Besides," Sheila added, "Tanya's nature might have nothing to do with what happened to her."

He looked at her askance. What was she talking about?

"Oh, come on, Canaan, you know what she's so afraid of. You know the other kids are behaving strangely. I'm sure Rohypnol has found its way to the reservation, just as it has everywhere else in the world. Some pervert could be using that drug to do who knows what to the children, and they won't remember a thing afterward. Is there someone on the school campus who might be a child molester?"

"Not possible."

"How can you be so sure? You know everyone that well?"

Again, he felt his jaw muscles tense. "Why are you suddenly so eager to place the blame for Tanya's illness on our school when we don't even know what's wrong with her yet?"

Sheila shook her head, obviously confused. She glanced over her shoulder toward the doorway, then turned back to him. "What have you and I been discussing since Friday night? You implied that there's a problem at the school. You're the one who's pulled old records of students who have died. You're the one who's suspicious of the recent deaths at the school, just as Tanya is."

"She is? And you couldn't have told me this?"

"Sorry, at the time it seemed like an overreaction by an impressionable young girl. She suggested a connection between my mother's death and Wendy's."

"Tanya did?"

"That subject comes up a lot. So will you please get down off your high horse and talk to me?"

That old, familiar phrase broke the tension, and Canaan felt himself relax. This was his old friend he was talking to, after all.

"I'm sorry," he said. "This whole thing has me a little tense. The staff works well together, most have been at the school for years and everyone is thoroughly screened before he or she is hired at the school."

"I wasn't. I wasn't asked a single question."

"It's possible my grandfather didn't want to question you. The screening process most often involves former coworkers, bosses, neighbors and school officials. He checks for any kind of trouble with the law."

"Well, then I'm amazed I've been allowed to enter the hallowed halls of the school if all those people from my life were questioned," she said, her sarcasm dripping from every word. "But can we take the chance that just one person has slipped beneath the radar? What if there's someone who's molesting not only Tanya, but other children, as well?"

"Would you please wait until the test results come back before you start talking like this? Word can carry fast, and that would be a dangerous rumor to start."

Frustration tightened the lines of her face. "It doesn't hurt to be pre—"

"Dr. York?" came the voice of the E.R. secretary from the doorway. "Dr. Balmas wanted me to show you these results. He says he'd like to talk to you about it as soon as he finishes with a patient."

Canaan took the lab printouts and read the results of the pregnancy test. For a moment, his relief was so powerful he wanted to shout. "Negative for pregnancy."

Sheila exhaled with a sigh of obvious relief as she joined him and glanced at the lab sheet. "What did the CBC show?"

He flipped to the next sheet. "Low platelets."

"How low?"

"It rates aggressive treatment of immunoglobulin G to stop the bleeding."

"But bleeding from what?"

"I'll talk to Dr. Balmas, but I think it's ITP, idiopathic thrombocytic purpura."

"Isn't that a bleeding disorder that usually happens with younger children after a virus?"

"Tanya isn't too old, even if it is less common for a child her age. At least I didn't accuse her of being pregnant."

"I didn't accuse her—"

"She wasn't feeling well a few weeks ago, probably a virus."

"This looks like she's just bleeding too much with her menses," Sheila said.

"The platelet count doesn't drop with excess menstrual bleeding—if anything, it will go up to compensate. This is something else, I think." He checked the comprehensive metabolic profile, which was normal. "I'll talk to Dr. Balmas about that immunoglobulin G."

"I'll go reassure Tanya," Sheila said. "I'm afraid I might have set her off just a little."

Canaan glanced at her sharply. "You didn't tell *her* she was pregnant, did you?"

"I'm sorry, I might have suggested it as a possibility when I was questioning her about what could have been wrong."

"Then by all means reassure her that she's still pure," he said. "Next time you want to try diagnosing a child without consulting me, keep your theories to yourself until you know for sure."

Sheila frowned. "I wasn't diagnosing."

"Tell her I'll be in to talk to her in a few minutes. Doc's on his way here with her medical records so I can double-check

*Double Blind*

her history." He nodded to dismiss her, and caught the flash of irritation in her eyes. "What's wrong?"

"Wouldn't it be best to treat her immediately? Canaan, she bled so badly she was passed out in the desert."

"If it'll make you feel any better, most of these kinds of cases are self-limiting."

"But what if she isn't—"

"You're going to have to trust me with this," he said, knowing his sharpness surprised her. "She's in the hospital emergency room. She can't get much safer than that."

Sheila nodded and left without another word.

He had been wrong to think that they had returned to their childhood friendship. Now he was her boss, and she would have to deal with that. So would he.

## ❧ Chapter Twenty-One ❧

Sheila stepped from the waiting room into the broad hallway that led to the E.R. She paused at the small window that revealed only a small section of the hillside beyond the hospital. This day had held a surreal quality from the time Canaan knocked on her door to their flare of words just now.

It was as if her presence here had set a series of events into play, and the relationship she had hoped would resume from childhood wasn't as comfortable as she'd expected.

She thought again about what she had said to Preston on Monday—that God might have a hand in everything that was happening. Of course, she knew that to be true, but these most recent moments seemed to be particularly significant.

Would it be better to never know what happened to her mother? And to herself? Was it too late to leave the mystery of her past as it had always been?

She closed her eyes and prayed for strength. As she prayed,

a rhythmic echo reached her. She opened her eyes to see Doc Cottonwood, Kai Begay and Jane Witherbe coming toward her, their footsteps echoing. Sheila smiled a greeting, ignoring Kai's cool gaze.

"How's our patient?" Doc asked, stepping forward to drape an arm over Sheila's shoulders.

She took comfort in his presence. "Tired. It seems Tanya's lost a lot of sleep lately."

"I could have told you that," Jane said. "She's up half the night pacing in and out of her room, keeping everybody awake."

"And what's wrong with her?" Doc asked Sheila.

"I don't think the exact diagnosis has been made yet," Sheila said. If she wanted to keep her job, she'd better let Canaan announce the diagnosis. "All I can say is that she's lost a lot of blood. Canaan thinks it's an aftereffect of a recent virus." There, she'd already said too much. Could she expect disciplinary action?

"When can we see her?" Doc asked.

"Give me a few minutes to talk to her. She wasn't in the best of moods earlier, and she said she didn't want to see anyone."

"That's okay." Jane held up a duffel bag. "Doc thought she might need some fresh clothes. When Canaan called, he mentioned our girl might have to spend the night."

"I brought Tanya's medical records for Canaan," Doc said, "though I had a dickens of a time finding them."

Sheila directed him into the E.R. and excused herself as she went to Tanya's room.

Tanya was asleep when Sheila entered, but she awakened with a start at the soft swish of curtains being closed. She blinked sleepily at Sheila.

"Feeling better?" Sheila asked.

Tanya watched her in silence for a few seconds, then gave a brief nod.

"I bet you'll sleep the night away," Sheila said.

"Where's Canaan? Are we going home now?"

"Probably in the morning," Sheila said. "Jane, Doc and Kai are here. Jane brought some things for you. They'd like to see for themselves that you're okay."

"If I'm okay, why do I have to spend the night, and why did they come to see me?"

"I'll let Canaan tell you what he and Dr. Balmas decide to do, but I have an apology to make to you."

Again, Tanya watched her silently.

Sheila took Tanya's hands, surprised that Tanya didn't resist. "Honey, you know what we talked about earlier?"

Tanya nodded. Her hands tightened in Sheila's.

"I jumped to a conclusion I shouldn't have, and I was wrong."

Tanya's lips parted, and there was no misreading the relief in her expression. "I didn't have a miscarriage?"

Sheila studied her expression. "No." Why the surprise? Was it possible that the child *was* already acting out? "I'm sorry if I frightened you. Canaan will call your parents soon."

Tanya suddenly seemed interested in avoiding eye contact. "Why? He doesn't have to call them. Everything's okay, right?"

"You lost a significant amount of blood, and he and Dr. Balmas will want to make sure that doesn't happen again."

Tanya glanced toward the curtain, then motioned for Sheila to lean closer. She whispered, "It was a warning from…from him."

Sheila didn't pretend ignorance. "The wolf didn't have anything to do with this."

"You don't know that. You don't understand."

"I understand more than you think. Canaan mentioned you were sick recently."

"Uh-huh. Wendy Hunt was in the clinic when I went to get some cough medicine one day, and she made me stay there and had Canaan come check me over."

"Did you have a high temperature?" Sheila asked.

Tanya nodded. "Wendy had me come back to the clinic a couple of times so she could check me, but I got well fast because of the vitamins Doc makes all the track kids take. They keep us healthy."

"Did Wendy know about the wolf you're so afraid—"

With shocking suddenness, Tanya gagged, then coughed. Sheila watched in stunned surprise as tiny droplets of blood spattered the crisp, white sheet beneath her chin.

Tanya gagged again. "What's—" she coughed more blood "—happening?"

Sheila grabbed a towel and held it to Tanya's face. "You're still bleeding. I'll get the doctor."

She rushed through the curtain and into Dr. Balmas's office, where Canaan and Dr. Balmas were studying a lab report.

"She's coughing up blood."

Canaan turned to Dr. Balmas. "You did check for plague and anthrax?"

"That's right, even though we know how rare those both are."

"It's still endemic," Canaan said.

"I just checked the blood under the microscope, and there's no evidence of boxcar or safety pin microbes."

"What about hantavirus?"

"That takes longer, but in the meantime we'll go with our assumption that it's ITP and begin immunoglobulin treatment and see if it helps. If it does, we'll know what we've got."

"May I suggest a chest X-ray?" Canaan asked.

"That's a given." Dr. Balmas turned to a nurse, who was already nodding and writing the order.

Sheila returned to Tanya, who had coughed more blood, and whose eyes were wide with terror. Sheila sat on the side of the bed and put an arm around the girl's shoulders. "Canaan and Dr. Balmas are going to want a chest X-ray, but that's just because they're checking all options, honey. Whatever this is, it can be treated, and you're in good hands. Obviously, you'll need to stay here until it's clear what's going on with you."

"By myself?"

"I'll be with you." She hadn't discussed it with Canaan, and in his sudden, bossy mood he might veto her decision, but if he did, he could be the one to tell Tanya that she'd be spending the night alone.

"Don't tell my parents," Tanya asked.

"I can't tell Canaan what to do."

Tanya coughed again.

"Don't try to talk," Sheila said. "Canaan will do what's best with your parents."

Tanya covered her mouth with her hand as she coughed again, then held her hand out, staring at the blood. "The wolf—"

"Tanya, you'll be safe with me. If some wolf tries to get to you, he'll have to get through me, and he'll be sorry he tried."

Betsy Two Horses sat in the late-evening shade of a piñon tree and watched the children play. Some children were still returning from their weekend, being dropped off by their parents.

There were often tears when the children returned for a new week, along with many words of love, promises to be good and to learn a lot. Sunday afternoons and evenings bustled and the activity continued through the week.

Navajo parents wanted their children at home, but they allowed them to stay through the week because Twin Mesas was such a good school.

The children who remained over the weekend either lived too far away to travel home every weekend or they were on the track team, participating in meets on Saturdays. Those who stayed were well fed and well loved; the staff cared deeply for the children. They were good, Christian people. At least, most of them.

Betsy watched the gymnasium door open and the track team file out for their evening run—all but Tanya. These were Doc Cottonwood's kids. To please him, they pushed themselves hard, running faster and faster. The two at the back of the line—April and Jamey Hunt, the orphans—didn't quite have the speed their older brother, Steve, had displayed last year when he won all those ribbons. Steve, who helped in the cafeteria this year, had been hit hardest over his parents' death this spring.

A student coach trailed behind Jamey, laughing, calling out encouragement to the runners. Doc had gone to the hospital to see about Tanya.

Sure, this wet-behind-the-ears kid could laugh and offer support, but tomorrow, when Doc came back, he would be shouting, pushing his young athletes into shape, sometimes demanding more than they could give. Doc was always happy when his kids performed for him. But Betsy felt sorry for the ones who didn't—or couldn't. Doc never hid his impatience and disapproval.

What amazed Betsy was the way all the kids idolized him, as if he were a messenger from the Great Spirit.

"Stupid," Betsy muttered. She was a jealous old woman, disgruntled because the kids used to hover around her in the cafeteria the way they hovered around Doc now. The way they had hovered around Sheila on Saturday morning.

So who had Canaan called when there was trouble this morning? Not Betsy Two Horses, but good old Doc Cottonwood. She'd heard others grumbling about it too, over dinner tonight.

The sun sank too low for warmth, and Betsy got up from her seat. Yes, she knew she was jealous of many of the teachers and dorm parents. Now, instead of adoration, she sometimes inspired fear in the kids, because of her age. One of the long-held beliefs of The People was that the aged held a magical power to life.

What a bunch of sheep scat. All the aged held was a strong will to live, to hold on to what pleasures life still offered.

She thought of Sheila, and a smile chased away her scowl, but only for a moment.

Sheila had her own problems now. When the time was right, Betsy would have to tell her what little she knew about Evelyn. Not yet, maybe. But soon, when Sheila was ready.

## ❧ Chapter Twenty-Two ❧

On Monday morning, May 16, Sheila leaned back against the headrest in Canaan's van. The beauty of passing scenery lulled her to the edge of slumber. The ocher and mauve of the peaks jutting at the horizon, the soft turquoise of the unbroken sky provided a landscape that had always drawn her heart back to this place. She allowed the colors to settle in her soul as her eyes closed.

The quiet hum of the engine droned on, mingling with Canaan and Tanya's chatting voices in the front seat.

Last night, Tanya's bleeding had stopped soon after the immunoglobulin G was administered intravenously. The X-ray had showed no mediastinal widening, which helped rule out the danger of anthrax.

During the treatment, Sheila had taken a long walk while the visitors from school had taken turns watching Tanya.

When she'd arrived back in Tanya's hospital room, she had found the girl sleeping peacefully.

Keeping vigil over the frightened girl required diligence and a strong heart. Nothing had come at them during the night, and Tanya hadn't had any obvious nightmares, nor a physical relapse or waking terrors. Sheila, on the other hand, had endured endless hours of taut nerves, an aching back and a tension headache.

When Canaan contacted Tanya's parents, he had apparently reassured them so persuasively that they'd opted not to cut their trip short to come home and see their daughter. Sheila had to remind herself that the Swifts' livelihood depended on those triannual circuits to sell the items they crafted during the rest of the year. She also wondered if Canaan had downplayed the seriousness of Tanya's problem.

She was so glad that Tanya had caring adults who were good stand-ins for her parents. Canaan was overworked, but he was there for Tanya when she needed an "exorcism." Doc, despite his military bearing, had a tender heart when it came to his kids. Jane worked so many extra hours with her double responsibilities as teacher plus dorm parent, but she spent extra time with Tanya for "girl stuff."

A trill of female laughter rippled through the van, and Sheila opened her eyes as Canaan was turning from the highway toward the school. Had she actually heard Tanya laugh, or had that been a dream?

She had discovered last night that Tanya had the admirable ability to shrug off the oppressive weight of her medical problems with simple faith in Canaan...and to a lesser extent, in Sheila. In that way, she was still very much a child, though her quick wit and surprising insight—which Sheila had discovered for herself during their long talk last night—showed a maturity beyond her years.

"We'll be there in time for lunch," Canaan said over his shoulder. He glanced at Sheila. "You probably want to freshen up, brush your teeth or whatever."

Sheila frowned at him, suddenly feeling grubby, tired and irritable. "I'd prefer a good 'whatever.'" She knew she was due for a proper orientation today, with a tour of the school and introduction to some of the students scheduled for physicals. What she needed was a hot shower, a long nap and a double dose of espresso. What she would get, besides a chance to brush her teeth, was anyone's guess.

She was ready to doze off again when she recalled something Tanya had said yesterday just before the coughing had distracted them. "Tanya, didn't you say something yesterday about Doc giving everybody on the track team vitamins?"

"Sure. They give us extra energy."

"All the kids get vitamins," Canaan said. "Doc just rides his kids harder to take them every day. He's a health nut, and he was the one who convinced my grandfather to give them to the kids in the first place."

"Do you know the ingredients?" Sheila asked.

Canaan's brow puckered. "It's just a multivitamin."

"Any megadoses?"

Canaan shook his head. "If you're wondering if there's anything in them to cause Tanya's bleeding, there isn't. I already checked these pills out at the source. They're not harmful in any way." He pulled the van to a stop in front of Sheila's apartment.

"Can I go to class today?" Tanya asked.

"No," Canaan said. "You need to rest, and someone needs to keep an eye on you."

"You said I was okay."

"But you shouldn't overdo it today. You can stay with Sheila in the clinic."

Tanya glanced at Sheila, then back at Canaan. "She didn't sleep last night, and she told me she hasn't had a bath in two days. Does she have to work today?"

Sheila grimaced, suddenly feeling like an absolute grunge.

Canaan also turned to look at Sheila, considering the question. "Maybe she should take the day off, too," he told Tanya.

In spite of it all, Sheila was touched by the girl's thoughtfulness. "I could use some downtime, I'll admit, but I know there's a lot to do in the clinic. Why don't I take off a few hours today, then work this evening?"

"And I can take a nap on her couch," Tanya said.

"You can stay with me in the office," Canaan said.

"But you'll be in and out all day, and that means I'll be alone."

"It's okay if she stays with me today," Sheila said.

Canaan opened the door and got out. "All right, Tanya, but only for a few hours. I do need Sheila's help in the clinic." He glanced at his watch. "First lunch has already started, but there's no rush.

Tanya slowly climbed out of the van and waited as Canaan opened the door for Sheila. "I don't want to go back to the dorm tonight." The girl crossed her arms over her chest.

"Of course you don't." Canaan shot Sheila a wry glance over Tanya's head. "You made that clear the last two times you ran away. Where do you plan to stay, if not the dorm?"

She stepped closer to Canaan's side. "I want to stay with you."

Canaan had the grace not to react to that charged suggestion. He reached out and smoothed the girl's hair. "I'm afraid that wouldn't work."

"Okay, then, with her." Tanya nodded to Sheila.

Sheila couldn't hide her surprise.

"I think I need some one-on-one attention," Tanya said.

"You mean you want to move in with me?" Sheila asked.

Tanya nodded.

"It's a one-bedroom apartment," Canaan said.

"But she has a sleeper sofa in the living room. I know because April told me. Please, Sheila? I'll be quiet. I don't talk on the telephone or have my friends over or play loud music or even watch television." She glanced toward the apartment. "Not that you have one."

Sheila looked at Canaan, who shrugged. She could almost read the gleam in his eyes. She'd been the one preaching to him yesterday about Tanya feeling abandoned. Now he was calling her bluff.

This had not been in the job description; not at all what she had agreed to. The suggestion was not alarming, however.

"Sure, Tanya," she said, and allowed herself only a few seconds to enjoy the sudden look of surprise on Canaan's face. "I'd love to have you stay."

With a squeal, the girl hugged her, then hugged Canaan, then pivoted in the direction of her dorm. "I'll get my things and be right back! Don't lock me out!"

"Take it easy!" Canaan called after her swiftly retreating figure. "You just got out of the hospital."

Tanya waved without looking back, almost as if she were afraid Sheila would change her mind if given the chance.

And she could be right.

Canaan's approval was obvious when he turned back to Sheila. "You didn't have to do that."

"I don't think you gave me much of a choice. I wasn't about

to turn her down. She doesn't need that kind of rejection after everything she's been through, and I know I'm being codependent, and I don't have good boundaries, but this is something I can do."

"You're that afraid of the wolf?"

"You're the one who exorcised the dorm for Tanya Friday night, and I'm guessing it was to frighten away the Navajo werewolf. Are you saying you don't believe in all the talk about the wolf?"

"I didn't say that."

"Do you?"

"You know about my suspicions that something is going on here, and may have been happening for many years. I can't put my finger on it. Yet. That's where I need your help. I've been praying for a break before the end of the school year."

"You mean some kind of great, dramatic revelation about the deaths and why they've happened?"

He nodded. "Or at least some extra hands to help me dig through the files and pick up on any clues that might be hidden there."

"If anything."

He nodded. "The way things are happening, it doesn't look as if that'll happen."

"Tell you what. I don't need lunch, because Tanya and I had a late breakfast at the hospital. Let me get her settled in, then I'll clean up and grab a sandwich and take it with me to the clinic for later. I can work through dinner."

He hesitated. "You need a rest."

"I'm a nurse. I'm accustomed to doing without sleep."

"You'd better be careful. That kind of schedule can age a

person fast. In fact," he said, leaning closer, studying her face, "now that you mention it, are those laugh lines around your eyes?"

She grinned up at him. "Watch the sarcasm. I can withdraw the offer of lodging for Tanya."

He returned her grin, and then his face fell back into its usual seriousness. "Thank you, Sheila. Your help means a lot. I'm still not sure you should be here, but since you're here, I'm simply going to go with the serendipity of your arrival."

She nodded. If it were anyone else, she would be tempted to think he was being romantic. But Canaan York simply used words like *serendipity* as a matter of course. He must know she didn't have purely unselfish motives for being here and helping him.

For that matter, she wasn't being unselfish by lodging Tanya. Loneliness motivated her more than she had wanted to admit. She felt uneasy alone in the apartment and in the dark silence at night. She'd become accustomed to living with Dad and his two friendly house cats.

At the pop of tires on gravel, Sheila looked around to find a very familiar vehicle slowing to a crawl as it reached her Jeep. Strangely, her first thought was that Canaan's prayer might just have been answered.

When Preston caught sight of Sheila and the well-dressed man standing far too close to each other on the sidewalk, he thought that if he were to continue driving forward, he might nudge the man out of Sheila's personal space with his bumper. Then both of them looked toward him.

He could swear a look of welcome flashed across Sheila's face just before her eyes narrowed into threatening slits. He waved, smiled, and then, against his better judgment, resisted the urge to take a swing at lover boy with his bumper. He pulled in beside Sheila's Jeep and parked. Sheila stepped away from the man—was that Canaan?—of her own accord.

Blaze, sprawled out in the passenger seat, bare knees braced against the dashboard, gave a low whistle. "Looks like competition, my friend. I told you to wear the dark red silk with your jeans today, but did you listen?"

"I refuse to be pretentious."

"You packed the shirt, didn't you? You saving it for date night or something? This guy's pulling out all the stops."

"If that's who I suspect it is, he's the acting principal of a Christian boarding school. He has to dress the part."

"Sure he does, especially when there's a beautiful woman to be stolen away from the most eligible bachelor in Hideaway." Without waiting for argument, Blaze pushed the door open and got out, arms open wide. "Hey, Sheila!"

She stepped off the sidewalk, a wide smile of welcome on her face. "Blaze Farmer, how on earth did you guys find your way here, and what are you doing here?"

"Mission trip. Didn't Preston tell you?"

"I thought you had another week or so in school."

"Not me. I'm done for the summer, but I'd sure like the chance to help out at a clinic somewhere around these parts. For the experience, of course."

"Changed your mind about prevet now? You want premed instead?"

"Covering my bases."

She walked into Blaze's open arms, and he picked her up and swung her around. The show-off.

Preston got out, walked over to Sheila's Jeep and kicked the tires, noting that the spare was on the right front. Even if she sent him packing after all the trouble he'd gone to, he would still replace the spare or buy her a new set of front tires if she needed them.

"Making sure it's travelworthy for your trip back?" came Sheila's dry, tired-sounding voice from behind him.

He turned to her with his most innocent expression. What had happened to her smile?

With Blaze in the background introducing himself to the well-dressed competition, Preston held out his arms. "Don't I get the same kind of welcome? After all, I was the one who saw to it Blaze got here safe and sound."

She did not walk into his arms. She put her hands on her hips and gave him a mock glare as the noonday sun illuminated lines of fatigue on her face, glinting golden lights from her dark brown hair. "You just had to bring the argument all the way out to Arizona."

"I'm perfectly willing to trade cars with you *when* I decide to go back home."

"What?" Blaze called from the sidewalk. "No way! Preston, we need to talk about this, I'm telling you. Sheila's car doesn't have AC, and I'm not riding all the way back home with a lovesick grump without AC."

"Sheila," Canaan called, "you didn't tell me you'd sent for reinforcements. This guy works at the hospital and he's prevet? Talk about an answer to prayers." He stepped from the sidewalk and nodded to Preston, obviously expecting an introduction. "And who's this? A doctor or something?"

Preston stepped forward and extended a hand, speaking before Sheila could say a word. "Preston Black. Sorry, no medical background at all, unless you count my sister, who's a nurse, and the time I spent in the hospital last year after a fire. You've got to be Canaan York. Sheila's told me a lot about you. It sounds like you have a heavy load right now, and we decided to offer our services, such as they are, to help until replacements can be found and you can be reinstated into your rightful job." He knew he was running off at the mouth, but a man had to establish his territory and set the ground rules quickly.

Preston wasn't sure what he'd expected when he met Canaan. In fact, he was about a foot taller, fifty pounds heavier, with much lighter skin and a friendlier expression. Preston especially hadn't expected friendly. Most especially, he hadn't expected—or wanted—the friendliness he'd observed when driving up, not after the trouble this guy had given Sheila about the dog.

"How long can we expect you to stay?" Canaan asked.

Sheila cleared her throat. "Well, to tell you the truth, they're only—"

"As long as we're needed," Preston said, avoiding her glare. "Or as long as Sheila doesn't send us back."

"There'll be no danger of that," Canaan said, gesturing to Blaze, who had returned to Preston's vehicle to start unloading luggage. "Leave that in the car until I've figured out where to put you guys. I'm thinking the best place would be with me. I have a guest room and extra bathroom in my apartment on campus. Would you two mind sharing a room? It's got two single beds in it."

Preston covered his reservations with sickeningly effusive thanks, wondering if Canaan's strategy was to keep the competition in plain sight. Better control that way. And of course, his magnanimity looked good. Sheila was impressed, no doubt, especially since Canaan seemed to be genuinely glad to see them here.

It remained to be seen how this little experiment in mission work was going to turn out.

## ∻ Chapter Twenty-Three ∻

In spite of ordering Preston, more than once, not to come here, in spite of knowing his presence could be awkward and in spite of her irritation that he didn't seem to believe she was capable of taking care of herself, Sheila could not deny her relief at his sudden appearance. But she wasn't going to let him know.

He had come all the way to Arizona. For her. He wanted her. A romantic gesture couldn't get much better than that.

And yet, when Ryan was alive, he had made huge, romantic gestures in an effort to control her. Unfortunately, it usually worked. She'd come too far, endured too much, to allow another man to repeat that pattern.

Everything she knew about Preston told her he wasn't a manipulative man. She had always appreciated his good interpersonal boundaries, in spite of his dysfunctional childhood. He was neither dependent on others to make his life complete, nor interested in forcing anyone to think or do what he wanted. She knew he had undergone some therapy to establish a more emotionally healthy outlook on life, and she appreciated the results.

And that was why his suddenly showing up shocked her. Of course, just because she had told him not to come didn't mean he had to comply. There again, she had no right to control him, either.

She turned to see Tanya carrying a duffel bag and what appeared to be a pillow and blanket from the dorm, while Canaan rushed to help her with it. Blaze hurried along beside him, obviously eager to make new friends, get the lay of the land and plunge into work—indeed, an answer to Canaan's prayers.

Prayers that Sheila, herself, would have gotten in the way of, ironically, if Preston had done as she wished. But then, who knew?

"Mad at me?" Preston asked from close behind her.

She suppressed the smile that sprang from deep within her. "I told you not to come, and you came anyway, dragging poor Blaze along as an excuse." And Blaze's present behavior suggested that Preston might have done some major soul sharing on the drive out, as well.

"Would you believe me if I told you it was Blaze's idea?"

She shook her head, watching Canaan, Blaze and Tanya step into her apartment.

"It's true," Preston said, waving his hand in front of her face to get her full attention. "He wants to do this, Sheila, and it looks as if you and Canaan could use the help."

She sighed and looked up into the blue-gray depths of those eyes she admired so much. "Don't you dare try to convince me that poor, defenseless Preston Black was bullied by mean old Blaze Farmer into escorting him out here. Nobody bullies you."

"Blaze doesn't have a car."

"If you were so gung ho for him to come, you could've let him use your Jeep. Better yet, you could've bought him a new one."

Preston walked in silence for two beats. "Okay, I didn't say he bullied me into coming, I just said it was his suggestion, and one thing led to another, and your phone calls cinched the deal for me."

Sheila stopped walking far enough from the closed front door of her apartment so no one inside could overhear. "My phone calls? Now you're blaming me?"

"I'm not blaming anyone. I'm simply trying to explain why I was willing to disregard your commands. I'm convinced you're in danger, and I can't just shrug off that feeling the way you seem to be doing."

"I'm not—"

"I know." He touched her arm. "Honestly, Sheila, the last thing I want to do is invade your space the way pip-squeak was doing when we drove—"

"What?"

"Sorry, I meant Canaan. You didn't tell me how well he'd outgrown that silly little name of—"

"Don't you dare call him that in his presence. I let that nasty nickname slip one time, and, of course, you would remember it."

"Of course. I can't help myself. He's the competition."

"No, he's not!" She spread her hands in exasperation and turned to march up the sidewalk. "You're here, and that's fine. In fact, it's more than fine, because we could sure use the help right now, but don't imagine there is some kind of a love triangle happening here."

"Okay, I won't. I won't even give you the purple daisies and dark chocolate Blaze told me to bring you."

She frowned up at him. "You didn't."

"Relax," he said. "I knew better. I'm not trying to seduce your emotions by coming here, I'm here because I couldn't stay away under the circumstances. I'll play nice, and I'll do anything Canaan York would like me to do. If he wants to put me to work scrubbing toilets, I'll do it. I'm not afraid of a little hard—"

"Don't be ridiculous. He's not going to do that. He and I have known each other since we were five years old, and—"

"Actually, five and a half," came a voice from the doorway of the apartment. The open doorway, where Canaan stood watching, with very apparent interest. "If I remember correctly, Sheila's birthday is in late October, so that would make her thirty-four and a half."

Sheila cringed. How much had he heard? If he'd caught that pip-squeak comment...

"Preston," Canaan said, "Blaze just told me you were a CPA. How did you guys know I'd need someone with your capabilities even more than another doctor? I've already reassured Blaze that he'll have plenty of one-on-one experience with patients, and when we get time, I'll take him to meet a shepherd I know who would be glad for the help of a prevet student."

"Well, that settles it," Preston said dryly. "Blaze will be here for the summer at this rate. You actually remembered Sheila's birthday?"

"Sure. I always got invited to her birthday parties, and she always got teased about being a Halloween baby. I was a Christmas baby." He rubbed his hands together. "Speaking of Christmas, that's what today suddenly feels like to me. You didn't realize what you were getting into, though I'm sure

Sheila will warn you about it when she has some time, but first, I'd love to show you all around, get you started doing those things you each do best."

"I'm game," Preston said. "And Blaze has been looking forward to this ever since Sheila left the hospital last week."

"Then let's get started," Canaan said, his eagerness obviously contagious to the guys.

Sheila waved a hand at Canaan. "Before you get carried away, you might want to give me some time to catch up on my sleep, since we do have the help we need, after all."

"You've got it," Canaan said. "Take the afternoon off, Sheila. We'll get better work out of you that way, anyway. Maybe you could join us in the clinic this evening?"

She nodded, realizing for the first time that, aside from her joy at having Preston and Blaze here working beside her—a comforting presence from home—they were going to carry their weight. And she did feel safer with them here. Definitely.

Just having Preston closer tended to chase away the excessive fears that had haunted her since her arrival.

Maybe Preston was an answer to some of her prayers, as well.

Canaan was conflicted. He now had not one, but three people to help him in the search for some kind of connection between those who had died. And these were people from afar, whom he could trust. And yet...

He glanced at Preston. From Canaan's earliest memories, any time he faced an important event or had a decision to make, he listed in detail every pro and con he could think of about the subject. That was how he realized so well that there were drawbacks in even the most positive experiences—nothing was ever totally black-and-white.

For instance, at one of his worst times—when Sheila had left—Canaan had been forced to fight his own battles. It was a lesson he should have learned much earlier.

And now that Sheila had come back—his heroine once again jumping into the fray, bringing friends along to help— the sudden, unexpected blessing was not without a few very obvious drawbacks.

It wasn't so much Preston Black's arrival that was disconcerting, it was the fact that his presence forced Canaan out of denial. He had to admit to himself that he didn't want to lose Sheila again.

And yet he didn't want to be jealous of the closeness she shared with Preston. A more mature man would have enjoyed seeing the happiness in her eyes when Preston arrived this afternoon. But Canaan couldn't help wondering about Preston's character. What kind of man was he? Why had Sheila told him to stay away? Was he forcing himself on her by coming and ingratiating himself here?

From what Granddad had said about Sheila's marriage, the trouble had begun with disagreements about her faith, and had escalated from there, until only a shell of a marriage remained when her husband was killed in an accident with the woman who'd been his last tawdry flirtation.

How many other flings had the loser had, endangering his wife's heart, as well as her life, with who knew what sexually transmitted diseases?

That aside, however, Canaan felt on the verge of true excitement as he settled with Blaze and Preston in the clinic. He showed Blaze the files and the multiple forms to be filled out when the children came through. He gave Preston a set of parameters to check while examining the medical histories of those who had died. Blaze would be a hit with the kids, and Preston was enough of a hunk that the older girls would love to catch a glimpse of him.

All in all, Canaan's current list was filled with pros. The cons were few.

So why did that very short list threaten to ruin his suddenly upbeat attitude?

## Chapter Twenty-Four

Dinner aromas permeated the air outside the cafeteria late Monday afternoon, drifting through the clinic, reminding Sheila that she'd had only a few crackers and an apple before her short nap—her very short nap.

The clatter of pots and pans and the occasional cry of a bird were the only noises she heard through the windows. Her attention was on the soft chatter of nervous children and Blaze's low voice behind the privacy screen, offering reassurance that he and Sheila were both very gentle.

Sheila's turquoise cross, in its setting of gold, danced in midair as she bent over a second grader. She fingered the stone absently, remembering Tanya's comment that the turquoise served as protection. She had gotten the idea from Betsy Two Horses.

Sheila couldn't think about that at the moment. The children were arriving in the clinic in small groups. Blaze was drawing blood, doing the basic checkups, and Sheila was providing more complete physical examinations.

Far from being put to work scrubbing toilets, Preston was, at this moment, in Canaan's apartment, at his kitchen table, poring over a stack of financial reports that Canaan admittedly didn't understand.

As always, Sheila loved working with the children, but not sticking them with needles. Fortunately, most of the kids were up to date on their immunizations, so very few injections were necessary.

So far this afternoon, she had discovered that the Twin Mesas children seemed happy and eager to please. There was no sign of a problem, and she wondered about Canaan's comment that there were children who seemed spooked. The only one who appeared spooked was Tanya.

Just as the last child was finished, Tanya walked into the clinic. Sheila was surprised to see her, and she didn't like the pallor of her face.

"You doing okay, Tanya?"

The girl nodded and stepped up to Sheila's desk. "I should've listened to Canaan, but I wanted to go to the surprise party for Kai. He's sixty-five today, and Betsy made him his favorite taco with extra cheese, and a chocolate birthday cake big enough for his whole homeroom class."

"But you're not in his class."

"No, but Jamey Hunt has been supervised by Kai since his parents died, so he was invited, and he said April and I could go, too."

Sheila dabbed at a streak of chocolate on Tanya's chin. "You don't look as if you feel very well. Too much cake?"

Tanya shook her head. She glanced back over her shoulder toward the door, then leaned closer to Sheila. "April's such a jerk."

"How's she being a jerk?"

"I wouldn't tell her what was wrong with me, and it made her mad. Then she found out I was staying with you, and so now she's all 'Tanya's studying to be a *biligaana*,' like it's some horrible crime."

Sheila reached out and felt Tanya's forehead, then her neck. The girl didn't feel warm, but she was bound to be tired and weak from her ordeal yesterday. "Do you want to go to Canaan's office for a while to rest?"

Tanya shook her head. "I'll stay here with you. I don't care what April says." She glanced around as a tall, slender boy around her age walked in, then she turned back and whispered, "That's Jamey, April's brother. He's not like his sister."

"Thank you. Why don't you sit down over by the windows. I have a form for everyone to fill out, and you might as well get that over with, too. I'll give you a checkup after the rest of the kids have gone," Blaze was saying.

A hint of a grin peeked from the girl's dark brown eyes. "Can Blaze do the checkup?"

Sheila chuckled. "Sure, he can take your vitals."

Satisfied, Tanya walked toward the far end of the large room, where comfortable chairs had been grouped together as a waiting area beside a bank of windows overlooking the playground and cafeteria. She slumped onto a chair near Jamey Hunt.

Another young girl stepped through the doorway, then paused and looked around. Her eyes appeared small, but that was probably because of the scowl on her face when she glanced Sheila's way. She was short, with black hair that clung to her scalp. As she took a seat between Tanya and Jamey, her thin, gangly arms and legs seemed to jut in all directions.

She whispered something to Tanya, giggled, then glanced at Sheila, eyes still narrowed.

Tanya shifted in her seat, obviously uncomfortable.

The newcomer turned back to Tanya and whispered something else.

"Stop it, April," Tanya muttered.

Sheila watched the girl a moment longer as she whispered to Tanya once more, reached across and pushed a chart off the bookcase behind Jamey. Then she shot Sheila a glare.

This would be interesting.

Once the rest of the sixth and seventh grades had arrived, Sheila handed out clipboards, each with a questionnaire and a pencil. It was a simple form, with easy questions, but as she passed out the sheets, she heard groans of foreboding. The children shot worried glances at each other.

"This test won't do any good, you know," April said when Sheila reached her.

Sheila held a clipboard out for April. "It isn't a test, it's a health history form."

April's dark eyes met Sheila's gaze with a bold challenge. Slowly, with deliberation, she took the clipboard from Sheila, then dropped it onto the floor, where it clattered loudly.

Sheila gave herself a moment to remember the last time she'd heard the clatter of a clipboard on the floor. It had been a week ago, when she had dropped one twice, herself, on the hospital floor in Hideaway. For her, the reason had been distraction. For April, the reason might be a little more complicated.

"I read in your file that you're a bright girl, April," Sheila said as she picked up the item of apparent offense. She considered offering April condolences over the loss of her parents, but decided that wasn't wise at this moment.

The girl's glare turned colder. "You read my file?"

"Sure. I'm in charge of your health care until the end of the year. I need all the information I can get."

"I don't care about this stuff, I care about running. If I can run fast, I won't have to worry about medical stuff. I'll be healthy." April leaned back in her seat, arms crossed in front of her.

"You don't run that fast, April," said her brother beside her.

"Shut up, Jamey."

"Then stop causing trouble and fill out the form."

Two pairs of matching, dark eyes locked in a silent duel for several seconds before Sheila stepped between the brother and sister. She gave Jamey a clipboard, then turned back to his sister.

"I'm flattered, April. I was under the impression you didn't like me, but now it looks as if you want to spend more time with me so I can give you a complete physical."

April's sneer drooped.

"Who knows?" Sheila continued as she handed April's clipboard to her once more, "I may have you here well after school is over for the day. Would you like to spend some time together after school? I'd love to get to know you better."

Warm color spread slowly across the girl's face. "You can't keep me here against my will."

"I wouldn't dream of physically restraining you. I can, however, discuss the situation with your principal and your track coach. I'm afraid your track activities would have to be curtailed until I get this form filled out."

"Doc wouldn't listen to a—"

"*Biligaana?*" Sheila allowed just a hint of warning to enter her voice. "He would listen to this one, because I ran on his track team, too, and he and I have known each other a long time."

The small eyes widened. Apparently not all the information about Sheila's history had circulated through the school. Fascinating. If this had been Hideaway, everyone on campus would have already known her mother's and father's full names, dates of birth and her mother's maiden name, and her parents before her.

"I'm sure Doc will understand that we have an important relationship to develop," Sheila continued. "I'll explain it to him after the final bell today."

April snatched up her pencil and leaned over her paper in an exaggerated show of eagerness.

Tanya shot Sheila a grin, and Sheila winked at her. April wasn't as tough as she thought she was. A hurting child acted out in a number of different ways. Later, maybe Sheila and April could have a long talk.

## ❧ Chapter Twenty-Five ❧

The dismissal bell had not stopped ringing when Canaan looked up from his desk and saw Kai Begay striding across the playground, ponytail bobbing, chin jutting forward and hands flexing in and out of fists at his sides. He walked like a man in a hurry. Kai seemed to be in a snit about something quite often now that Sheila was here.

Kai jerked open the door to the office, barreled through, then stood staring at Canaan as the door slammed shut behind him. Canaan feared for the frosted glass in the windowpanes.

"You didn't come to my party," Kai said.

"I'm sorry. I thought it was only for you and your kids."

"Betsy made a giant taco with fry bread, thick as my arm. Everybody at the party got some." He sank down into the chair in front of Canaan's desk.

Canaan leaned forward, elbows on the desk. "I can tell you have something besides birthday parties on your mind."

"Tanya was there," Kai said.

"I know. She was invited, and I didn't have the heart to tell her she couldn't go."

"She going to be okay? She didn't look so good."

"It'll take her some time to recover."

"You sure she's recovered?" Kai leaned closer. "The principal died of some kind of virus. April mentioned she saw a mouse in their cottage last week. What if Tanya's got something contagious?"

"Do you have any reason to suspect she has?" Canaan asked.

"It isn't up to me to find that out."

"Do you know how many viruses there are? It's impossible to check everyone who gets sick for every possible infection, and they're difficult to isolate."

"What about plague? Hantavirus? The usual?"

"If Tanya had either of those she'd be worse instead of better."

"Did they check her out there at the hospital yesterday?"

Canaan suppressed an exasperated sigh. "For what, Kai? We have nothing to go on. No one else at the school is sick, and so this problem with Tanya is obviously not contagious."

"If you don't think she's contagious, why did you let her move out of her dorm?"

"I feel she needs some adult attention."

"From the only white woman on campus? Why?"

Canaan felt a flash of defensive anger. "She's with Sheila, Kai. You know Sheila. She's not going to hurt Tanya, for Pete's sake, and she's a nurse. If you're worried about the child's health, you should be glad she's in the care of a medical professional."

"How does Sheila feel about having some strange child forced on her before she can even get her bearings?"

"She agreed to keep Tanya."

"I didn't ask what she agreed to, I asked how she felt about it."

Canaan studied Kai's expression, the arms crossed over his chest defensively. "I haven't had the impression that you would be concerned about Sheila's feelings over anything."

"If she resents Tanya moving in with her, that could be hard on Tanya."

"Believe me, Tanya will not hesitate to let me know if that turns out to be the case."

"If Johnny Jacobs knew—"

"He'll know about it as soon as I tell him, unless you decide to beat me to it." Canaan took a slow, measured breath and let it out. Kai was a driving force in this school, and Canaan appreciated him. Still, sometimes the man tended to overstep his authority. Yet if Canaan had been an authority figure here as long as Kai, he would have the same attitude, he was sure.

"I'm just curious why you didn't have Tanya move in with one of our own."

"Our own?" Canaan snapped. "Sheila is one of our own, Kai. Would you at least give this situation some time?"

Kai studied him, his granite face showing no expression for the moment. "If that's the way you want it, fine. Now tell me about today's newcomers."

Canaan resented Kai's assumption that he had the right to grill him this way. "Preston Black and Blaze Farmer are friends of Sheila's from Missouri who have volunteered their time and expertise to help us get the clinic and this office organized."

"If you needed help, why didn't you ask for it here at the school, instead of sending for it from another state?"

"I didn't ask, but it was offered, and I've accepted it."

"Where are they staying? The dorms are full. Sheila took the last apartment and—"

"They're staying with me, Kai. I've got a guest bedroom."

It was obvious this news didn't sit well with Kai, but Canaan doubted anything would at this moment.

"Tell me, Canaan, how were you treated when you went to college?" Kai asked.

"I was treated very well."

"That's hard to believe. You never heard any remarks about us 'educated Indians'?" Kai's lip curved in a sneer. "It wasn't suggested that 'heathens' like us didn't have enough brains to think for ourselves?"

"Those are ignorant opinions of ignorant people a long time ago. Things have changed."

"You're telling me you didn't feel it, too?"

"Sure, I felt it from both sides," Canaan said. "Many of my classmates believed I was receiving special privileges because of financial incentives and grants in college. Many others treated me with honor I didn't deserve, specifically because I was part Navajo."

"You trying to tell me that didn't affect you?"

"I became more suspicious of people who were kind to me, and less patient with those who were unkind simply because of my blood. I try not to let it get in the way of my job performance."

"Then you were one of the lucky ones, because it affected my whole career. At the university in Flagstaff, I was blessed with a Hopi professor who hated me because I was Navajo. He influenced the university bureaucrats to have me black-listed, the same kind of thing the Hopi are doing to us here on the reservation." Kai sat rigid with remembered anger, as if four and a half decades had dropped away. "That's what racial prejudice did for me."

"And so now you're doing the same thing to Sheila," Canaan said. "Didn't you learn from that experience?"

Kai shook his head. "I'm not trying to take all this out on her."

"You could've fooled me."

"I just don't want people from other cultures coming to this school and ingratiating themselves with our kids. We have enough trouble keeping the younger ones on the reservation as it is."

"I heard you once tried to leave the reservation. How can you blame others for the same desire?"

"I wanted to be a physician. The initials *M.D.* would have earned me acceptance into the white man's world. I was premed all the way, and I made the grades. I graduated early and was told that I'd been given glowing recommendations." Kai's short, thick fingers dug into the deep pile of the chair. "But no med school would even consider me. So don't talk to me about racial prejudice."

"Do you hate it here so much?" Canaan asked.

Kai looked down at his hands, and his grip eased on the chair. "No."

"You love the kids, and they obviously love you. I don't know many kids who go to all that trouble for their teacher's birthday."

Kai returned Canaan's gaze. "People change. I've changed over the years."

"Maybe you should think about changing a little more," Canaan said gently.

Kai held his look for a long moment, then looked away. "You'll have trouble if the parents find out Tanya's staying with Sheila."

"Times have changed, Kai. You're looking too far into the past."

Kai shook his head and got up. "It's no use talking to you, is it? You're not going to listen."

"I wish you'd listen to yourself for a moment, Kai. You're a Christian. You know we are commanded to bless our enemies and forgive them. Sheila isn't even the enemy. You've allowed a root of bitterness to grow inside you, and it's affecting everything around you. Why can't you let it go?"

For a moment, Kai stood still, staring at the door. "I'm getting old, Canaan. Some things are still hard to change."

"Try, okay? Sheila's done nothing to deserve your resentment."

Kai shot him a sharp glance. "It isn't Sheila as much as…" He shook his head, pulled the door open and left, letting the door slam shut behind him.

Canaan made a note on the pad in front of him. He had a meeting to attend in Flagstaff at the university next weekend. Old Doctor Whitter was a professor there, and he was Hopi. He'd been there for probably fifty years and was likely to have had Kai Begay in a class or two. Maybe he even knew something about Kai's bitter anger. It was time to find out.

Preston carried a stack of files through the sliding-glass door of Canaan York's apartment onto the second-floor balcony, shaded from the sun by a vine trellis overhead and several potted cacti along the perimeter. The temperature here was probably about the same as in Missouri, but the dryness of the air made it feel ten to twenty degrees cooler, especially out here, with the breeze coming in across the desert.

With the frenetic pace of the day, there had been no chance

for Preston to really talk to Canaan. After giving a tour of the campus, the doctor-turned-principal had handed Preston a stack of files and explained that his predecessor had been in the process of compiling the year-end financial report. Canaan, who did not have a head for finances, had been shoving the project aside until he could find time for it.

Judging by the lack of organization Preston had seen in the files, he gathered that Canaan intended to pay a CPA to attack the mess when the need became too great to ignore.

An expensive option.

Canaan had said that Preston and Blaze's arrival was an answer to prayer, but Preston dismissed that. He didn't remember anyone ever before implying that he was an answer to prayer.

In the files, Preston found some discrepancies that he thought could be explained if he had more information. At the moment, however, it appeared that several of the staff weren't salaried, but worked for room and board and a minimal stipend every month. Kai Begay was one. So was Betsy Two Horses and Jane Witherbe. Doc Cottonwood also earned a particularly low income, and though none of the staff was paid enough to build a comfortable retirement, these people appeared to be at this school simply for the joy of serving the kids.

When Preston had first discovered the anomaly, he'd thought he must be missing something. Perhaps stock options were being provided, or another incentive he hadn't yet discovered. Thinking about it, he supposed it was possible for the staff to see the work purely as a labor of love—the way he did with his cabin in the woods—to be dedicated to the jobs and the children they served. But what if something else was going on?

As he continued to ponder this puzzle, he heard voices down at the edge of the campus. A man in red gym shorts and a white T-shirt with a coyote insignia across the chest called to the children who ran in a line beside him.

"That's right, Jamey, swing your arms," the man said. "Swing them hard. You, too, April. See how those vitamins helped?"

Moving his chair closer to the edge, Preston peered through the cactus screen and saw a tall, dark-haired boy and a very skinny girl about the same age as Tanya Swift.

The boy's face reddened beneath the deep brown of his skin, which already dripped moisture. This one was a fast runner, but he obviously wasn't focused on what he was doing. He tripped twice, and nearly ran over the coach.

"Watch it, Jamey," the man snapped. "You've got to concentrate, watch where you're going, make every step count."

"Sorry, Doc."

The man named Doc turned to shoot a fierce frown at his one lagging team member, far behind the others. "Dahlia, what's this talk about winning a race this year? You couldn't beat a rock at that pace."

The girl placed her hand on her abdomen and grimaced.

He sighed. "You want to run in a competitive team, you can't let anything get in the way. Push past it," he called over his shoulder, increasing the pace. "Come on, you'll feel better if you get moving. Okay, everybody, pick it up. Keep up with me. Our people are nothing without speed. Run with the coyote. Visualize. You're the coyote, chasing your prey across the earth."

They ran faster, faster, breathing heavily, kicking hard over a dirt track that wound out into the desert, then back again. Even Dahlia kept up, carried by the cadence of the coach's voice.

Preston found himself wishing he could run into the desert, feeling the warm sun on his skin, the sweat of exertion, the thrill of the race. There was something about this place—so vastly open and overwhelmingly silent that the shouts of the coach, voices of the runners and laughter of the children on the playground seemed inconsequential.

How different it was from the Ozarks. The distances were deceptive here, the spaces so great. In Hideaway, a half-dozen varieties of birdcalls could be heard at one time, along with the splash of fish in the lake, the roar of boat motors and the voices of neighbors hailing one another. Here, the calls of birds and children seemed hushed by the very atmosphere.

The coach called, "Okay, cooldown time. Let's walk." He seemed satisfied, at last, with his runners.

The dust quickly settled as the runners caught their breath. The skinny girl with short black hair and skinny arms and legs started giggling and whispering to Dahlia. Her voice grew louder, and in spite of himself, Preston strained to hear what she said.

"See that?" She pointed toward a column of drifting smoke on the horizon.

"Sure I do," Dahlia said. "The death hogan is out there. Is that where the smoke is coming from?"

The skinny girl nodded. "That means somebody's being called."

"What's that?"

"It means someone at the school will run out to the hogan tonight."

"But why?"

"For the special ritual that will help whoever is called to run better than ever before. You must never follow its call on your own, but when you're called, you must go."

"Have you ever been called?"

"No, but I will."

"Why is the hogan haunted?" Dahlia asked.

"An old chanter died there many years ago, and his bones were found months later. The entrance was boarded up, but later someone came, took the boards away, and then left the valley forever—to escape ghost sickness. Now whoever is called and goes there comes back with special powers."

"But isn't anyone who goes there afraid of ghost sickness?"

"I'm not afraid."

"April, that's enough," came the sharp voice of the coach. "Concentrate on your breathing. Enough chatter."

Preston sat back in his chair. Haunted hogans, ghost sickness, special powers? He was certainly a long way from home.

## Chapter Twenty-Six

Betsy Two Horses freed her braid from the hairnet and left her helpers preparing dinner. She sat down alone in the empty dining room with her taco. She never had time to eat when the others did; there was always someone wanting her to fix something special, someone wanting her to tell a story or explain something about the old ways. She hated to talk and eat. That was why she stayed so skinny—there was always someone who needed her time.

Even as she raised her taco to her mouth, the dining room door opened with a quiet swish. She turned, then dropped her food back on the plate when she saw the beautiful woman with the large, sad eyes.

Sheila waved at Betsy from across the dining room. "Got some time? I need to ask you a few questions."

Betsy nodded. Some time. Not a lot.

"Go ahead and eat."

"I plan to," Betsy said, though she was already losing her appetite for the taco. She had tried a new flour for the fry bread, and it tasted too sweet to her.

She must be getting old; nothing tasted good to her anymore.

She took a few small bites while Sheila went into the supply room that was used by the staff to stock their apartments—items such as paper towels, coffee, soap, laundry detergent and toilet paper were always on hand. By the time Sheila returned with a paper bag filled with supplies, Betsy had pushed her plate away.

Sheila sat down across the table. "I'd like to visit with you, but I can't stay long. Tanya Swift is staying with me for a while, and I don't want her to be alone."

"Where is she now?"

"With Canaan."

"I heard rumors about her staying with you," Betsy said.

"Word seems to have spread quickly. I don't see why it's a big deal."

"Neither do I, but others may hurt you and Tanya with their words."

"You mean like your helper, Steve?" Sheila gestured toward the kitchen serving window, where Steve Hunt worked in front of the stove. "He doesn't try to hide his resentment when I'm around. I'll get used to it. I just wish the children wouldn't taunt Tanya for staying with a *biligaana*."

Betsy grunted. "Since she received no punishment for running away…" She shrugged.

"She was punished, Betsy. Believe me." Sheila's fingers absently toyed with the cross at her throat.

Betsy had yet to see Sheila without that necklace. "You seem to like that thing," she observed.

Sheila's movements stilled. Betsy noticed her eyes had darkened to a deep golden color, almost brown.

"Your eyes were that color a lot just before your Dad packed up and moved you to Missouri," she told Sheila.

"My eyes?" Sheila shook her head, not comprehending.

"They darken when you're upset."

"You remember that?" Sheila leaned forward, as if she'd been waiting for this opening. "What else do you remember? You knew my parents well."

Betsy nodded. "They were hard workers. So were you, doing well in school, playing well with the other kids."

"What was it like here then?"

"A lot like it is now, except the buildings were old, falling apart, overrun with mice. The people were the same. Most of the staff has remained over the years."

"What was my mother like?"

Betsy frowned. "Your mother? You were old enough you should be able to remember her well."

Sheila grimaced and shook her head.

"Your father didn't talk about her?" Betsy asked.

"No, Daddy always seemed irritated when I asked questions about her, about what happened. I couldn't remember much of anything." Sheila leaned forward, folding her arms together. "It's as if some thick fog settled over everything after her death."

"The fog never lifted?" Betsy wondered if she should reveal anything at all. Maybe some things were best kept concealed.

Sheila shook her head. "What do you remember about her, Betsy?"

"She was my friend for five years. I remember many things."

"Tell me the good things. I need to know the good things."

Betsy relaxed. She would gladly share the good things.

* * *

Preston knocked on the door marked Principal, then let himself in to find Canaan bent over an open file drawer in the far corner of the office.

"Come on in, have a seat," Canaan called without looking around. "What can I do for you?"

"I just need my curiosity satisfied," Preston said.

Canaan turned at the sound of his voice, then glanced at the file in Preston's hands. "Find something interesting?"

"Do you know anything about the staff salaries?"

Canaan grimaced. "Pitiful, I'll tell you that. All of them deserve much more."

"Including you."

"This year was an anomaly for me. I came here as a favor to my grandfather, and he doesn't expect me to stay for another year. That's a good thing, since I'm paying for a house, and my salary here barely covers those payments, much less living expenses." Canaan sank into the chair at the desk and gestured for Preston to have a seat. "So what did you need to know?"

"There seem to be some staff members who don't get paid at all. Volunteers?"

"You're talking about Kai Begay and Doc Cottonwood and some others," Canaan said. "Since this is a mission school, the staff members consider themselves missionaries, and some of them arrange for their own support through churches in the region."

"I'm afraid I'm totally out of my element here. This is a different state, as well as a Navajo reservation. Do we need to do a breakdown of the income these individuals receive from other sources?"

"No. All our contributors need is a report on how their

funds were utilized. Bob Jaffrey used to do a pie chart to show them the breakdown of resources."

"Great. I'm sure the computer has a spreadsheet for that," Preston said.

Canaan leaned back in his chair and studied Preston while Preston made a show of studying the top file on the desk.

"I told you when I gave you the tour that there was a lot of work to be done in a short time," Canaan said.

"I'm convinced."

"So you can do the pie chart?"

"Of course," Preston said. "May I ask you something?"

"Yes."

"I'm curious about Johnny Jacobs."

"What do you want to know about him?"

"Forgive me for saying so, but I've read about religious schools or mission settings where all but a selected few sacrifice everything for the cause, but those few live in luxury supported by others."

Canaan's sudden stillness and the grip on his pen revealed that he did not like the implied criticism of his grandfather. Still, he smiled. It was not one of his best smiles. "I've read about them, too, but it isn't something I've ever seen personally."

"Never?"

"Believe me, my grandfather is not one of those people." There was some heat in Canaan's tone.

"I don't want to offend," Preston said, wondering if that was the truth, or if, deep down, he had hoped to get a rise out of Canaan. "I should probably have warned you that I've been cursed with a strong dose of doubt about certain missions in general."

"And perhaps the Christian faith in particular?" Canaan suggested.

"I was raised in a strong Christian environment that was also painfully dysfunctional. To me, it appeared as if my parents used their faith as a lifeline because their lives were so hopeless."

"You saw their faith as a crutch," Canaan said.

"That's an old cliché, but it works."

"And you reject being dependent on that crutch."

"I fail to see what good it did in their lives."

"But what about their hearts? That was the important thing."

"I saw their hearts broken by the unkind acts of some of God's own people, and I vowed I would never become one of them."

"Now I see what Sheila meant about the good friend who kept her life very interesting," Canaan said. "She obviously cares a lot about you. But I can also see why she still calls you only a good friend."

Preston blinked at the sting of the man's words.

"Why did you really come to Arizona, since you obviously have no interest in helping out at a Christian school?" Canaan asked.

"But I do want to help, or I wouldn't be wasting my time on the poorly kept records. But you're right, my main reason for coming out here is to make sure my *good friend* remains alive long enough to come back home to Hideaway, where she belongs." Preston heard the heat in his own words and didn't regret them.

"How do you know she belongs there? She grew up here. She has some good memories and some good friends from this part of her life."

"I don't doubt it, but she also obviously has some very horrible memories that make me wonder if there isn't more danger here for her than anyone wants to admit. I want to be here to protect her, if necessary, no matter what."

"Do you think you can control her decisions about her future?"

"I don't think that's what I said."

"She's an adult," Canaan said. "She can take care of herself, and I'll do everything I can to make sure she stays safe."

Okay, the man had claws and a bite. Definitely one of those in-your-face Christian soldiers. Preston could respect that. He couldn't leave it alone, but he could respect it. "I hear you're divorced."

"That's right, though it really isn't anyone's business."

"You know, they say divorce is never the fault of just one person."

"That's right. And you?"

"Never married."

"You don't believe in Jesus, you don't believe in marriage."

Preston could hear the unspoken words in his head. *What makes you think you're the man for Sheila?*

"Oh, I believe in marriage," he told Canaan softly, "just not broken ones."

To Preston's extreme frustration, there was a knock at the door, and Tanya walked in. "Hi, Canaan. Sheila's not in the apartment. I thought I'd hang with you until she shows up. That okay?"

Canaan and Preston locked gazes for a long few seconds, then Canaan nodded at Tanya.

This very interesting discussion would resume another day. Preston was pretty sure he could count on that.

## Chapter Twenty-Seven

Sheila leaned her elbows on the table. "I always had the impression from Daddy that he was sort of mad at my mother for dying," Sheila told Betsy.

"Did he stay mad?"

"He just refused to talk about her. It seems everybody's refusing."

Betsy sat back in her seat, studying the delicate lines of Sheila's face. At first glance, Sheila looked like Buster, with the same dark brown hair and golden hazel eyes. The more Betsy looked at the girl, though, the more she saw her mother in her. That could be a frightening thought...

"Your mother loved the children the way you do," Betsy said. "She liked their company, and she liked to come into my kitchen and fix them special treats. But you were most important to her."

"Did everybody here like her?"

Betsy hesitated, then said carefully, "Most of the people saw a friend in her."

"Didn't anyone resent her because she was white?"

Betsy hesitated longer this time. She shook her head. "I don't remember anyone complaining about that."

"Not even Kai Begay?"

Betsy smiled. "Your mother was a beautiful woman. Kai was a younger man then." She shrugged, grinning at Sheila. "Men are men."

Sheila rested her chin in her cupped hands. "Can you tell me about the day she died? What happened?"

The suddenness of the question stiffened Betsy's spine. "I thought you wanted to hear the good things. I have many more good memories of her than bad ones."

Sheila's eyes narrowed slightly, then she nodded. "Okay, did she love dark chocolate the way I do?"

"She loved tea and coffee. She stopped in the cafeteria several times a day to share a cup with me. She couldn't eat chocolate very often because of her diabetes. She loved flowers, and she loved to collect old perfume bottles. She wasn't much on wearing perfume, because she said it set off allergic reactions in some people, and she didn't want to make anyone else sick just so she could smell good. But she loved scents, and she loved to taste new foods, try new things."

"Canaan mentioned that I used to go walking in the desert," Sheila said. "Did my mother ever walk with me?"

Betsy hesitated. She knew what was coming next. The girl would not get past the need to know about her mother's death.

Sheila reached out and touched her arm. "Please, Betsy, can't you tell me anything? There's something about that time that still bothers me."

"Your mother died. It was a shock. It's always going to bother you."

"It's more than that, and I think you know it. I need to know what happened. You were here. You were one of my mother's best friends. She probably told you more than anyone. I was just a little girl. All I remember is a blur. If it weren't for pictures Daddy kept, I wouldn't even know what she looked like."

Those words, more than anything, broke Betsy's heart. "Then you don't…" Betsy hesitated.

Sheila looked up. "Don't what?"

Betsy was sorry she had begun. Sheila would persist until…

"What am I supposed to remember?" Sheila asked.

"Okay. You don't remember the fighting?"

"What kind of fighting? Who fought?"

"Your parents had some trouble getting along, just before she died. That made it harder on Buster afterward."

Sheila frowned and touched her temple, as if to bring forward a lurking shadow of memory. "I don't recall any of that. Many of my memories are in snatches, in awful dreams…"

Betsy caught her breath. "Dreams?"

"Bad ones."

Betsy's attention sharpened, and she felt the thrust of familiar fear. This was worse than she'd thought.

"Betsy?"

"Nothing. It's got to be nothing. Just an old woman's imagination."

"Uh-uh. It's something. Say it. I need to know about my mother, to remember her, to understand why she left me."

"She didn't leave you, she was taken."

Sheila frowned, her attention caught by Betsy's choice of words. "Taken? By whom?"

"By death. The way all of us will someday be taken."

"Why do my dreams cause you concern?"

Betsy sighed. Might as well get this over with. "Sometimes nightmares are a sign of witchery. Victims of witchcraft have them."

Sheila stared at her. "Lots of people have bad dreams. That doesn't mean somebody's casting spells."

Betsy put her hand on the table again, prepared to stand. But she didn't. Perhaps there was more Sheila needed to know. "You're right. And Navajo witchcraft works only on Navajo, so you should be immune."

"In my nightmares, I see the Twin Mesas, a hogan in a valley and a wolf."

Betsy stiffened. "A wolf? Are you sure?"

"I'm sure."

Betsy scooted her chair back and stood.

Sheila reached out. "What about the wolf?"

"They need me in the kitchen. I'll have to think about this." She avoided Sheila's questioning eyes. "We have tacos tonight, and Steve never cooks the meat enough."

"Please, Betsy. It's important." Sheila got up and came around the table. "You do know what I'm talking about."

Betsy felt a wave of panic. She glanced around the cafeteria. There could be listening ears. "Don't talk about it. Don't summon it." Why was Sheila remembering these things now?

"Of course I'm not summoning it."

"Push it away from you, force it from your thoughts. If it is witchcraft, it can be dangerous for you. Deadly."

"Did my mother have these dreams?"

"Stay away from it, Sheila."

Sheila held up a hand. "Okay, so forget the wolf for a minute. Can't you tell me what my parents fought about?"

Betsy saw the need to know in the depths of Sheila's eyes. "They fought about what time to go to work in the morning, what time to go to bed, how to raise you. Near the end, they fought about everything. Your mother decided she didn't want to be here. She wasn't sure how she felt about Buster's dedication to helping our people. She was more like me."

"How like you?" Sheila asked.

"She was sometimes confused by Christianity. She wasn't as sure as Buster about whom she served."

"My mother wasn't a believer?" The idea seemed to shock Sheila more than Betsy expected.

Betsy shrugged. "Who can know?"

It took Sheila a few seconds to digest this. She swallowed audibly. "I don't believe that."

"You should ask your father about these things."

"Like that's going to happen," Sheila muttered. "One more question."

Betsy braced herself. What next?

"Where was I the day Mom died?"

So Sheila didn't remember this, either. Betsy reached out and touched the girl's cheek. "You're the only one who knows that, honey."

"But I don't remember. I've been told that I was carried in from the desert, but I don't recall anything about that day. Or several days afterward, for that matter."

"All I can say is that no one knew what happened. Your mother came running into the kitchen, upset because you had not come home from school. We all started looking for you. You used to like to walk out by yourself on the desert, and that was where we all looked, the staff and some of the older kids."

"I was told Johnny Jacobs found me."

"He did, two hours after your mother started looking for you. You were lying in an arroyo, sick, half-delirious. You didn't know where you had been, but you were crying for your mother. Then we couldn't find her to tell her you were okay. Your father found her an hour later, dead, in an old hogan in Piñon Valley. It was thought that she died from insulin shock."

"I know what Doc thinks, but nothing was ever proved."

"We thought maybe she had found you in that hogan, and the exertion of her walk, with nothing to eat, had killed her before she'd gotten help. And you had seen her die."

Sheila closed her eyes. Her face lost some of its color.

Betsy reached out and squeezed her arm. "Sometimes there is a reason for the loss of memory. Sometimes what happens in our past must stay there."

"But all these years…" Sheila looked at Betsy. "What would my mother have been doing in an old hogan in Piñon Valley?"

"I think that was what upset Buster so much. He never knew. I told him that people do strange things when they're upset, and she had been…upset lately."

"About what?"

"Their fighting, of course." Betsy gestured toward the cross that hung around Sheila's neck. "Do you still remember what the necklace was for?"

Sheila didn't answer right away. The silence made Betsy uncomfortable. There was a certain watchfulness in the young woman's expression. Caution.

"Sheila?"

"You told me it was to remind me that I was never alone."

"Yes. You are to remember that someone loves you."

"And that's the real reason you gave this to me?"

"Yes."

"And it isn't to protect me from whatever killed my mother?"

"I don't think it can. I seem to have lost faith in any kind of magic."

"Then maybe you should give God another try."

Betsy stared at the cross for a moment, and then she nodded. Maybe she was making other things more important than the God she was here to serve.

"I'll do that," she told Sheila.

Late Monday night, as Tanya put sheets and blankets on the Hide-A-Bed sofa in the living room, Sheila unhooked the chain that held the turquoise cross around her neck. She held the delicate jewel to the light, admiring its beauty.

She had been a frightened child when Betsy had given this to her, but she was no longer that child.

She walked into the living room and sat on the plush chair beside the coffee table that held the sculpted sheep head. "Tanya."

The girl turned to her.

"I have something I want to give you." She held out the necklace.

Tanya's lips parted, eyes widening. "But this is your protection."

"I explained to you that it isn't some supernatural protection, it simply reminds me that I am loved by the most powerful Spirit that exists."

"But I'm not a Christian, and so—"

"That won't stop this Spirit from loving you, Tanya. Even if you don't believe in Him, He believes in you." She laid the chain in Tanya's open palm. "Remember that anytime you're afraid."

Tanya studied the cross, turned it over in her hand, clasped it tightly and held it to her chest. She closed her eyes. "I love it. But I know someone who might need it more than I do."

"Who's that?"

"Jamey Hunt."

"Is he also afraid of the wolf?"

"I don't know, but he's having a lot of trouble right now."

"The necklace is yours to do with what you want."

Tanya held the necklace out to Sheila. "Would you fasten it around my neck? I'd like to wear it, at least for tonight."

As Sheila obliged, she couldn't help wondering again how many children were affected by this terror of the wolf.

## Chapter Twenty-Eight

Sometime in the dark hours of early morning, I awake with a start, falling, crying out, grasping through the black air for something that vanishes with my return to consciousness. I hit the floor with an impact that knocks away my breath.

I no longer soar with the spirits—I am unable to feel my own spirit. Something tickles my cheek and I claw at it, only to find tears trickling down my face. Perspiration drips from my body.

Invisible spirits jeer at me, surrounding me. I huddle against the side of my bed, stiff with terror. They are waiting for me. One move, one wrong sound, and they will come for me. I squeeze into myself, ducking my head between my bent knees. The terror is a familiar feeling, yet I have no memory of this ever happening before.

I cringe in this cowardly way for endless moments, waiting for the spirits to stop hovering around me. I shouldn't be afraid. Don't I command those spirits? Don't I control them?

With my knowledge, haven't I summoned the most powerful spirit of all, the spirit of the wolf?

Gradually, I grow aware of a whisper that echoes through the blackness—a childish whisper, like a little boy at play:

*"Racing Deer is running, racing, Racing Deer is running far from here."*

"Who's there?" I call out, my voice quivering so I barely recognize it.

*"Racing...racing...racing...*

*"Running...running...running...*

"No," I whisper.

The voice grows louder: *"Racing Deer is running, racing, running. Racing Deer is running far from here."*

"No!"

Louder: *"Racing...racing...racing...*

*"Running...running...running...*

The voice echoes around me, chanting the same words over and over, growing louder, deeper, stronger. I cover my ears, but the chant pounds through my head.

*"RACING...RACING...RACING..."*

I whimper, then groan, but the sounds grow louder, closer, swelling and throbbing through my brain.

I find myself repeating the words as if I have no will of my own.

As if I haven't for a long time.

*"Racing deer is running...running...running..."*

My own voice echoes in my ears, and I discover that this makes the other voice fade.

I fall silent.

The pain slowly goes away. Soft echoes of the child's voice dwindle and die. With them go the hovering spirits, drifting off with the wind.

When I raise my head, the darkness of the room crowds around me, but it's an empty darkness now.

I pull myself from the floor, still trembling, and sit on the bed. My sheets are drenched.

I swipe at the sweat dripping from my forehead. What's happening to me? Whose voice was that, and why this sudden attack? Haven't I served to the best of my ability? This is to be my doorway to riches and ease, and the spirits are supposed to be happy with my work.

Sheila. Spirit of the white woman. She knows things she shouldn't, things she learned as a child. Has she brought the spirits to hover around me?

Sudden, sharp anger urges me out the front door to glare at the sky. Gusts of cold air catch at my bare arms, and almost…almost I can hear again that voice on the twisting currents of the air.

She has to be stopped. Hasn't the spirit already warned me about her? And haven't I resisted what I've known needed to be done ever since she arrived?

I go back to my apartment long enough to pull on my night walking clothes, then I set out on my two-mile trek to the hogan.

The death hogan.

Something tickled Preston's nose. He brushed it away, but it came back. Finally, awake enough to think straight, he realized he wasn't in his own bed at home; he was staying in the home of his rival for Sheila's affections.

And then he thought about mice.

He shoved the covers away and leaped from the bed, thinking of plague and viruses and dangerous fevers that could kill before a man could get to help.

Then he remembered, of course, that a doctor slept down the hall. And he realized that the tickle he'd felt on his nose was most likely a corner of his sheet being ruffled gently by the breeze that shot through the room from the open glass door.

He glanced at the other twin bed in the room, and saw the white sheet where the blanket had been thrown back.

"Blaze?" he called softly.

"Shhh!" The command came from the deck.

"What are you doing out there?" Preston stepped to the open door and peered out at the moonlit desert.

"You see anything moving?" came a whisper no more than six inches from his ear.

"What am I supposed to see?"

Blaze raised an arm and pointed west. "That little figure walking away from the school. See it out there? It's all in white."

Preston peered into the darkness, and he did, indeed, see a flicker of white. "Could be a dog," he said, then grinned. "Could be the ghost of the dog that got killed on the road last week."

"Don't joke about something like that in a place like this," Blaze muttered. "It might be too close to the truth."

"Okay, I give up. Why are we up in the middle of the night spying on people, or ghosts or whatever?"

"Nothing better to do. Couldn't sleep."

Now that was strange. Blaze Farmer was rumored to be able to sleep sitting up in class and in church without anybody being the wiser. "What's wrong?"

Blaze kept watching the desert. "Weird stuff going on around here, kids telling stories about haunted places and ghosts and—"

"You're letting little kids scare you now? Maybe you're right, after all. Maybe you should stick to animals."

Blaze grunted. "You said it. I woke up and heard someone singing, like a little kid. Then that stopped and I heard a door open and close and someone went walking out into the desert."

"The ghost in white?"

"No, all I saw was a shadow."

"So there are two ghosts walking out in the desert?"

"Don't know about no ghosts, but there's a couple of somethings out there."

"It might be Tanya running away again, but if she was the one singing, then Sheila sure would've heard it. You want me to call Sheila on her cell and see if her houseguest has escaped?"

"Nope." Blaze stepped to the edge of the deck and looked down, then around, then back at Preston. "You need to stay in Sheila's good graces, and waking her up in the middle of the night won't help you none. Besides, I had a little talk with Tanya last night."

Preston stepped back inside. "I don't suppose you've noticed it's cold. Come back in. Whoever's walking in the desert is probably someone we don't know, and it's none of our business who wants to take a walk."

Blaze came back in and slid the door shut silently. "Tanya's another scared kid. I think you're right—something's wrong in this place, and I think Canaan thinks the answer can be found in the medical records."

"He told you that?"

"He and Sheila were in the clinic until late last night."

Suddenly, Preston didn't feel so great. "Tell me about it."

"So while you were up here working on the finances—"

"Which are coming along nicely—"

"And they were in the clinic with piles of folders stacked around them—"

"And that's all?"

"That's all. Anyway, while everybody else kept busy, I finished up my lab work and went to see if I could get something to eat in the cafeteria, which doesn't keep very long hours."

"It's a Navajo boarding school," Preston said. "You can't expect this place to be a modern metropolis like Hideaway."

"*Anyway,*" Blaze said, shooting him an irritable look, "I saw Tanya talking with this guy who was cleaning up—she told me he was the son of the people killed in the fire and she got me something to eat. We sat and talked until that old lady with the long hair ran us out."

"That's Betsy Two Horses. She was here when Sheila was a little girl."

"Well, I don't think Tanya's going to bolt again. I think I convinced her she might've died if Canaan and Sheila hadn't found her when they did."

"In case you hadn't noticed, I've been buried up to my eyeballs in finances and pie charts ever since we got here."

"And you thought you'd be scrubbing toilets."

"My point is, I don't know what happened to Tanya."

Blaze gave him a quick rundown of the child's escape, her rescue, her hospital stay.

"Okay," Preston said, "did Tanya happen to mention what they tested her for?"

"You're thinking hemorrhagic fever of some kind," Blaze said, nodding. "No tests for that in a small hospital. The equipment needed to test for viral infections is too expensive."

"Plague?"

"That's fairly characteristic under a microscope, because it isn't a virus," Blaze said. "Anthrax would show up, as well, but hantavirus, being a virus, wouldn't show up under a regular microscope. Find anything strange while you were making that pie chart on your computer?"

"I don't know, maybe wacky expense sheets, money being used for supplies that weren't actually delivered, unknown sources of income."

"What kinds of supplies?"

"Dog food," Preston said. "But there aren't any dogs around here."

"Hmm. Weird, huh? I found some notes in a file for one of the kids I'm supposed to test today," Blaze said. "Probably written by the woman who was killed in the fire. Wendy Hunt."

"What did it say?"

Blaze hesitated. "You know, this is confidential information."

"Of course, but the financial state of the school is also confidential information. Canaan obviously trusts us both to keep our mouths shut."

"Could be, but it seems to me he's just desperate."

"It's all school business, and in this case I think we need to share as much information as we can."

"Okay. Looks like Wendy was planning to send blood samples from four different kids to the CDC."

Preston whistled softly. "The Centers for Disease Control? Big guns."

"Yep, that's what her note said. So I figured the CDC would've had time to check out that blood and send the reports back."

"Did you find anything?"

"Nope." Blaze shook his head in puzzlement. "I was going to tell Canaan about it, but I got tired of waiting for him and Sheila last night. I'll tell him this morning, and you know that lab? I know how to use it. I can't wait to run a few more tests here at the school."

"You drew blood on those particular kids?"

"No, but they're scheduled to come in for physicals today. I found their files and sent a special request to the teachers."

"But you don't know what to test for. If she sent samples to the CDC, then she obviously thought there was something in the blood that she wouldn't be able to pick up with the equipment here."

"I said she was planning to send those samples. If they got sent, then nothing must've been found out of order. But they might not have gotten sent before she died." Blaze stared out at the night desert for a moment. "You're right, I probably won't find anything, but judging by some of the other notes I saw from Wendy, she was afraid Bob Jaffrey's illness might be something dangerous to the school. I'll check those kids tomorrow and see."

When I reach the hogan, I step in with the knowledge that I am stepping into an altered world. The entrance of a Navajo hogan traditionally faces east, to catch the rising sun. This one faces west, to catch the sun's death—my entrance into the haunted hogan of Piñon Valley.

Though the hogan is close to the school, few know of its exact location, protected from sight as it is by rolling hills and piñon and cedar trees.

It is time to prepare.

I build a fire with the cedar chips already set in the fireplace, then gather my pouches of colored sand to repair the damage that has been done to the sand painting since I left it last— stray wisps of wind drifting down through the central smoke hole to smudge lines and colors.

Before I begin repairs, a sound reaches me, like the scuff of shoes on the ground. I freeze, holding my breath, cursing the crackle of fire as it catches and casts its light through the hogan.

When I hear nothing else, I go to the door and look outside. Nothing. I've let the dream of that taunting little boy follow me here. It was only a dream. It was only my imagination.

Back inside, I study the sand art in the far corner of the hogan.

I am no artist, which is why the sand painting here in my hogan remains as it is. Traditionally, my people make their sand paintings during the day, use up its medicine and scatter the sand before sundown. To do otherwise is dangerous, risking the wrath of many gods. But I court that danger. The spirits to whom I send my chants prefer to be entreated in the darkness, just as I prefer to work under the cover of darkness.

The retouch of the sand painting completed, I step to the doorway and look up into the sky. The stars have begun to fade in fear of the approaching sun. I must hurry.

I send a curse into the whipping wind, and find myself wondering if the words I speak will work if my heart is not in it. Because the power of this curse on Sheila Metcalf is not a product of my heart.

## Chapter Twenty-Nine

Preston sat nursing his third cup of coffee in the cafeteria barely three hours after the early-morning awakening. Following the talk with Blaze, the kid had been able to fall back asleep almost before his head touched the lumpy pillow on his twin bed.

Unsettled by their conversation, Preston had kept watch until the sun rose with a sudden burst of gold across the eastern horizon. The sunrise here wasn't like in Hideaway. This country may be beautiful in a stark, dramatic way, but he preferred Missouri, with the gentler hills, tree-lined valleys, lakes, streams and humidity.

"I thought I might find you here," came a very welcome voice from behind.

He looked up to see Sheila sliding into the seat beside him as she placed an overloaded food tray onto the table. If he wasn't mistaken, there was a huge, sugar-crusted doughnut on one plate, topped by two slices of bacon.

"Where's the hole?" he asked.

"It's Navajo fry bread rolled in sugar and cinnamon."

"It's dough fried in hot oil, right? So essentially, it's a doughnut. If you eat all that you'll get fat."

"I guess I'll get fat, then." She bowed her head.

Watching her, it occurred to him that he had always held a deep respect for the way she practiced her faith—never shoving her convictions down his throat, but also not curtailing her daily acts of devotion for his benefit or anyone else's.

It surprised him to realize that it just might be the very strength of that faith that drew him to her. Yes, she was beautiful to him, fun and thoughtful, and they were compatible. He adored her. But the quiet faith that lived in her and directed her life was irresistibly alluring to him.

He wasn't about to tell anyone that. It would give Blaze an opening, and Preston didn't need a sales pitch for Jesus. He'd heard the pitch so many times, he had learned to recognize the certain look, words and change in attitude that always signaled the canned "Jesus is your Savior" speech, instilled into groups of people before they were released into the unsuspecting populace. Jesus wasn't a vacuum cleaner for sale. The ad campaign just didn't work for Preston. He was thankful that Sheila had never tried the canned speech with him.

Sometimes he wondered if it wasn't church attendees, themselves, who turned him off so much—with their infighting, self-righteousness and the way they made any man who questioned the Christian status quo feel like a second-class citizen.

Once, when Preston was a teenager at church services with his family in a small country church, a man had sought them out during the postsermon invitation to approach the altar. The man had had the gall to inform his parents that Mom's schizophrenia was evidence of continued sin in their lives, as well as a lack of faith.

Preston had called the man a couple of derogatory names and then punched him in the mouth, right in front of the whole congregation. Though the hit had stopped the singing, the organ music had continued while Preston stormed out of the chapel, his sister, Willow, following close behind.

By mutual agreement, that was the last time Preston's family had attended services in that church.

Sheila picked up her fork, gave him a sly grin, then slid the plate of fry bread and bacon in front of him.

As Preston accepted the extra fork she handed him, and was prepared to dig in to this interesting new taste experience, a young man in coveralls approached their table.

"Are you the new nurse who had the flat tire last Friday?" he asked Sheila. When she nodded, he said, "I'm Lew Bowie. You're going to need a new tire." He glanced around, then stepped closer. "There's a piece of steel lodged in the rim. Did you make somebody mad?"

For several seconds, there was silence. Preston saw Sheila's look of surprise.

"Are you saying you think it was a bullet?" Preston asked.

The guy nodded, looking around the near-empty cafeteria nervously. "The chunk of metal was smashed against the rim, but it sure did look like a bullet hole through the tire."

"Okay," Sheila said, sounding as if the wind had been kicked out of her. "Thank you for telling me."

"Lots of deaths here lately. You might want to be careful. Or maybe leave."

"Have you told Canaan?" she asked.

The guy nodded. "He called the tribal police, but they won't have anything to go on. Can't even tell it's a bullet for sure."

She thanked the young man again, told him she would be fine, and kindly dismissed him, while Preston struggled with all his might not to grab her and throw her and Blaze into his own vehicle and drive them back home. To Hideaway. Where there hadn't been a murder in several months.

"You mind telling me what that was about?" he asked when the man left.

Her face had turned considerably paler. "The dog I saw in the desert just before my blowout? She was running, and then suddenly she seemed to disappear in a puff of smoke. What I thought was smoke was probably dust flying up from the ground when a bullet struck. At least now I know I'm not losing my mind."

"Oh, sure, you just almost lost your life instead. Sheila, this is not going to work." He gritted his teeth to keep from slipping into I-told-you-so mode.

"I thought Friday night that there could have been two dogs," she said. "Maybe one I didn't see, which would have been Moonlight. You know how dogs always form a pack when they're left to run free. I was so distracted by the dog in the desert that I just didn't see the one on the road."

"Or there wasn't one on the road, and you've been convinced that you hit a dog, when in actuality you never even got near that dog. Maybe she was dragged to the road, or left for dead and she crawled to the road before she died, *after* your tire was shot."

"The question is, why would anyone want to shoot a dog?"

"Or you?" he asked, irritated that she still failed to focus on the threat to herself.

"Maybe the dog was killing sheep," she said, reasoning out loud. "There are flocks of sheep in this area."

"Why are you more concerned about dogs than you are about yourself? Why would anyone try to shoot you?"

"Ricochet."

"I'm not buying it. No one in his right mind would be shooting at dogs—I don't care if twenty sheep were killed—when there's a car driving by on the road. This is not a good place for you, Sheila."

She didn't look at him. "I need to be here," she said quietly. "If you came out here to drag me back home to Hideaway—"

"That isn't why I'm—"

"—then you can turn around and—"

"Blaze and I can stay and help Canaan. You're the target. You aren't safe here. Drive my Jeep back home."

She looked at him then, and what he saw in her eyes nearly stopped his heart. There was such tenderness in her expression, mingled with sadness.

"I love you, Preston."

He stopped breathing.

"You're my hero," she said.

He forced himself to breathe again, but with difficulty.

"You're the kind of man who will rush into a burning building if people are in danger." Her gaze traveled over his face, and paused at the scar on his chin from a burn. "I should've known that if you thought I was in danger, you couldn't just sit home and worry about me. You're a man of action."

"I'm sorry. I can change if I have to, but right now—"

"I'm not asking you to."

"And yet if I don't change in one basic way, this thing we have together—"

"It's called a relationship. And your total honesty about your feelings on the subject of Christianity is one of the reasons I love you."

Preston stared down at his beautiful doughnut and wondered why he wasn't more ecstatic when the woman of his dreams was telling him she loved him. Perhaps the sadness in her voice and the knowledge that someone had shot at her recently overwhelmed the romance.

"I'm not leaving this school because of a piece of metal in my tire," she said. "Get used to it. I really don't think anyone was shooting at me. That young man looked to be barely out of his teens, which means he's probably as excitable as everyone else has been around here lately."

"The tribal police will check it out, I'm sure," Preston said.

Sheila grinned up at him, though the grin was notably wooden. "So who do you think will handle the case, Jim Chee or Lieutenant Joe Leaphorn?" She was joking, referring to characters created by Preston's favorite author.

"I'm thinking the lieutenant will take it on as a private case."

She nodded and picked up her fork, her smile losing its power completely. "If the brilliant lieutenant does discover anything, I want to find out why I was shot at, and I want to know if it has anything to do with my mother's death, or with the recent suspicious deaths here at the school and the deaths of other school graduates that Canaan believes are suspicious, as well."

"You don't want much, do you?"

"Only the truth."

"Then I'll have to stay to make sure you remain safe."

She picked up his hand and kissed his knuckles.

He loved this woman. He would die for her. He only hoped that wasn't going to be necessary.

Canaan sat staring at the note Blaze had just plopped onto his desk, saw the letters *CDC* and leaned back in his chair as he listened to the young man's explanation about what he'd done the day before.

First Lew Bowie had come in with the information that Sheila's blowout could have been due to a bullet in her tire, and now this. Things seemed to be coming to a head more quickly than he'd anticipated.

"I'm sorry I didn't tell you about it yesterday," Blaze said in conclusion. "But I never could catch you alone and I didn't think you wanted anyone else to know about it until you'd had a chance to get to the bottom of things."

"So you got the legwork out of the way." Once again, Canaan marveled at this answer to prayer.

"I couldn't find any evidence that the CDC ever got the vials. In fact, I can't even find evidence that they were actually sent. I was going to retest the kids today."

"You know it probably won't do any good."

"Something that I think did do some good, though, was going through the computer files on the kids," Blaze said.

Canaan studied this young college student who had dropped in unannounced yesterday. "If you ever decide to become a medical doctor instead of a veterinarian, look me up. Someday I want a practice with a partner who does all my work for me."

"I'll never change my shingle. Anyway, you saw where Wendy noted that all four kids had been in the clinic with viral symptoms a week or so before Bob Jaffrey got sick?"

"Yes, and I remember seeing them, but there was a virus

going around at the time. We took precautions, and none of the children got worse."

"Only Bob Jaffrey," Blaze said. "And when I checked the files on these kids, none of them missed school. You'd think, if Mr. Jaffrey died from the virus, the kids would have at least been sick enough to miss school."

"There could be any number of explanations for that," Canaan said. "Bob could have had a compromised immune system for some reason."

"You mean from the chemo he had last year for colon cancer?"

"That wasn't in his file," Canaan said.

"No, but I was talking to Jane Witherbe, who was friends with his wife. She told me about it when she came in yesterday for something for her headache."

"At any rate, even though I was concerned, the family would not allow an autopsy."

"Well, what would it hurt to test the blood of those kids? They had it at the same time, could have easily been the same strain, so the antibodies would still be present."

"Wait until after I've called the CDC to find out if there's any new information before you draw blood on those kids again."

"Gotcha. Glad you're on it, Doctor. I knew I wouldn't get past the CDC's answering machine."

"In the meantime, keep testing, and keep very thorough documentation on everything, whether it looks notable or not. And, Blaze, stay close to Sheila today."

"Will do, chief."

## ❧ Chapter Thirty ❧

Tuesday afternoon Sheila burst into her apartment with an armload of supplies and a sandwich she had snitched from the cafeteria. What a miserable day this was turning out to be. She couldn't believe she'd finally escaped her guards. When Blaze wasn't nearby, Preston found a reason to work on the records in the clinic, or Canaan decided to join her and help with the physicals. She could barely go to the bathroom in peace.

She shoved the door shut with her foot, turned toward the coffee table and dropped the supplies as she gasped and stumbled back against the wall.

A wolf head with its teeth bared was in the middle of the table, carved lips pulled back to expose vicious, oversize fangs. The eyes were nearly closed in brooding hatred, hackles raised on the back of the head.

For a moment, Sheila could only stare at the monster, as if her nightmare had suddenly materialized right in front of her.

She took a slow, deep breath, relaxing the suddenly tensed muscles in her neck and shoulders.

She picked up the items she had dropped and forced herself forward. This wolf head had the lovely sheen of polished wood, and it was no imaginary nightmare image. Someone had to have brought it here since she left this morning.

She glanced around the room to see if anything else had been disturbed. All looked the same. Someone had apparently just brought this nice little wood carving into the apartment to cheer her up. Anyone could have done it, because half the time she didn't bother to lock her door.

As she moved around the apartment, putting things away, she felt the presence of that head; tiny hairs prickled at the back of her neck. It seemed to have a spirit of its own, and yet Sheila knew she was personifying it with her own fear.

She changed into a pair of jeans and went back into the living room, half expecting to find that the carving had moved. But it was in the same place, lips drawn back in a permanent snarl, wicked fangs protruding. Sheila stared at the realistic eyes, mesmerized by them. She picked up the sculpture gingerly, and glanced at the bottom. *CY. Canaan York.*

It was a good thing Tanya was still in class, or she could have been the first one to see this.

There was no way Canaan would have placed this here, but maybe he could find out who had.

Canaan received the return call from CDC, then hung up with dismay. He looked up at Blaze, who had popped his head through the door periodically throughout the day, especially when the telephone rang.

"Nothing," Canaan said. "Whatever Wendy intended to do, it didn't get done."

Blaze shook his head. "Well, I don't know much about all this, but I don't like coincidences, especially since she and her husband died in a fire the same date she wrote this note."

Canaan agreed.

"Did the police pick up that wheel from Sheila's Jeep?"

"Yes, but I haven't heard anything yet. Where's Sheila?"

"She went to her apartment. She threatened me with my life if I tried to go with her. Said there's certain things a woman's got to have, and one of those is privacy from time to time."

"How are the checkups going? Have you found any sick kids?"

"Tanya still doesn't feel a hundred percent, but a couple of the teachers and a dorm parent came in asking for something to settle their stomachs. Temps were up a little, so they could have a virus that's going around, or they might've eaten something that didn't agree with them."

"Let me know if they come back. We'll need to do blood cultures. Can't be too careful after what happened to Tanya Sunday."

"Will do, chief."

The door flew open and Sheila came marching in, breathless, eyes wide, holding a pillowcase in front of her, with something obviously in it.

"Do you have a practical joker at this school?" she asked Canaan.

"We've had a few from time to—"

"Here's a joke that isn't funny." She withdrew the pillowcase to expose a very familiar carving of a wolf head, fangs bared, eyes malevolent.

"I didn't carve that as a practical joke," Canaan said, "but what are you doing with it?"

She set the carving on his desk. "It would be nice to think that since I admired your other carvings so much, you thought I'd like to see this one, too, and so you set it on my coffee table. But I don't think—"

"Sheila, where did you get this?"

"The little fellow was waiting for me when I got home today."

"This was in your apartment?"

"My door was unlocked. I leave it that way half the time."

"Smart, Sheila," Blaze said with some sarcasm. "So what's the big deal about a wolf?" He picked up the carving and studied it. "Nice work."

"Thanks," Canaan said. "I keep it at home because the wolf scares the kids."

Sheila sank down into the chair in front of Canaan's desk. "Which means someone else was in my apartment today."

"That's what you get for leaving your doors unlocked," Blaze said. "Here we've been playing bodyguard all day, and you pull something like this."

"Do you think one of the kids left it as a joke?" she asked.

"Could be," Canaan said. "Or maybe someone was trying to make a statement about Tanya staying with you."

"Why would anybody care about that?" Blaze asked.

"Prejudice," Sheila said. "I'm white."

Blaze grinned. "Don't that beat all. For once, I'm not the only one in the minority."

The tension eased in Sheila's expression for a few seconds as she looked at her friend. "Enjoy it while it lasts."

"I've been thinking about that," Canaan said. "I don't think

Sheila's color has that much to do with it. My grandfather's white, and—"

"Your grandfather has earned the right to be respected," Sheila said. "I'm a newcomer to most of the people here. And there are still those at this school who distrust most whites."

"That's not a good reason to try to terrorize you," Canaan said.

"So what's the big deal with the wolf?" Blaze asked.

"That's what we're trying to find out," Sheila said. "Canaan, this piece is so different from the other two carvings in my apartment. What inspired you to do it?"

"My inspiration for this originally came from one of the kids' silly coyote skinwalker stories, but instead of the human coyote, I thought about the Navajo werewolf."

"Werewolf!" Blaze exclaimed.

"You caught the mood," Sheila said.

"It was almost…like something I had to exorcise from my own mind."

"Here we go with the exorcisms again," she said.

"Only a figure of speech," Canaan told her. "And since when did you have any idea about the mood of a werewolf?"

"Since I began having more memories of my childhood, and some nightmares, and spending Sunday night with a young girl very frightened of this beast," she said. "Did your exorcism work for you?"

Canaan shook his head.

"I think I understand what you intended, though," Sheila said. "It's almost as if you can get rid of your fear if you expose it to the light of day."

"So it's therapy," Blaze said. "Tanya's afraid of the Navajo werewolf, right?"

Sheila and Canaan both looked at him.

He spread his hands. "It really could be just a kid's prank. They know she's staying with Sheila and that she's afraid of the wolf."

"But Tanya isn't the only one who's afraid," Canaan told him, looking at Sheila. "And it isn't just Tanya and Sheila. Now I'm trying to figure out why Sheila and Tanya both have terrors about the wolf. I can't understand why the fear would cross cultural lines, why the wolf would frighten a white woman."

"Real monsters frighten everyone," Blaze said. "There are people dying here, and Sheila's getting shot at."

"Thanks for reminding me, Blaze," she muttered.

"You want to know what I think?" he asked. "I may not know much, but if I was getting shot at and there was a death scare, I'd be locking my doors all the time. Who got into Canaan's apartment to get the carving?"

Canaan grimaced. "That could have been anyone, as well. I'm afraid I'm as bad about locking my doors as Sheila is."

Blaze clucked his tongue in reproach. "What's it gonna take for you guys to learn?"

Tanya Swift leaned back in her chair and stifled a yawn, trying hard to concentrate on what the teacher was reading. In spite of her sleepiness, she enjoyed being back in class. It felt normal, and she wanted everything to be normal again.

Jamey Hunt sat beside her, propping his feet against the bar on her chair. As usual, he was slumped far down in his seat behind Lan Marcell, the tallest kid in this class. She knew Jamey didn't want the teacher to call on him to read, because he hadn't been feeling well and all he wanted to do was sleep.

Tanya felt bad for Jamey. He hated reading, especially in front of others. Nobody in this class could read much better than he could, but his shyness made it much harder for him, especially since his parents had died.

He'd told Tanya that she was the only one who ever helped him with his homework anymore. His older brother was busy all the time, and April just teased him for needing help.

Because Jamey was so gentle, he let April boss him around all she wanted, and their parents weren't there to stop it. Tanya knew he had to do the laundry and keep the house clean because Kai was supervising them, and Kai wouldn't stand for a dirty house. Jamey'd have to do the cooking and dishes, too, if they didn't eat in the cafeteria.

"Jamey Hunt," the teacher said, "please read the next page for us."

Tanya glanced at him. He looked like a scared cat caught in the beam of a flashlight.

April, sitting behind him, slapped him hard on the shoulder. "Stupid!" she hissed. "Pay attention."

"Jamey?" the teacher called.

He looked up at her, his face flushing deep red.

"Page forty-two," she said.

Tanya saw that he hadn't even opened his book.

He looked at her and grimaced.

She passed her book to him, but he shook his head and slumped down farther in his chair.

Tanya knew the teacher would let him get by with it, because he was an orphan now. But how long could this go on? He could read. Why wouldn't he try? Before the teacher could say anything more, the bell rang. Jamey sat where he was while the others jumped up and rushed out.

April slapped him hard on the head when she went by. "Stupid! Why did you have to be born?"

Tanya saw the tears in his eyes, and she reached over and rubbed his arm. It felt hot. "It's okay, Jamey."

He shook his head and looked up at the teacher, who was gathering papers from her desk.

"I know it isn't now, but it will be," Tanya said.

"How do you know?"

"Because Sheila Metcalf's mother died when she lived here, and Sheila's doing okay."

"Did she have a sister like April?"

Tanya sighed. He had her there. "Maybe April will get nicer."

"She's never been nice before. Why would she change?"

"I don't know. People change, I guess. Sometimes."

Jamey looked at her. "What's it like living with Nurse Metcalf?"

"It's okay. I like her."

"You didn't at first."

"The difference between April and me is that I can admit when I'm wrong."

Jamey gave a slight grin, but it didn't last long.

"Is everything else okay?" Tanya asked.

He shrugged, then got up. "It has to be. I can't be sick today. Or even this week."

"You can be sick if you're sick. You don't have a choice. Why don't you go to Blaze and have him check you out? You don't want to have to be doing push-ups and sit-ups when you're trying not to puke."

"I'll just have to tough it out."

"Okay, but first I have something for you."

Jamey turned back. He didn't seem to know what to think about that. "The others are leaving. I'd better get—"

"Don't worry, this isn't going to take a lot of time."

She reached up and touched the cross that rested against her chest, then fumbled with the clasp.

"What are you doing? Giving me a girl's necklace?"

She held it out for him to see. "You know who gave this to me?"

He shook his head. "I think I should be going."

Tanya ignored him. "Sheila Metcalf. And you know who gave it to her?"

He frowned at her. She knew he never liked questions he didn't know the answer to. "Betsy Two Horses, many years ago when Sheila was a little girl, younger than us."

"Why?" he asked.

"Well, at first I thought it was because turquoise was supposed to scare off the evil spirits, but Sheila says it was to remind her that Jesus loved her, and she gave it to me to remind me of the same thing."

"But you don't believe in Jesus."

"She says that doesn't matter. But I'm giving it to you, anyway. I mean, you're a Christian and all, so it should work on you better."

Jamey reached up and touched the cross. Golden strands bound the turquoise and connected with the gold chain. "It's pretty."

Tanya laid the necklace on the desk and pushed it toward him. "You need it more than I do."

"What'll I do with a girl's necklace?"

"You stick it in your pocket, and when you reach in and feel the cross, you'll remember you're not alone."

Jamey stared at the necklace. "Doc's waiting."

"Doc won't be mad at you. You can get away with anything right now. Just take the necklace."

"If anybody sees it, I'll be laughed at."

Tanya wanted to smack him. How hard could it be just to accept the stupid gift? "It's not for anyone else to see, it's just for you. Take the necklace!"

He stared at her for a minute.

"Just keep it for me, okay? Every time you look at it, remember what it means. And if you decide you need someone to talk to, remember me." She inched it toward him. "Go ahead, take it."

Jamey touched the chain, then picked it up and held it in his hand. "April can't see this."

"Keep it hidden. I can't believe I ever thought she was my friend. She's mean."

"I hear her crying in her bed every night, when she's at home."

"When isn't she at home?"

"She sneaks out a lot. When I caught her one night, she said she was looking for Mom and Dad's spirits. I told her they're in heaven, but she's got this weird idea that they wouldn't leave us here alone, and even if their spirits are evil now, it's better than not having them at all."

"But it's so stupid to go out like that."

"I know." Jamey slid the necklace into the front pocket of his jeans. "Thanks, Tanya. If anybody sees it, I'll say my girlfriend gave it to me to keep it safe."

Tanya sighed. "Whatever." Giving gifts wasn't as much fun as she'd thought it would be. "Just remember what it means."

## ❧ Chapter Thirty-One ❧

Another one comes tonight. Still so many to initiate, and so little time left. I don't know how much longer I'll be able to continue this. Suspicions have been raised, and authorities are searching for the shooter. So far I have them controlled, but I can't know how much longer that will work.

The blood. It's always in the blood, the life of the person. I am so filled with tension that my skin tingles with it. But with this night could come great power, if only the child will respond well.

The wood chips smoke. Thick clouds of it drift past me before finding the smoke hole in the center of the roof. I inhale, spreading out my arms to catch the blessing of the smoke on my skin. I breathe deeply, the tension increasing with every breath. I must be gentle with this one. Less is remembered when the pain is not so bad.

A whisper of sound reaches me from outside. I stiffen. That will be Jamey. It is time. At the opening, I find the boy standing in the moonlight. His immature body, bare above the waist, glows with the film of perspiration of his run from the school.

Jamey shows no surprise at my appearance. I have already planted in his mind the route here, the things to expect.

"Are we ready?" The boy's voice shakes.

"Don't be afraid." I hold out a hand. Jamey takes it, and I relax. The boy trusts me or he wouldn't have come out into the desert alone to find me. It's all going to be okay.

"What do I have to do?" he asks.

"You need only do what I tell you and nothing more. You must understand the importance of these meetings. They will bring great power and riches."

"To you or me?" Jamey has the audacity to ask.

Losing patience quickly, I take the boy's arm and lead him inside, where a breeze thickens the smoke from the cedar wood. The fire's glow lights the room. At the sight of my wolf-sculpted face, the boy catches his breath, his grip growing tighter.

"What are you? A wolf?"

"This is my identity tonight. Come to the altar."

He does not move. "What kind of altar is it?"

"Mine."

"What do you mean?"

I am not accustomed to such noncompliance. What is wrong with this child? "This is where we pay homage to the spirit that resides in me." I reach for a section of peyote button beside the altar and hold it out for him. "Take this in your mouth."

Jamey's head comes up, his dark eyes more alert than they have been in days. "What is it?"

"It's something that will help you in the ritual. Don't worry, it's safe. I take it myself."

"We have to do this?"

Foolish child! "It's not for you to question the ancient spirits that draw you!"

"Ancient spirits? But—"

"Only an expression, Jamey. This is a natural, time-tested way to increase your endurance. You want that, don't you? As a member of the track team you want to make Twin Mesas famous so Doc will be proud of you."

"Yeah."

"Then we will continue." What's wrong with the boy tonight? Why is he so inquisitive and resistant?

"Open your mouth."

"But Doc says—"

"I know more than Doc knows. I am the one you must listen to and trust. Tomorrow you will be glad you did this."

The boy obeys at last. I place the piece of peyote on his tongue. "Chew and swallow. It is very bitter."

I watch Jamey's face screw up.

Patience. Mustn't move too quickly. The drug will work, given time. I prepare my utensils. I will make this as painless as possible.

Within moments, Jamey's muscles relax. He sways ever so slightly.

"The spirit is coming now." My voice takes on the low, rhythmic tone of a chant. "The spirit will take us both in its grasp and suck us up, drink us dry, then fill us with power. Let your mind flow with the spirit that guides you."

I reach for another piece of a peyote button. "Open your mouth."

With a slightly dazed, reluctant glance at me, Jamey obeys. It's almost time. Almost. But I must not take chances with this one.

Soon his barricade of mental defenses will weaken.

Jamey takes a deep breath and sways backward. I smile as I reach past him for my utensil, but then he tenses. His half-closed eyes open wide and his head comes up.

"What...are you doing? What's happening?" For a moment his gaze sharpens.

"The spirit is ready," I say as I ease the boy forward. "Study the flames and discover what the spirit of the wolf is telling you."

"Wolf? But the wolf is evil."

"The wolf is the most powerful spirit in our world. He is a spirit of darkness, but will come to you through the light of the fire. He will be your power. No need to fear him, if you obey." As my voice drones on, I watch the drug working the boy's mind.

"You must never reject the spirit, because if you do, it will follow you, haunt you and take every chance to harm you and those you love. Accept the spirit, Jamey. It will fill your life. It will make you strong."

Jamey shakes his head.

This is not working as it has before.

Jamey backs away from me. "I want to go home."

"No!" Harsh from smoke, my voice grates even more deeply than the power of the spirit that controls me. "You have begun. You can never turn back."

"I'll never listen to this spirit. Just let me—"

"No! Look into the fire. Give me your hands." I grab his clenched fist and his hand opens. In his palm is something golden and blue. Something familiar.

It's as if I've been dashed in a snow stream. I am staring at a turquoise-and-gold cross. Sheila Metcalf's necklace.

But this can't be. Does she know about me? What other

reason could she have for giving this necklace to Jamey on the night he is due to see me?

I stumble backward. Jamey is protected by the enemy! I must trust that he has enough of the drug in his system to forget everything that has happened. He will wake up in the morning, at worst thinking he's had a bad dream.

"Who is the spirit that controls you?" I demand.

Jamey says, "Jesus."

"Get out. Take your cross with you. You are an enemy of the spirit of the wolf!"

Sheila lay on a hard table, with a bright light shining on her from somewhere above. How had she gotten here? What was happening?

She heard chanting, and she tried to get up, but something held her down. Smoke filled the room and drifted upward and out through the smoke hole in the center of this hogan. She knew enough to realize that someone hadn't built the fire right, or it wouldn't be so smoky. Dumb people.

The room blurred around her, and she closed her eyes and allowed her mind to drift. She could feel herself racing through the piñons like a jackrabbit or a coyote.

The chanting grew louder. She kept her eyes closed. A woman's soft voice reached her, and she opened her eyes again. Across the fire, through the smoke, there was a shadowy image. A woman stood beside a doorway, her features blurred, but Sheila could see long, light hair falling over a shoulder clothed in white.

A sibilant chant, barely discernible from the wind, reached her. It sounded oddly familiar, yet like none of the Navajo words she knew. It sounded like someone singing backward, familiar Navajo words inverted in a discordant invocation that grew louder as her breathing quickened and her heartbeat pounded through her body.

A deep, guttural voice—she could not tell whether male or female—throbbed through the room, with the steady pulse of some hovering force that filled the hogan and spilled out into darkness beyond.

The voice wavered and fell silent, to be replaced by a deep growl.

Fear paralyzed her. The smoke choked her. She gagged. Rough hands grabbed her as she retched.

She turned toward the one who touched her, terror paralyzing her lungs. The face of the wolf leered at her, long fangs bared, eyes shooting flames of hatred at her, singeing her.

She cried out, even though she knew no one would hear.

The wolf whimpered, then spoke softly, gently, entreating.

Sheila opened her eyes and saw a shaded room, lit by a lamp in another part of the apartment. Perspiration filmed her skin, soaking her hair and nightgown. Another dream.

She saw Tanya leaning over her, eyelids still swollen with sleep, long black hair tangled.

"Bad dream?" Tanya's voice trembled as the sour breath of a long sleep wafted through the air.

The brisk temperature chilled Sheila's perspiring skin, waking her as if she had been doused in a winter lake. Relief flooded her as the dream vanished. She stared around her at the faint glow of the living room lamp, forcing herself to take slow, deep breaths. *Be calm. Recover. It's early Friday morning, and you're safe in your apartment.*

"I'm sorry, Tanya." She sat up, wiping at her forehead. "I hope I didn't scare you too badly. Was I making a lot of noise?"

Tanya nodded.

"Maybe we need to get you some earplugs. Do I snore, too?"

At last, Tanya's face relaxed slightly. She shook her head. "Are you okay?"

"I'm fine." Most times, the relief was so palpable when she awakened to find that it was only a dream that she felt instantly better. This time, there was a lingering apprehension that wouldn't totally leave her.

She took a deep breath and fought a spasm of chills. "It's gone now. I'm sorry if I frightened you." She noticed that Tanya's eyelashes sparkled with tears.

The girl nodded, then hugged Sheila, burying her head against Sheila's sweat-dampened shoulder.

"You know how, when you have a bad dream, you try to scream and you can't?" Sheila asked. "I make some funny noises sometimes. My husband used to laugh about it." She smoothed Tanya's tousled hair.

Tanya sat back, obviously curious, but with a residue of fear still lurking in her eyes. "Are you divorced?"

"No, my husband died two years ago."

Tanya nodded. "People are always dying."

"I know it feels that way sometimes, doesn't it?"

Tanya nodded. "What do you dream?"

Sheila hesitated. Ordinarily, she wouldn't think of burdening Tanya with the truth, but since Tanya was so terrified of this evil being, and since Sheila recalled her own loneliness as a child, she decided to take a chance.

"I dream about the wolf," she told Tanya.

A quick intake of breath.

"I'm convinced now that my dreams are connected to my experiences here long ago," Sheila said.

"The wolf was here then, all those years ago," Tanya said.

Sheila nodded. "I learned to block the dreams from my mind almost as soon as I awoke from them."

She found herself wondering where she had acquired this ability to forget at will the things that most upset her. How long had she been practicing this? Decades?

"Do you remember your dreams, Tanya?"

Moving cautiously, as if to avoid stubbing her toe in the meager light, Tanya circled the bed and climbed in on the other side. She crossed her legs and leaned back against the headboard.

Sheila's interest quickened. Tanya was stalling. And she was obviously too upset to go back to the sofa to sleep alone.

"Do you have nightmares?" Sheila asked softly.

Tanya looked down at her hands. "Sometimes." She reached down and drew the covers up to her chest, then pulled them around her shoulders.

"Does the wolf follow you into your sleep at night?" Sheila asked.

Tanya nodded and pressed her lips together.

"I don't remember having the dreams when I was a child." Sheila settled back beside Tanya in the bed. "I don't remember ever having them when we lived here, but there are many things I can't remember about the last year or so that I was here."

Tanya darted a brief glance at her, betraying both hope and apprehension.

Following Tanya's example, Sheila covered up with the blanket. The air was chilly, and it felt safer beneath the blanket.

"What was it like when you were here?" Tanya asked.

"It hasn't changed a lot. When did you first know the wolf was here?"

Tanya hesitated, cleared her throat. "About a year ago." She shifted beneath the blankets. "Let's not talk about it. Not now. It's too dark, and—" she darted a glance out the window into the night "—talking about him could call his attention to us."

A tiny pinprick of foreboding stabbed at Sheila once more. With her heartbeat, the feeling pulsed and grew. Blood pounded louder and louder in her ears. Memory pushed at the edge of her defenses.

Tanya's wide eyes searched the room, the doorway, the shadowed window.

Sheila's heartbeats increased, then the sounds separated, as if doing double time. For a moment, she thought she was actually identifying so closely with Tanya that she could hear both their hearts.

Then the sounds changed. Running feet. Someone was running past outside.

Tanya grabbed her arm. "He heard us! He's coming here! He's going to—"

Sheila grabbed the girl's hands. "Hush. The wolf is not human. He doesn't run like a person." She thought she could hear the labored breathing of someone who had run a long way.

The bed shook with Tanya's struggle to hold back deep sobs of fear.

Sheila put her arms around the girl and pulled her close. "It's okay. We're here together. He won't hurt us if we're together."

They listened as the footsteps diminished.

"Hear that? It was just someone running by. Whoever it was didn't even stop." Her voice was unsteady.

"He'll be back," Tanya said. "He wants to scare us. He wants to make us suffer, to think about what he's going to do to us."

"I've thought all I want to think about that." Sheila slung back the blankets.

"What are you doing?" Tanya cried, still clinging to Sheila's arm. "Where are you going?"

Gently, Sheila disengaged herself. "Shh. I'm going to take a peek outside, just to reassure myself."

She went to the front door and peered out the window. In the darkness, the stars shone down like white glitter. The road in front of the apartment stretched from the school out into the desert, empty.

With a catch in her breathing, she unlatched the door, opened it and stepped out, her feet cringing on the cold concrete. She had nothing to fear, had she? Only her own imagination, and that of—

"What is it?"

Tanya's voice directly in her ear startled her so badly she yelped.

At the edge of her vision, a movement in the darkness caught her attention. She looked out again.

At the end of the school grounds, where April, Jamey and Steve lived in a small house, a shadowed figure stepped onto the porch.

The door opened, and a sheen of light from inside silhouetted the dark figure. Sheila couldn't be sure, but she thought it was Jamey.

Her pounding heart slowed. She blew out a sigh of profound relief. "It's one of the kids practicing for track." Amazing how the mind could be so deeply affected by no more than the suggestion of fear.

"Let's go to bed." She laid an arm over Tanya's shoulders. "We're letting our scary talk get out of hand."

Tanya hesitated. "Can I sleep with you? Just for tonight?" Her voice wavered with lingering fear.

"Of course, honey. I could use some company myself tonight. I just hope I don't dream again and scare us both."

Tanya climbed back beneath the covers, her gaze following Sheila around the bed. "Pray."

Sheila hesitated as she sat on the edge of the bed. "What?"

"Pray, like Canaan does. He says as long as we keep our hearts and minds on God, and pray, our hearts will be safe from the evil ones who stalk the land at night. It didn't work for me the other morning because I was alone, but we're together now."

"Did it help you when Canaan prayed?" Sheila asked.

"Yes. I shouldn't have run away again. I should have trusted Canaan more. I should have trusted God. Maybe I wouldn't have gotten sick. I should have allowed the Spirit of Jesus to have control of me—"

"Tanya, you were sick. That illness might even have affected your imagination to make you more afraid."

"Please, Sheila." Tanya took Sheila's hand. "Please pray."

"Of course, honey." Sheila squeezed Tanya's hand and bowed her head, and together, they prayed.

## ❧ Chapter Thirty-Two ❧

Betsy Two Horses unlocked the kitchen door before the sun had begun to touch the sky on Friday morning. Her aching body, which had complained all week long about the extra work she'd been doing, threatened to betray her. She'd barely been able to drag herself out of bed this morning.

A few aspirin would have to carry her through the early shift. The others could take over for the lunch preparation.

She had put off getting her monthly shot from Canaan for her rheumatoid arthritis, hoping she could wait until this afternoon. She knew she would have to get it soon. The body aches had led this time to a headache, which made her sick to her stomach.

Before she had even reached into the upper cabinet for a mixing bowl, there was a knock at the door. She turned to see Jane Witherbe stepping inside, her usually cheery round face in a grimace.

"You feeling okay?" Betsy asked.

Jane nodded. "I just need some painkillers. Got any aspirin? Maybe some crackers?"

Betsy pointed toward the supply room. "How bad?"

"Probably just something I ate. None of my kids are feeling bad."

"It'll pass."

Jane agreed. She got her supplies and left, and Betsy got to work. She felt bad for Jane, mothering her dorm girls while feeling sick.

Betsy hated illness in any form. She should've been a doctor.

Sheila stepped from the bathroom after a quick, hot shower. "I need to get dressed and go to the clinic for a little while before breakfast," she told Tanya, who sat at the kitchen table. "Will you be okay here alone for an hour or so?"

"I'm not a little kid, you know."

"Of course you aren't."

"I could go with you and help."

"No, I've just got to do some paperwork I didn't get done last night."

"All you've done is work this week. You hardly eat."

The girl was right, and Sheila felt bad for not being around for her. "I notice you've spent a lot of time helping Blaze with the other kids. You might grow up to be a doctor, too."

A smile transformed Tanya's features. "Or maybe I'll marry Blaze and become a veterinarian, and we can work together."

Sheila chuckled. "You'd better be prepared for competition."

"He said he doesn't have a girlfriend back home."

"I know a lot of girls back home who see the same things in him that you see, though. He's so busy with school and work that he doesn't have a lot of time for anything else."

"Then what's he doing out here?"

"Working and learning. Blaze doesn't depend on teachers alone to give him the education he needs. This is a learning experience for him, kind of like your remedial reading class, where you're supposed to read books on your own time for fun."

Tanya made a face.

Sheila laughed. "Why don't you try to get a little more sleep? You can climb into my bed. It's still warm."

"I guess I could take my book to bed and read."

"Good girl. Veterinarians have to read a lot."

As Sheila walked to the administration building across the central courtyard of the complex, she thought about this past week, working closely with the children, living with Tanya. She loved it. Of course, that could partially be because her biological clock was ticking double-time and her future for motherhood looked bleak right now.

For as long as she could remember, she'd wanted to have children. She'd hoped for children for so long with Ryan, but after a miscarriage, there had been no other pregnancies. Eventually she'd discovered that Ryan had had a vasectomy after her miscarriage. To carry on his affairs without getting caught, she suspected, since he wouldn't have wanted to take the chance of making another woman pregnant.

Even after two years, she battled bitterness that arose at unexpected times. It had become a habit for many months after Ryan's death to blame all her problems on his actions. She had discovered early on that forgiveness was an ongoing struggle, even though she knew he'd paid the ultimate price for his choices.

When she unlocked the clinic door and stepped inside, she caught a faint, familiar scent.

Cedar.

At first, she thought she or Blaze must have left a window open last night, but all the windows were closed. She peered around the sunlit room, recalling clearly this morning's dream.

She stepped around a privacy partition to her cubicle, and saw something lying in the center of her desk. Switching on the lamp, she moved closer, then scrambled backward with a gasp. A picture lay faceup, the torso of a man with the head of a wolf. Scattered around it were wood chips and a handful of colored sand.

The snarling face with bared fangs, the posture of the body, the yellow animal eyes called forth an echo of memory so real she had to close her eyes.

She could almost envision the photo taking on substance, the animal rising up from the flat surface of the page, materializing into the monster that haunted her dreams. She clutched the file cabinet behind her, then turned to scan the room.

It had followed her here.

A door closed somewhere outside, replacing the barrier between dream and reality. This was nonsense. She stepped forward to pick up the picture.

Her fingertips tingled from the touch of the smooth paper, as if she had come into contact with the spirit of the wolf, captured within the photograph. The picture slipped to the floor, and the barrier faded again.

She shivered, looking around the room and out the windows to see if she was being watched. She didn't see anyone.

This was only another wicked joke, and she couldn't allow it to work. But the picture lay faceup on the floor, the wolf's face leering at her.

Last night's dream came back vividly—a smoky room and chanting. And a woman, briefly. The light-haired woman.

The woman was a new part of the dream—more frightening, for some reason, than anything previously retrieved, and something Sheila needed to explore. All she had to do was let herself remember, but right now was not the time. Not when she was alone and vulnerable and confronted with a hostile message.

Sheila squeezed her eyes shut. Not yet.

"Hey, you, what's up?" A man's voice, warm, personal and, right now, very welcome.

She turned to see Preston stepping through the doorway. His smiling expression changed when he saw her face.

"What happened?"

Before Sheila could stop him, Preston sauntered closer, saw the picture on the floor. "What's this?"

"It seems I've been the recipient of another practical joke."

He snatched up the picture. "The wolf again."

She took the picture from him, resisting the urge to hold it by the corner as if it pulsed with life. "It was with that other stuff." She gestured toward the desk. "I found it here when I walked in the room. It's nothing. Just a hoax."

"By whom?" he asked, stepping closer to the desk, frowning at the debris scattered over it.

"Great question."

"It doesn't strike me as a friendly gesture," Preston said.

"A childish joke. Not all the children are friendly, but that doesn't mean they have evil intentions." And yet evil was what she felt in this room and her hands shook…. Her whole body trembled.

What child would know how badly the wolf could terrify her? What adult would stoop to such childish pranks?

Preston pulled out a drawer, where colored sand and wood chips had also been poured. "What *is* all this?" he asked.

"You're looking at items used in a Navajo sand painting."

"And why would these be used to frighten you?"

"I wish I knew for sure."

He turned back to her, and this time his attention focused totally on her. "It does frighten you."

She nodded. "It terrifies me."

He held his arms out—his strong, protective arms—and she stepped into them and allowed him to draw her close. She pressed her forehead against his chest and closed her eyes. For this moment, she just wanted to stay right here and forget.

As if reading her mind, he remained silent, his breath reassuring and deep, his arms steady.

She could very easily get accustomed to this. More and more in the past months, she had found herself craving his nearness, the sound of his voice, his touch. So much so that it was difficult to think straight when she was with him. But right now, she didn't want to think straight.

"Please don't say 'I told you so.'"

His arms tightened around her, and she thought she detected a light kiss on the top of her head. "For your sake, I'm trying to delete that phrase from my vocabulary."

"I feel violated."

"Of course."

"And hurt."

"Yes," he said. "You came out here to help these people, and this ugly trickery is the response you get."

How she adored this man. They spoke the same language. They understood each other.

She stepped out of his arms, and he released her. She looked up into his serious gray-blue eyes and was touched by the tenderness she saw there…and something else. The something else was the reason she'd attempted to keep space between them for the past few months. It was so difficult.

"I'll tell you what," he said. "You go get some breakfast, because I know you worked too late last night to get anything from the cafeteria."

"I had a piece of cheese when I got home."

"I'm going to take care of this mess while you're gone, but first I'll show it to Canaan."

"Okay."

"Then you and Blaze and I will pack our bags and hightail it back to Missouri, where we belong."

She wouldn't admit that the idea tempted her. "I knew you couldn't resist. And you know I can't go."

"Then neither can I." He pulled his cell phone out of his pocket. "Now go get some breakfast while I take some pictures of this mess. I'll see you later."

She wanted to kiss him. "Have I told you lately how special you are?"

"That could be taken in one of several ways," he said with a grim smile. "But thanks. Now go."

## ✒ Chapter Thirty-Three ✒

The first thing Canaan did when he stepped into the cafeteria early Friday morning was check out the dining area.

Empty. As usual, he was the first one here. He would attempt to eat his breakfast and be gone before the usual complainers could surround him and ruin his meal. That happened a lot. He'd never realized the weight of responsibility Bob Jaffrey had carried when he was alive—or how much trouble one little boarding school could be.

The folded sheets of faxed information in Canaan's front pocket proved that. He was confused. When he'd first received the fax and seen the return address of Keams Canyon, he'd known it was the results of Tanya's blood tests. Nothing unusual. Because the hospital's lab was not equipped for a qualitative screening, samples of her blood had been sent to a regional lab, hence the longer turnaround time.

Canaan picked up a tray and slid it along the counter,

selected silverware as he pondered the one disturbing result. Tanya's blood had tested positive for GHB, gamma hydroxy-butyrate, a drug with a couple of uses. Though it wasn't the most common date rape drug, it was sometimes used for that. It was also used by athletes to improve their performance. Tanya was on the track team, but she wasn't particularly passionate about being an athlete.

This was what made Tanya's fear of the wolf that much more disturbing—and that much more understandable. What if someone was using the drug to take advantage of her?

Questioning her would do no good. And it was not feasible to test the blood of every child in this school for the drug, but he was suddenly thankful once more for the extra help he had received this week, no matter that Preston's presence made him somewhat uncomfortable.

He wouldn't mind keeping Blaze around for a while longer, though Canaan didn't know where he himself would be at the end of the summer. He didn't want to leave Granddad in the lurch, and he would not, but one school year here was enough.

His thoughts were suddenly interrupted by a greeting from Betsy Two Horses. Her dark gaze scanned his face as she served him sausage and scrambled eggs. "She'll probably be here any time."

Canaan blinked at her. "Who?" He took the new purple ball cap from his head and tucked it under his arm.

"Give it up. These old eyes don't miss much."

"Better make an appointment with an eye doctor, Betsy. You're seeing things."

"That's good to hear, because we wouldn't want our respected principal to get into a brawl with a man over a woman who doesn't belong on the reservation."

Canaan placed milk and coffee on his tray.

"She doesn't belong here, Canaan," Betsy said.

"Who would that be?" he asked. This was one of the reasons he was more than ready to leave this school. He certainly didn't command any respect as a doctor or as an interim principal with the elders who'd known him as a child.

"Who are you spending all your time with this week?" Betsy asked.

"I thought you liked Sheila." And it was none of Betsy's business why he was spending time with Sheila.

"I love her, but this isn't the place for her. Did you notice she's working herself to death the past few days?"

"We all are, but it'll be over soon." He hoped.

"Did you ever find out who shot her tire?"

"Yes, it was a boy protecting his sheep. The police called me just a few minutes ago." And in his consternation over the fax from Phoenix, the news about the shooter had been pushed to the back of his mind.

"He needs to be punished."

"He will, I'm sure."

"She still needs to leave, Canaan. That man of hers should take her back to where they both belong."

He walked away without replying. Even though he understood what Betsy meant—that he and Sheila were from different worlds—he wasn't up to discussing the subject this early in the morning, and he certainly wasn't in the mood to listen to Betsy shove her opinions down his throat.

Yet another reason why he didn't make a good administrator.

He found himself carrying his tray toward the table in the corner, where Sheila usually sat when she ate in the cafeteria. Halfway there, he changed his mind and took a seat on the other side of the dining area. As the old TV sitcom character Barney Fife would say, "Nip it in the bud." Why start rumors? And why allow himself to become emotionally attached again, when he knew Betsy was right?

The door opened and Sheila stepped inside. She searched the dining room, her gaze stopping at Canaan.

With all the finesse of an awkward adolescent, he tipped half a glass of milk into his coffee, spilling a stream of it across the table, and as he reached to catch it, he dumped the sugar onto the floor with a clatter of kidproof plastic.

He had the mess nearly cleaned up when she joined him, and a good thing, because the children started drifting in with their dorm parents. Kai Begay was the first, with his group of boys behind him.

"Dare I say good morning?" Sheila asked.

"Please do, I could use it." He looked at her closely. She looked agitated, her gaze darting around the room.

"I received a call from the police this morning about the bullet in your wheel," he told her.

The gaze suddenly riveted on him. "They have a lead?"

"More than that, they solved the problem. They questioned some locals, and a shepherd confessed that his son was out tending a flock of sheep when some wild dogs got after a lamb. The boy shot at the dog, but missed. He didn't see the Jeep until after he shot, and then he was afraid to say anything."

"How old is the boy?"

"Eleven."

Sheila's eyes narrowed, and he could almost hear her wondering what moron would allow an eleven-year-old to carry a rifle.

"The father has promised to pay for a new tire and wheel," he said. "The boy got the scare of his life when the police threatened to haul him to jail."

"But they didn't, right?"

"That's right, but I don't think he'll try something like that again. His father also promised never to let him carry a rifle until he's older and has taken a gun safety course. I'll go talk to them myself. I know the family."

Sheila leaned back in her chair. "Thank you. I needed to hear that. Now maybe my bodyguards will relax their efforts a little."

"Not likely. I have a feeling one of those bodyguards is just looking for a reason to be near you."

Sheila nodded.

Canaan discovered he wasn't interested in exploring that subject further. "Tanya still doing okay?"

"Healing very well, I think. Physically."

"She still having trouble emotionally?"

"Yes." Sheila poured milk over her cereal, not spilling a drop.

"How did you sleep last night?" he asked.

She darted a quick glance at him. "I look that bad, huh?"

"You look as if you could sleep a couple more hours."

"Thanks so much. Did Preston talk to you this morning?"

"No, he was already gone when I got up."

She straightened and looked at him. "There's something he wants you to see in the clinic."

"What?"

"The wolf man struck again, this time on my desk." She sounded almost nonchalant, but he caught the faintest quality of fear in her voice as she described what the vandal had done.

He pushed himself away from the table.

Sheila placed a hand on his arm. "It can wait until after

breakfast. I'll call Preston on my cell and see if he'll join us. We can talk about it."

Canaan agreed. He was hungry and not eager to face the vandalism on an empty stomach.

"The wolf again," he said.

"Something happened here in the past," she said. "I can't help thinking that same thing is still here—or it has returned. I keep having dreams about this place and new memories."

"Anything significant?"

"I remember the smell of cedar smoke, and this morning, when I saw the wood chips and colorful sand on my desk, with the wolf head, I knew exactly what it was all for. I was able to explain to Preston when he asked."

Canaan shook his head in dismay, then nodded a greeting at Jane Witherbe, who had stepped in with her little girls. She wasn't moving as quickly as usual. While Sheila called Preston from her cell phone, Canaan studied Jane's long face and sickly pallor. Not for the first time, he wondered why she had been given double duty as both dorm mother and teacher. It had to be an overwhelming responsibility, but he knew this school was her whole life.

Sheila folded her phone, and Canaan returned his attention to her. "Is there anything else you remember about these dreams?" he asked.

"I'm a child in them. This morning, I awakened from another repeat of a recurring dream, but this time there was a woman."

"What did she look like?"

"My impression was that she resembled my mother."

"Do you think this is just an overactive imagination jumbling a lot of thoughts together?"

"Very possible," she said, and yet there was doubt in her voice.

"You think it's more of a memory?"

She nodded.

"Look at you two." Doc Cottonwood's voice came from behind them, and Sheila and Canaan both started in surprise. "You're not eating enough to keep a kindergartener alive. Come on, eat up!" He set his tray down across from them and pulled out a chair.

"Why don't you join us, Doc?" Canaan said dryly.

"Sure, now that you asked." Doc's voice was just as dry. "Looks like you need some serious prodding. You know what I always say—a good breakfast keeps you from burning muscle instead of fat." He sat down, pulled a bottle of tablets from his pocket and set it on the table. "Now if I could just convince the student body and staff to be a little more reliable about taking these every day, we wouldn't have any need for a clinic." He leaned forward and looked at Sheila. "What's got you two looking so serious?"

"Just reliving old memories," Sheila said.

"Must not be good ones," he said.

"I just don't like the way I keep being reminded of them," Sheila said.

"Well, you just tell your Uncle Doc all about them, and maybe I can fix it for you."

## *Chapter Thirty-Four*

Preston looked for Sheila as soon as he stepped into the cafeteria. She was sitting beside the track coach, across the table from Canaan. They looked deep in conversation, and he could only hope they were figuring out who might have been pulling these scare tactics on Sheila.

Preston went through the food line, hearing sixth-grade boys on both sides of him talking about a television show. Preston hadn't seen a television since he'd been here, but the dorms must have them.

To his disappointment, sausage and eggs were on the menu, fry bread was not. Although the lady who ran the cafeteria, Betsy Two Horses, didn't appear as bright and cheerful as in days past, she had greeted him with an increasingly warmer smile every day. Today was no exception. He discovered yesterday that this was because she had been told he was Sheila's good friend.

He remembered what Canaan had said to him on Monday:

Good friend might be all he ever would be to Sheila. To Preston's surprise, Canaan hadn't brought up the subject again, and Preston, in turn, had taken pains not to ask pointed questions about Johnny Jacobs's business practices. He didn't see a need to further irritate his host.

He had, however, become curious about one anonymous financial supporter, and he had made an effort to discover the benefactor's identity. All he'd discovered was that the donor was exceedingly careful to remain anonymous—and this was by far the most generous donor of all. The multimillion-dollar contribution over a year ago must have made it possible for these new buildings to be erected.

Preston had decided not to tell Canaan about his search. After a few financial discussions with the man, Preston knew economics wasn't dear to Canaan's heart, nor a subject that he grasped easily. As a professional financial advisor, Preston had discovered that many of his clients in other professions were not financially savvy.

Preston walked to the table where Sheila was in a serious conversation with Canaan and Doc, and placed his tray beside Canaan. Sheila was describing this morning's discovery in the clinic. Doc was suitably outraged, and Canaan was voicing his conviction that the children needed to learn that vandalism was an unacceptable form of expression.

Preston listened for a moment, startled when Canaan asked Doc a pointed question.

"Have you ever caught anyone on your track team taking illegal supplements?"

"No way. Not my kids," Doc said. "They all know the danger to their health, and that if I ever caught anyone doing something like that, he or she would be expelled from the team, not just suspended. Why do you want to know?"

"Just wondering if the hoaxes pulled on Sheila could be because a drug of some kind is influencing one of the kids."

Doc pursed his lips, considering the question. "Could be an angle to check. Or it could just be some of the kids daring each other."

As Canaan explained the shooting incident and its conclusion, Preston lost his appetite. Though relieved to hear that there was no crazed killer out to hurt Sheila, he was discovering more reasons why she should not remain at the school. What were the odds that Sheila had been driving by at just the moment a shepherd boy decided to shoot at a sheep-killing dog?

On the other hand, what were the odds that an eleven-year-old shepherd boy had decided to shoot at her for no reason?

Their conversation was overheard by a few nearby diners, and soon all of the teachers and dorm parents knew about the wolf head and the vandalism in the clinic. Everyone had an opinion about what needed to be done.

Preston ate a few bites of his meal. It just wasn't the same without fry bread.

He was finishing his coffee when Canaan turned to him. "I'll go look at that mess in the clinic, then I'll clean it up. I found that pie chart on my desk this morning. Thank you. If you're up for more work, I need a courier to drive to Phoenix for me today."

Preston hesitated. Was this Canaan's way of telling him his presence was no longer needed here, or did he really need a courier?

"I'll let you drive my luxury car," Canaan said with a grin.

"The van?"

"It may not look like much, but I bet it gets better mileage than your Jeep."

"You'd have to prove it to me," Preston said.

Canaan pulled a set of keys from his pocket. "Does that mean you'll go?"

"I told you I'd do whatever you needed." It was frustrating, however. Preston wanted to stay and study the financial records of past years—a job Canaan had given him as soon as he'd completed the pie chart yesterday.

"Did you have a chance to look over the old records?" Canaan asked, as if reading Preston's mind.

"Just a preliminary overview, but I found a few interesting discrepancies—if you could call them that."

"Such as?"

"I'm curious to know if your anonymous donor, who literally made it possible for the new school buildings to be erected, was the same anonymous donor who helped so much with the initial financing of the school, and then practically dropped off the radar about twenty-three years ago."

"That's a good question. Unfortunately, I can't answer it. I know my grandfather was enormously relieved by the renewed influx of money. For a couple of years, he thought he might have to close down one or more of his schools. He considered the sudden windfall an answer to prayers."

Again, Preston knew better than to argue with God—or at least with a person's faith in God. In fact, Preston found himself envying Canaan's faith in the face of the challenges the man was being forced to tackle.

"So this donor is giving equal amounts to each school?" Preston asked.

"That's right. Granddad could have kept two or three of the schools up and running without the help, but we wouldn't have these new buildings or our modern clinic."

"I'll be ready to leave for Phoenix in an hour or less."

"Good. That'll give me time to prepare my package, and if you drive as fast as Blaze tells me you do, you should be back to the school in time for dinner." Canaan clapped Preston on the back as he walked away.

Sheila stepped out into the desert, delaying the return to her desk in the clinic as long as possible. Right now, she craved sunlight and fresh air and time to talk things over with God. Or, at least, to share her thoughts with Him.

For instance, she had come to Arizona to help Canaan finish the school year with continued good medical care for the students and their families. The families would begin collecting the children for the summer in a couple of weeks, their arrival schedules staggered so that anyone who wanted a physical checkup could receive it, free of charge. Those who required further treatment would be scheduled to return after the children had all gone home. The clinic would stay open for as long as needed, even if that meant all summer.

This was a great benefit to the families who couldn't afford or were unable to get to good medical care otherwise. This service was the brainchild of Johnny Jacobs, funded by the donors who supported this school and the others like it on the reservation. It was why Sheila had the utmost respect for Johnny.

So why did she suddenly feel a strong urge to do as Preston had suggested earlier, and pack her bags and go home, without completing anything she had come here to do? She would resist the urge, of course.

"There you are," came Preston's voice from the edge of the school grounds.

She turned and waited for him to join her.

"I should have known not to make promises I might not want to keep," he said when he reached her. "Canaan needs me to be a courier today. I'm driving to Phoenix."

"Good. You're the only nonmedical person he knows he can trust, and he needs to send more blood samples to the lab to—"

Preston waved away her words. "I realize that. I just don't like leaving you here when someone is still obviously hostile toward you."

"Blaze is going to work with me in the clinic today, so don't worry," she said dryly, "I'll be well guarded."

"Canaan and I cleaned up the mess, and your clinic is ready for you again."

"It isn't my clinic." She turned and started walking again.

"Have you considered studying to become a nurse-practitioner when you return to Missouri?" He fell into step close beside her, due to the narrowness of the track. "Blaze and Canaan keep telling me how good you are with the patients."

"I already work with patients."

"But you have that something extra."

She smiled at his encouragement. Preston Black would support her if she decided to become President of the United States.

"I need to talk to you about something," she said.

"So talk."

She looked up at him, admiring the strength of his silhouette, the determination she knew was in his heart. This week, she had known she could trust him with her life.

"I'm struggling with something right now," she said. "I've been praying about it, but I also need to bounce these thoughts off someone with skin, and that doesn't mean I need you to fix anything for me, just listen."

He gave her a sideways glance. "I don't know, honey, that's a difficult challenge."

She smiled and took his hand. "Okay, but try. Here's the problem. For as long as I can remember, my mother has been a forbidden subject in our house. Her death is shrouded in mystery, and I've always felt this hunger to know what actually happened to her."

His steps slowed. "This much I know. You came out here not only to help a friend in need—which is part of your giving nature—but because you also had a need."

"And now I'm afraid," she said.

"Of what you might find?"

She nodded.

"You love your father very much, don't you?" he asked.

"Of course."

"Then don't you want to understand him better? He's a bit of an enigma, isn't he?"

She looked up at Preston again. "He always has been. He's a wonderful father, a great supporter, a man of God, but he just wouldn't discuss my mother."

"Don't you think you owe it to him to find out why?"

She thought about that for a moment. What was he saying? Did Preston honestly believe she had done the right thing in coming here? Did he feel she should stay until she found her answers?

"I'm beginning to remember some things about Mom," she said. "And I'm beginning to wonder if they will turn out to be good memories."

He reached out and touched her arm. "Hold on a minute. Haven't you suspected something disturbing all along?"

She stopped, midstride. "What?"

"Your father is a practical man. He doesn't do anything without good reason. He doesn't like me because he doesn't believe in marriage for a couple with different spiritual views. And he most likely didn't want you to come out here because he didn't want you to discover something about your mother that would hurt you."

Sheila digested this in silence.

"So it stands to reason that you'll discover something you don't want to know," he said. "You came here, aware deep down that this could happen. It's too late to turn back now, don't you think?"

"You mean you don't want me to leave?" she asked.

He gazed at her tenderly. "What I want has never been a part of the equation. You have a need to be here and a need to know. I'm here to help you—"

"You guys!"

They turned. Tanya was rushing toward them, face flushed, dark brows lowered.

"You're not going to believe this! Do you know who played those awful tricks on you, Sheila? April Hunt! I'd like to yank her head bald!" She turned and glowered toward the school. "I just might do it, too."

"You mean she admitted it?" Sheila asked, feeling a sudden rush of relief.

"Jamey told me. He said he got home really late last night—

you know when we heard someone running outside, and you said you thought it was Jamey? Well, it was. And he was sick and had to get some aspirin from the bathroom. He went past her little room and she wasn't there, so he went looking for her. He caught her trying to sneak back in the house just before dawn. He said he overheard you guys talking with the teachers about a wolf drawing in the apartment, and he knew she'd been out. You know, she has a key to a lot of the buildings because she cleans? Well, she admitted to Jamey that she used her key to get into the clinic last night, to set up that stuff."

"But why?" Sheila asked.

"She told Jamey it was because the wolf wanted her to." Tanya grasped Sheila's arms. "I think he's gotten to her, too. He's everywhere we turn!"

## ❧ Chapter Thirty-Five ❧

Canaan paced in front of the main office entrance at the Northern Arizona University at Flagstaff, tension tightening the muscles in his shoulders as he prepared to betray someone he had known most of his life. But when it came to a choice between Kai Begay and the good of the school, the school won.

He wasn't actually betraying Kai, anyway, he was simply doing a more thorough background check than might have been run on him when he first became a member of the staff. Maybe Doctor Whitter couldn't tell Canaan anything about Kai that he didn't already know. What a relief that would be. Perhaps.

An elderly Native American with a brisk step approached him and smiled. "Dr. York? I'm Eyotah Whitter." He held out his hand. "I knew you instantly. You look very much like your mother."

Canaan took Dr. Whitter's hand. "My mother used to talk

about you often when I was growing up. You were one of her favorite professors here."

"Why don't I remember having you as a student?"

"I've been here several times, but I attended university and medical school in Phoenix."

The man had the broad features of the Hopi tribe, and Canaan remembered Kai mentioning that one of his professors had been Hopi. A Hopi college professor was very rare in the days Kai had gone to school.

"I come from your part of the country," Doctor Whitter said. "From the Hopi reservation in the center of Navajoland."

Shorter and more slender than Canaan, the older man exuded an energy that seemed to burst at the seams of his reserved demeanor. Rather than inviting Canaan into his office, he suggested they talk as they strolled around the campus, though Eyotah Whitter's stroll was more like a jog.

"We'll have more privacy this way," he explained, absently pushing his shaggy black hair from his forehead. "Everybody wants to drop in for a visit when I'm working on Saturday."

They stepped across a concrete courtyard, the cool, fresh air so clear that the dark green needles of the pines and white bark of the aspens looked painted on a canvas of blue velvet. Unlike the desert of the Navajo reservation, Flagstaff eased beautifully into summer, due to the higher altitude. Here pines grew tall and straight against the backdrop of the San Francisco Peaks. Not for the first time today, Canaan wished he were here simply for pleasure.

He turned to Doctor Whitter. "As I asked you over the telephone yesterday, do you remember a student you might have had thirty-five or forty years ago named Kai Begay?"

Whitter's mouth pursed, and his steps slowed. "And as I

told you yesterday, we're talking about a lot of years. I've been curious about why you want to know."

"He's a teacher at our school, at Twin Mesas, and he mentioned a Hopi professor. I thought of you—"

"He works with children?"

"He's one of the school favorites, and has been since I was a student there. Does that concern you?"

"I'm not sure you're talking about the person I'm remembering, though the name is familiar. Tell me more."

"He was a premed student. He feels that he was held back by a Hopi professor at the time."

Dr. Whitter stepped over to a concrete bench and sat down heavily. He looked at Canaan in silence for a moment, as if considering his words carefully.

Canaan got the distinct impression he wasn't going to appreciate what Dr. Whitter had to say.

"If it's the Kai Begay I remember," Dr. Whitter began, "I thought he was out of the state. I was told he had left the area. I can't believe he's been working with children all this time, so close by." He raised a thick, dark brow at Canaan. "May I ask what problems you have had?"

Canaan joined him on the bench. "It's complicated. Some of my suspicions are based on nothing but intuition. There is a distinct mood of unease at the school. The kids are jumpy, some are waking with bad dreams, others are starting fights." He briefly told about Tanya's terror of the Navajo werewolf, the pranks played by April and Sheila's recollections of the past.

"You say the twelve-year-old had severe bleeding?" Dr. Whitter asked.

"Yes, but we got her to medical treatment in time, and she's fine now."

"Any evidence of sexual abuse?"

"None, and she had not been pregnant, but I did receive test results showing she had GHB in her system, which would indicate something nefarious, particularly since I know this child, and I don't believe she would willingly take the drug. I have no way of knowing how many of these events are connected and how many are coincidental."

"You said Kai was a teacher there when you attended the school?"

"Yes. But so were several other staff members. I'm not sure why I've begun to suspect Kai, except for his attitude toward Sheila Metcalf, who has returned to help me in the clinic. She was a student there, and she, too, was affected deeply by this crazy superstition about the Navajo werewolf—"

"If not for these other problems, the wolf would not concern me too much." Dr. Whitter shaded his eyes and watched Canaan. "With white civilization pushing in at every opportunity, I think superstitions are becoming more prevalent. Our traditions are becoming anachronisms. I left the world of my parents many years ago, but I still cling to some of the old ways. Just because I don't live by tribal customs doesn't mean I don't honor them in my thoughts."

"The Navajo werewolf is not a custom, it's an ancient evil," Canaan said. "I encourage the children to be proud of our Navajo heritage. What's been happening the past few years seems to be an undermining of the basic beliefs our school has attempted to teach our children for the past thirty years."

"Twin Mesas is a Christian school," Whitter said quietly. "Some people might say the Navajo heritage has already been undermined there for thirty years."

"Our Navajo heritage has never been hostile toward Christianity," Canaan said. "So would you be one of those people, Dr. Whitter?"

Whitter spread his hands. "I know Christians mean well. But you didn't come to see me to debate Christianity. You came to find out if it's possible Kai Begay is causing the trouble at your school. I believe he could very well be."

Canaan leaned forward, alarmed. "Tell me how."

Before Dr. Whitter could reply, they were interrupted by one of Dr. Whitter's students. Frustrated, Canaan checked his cell phone messages while Dr. Whitter conferred with his student.

This morning, before leaving the school, Canaan had left messages for the principals of his grandfather's three other reservation schools, requesting information about possible difficulties they might be having. As he listened to his voice mail, his concern grew.

Neither of the principals mentioned any concerns about the Navajo werewolf. One, however, reported that just this morning three of the dorm parents had visited the clinic, too ill to return to their dorms. An investigation was under way, but tests were inconclusive at this point.

Canaan needed to complete this interview and get back to the school.

Sheila missed Preston. She hadn't realized how much she looked forward to seeing him every day until she'd looked for him in the cafeteria at early lunch and remembered he was on his way to Phoenix.

She looked at her watch as she returned to the clinic. He would be back in another hour or so, if he hadn't been stopped for speeding.

"I thought you'd never get here," came a voice from the shadows at the far corner of the waiting area.

Sheila recognized that voice. She turned on the light and saw Betsy in a chair, hunched over. She didn't look good.

"I looked for you in the cafeteria," Sheila said, "but Steve told me you'd taken the rest of the day off. You look sick."

"Nothing a good shot of my arthritis medication won't cure," Betsy said. "It's been a month, and my over-the-counter stuff isn't working anymore."

"A month? Betsy, what are you talking about?"

"Canaan didn't tell you? I have rheumatoid arthritis. He's got a standing order for me to have a shot of etanercept once a month. Check my file."

Sheila reached for her thermometer and stethoscope. "Come into the exam room with me. Why didn't you say something sooner?"

"How much sooner?" Betsy got up and followed. "I never tell Canaan ahead of time, I just come in when I start feeling achy, and get the shot."

"When did this pain first start?" Sheila asked.

"About twenty years ago. Guess the weather's acting up. It's not usually this bad."

"Lie down," Sheila said. "I can listen to your heart better that way."

"You don't need to listen to my heart, you need to listen to me. There's nothing wrong with me that my medicine won't fix."

"Fine, let me get your file and set up your shot," Sheila said.

"Figured you'd go stir-crazy today, with Preston and Canaan both gone," Betsy said as she sat on the exam table. "Maybe I'll watch."

"Or maybe you'll go home and go to bed," Sheila said.

"People with autoimmune disorders are supposed to rest when they feel bad. I don't ever see you rest. No wonder you're hurting."

"That would bore me to death. What are you trying to do, play those two good-looking men against each other?"

"I'm not playing anyone against anyone. I came out here to help in the clinic."

"And to find out more about your mother," Betsy said.

"Right now I'm here to help you feel better. When did you start feeling the pain this time?" Sheila asked.

"It's been coming on all week. Have you found out any more about your mother?" Betsy asked. "Has being here stimulated your memories?"

Sheila placed the syringe of medicine on the stainless-steel tray table and opened an alcohol swab packet. "Maybe another memory, though I'm not sure. Just sit there and relax."

"I am relaxed. You mean a dream?"

"That's right."

"Tell me about it."

"All I can tell is that I was having the same dream as before, only this time I saw a woman standing in the doorway of a hogan. She had long, light hair, and she wore white. So I was either dreaming about an angel, or that woman was my mother."

"You saw your mother at the same time you saw the wolf?"

Sheila nodded. "Do you want the injection in the arm or hip?"

"Hip. It's nice to have a woman doing it again. I don't like baring my bony behind for just anyone, you know." She bent over the exam bed and slid down the waistband of her slacks.

Sheila swabbed the site.

"You should have seen our poor little April Hunt when

Doc questioned her about those nasty tricks she played on you," Betsy said.

"I hope he wasn't too hard on her."

"He needed to be hard. It's witchcraft, you know."

"The picture?"

"The cedar and sand. The picture was only a childish taunt."

"But that was what frightened me."

"Because you're afraid of the wolf. The wolf is the source of evil, but not the picture," Betsy said. "The sand was probably what the witch used in a dry painting to conjure the wolf spirit."

"I guessed it was something like that."

"There is a power in the prank that was played on you, because your fear weakens you, leaves you more open to the power. I have tried to stop it."

"Prayer is the only way to battle it, Betsy." Sheila slid the needle into the muscle and injected the fluid.

"I know this is a Christian school, but it's hard for some of us to give up all our old beliefs. My husband never liked it when I continued to practice some of the old ways, even after I became a believer in Christ."

"It's hard, sometimes, to change your whole belief system all at once," Sheila said. "Okay, I'm done. Betsy, you need to rest until you're feeling better."

Betsy ignored her. "That was why he gave me that necklace I gave you. He wanted me to remember where the real power came from"

"Jesus Christ is the only One with power," Sheila said. "If April left those things, that could mean she knows who is practicing Navajo witchcraft in this area."

Betsy nodded. "That's right. It's even possible the witch told her to try to frighten you."

"But why? I've done nothing to hurt anyone."

"I think you might have frightened someone. It's possible this person thinks you know how your mother died. It's possible whoever wants to frighten you killed your mother."

## ⤲ Chapter Thirty-Six ⤲

To Canaan's relief, the professor was finally free to walk with him again. "Dr. Whitter, can you tell me more about your experiences with Kai?"

"Please call me Eyotah. You are not a student."

"Thank you, Eyotah. I am Canaan."

Eyotah regarded him for a few seconds. "Certainly not a Navajo name."

"I am half white. I was given my name by my Christian grandfather, who founded four mission schools on Navajoland."

Eyotah took off his jacket and slung it over his shoulder. "Did Kai mention what classes he took under my instruction?"

"He didn't even mention your name. He referred to you only as a Hopi professor he'd had."

"He would be bitter. He didn't get his way with me." Eyotah's voice hardened. "I was stronger than he was, as few were."

Canaan frowned. "Stronger?"

Eyotah nodded. "I'm a professor of psychology, but I am also considered an expert in Native American legend and customs. My father was the holy man of a large tribe, and he taught me his ways. He also taught me of the dark spirits so that I would know how to shield myself from them."

"Witchcraft?" Canaan exclaimed. The Hopi were known for their power and expertise with witchcraft, far exceeding that of the Navajo.

"Yes, but I never used the dark power."

"I've never been able to see a difference between what you call the dark and light sides of the power," Canaan said. If the power came from the same source, it was the same power.

"You Christians are entitled to your opinions, but have you ever seen an evil that heals?"

"I've seen evil masquerade as light to seduce people. By the time they realized the mistake, it was too late. But tell me about your spiritual medicine. Did you teach it to Kai?"

A weary sadness pulled at Eyotah's expression. He nodded. "Had I known, I would never have shown him." He shook his head. "I thought he was sincere in his quest for knowledge of Navajo customs, and he knew I had studied many things about the Navajo. He showed so much interest in psychology classes, and he was so adept at anything he undertook, I was drawn to him. Of course, his Navajo heritage, with so few Native Americans in college those days, also attracted me. He was a brilliant, hardworking student for the first three years he was here. He was, as you said, a premed student, and I encouraged him, praising him to my colleagues at every opportunity."

"What happened?"

"I'm not sure." He turned to Canaan. "But for the first three years, he never returned home, even though it was only a five-hour drive away. He never mentioned his home, though I knew he came from the Black Mountain area. It was as if he wanted to wipe the past from his memory."

"Did you ever find out why?"

Eyotah shook his head. "I have only theories. During the summers he took night courses, worked, and saved his money. I hired him for several research projects on the Apache nation. But the summer before his fourth year, his father died, and he returned to Black Mountain. He stayed the whole summer. When he came back that fall, it was as if some darkness had entered his spirit." Eyotah shuddered. "It frightened even me."

"You have no idea what happened?"

"Only the barest inkling. There was an incident at Black Mountain, many years before you were born. An old man named White Wolf was shot for practicing witchcraft. It made the news because he was one of the last witches punished by death in the Navajo nation, and the police found out about it."

"I remember hearing about it. My grandfather told me."

Eyotah loosened his tie. At the next concrete bench, he tossed his jacket onto it, but didn't sit down. "I know I don't have to tell you how Native Americans resent outsiders meddling in our affairs, and for many weeks the Feds investigated White Wolf's death. They never found out who shot him, and for that I'm glad. From a small investigation I did on my own while studying the Navajo, I came to the conclusion that White Wolf truly was a witch, and that whoever killed him was a hero to the Navajo people."

"You think this somehow affected Kai?" Canaan asked the older man.

Eyotah nodded. "I know the educational system and white

society tell us that the spirits don't exist, but the beliefs of my nation go back many centuries. I'm convinced that demon spirits could enter some people—as it might have infected Kai when he returned to Black Mountain that summer."

"Or perhaps someone in that community was infected, who, in turn, somehow reached Kai that summer," Canaan suggested. "What was Kai like when he returned?"

"His whole character had undergone a metamorphosis. He changed from a brilliant, hardworking student to a trouble-maker in just a few weeks. He became very moody and volatile when denied what he wanted."

Canaan listened with growing alarm. "What kind of trouble did he cause?"

Eyotah sat down on the bench. "Other than temper tantrums and delusions of extreme self-importance, Kai nearly destroyed one freshman girl his senior year."

Before he could explain further, they were interrupted again. Canaan bit back his frustration and checked his messages once more. Nothing. He waited.

Betsy Two Horses was a tough woman who seldom admitted to weakness. That concerned Sheila. She offered pain medication to help Betsy until her injection kicked in.

Betsy turned it down. "What you've given me works well, and it won't take long. I'm still curious about what you remember of your mother. Tell me more."

"Just because I remember my mother's presence in the same place as the wolf doesn't mean she had anything to do with him."

"A witch—usually a Navajo male—can find his power through many spirits," Betsy said. "He can manipulate children.

He controls their minds. He can also control the minds of adults if his witchcraft is powerful enough."

"I don't believe anyone could have controlled my mother's mind enough for her to allow someone to hurt me."

"What if she'd been convinced you weren't being hurt? What actually was done to you?"

Sheila didn't know. "I remember great pain and fear, but nothing specific."

"And no memory of who this wolf was, or where the pain was in your body?"

"None. Wouldn't a mother know if her child was being hurt?"

"Children can be frightened and in pain from things that adults understand and accept without a problem."

"Tell me more about my mother's behavior at that time," Sheila said. "Maybe that's the key to understanding what happened."

"After you grew a little older, began making friends and weren't so dependent on her, I think she needed something to occupy her free time."

"I remember she was gone a lot when I arrived home from school."

"You spent a lot of time with me in the cafeteria then."

"I remember. I went there a lot, because I didn't want to go home to an empty house. Since we lived on campus, it was easy to walk over and talk to you."

"Evelyn kept busy in the clinic, but your father worked much longer hours than she did, often traveling to remote areas of the reservation for days at a time. She got lonely. I could tell."

"How lonely?"

"I saw her spending time with some of the other men on campus."

Sheila winced at these words. "Please don't tell me my mother had an affair."

Betsy hesitated. "There were rumors, but I never listened to those. Because we are so far from everything, and it's hard to support a family on the wages here, a lot of our staff are single. There were a lot of single men working here at the school when you were here, too."

"So she might have had an affair without your knowledge?"

"There were times when she was overly bright and a little too friendly, but I never saw anything that made me think she was doing something she shouldn't be doing."

"You told me that my parents fought."

Betsy closed her eyes, grimacing.

"Betsy? Are you feeling worse?"

The older woman shook her head. "I had hoped I wouldn't have to tell you all these things. I wish you wouldn't ask."

"I'm asking. I need to know, if for no other reason than to understand my father better."

"She was unhappy in her marriage," Betsy admitted at last.

"She told you?"

"Of course. We were friends. She talked to me a lot. She even talked about taking you and leaving Buster."

Sheila felt a pang of sympathy for her father. "Did he know?" Was that why he resisted talking about Mom?

"Your mother was never one to hide her feelings."

"Poor Daddy."

Betsy's dark eyes softened. She reached out and touched Sheila's arm with awkward compassion. "Tell me again what you remember about your mother's presence in the hogan."

Sheila closed her eyes as a memory of the dream flashed through her mind. Forcing herself to focus, she saw a few more details. "As always, I'm lying on a hard bed or a table in a hogan with a smoke hole in the middle. The hogan is smoky, and I always feel nauseated."

"Why nauseated?"

Sheila shook her head. "I don't know. I have a bitter taste in my mouth."

"You experience the sense of taste in your dreams?"

"I don't know if that's actually in my dream, or if it's just a memory. It's as if I've eaten something foul.... That's it, Betsy. I remember getting sick in my dream."

"But from what?"

"Something I chewed and swallowed. It was bitter. And when I was sick, the wolf got angry, but he turned me over so I wouldn't choke."

"Are you sure it's the wolf who turns you over? Maybe it's your mother."

Sheila thought about that, but the memory wouldn't focus clearly.

"Sheila, do you know anything about peyote?" Betsy asked.

"It's a cactus with hallucinogenic properties used in ancient rituals."

"Some still use it. What if the bitter taste was from peyote? It's about the size of an overcoat button, and it's bitter. It could have made you sick. It would also have made you hallucinate, so that later you wouldn't remember what happened."

"But I remember a hypodermic needle, as well. What would that have been used for, if not to make me forget?"

Betsy sighed and spread her hands across her lap. "Evelyn gave herself insulin shots."

"In last night's dream, as I try to recall it, she isn't the one holding the needle. Why would someone else be holding it?"

Betsy winced. "For a lot of years, many have thought that Evelyn died of an insulin overdose. I never believed it, because she was always very careful with her medication. But what if that was how she died, only not by her own hand?"

"The only other image I ever see in my dreams is the wolf."

Betsy watched her in silence.

Sheila held her gaze. For a long moment, neither spoke.

"Why would the wolf want to kill my mother?" Sheila asked.

"There are all kinds of reasons for murder. Passion is one."

"Or fear. My mother might have seen something she wasn't supposed to see."

"Such as what?" Betsy asked quietly.

Sheila didn't want to guess.

"Find out who is practicing the wolf's vile craft on this campus, Sheila, and you may find the person who killed your mother."

The clinic door opened, and both women started.

"Hey, boss," Blaze called in the outer room, "you here?"

Sheila motioned for Betsy to stay where she was, but Betsy shook her head.

"I'm going home."

Sheila sighed. "Okay, go on home. But be sure to rest."

Betsy saluted and walked out the door.

## ❧ Chapter Thirty-Seven ❧

Halfway between the administration building and my apartment a whisper brushes at me through the air. I stop. I listen. Silence.

Is this the same little boy who taunted me before? I might suspect it to be Jamey, but this voice doesn't hold a human quality.

I walk on a few steps, hear the whisper again, this time more like a voice than the wind. Again I stop, and this time the whisper grows louder, becomes a childish chant:

"*Racing Deer is running, racing,*
*Racing Deer is running far from here.*"

Shocked, I whirl around, but find the road deserted. The children have all gone to their dormitories.

It's the same taunt that dragged me from sleep several nights ago. A child calls to me, but what child? And why?

I turn and continue to my apartment, the whisper echoing

around me, mingling with the wind. *"Racing Deer is running,*
*Racing Deer is racing, Racing Deer…"*

The voice becomes the wind that grabs at my hair and
clothes, that whistles across my ears, then turns to whispers
again. It's so often hard to tell if the spirit is wicked or
benign.

I force myself to ignore it, gritting my teeth as I walk faster.
I refuse to give in this time. There is no need to be afraid.
Unless spirits take a form, they cannot harm me. And a child
is no match for the wolf.

The voice stops abruptly when I enter my apartment.

I gather food and water and place them in my jacket. I go
to the chest beside my bed and pull supplies from my top
drawer. I take the silver-and-turquoise knife from the hiding
place where it has waited for so long. White Wolf's knife,
passed on to me from another. The power has waited within
this knife all these years. Now it is time.

I slide the knife from its leather sheath, caressing the bright
pattern of worked silver where the five-inch-long blade joins
with the handle. It is a good knife, beautiful, full of power.
Tonight, if I must, I will use it to draw every drop of life from
her body.

But she mustn't come for me here. I wouldn't be safe. If she
doesn't find me here, she will know where to go. If she doesn't
know, then I will still be safe, and the knife will not be necessary.

I hope the knife is not necessary.

Eyotah rejoined Canaan. "I'm so sorry. This is a busy day
for me, even though this is my free hour. Often it's busier at
this time of day than during class time."

"I understand," Canaan said. "Black Mountain is not that far from Twin Mesas. I think I'll drive there."

"You would most likely get much more information from Kai's clan than I could ever get."

"I believe you're right."

"Be forewarned that you will have faulty cell phone reception there, at best."

"I'm accustomed to that," Canaan said. "It's spotty in our area, as well. Please tell me more about what you know."

"Kai always displayed an interest in the occult, in mind control, in anything concerned with human emotions, which was why he was so interested in what I had to teach him. He became a member of the Native American Church for a while—drawn, I'm sure, by the sect's use of peyote—but he had no interest in that brand of religion. He was seeking something, but I don't think he found it there."

"And he used his newly acquired mind control methods on a young woman?"

"Yes. From his studies with me he learned enough about hypnosis to guide this girl into a trance state. She thought she was in love with him, and she did anything he told her to do." Eyotah shook his head sadly. "Really messed her up for a while. She attacked a teacher who had reprimanded Kai for talking during a lecture. This girl tried several times to kill herself after he lost interest in her. Kai didn't know what he was doing. He had no right."

"Was all this in his file?"

"In my files, yes, along with my suspicion that the poor girl might have been a victim of Kai's practice of witchcraft. For a long time she spoke of the wolf within her, the wolf stalking her."

"Wolf...the witch. How did Kai get a job at our school? Surely my grandfather checked him out."

"As I said, Kai could be a charmer. He was intelligent, attractive, with plenty of charisma. Other professors on our staff didn't agree with my opinions, nor did they believe in any of the customs of my people, or Kai's." The lines in Eyotah's face deepened. "They were offended by my allegations against him, and since I had no proof, they ignored me."

"You mean he got away with what he did?" Canaan asked.

"For me, it was even worse than that. I tried to help the girl, since no one would accept my theory about her problem. The dean found me practicing a private Hopi ceremony with her to try to repair the damage. The board members were outraged. I nearly lost my job. In spite of my pleas for them to help me stop Kai, they graduated him early to get him out of my way, then told me he had left the state."

"They lied to you, then," Canaan said.

Eyotah nodded.

Canaan was amazed that such an educated man could be so duped.

"When I went to Black Mountain to verify what I'd been told, no one would speak to me about Kai. It was as if he were dead."

"Perhaps no one would talk to a Hopi about him," Canaan suggested.

"That's likely."

"That doesn't explain everything," Canaan said. "My grandfather is an astute man. He does background checks on every applicant."

"As I said, what I've told you isn't in his school records."

"But Kai's behavior all these years has not been anything like what you're describing," Canaan said. "Many years have passed without incident, until recently. I'm at a loss to understand why."

Doctor Whitter studied his hands for a moment. "Does Kai still have an aggressive personality? Does he like to be in control?"

"Yes, but it isn't as if he runs the school." What Canaan was hearing did not ring quite true about the Kai who had been known and loved at the school for so many years. Was it possible that Kai could have been able to fool so many for so long?

"What about your school directors?" Eyotah asked. "Have you had a large turnover?"

"Yes. No principal seems interested in staying for long."

"Maybe Kai did a good job with the children as long as he was allowed to dominate—and with a new principal, that's easier to do. It could be that as long as he got his way, he didn't feel the need to strike out. You see, Canaan, it has to do with power. There are people who dry up and die inside when they lose their ability to manipulate others."

"You're saying our former principals may have left because Kai never allowed them to do their jobs?"

"Did you have complaints about him?"

"Not many. Most of the complaints lodged with my grandfather over the years were not about Kai specifically."

"What were the complaints?" the professor asked.

"In several exit interviews with principals, my grandfather heard that they felt unable to make changes, even in small matters."

"Who directs the school now?" Eyotah asked.

"Our principal died recently from an unexplained illness. He was a good man, and he had a strong hand in everything."

"Then perhaps Kai's need to control was displayed in his

interaction with his students. Maybe you can find something out at Black Mountain after all these years." Eyotah leaned forward and held Canaan's gaze intently with his deep black eyes. "Canaan, if he's influencing the children, I think you should get him away by any means possible. If he's the same Kai Begay I remember, he could be stirring trouble you don't even know about."

"I'll get him out of there, no matter what it takes, as soon as I get back from Black Mountain." Canaan helped Doctor Whitter with his coat. "I want to know what I'm dealing with first."

"I don't believe you've had time for lunch. Our cafeteria is very close, and I would be glad to treat you."

"Thank you, Eyotah, but perhaps another time. You've been most helpful to me." Canaan said his farewell and rushed from the campus. There would be time for food after this ordeal was over.

## ✦ Chapter Thirty-Eight ✦

I replace the knife in its sheath and put it with the other things, then wrap my jacket around it in a secure bundle. I must hurry. There is no time to get another jacket to protect me against the coolness after the sun sets tonight. I will be able to run back and stay warm.

I am slinging the bundle over my shoulder as I jerk open the front door. I nearly collide with Steve Hunt.

"What the—" Instinctively, I take a step backward. "Steve, what are you doing here?" I hope I'm keeping the panic from my voice.

Steve doesn't speak, but crosses his arms, dark eyes burning with such hostility that I feel forced to take another step backward.

I swallow and force my breathing to slow, returning glare for glare. "Something bothering you, Steve?" I keep my voice cool and low. Could the earlier visitation by the young chanter have been warning me about this?

Steve's eyes narrow further. "Going somewhere? Maybe to your haunted hogan down in the valley?"

My skin pricks with sharp needles of foreboding. A faint whisper reaches me, blown by the breeze.... *"Racing Deer is running..."*

Steve steps forward. "You thought I didn't know?" Anger infects his voice as heavily as onions from lunch infect his breath. "You kill my mother and father and you try to seduce my little brother, and you think I'm going to watch from my safe job in the cafeteria and let you get away with it?"

I finger the bundle of my jacket.

"Why did you kill my parents?" Steve demanded.

"I am sorry about your parents," I tell him, admitting nothing. Killing is not why I do what I do.

"How can you say that!" he shouts, pressing closer to me. "You're not sorry, or you wouldn't have—"

"You're upset, and you need someone to blame. I don't know why you've decided to blame me so long after the—"

"Because I know. My father knew. My mother knew. I heard them talking. I heard my mother tell my father about sending blood samples to the CDC, and somehow you knew, and you killed her."

I am so stunned I can only stare at him. This can't be happening. What if the Centers for Disease Control has received those samples? What if they know?

"What did my mother see that made you kill her?"

"I don't know what you're talking about," I say.

"You know, all right. You know."

I can honestly say that I do not, but I realize that Steve will not believe me. I think quickly. If Wendy sent blood samples to the CDC, the results would be back, and the Feds would be crawling all over this region of the country by now. Her death must have stopped her from following up on her plan.

*Racing Deer...*

The voice calls to me, distracting me when I dare not be distracted.

I force my attention to Steve's angry scowl, the mask of misery that has covered him since his parents died. "Steve, your parents were good people. Don't tarnish their memory by trying to place blame where blame is not due. Their death was a tragic accident."

"No," he says through gritted teeth, shoving me backward. The thrust of his growing anger stirs my panic again. "You killed them. And that wasn't enough. You tried to hurt my brother."

"You've been listening to wild talk, Steve." I bring the bundle down from my shoulder and cradle it in my arms.

"Yes," he hisses. "The tales are wild. But true. True tales about an evil witch who commits murder and abuses little kids at a Christian school, where everybody is so trusting, it's impossible to believe what kind of creepy monster lives here."

*Racing Deer is running...*

I swat at the air to stop the voice, and Steve tenses, obviously ready to do battle with me.

"I'm not going to let you hurt my family again," he warns me. "You and your nasty witching sand that my sister took the blame for."

"Your sister is obviously confused. I don't know why she pulled those pranks, but I knew nothing about them."

"You're going to leave us all alone. Until Canaan returns, I'm staying here to see that you do."

I take another step backward, this time intentionally. I will see how strong this young buck really is.

Only the whispers come again. I have to talk to drown out the sound. I'm surprised Steve doesn't hear them. "You were a good athlete when you were in school, Steve. I don't understand why you didn't go on to college. Your brother and sister would have been well cared for here. You didn't have to stay and work. If you were to talk to Canaan about these crazy theories of yours, you might be disappointed to find that he is more likely to believe me than you."

"Not if I tell him everything. Not if Jamey tells him what you did to him."

"Why would he believe you? All you do is lurk in the kitchen, glaring at everyone who comes into the cafeteria. You're obviously half-crazed with grief, and the burden of caring for your family has sent you over the edge. Not a good environment for Jamey or April, I wouldn't imagine. It might even be possible for you to lose your family."

I back farther from sight of the open door.

Steve follows me, his gaze locked with mine, his chin inches from mine. "It doesn't matter what happens to me after this. All I have to do is raise an alarm."

I wish I could close the door, but Steve is alert to my thoughts, my every move. I feel as if he can read my mind.

I slip my hand beneath the flap of my jacket bundle and feel the cold, hard handle of the knife. The whispers grow and echo in my head: *Racing Deer is running...racing...*

The knife warms immediately to my touch as I slip it from its sheath. I can feel the power surge into me from the knife; I can even control the whispers. It makes the spirit angry, I can tell, because it tries to take form, undulating in an aura around Steve.

As my focus narrows, my eyes narrow, and Steve's eyes mirror sudden confusion.

I know just where to thrust the blade, and my mouth waters with anticipation as I think about the power this will give me. I need this power.

Perhaps the spirit has even sent Steve here for me.

I grasp the turquoise handle tightly in my right hand, my gaze darting toward the spirit as it floats around Steve.

In one fluid movement, I bring the knife out of its hiding place, thrusting the blade into Steve's chest.

With a low, guttural cry, he bends forward. His eyes glaze with pain. I tighten my hand to remove the knife.

But a white-hot stab of fire streaks through me. The undulating aura around Steve disappears, and my vision clears. I hold tightly to my knife as Steve stumbles back against the wall. As I step away from the boy, the pain in my gut shoots the length of my body.

I drop the turquoise handle and clutch at my abdomen, doubling over. My fingers skim the wooden handle of a kitchen knife. I look at Steve, and see a gleam of triumph mingle with the pain in his expression. He has come prepared.

His face presses into the wall, and a groan escapes him as he falls to the carpeted floor.

I'm still the stronger one, after all. Only half the kitchen knife blade penetrates my abdomen, and though sticky blood covers my hands, I can't be sure how much is mine and how much is Steve's.

Gritting my teeth against the pain, I wrap both hands around the wooden handle and jerk the knife free. A scream of pain spurts from my throat, quickly bitten back. For a moment, I think I will join Steve in his death throes on the floor, but the wall steadies me. I take deep breaths. It will be okay. I just have to stop the bleeding and get to the hogan.

I hold the knife up and examine it, shiny with blood, coated with the energy of my own life force. The hogan. I must get to the hogan.

Preston stepped from the cool interior of the laboratory into the bright, hot Phoenix sunshine, only to be accosted by a masked man. Not only was he masked, he was gloved and in goggles.

"Sir? Didn't you just drive here from the school at Twin Mesas?" the mask asked.

"That's right."

"Would you please come with me?"

"Why? What's wrong?"

"Dr. Sheridan needs to speak with you before you drive back."

"Okay, but if he needs information, I'm not the man for him. I was sent on this mission specifically because I don't have medical knowledge."

"Why is that?"

Was it Preston's imagination, or was this man beginning to sound more like a police officer than a member of the scientific research staff? "They've got their hands full at the clinic doing year-end physicals. The person he needs to talk with is Dr. Canaan York."

The man nodded, though Preston could not, of course, see any expression on his face.

"Would you please just step this way for a moment?"

Preston relented and followed the man around the corner of the building and into a side door. He hoped this would not take long; he wanted to get back to the school. In spite of the mysteries that seemed to have been solved, he felt uneasy about this whole situation.

The man in protective gear led Preston to a large office lined with vials, books, a microscope of impressive proportions, all in organized chaos. Behind a sizable desk sat a blond-haired man with a ponytail, an earring and linebacker shoulders.

He stood and shook Preston's hand, introducing himself as Dr. Tim Sheridan. "Canaan told me he was sending a courier today, but he tells me you've been at the school this week?"

Preston took the chair Dr. Sheridan indicated. "Yes, but as I told your masked friend, I'm nonmedical."

Dr. Sheridan waved a hand at the masked man dismissively. "Don't mind him. He always dresses like that. He sees a virus behind every test tube. He was doing some lab work when he found out you were here. He knew I wanted to talk to you, so he ran out without removing the gear. I think he secretly likes to freak people out."

"He should be pleased, then," Preston said. "It worked."

"I spoke with Canaan for a few minutes this morning, but I didn't have much time. Was anyone sick when you left the school earlier today?"

"Uh, sick? No."

"The clinic didn't see anyone with a bad headache, high fever, severe body aches?"

"The clinic staff was giving regular physicals. I was in the cafeteria for breakfast, and all I heard was everyone speculating about who had played the latest hoax on the school nurse."

"I understand the principal of the school died recently of an unexplained illness," Dr. Sheridan said. "Unfortunately, there was no autopsy done on the body. And yet we're getting all these vials of blood to test on other people."

"I think Canaan's worried about a rash of recent deaths there," Preston said. "Two were accidents, not an illness. In fact, the whole student body seems pretty healthy to me. A young man who is helping out in the clinic told me four students reported sick around the same time as the principal, but they're fine now. I watch the track team running in the desert every day. They all look healthy."

"I believe the blood we've just been testing is from members of your track team. In light of your news, I've decided it isn't necessary to quarantine you." The doctor grinned at Preston.

Preston frowned at the doctor. "What aren't you telling me?"

"We found something on our electron microscope just a few minutes ago," Dr. Sheridan said. "A filament-shaped virus that is on the watch list for bioterrorism. That particular shape could belong to Ebola or Marburg."

Preston felt his heart begin a dance in his rib cage. "I've heard of Ebola, but not Marburg."

"Neither is endemic to this country, which is one reason I'm questioning you. If those children had either virus, they wouldn't be running out in the desert with their track team, they'd be dead."

"Do you think there's been some kind of mistake? Who would strike an underpopulated region of the country? It doesn't make sense."

"Canaan told me this morning that no one at the school has traveled out of the country in quite some time," Dr. Sheridan said. "No one from another country has visited the school."

"Where, specifically, would the visitor have come from for this infection to have been carried?" Preston asked.

"Africa. Canaan also vouched for you this morning, which

means I can trust you not to share this information with anyone except medical personnel at the school, until it's definitive."

"That's correct."

Dr. Sheridan nodded. "Good."

"How dangerous are these viruses?"

"In my opinion, they are the most deadly diseases on the planet. Latest studies show a mortality rate of ninety-two percent for Marburg virus. With every outbreak, that rate increases."

"There's no cure?"

"How'd you guess? However, with advance warning and proper, aggressive medical support, I believe those numbers can be much better."

"I'll be sure to raise the alarm if I so much as hear someone sneeze at the school."

"There is one other possibility I will need to check out before I call Canaan," Dr. Sheridan said. "The members of the Filoviridae family, Ebola and Marburg, closely resemble viruses of the family Rhabdoviridae, which I am hoping is the case with this. I'll have to run the PCR test to be absolutely certain it isn't Ebola or Marburg."

"So if it's the other virus you mentioned, the rab—"

"The rhabdoviridae," the doctor supplied.

"Okay, if it's this virus, it's no big deal?"

"It's a big deal, all right, but much more believable. It's rabies."

Preston closed his eyes. So it possibly wasn't bioterrorism, it was possibly rabies. How could it get much worse?

"I'll be sure to let Canaan know as soon as I get the final results," Dr. Sheridan said.

"Would you mind calling me, as well?"

"I will, but remember, we cannot afford a panic on our hands. No one must be told about this until we know for sure.

Then, depending on the results, I could be calling in the CDC in quick order."

"My friends traveled from Missouri to Twin Mesas to help with the shortage of medical staff. They can be trusted to keep their heads."

"Okay, but no one else. I'll have to contact the CDC and send samples to them for further testing. Until we know something for sure, you need to lie low. However, I can call in the Rapid Response Deployment Team from the CDC if my findings are confirmed for Ebola or Marburg."

"Meanwhile," Preston said, "I'll get back to the school so I can pack my bags, grab my friends and get out of the state."

Dr. Sheridan smiled as he came out from behind his desk and slapped Preston on the shoulder. "As you said, no one at the school is sick right now. We can hope for the best. Have a safe trip back."

# Chapter Thirty-Nine

Preston had never much cared for cell phones. Back home, it seemed that when he needed to use his, he was either out of range or out of juice. Today he'd at least thought to bring his phone, but in an effort to beat the mad Friday-afternoon rush out of the city, he'd delayed trying to call Canaan. Now that he'd finally escaped the traffic, he found that Canaan was either out of range or had his phone turned off.

So he called Sheila. It was so good to hear her voice.

"Are you on your way back?" she asked.

"That's right. I'm riding the wave of speeders right now. They do like to test their engines out here in the wide-open spaces, don't they?"

"I wouldn't know. According to you, I drive like a granny."

"And I appreciate that in a woman. Have you had any sick patients since I left there today?"

"Not a one, although we've had a lot of healthy patients, and one who needed a shot."

"A shot?"

"Standing orders from Canaan for shots once a month."

"Good. Sheila, you need to be careful. You and Blaze have to take precautions if anyone comes in sick."

"I'm pretty sure we'll be okay. Why the sudden concern?"

"When I was at the lab, a Dr. Sheridan questioned me about the vials of blood he's been testing." Preston told her about the Ebola/Marburg/rabies concern.

"Well, rabies would make sense," she said. "I'm sure that's what he's seeing. You need to get the infected child started on the rabies shots as soon as possible."

"Okay, but just to put my mind at ease, you're sure you never touched a dog on the road the other day, or an animal of any kind, or—"

"That's right, so relax," she said.

"Just take precautions, okay? I'll keep riding the wave of traffic. If it keeps going as it is—"

"You know, I wouldn't mind if you drove a little more like a granny and got here alive."

He told her again to be careful and disconnected. Whatever squiggles Dr. Sheridan thought he saw in his high-powered microscope, Preston wanted to have faith that he would find no problem next time he looked.

Canaan had never been a speeder, but this afternoon he'd driven from Flagstaff to the vicinity of Black Mountain in record time. Cell reception had been undependable, and now he would be out of range, but he needed a little more information to go on. If he remembered correctly, at least four staff members came from the Black Mountain area. Kai Begay, Betsy Two Horses, Doc Cottonwood and Jane Witherbe had common backgrounds, though they were different ages. All had been with the school at least since before Evelyn Metcalf's death.

Dr. Whitter had given Canaan good directions to the tiny settlement, and a man on horseback pointed him to the house where Kai Begay's younger sister, Sara Pringle, now lived.

When Canaan reached the dwelling, he decided *hut* described her home more aptly. Covered in tar paper, it crouched behind several scrawny piñons. Two gray-snouted stock dogs erupted from those trees, barking at the sight of Canaan's sedan. An old, wrinkled woman sat on a wooden chair that barely fit onto the rickety planks of the front porch. She yelled at the dogs, then nodded at Canaan as he approached.

He returned her nod and introduced himself. "I came to talk to Sara Pringle. Do I have the right place?"

Before the woman could answer the front door opened, emitting the aroma of mutton and frying onions. A plump, middle-aged woman leaned out, her black gaze settling on him in a familiar intent stare. She looked to be at least twenty years younger than Kai.

"Are you Sara Pringle?" he asked.

She looked him over for a moment, then nodded.

"I'm Canaan York, principal at Twin Mesas School."

She frowned. "Why are you so far from your school?"

"Your brother is a teacher there," he explained. "I had hoped to ask you a little about him."

Her eyes clouded with confusion. She stepped out onto the porch, her heavy footfalls making the wooden slats creak and groan. "My brothers are both guides at Canyon De Chelly."

Canaan nodded. He knew Kai had younger twin brothers. "I mean your older brother, Kai," Canaan said.

"I have only two brothers," she said. "You must have the wrong Sara Pringle." She turned and stepped back in the door.

The sound of many small animal footsteps filled the silence, accompanied by the bleats of sheep and goats.

Canaan tugged at the bill of his cap and sighed in frustration. He turned from the door to stare at the ghostly white shadows spilling around the side of the house in the murky darkness. The two stock dogs bounded from the porch in silence to herd the flock of sheep to the back.

"Don't blame Sara," the old woman said from her perch behind Canaan.

He turned to regard her. What did she know about Kai?

The woman pulled a brightly woven green-and-yellow blanket more snugly around her stooped shoulders. "She was a young child when Kai left. She doesn't remember him and his name was never mentioned after he was forced away like an unwanted dog."

Canaan studied her. "Are you related to Kai?"

"I was his mother's sister. She died last year. He doesn't even know."

"I am sorry. I didn't come here to cause your family trouble, but to help my students. What happened to Kai? What did he do?"

The woman bowed her head, as if ashamed. "It was not all his fault. We think the wolf got to him early, right after the twins were born. My sister had too much to do, with Sara and the twins so little. I had my own children to watch. We didn't know…"

"Didn't know what?"

A slight breeze stirred the woman's gray hair, and she pulled her blanket closer. "You say you know Kai?"

"Yes, he's a teacher who works with many of the children every day." Canaan squatted before her. "It's important that I know what happened to him, what he did."

"He always wanted to be a doctor, you know. He was always exploring science, interested in things he couldn't learn around here. There was an evil chanter who used to live in a cove near the foot of the mountain." She gestured in the direction of the ridge Canaan had seen on the way here. "After the twins were born, Kai spent less time at home, and I think he sought the chanter, to learn more of his ways. This chanter sought the children, and we had to be careful, and keep our kids away."

"I heard that White Wolf was the last of the witches to be put to death by The People."

"Yes, but not before he infected many of our children." She nodded and stared into the distance. "He always sought the young ones."

"What was it Kai did?"

For a moment the old woman didn't answer. Her lips folded together in a bouquet of wrinkles. She straightened her shoulders and met Canaan's gaze. "He abandoned the way of his people."

Canaan stared at her.

"He told me of the great sorrow he felt over the things he had done in service to White Wolf. So he sought the way of the white man. The white man's God stole his spirit."

"How did this happen?"

"There was a missionary who held some tent meetings in the area when Kai was here. He gave in to the missionary's God."

"You mean he became a Christian?"

The old woman nodded. "He renounced his standing in the clan."

"Why would he have to do that?"

"Many families here have hated the white man for many years because of White Wolf."

"Are you saying the wolf was a white man?"

"That's what I'm saying."

"So they wouldn't turn against Kai for his involvement with White Wolf—a Navajo werewolf—but they evicted him from the clan because he accepted the white man's God?"

She shrugged. "Everyone knows the white man's God is more powerful than any wolf."


The sounds of chattering children and thundering footsteps had long ago subsided late Friday afternoon. Most of the children who were going home for the weekend had been picked up and many of the teachers had gone into town.

Sheila knew that the school ran only a skeleton crew on the weekends. On a campus that housed a hundred and fifty adults and children during the week, perhaps only thirty were remaining this weekend.

Sheila stood holding the telephone as she waited for Betsy to answer. "I've tried twice in the past three hours," she told Blaze. "No answer."

"Maybe she's trying to sleep," Blaze said. "And maybe she's using earplugs so nobody'll bother her. When I'm not feeling well, I don't answer the phone, either."

Sheila scowled at Blaze as she disconnected. "I'm going to her apartment."

"Okay, but didn't you tell her to rest? How can she rest if she keeps getting interrupted? You might just make her mad."

"I'd rather make her mad than take chances." She picked up a medical bag and hurried to the door. "I'll probably be right back with my tail between my legs."

"Okay," Blaze said darkly, "but don't come crying to me if she kicks that tail."

## ❧ Chapter Forty ❧

What is it about Sheila's presence in this place that causes trouble? It's all gone wrong again. The deaths…why do there have to be so many deaths?

I know Sheila can't be blamed for everything that has happened. If the Hunts had not grown suspicious of the time their son spent out in the desert at night—if Tad had not followed his son—they would never have died. If Steve had not come to me today, he would still be alive.

But then…if Tad and Wendy had not died, I would not have stopped Wendy from sending those samples. I never wanted to kill them, but it was necessary.

It is taking me so long to reach the hogan this time. My legs don't want to work. I stop often to rest. It is so hot, even though a bank of clouds covers the afternoon sky.

It will grow dark early tonight.

Sheila is beginning to remember too much. I knew she

must never come back to the school. I knew the spirit I serve would order her death. But what if I can make her forget again? I was able to control her once before.

I reach the hogan at last, where there are medical supplies. I take several thick gauze squares from the medicine drawer, dampen them with peroxide and place them in the band of my pants, over the wound, gritting my teeth and moaning with pain. My whole body burns with fever, and it cannot be from this fresh wound. What I fear is something much worse.

I take an elastic bandage and wrap it around the wound to hold the gauze in place. I can get through this. The spirits are all around me, I can feel them. I am strong and able to endure great pain.

I eat a peyote button. This will help with the worst of the pain. I have to do what I was sent here to do. I must find the power to stop these discoveries and get on with my work.

Power and wealth await.


Canaan left the canyon behind. It was not yet dusk, though a bank of clouds made it seem much later. It felt so dark to him—the history of Black Mountain, as well as the attitude he'd sensed in the people. No wonder Kai hadn't wanted to return home during summer breaks.

For the first time today, Canaan began to doubt the wisdom of his fact-seeking mission. Was he on a wild-goose chase? Had Sheila's memories and the paranoia of the children diverted him from what he should have been doing today at the school?

He considered calling Eyotah Whitter and asking him about other former students who were now staff members at Twin Mesas. If the professor had had such insight about Kai, what might he know about Doc? Or Jane? They were both from Black Mountain and had been at the school when Sheila's mother died.

Had Eyotah instructed them in Navajo legends and customs and hypnosis techniques? Certainly a Navajo werewolf—or a white witch embedded in the Black Mountain culture—could have gotten to either of them as effectively as Eyotah suspected Kai had been influenced.

As soon as Canaan had cell reception, he called Eyotah, only to be bounced to voice mail. He decided not to leave a message.

Was it just wishful thinking to believe that Kai had truly experienced a change of heart all those years ago, when he attended that missionary meeting? Yes, he still struggled with the need to control, and he still resented whites, but considering his childhood and the hostility he'd been raised to believe was normal, he'd come a long way.

While Canaan still held the cell phone in his hand, it chimed. He answered. It was Preston.

"Did your friend Dr. Sheridan get in touch with you?" Preston asked.

"No, I just got back into cell range."

"You'd better check your messages, because I'm sure he'd have called you about his findings. Ever heard of Marburg virus?"

"Marburg? I think that's something like Ebola, which originated in Africa. Why would—"

"He found Marburg in the blood he received earlier this week," Preston said. *"All four boys."*

Stunned, Canaan gripped the steering wheel and stared at the road ahead of him. "But that's impossible! We're on the other side of the world! There's never been a single event of—"

"It's confirmed," Preston said. "When I was there, he wasn't sure if it was rabies, Marburg or Ebola, because the shape of the virus is very similar, but he has since called me. He isolated Marburg. From what he told me, that virus appears to have a higher death rate every time there's a new outbreak. I have to tell you this scares the dickens out of me."

"But we haven't had an outbreak," Canaan said. "Nobody's been sick enough for it to be a killer virus."

"Bob Jaffrey," Preston said.

"One man, and he had low resistance due to a preexisting condition. No caretakers fell ill, no coworkers, which is what would have happened with an outbreak." Marburg? How was it possible?

"Those four boys had been sick."

"Very mild cases," Canaan said. "Nothing deadly."

"Canaan, listen to me," Preston said. "Dr. Sheridan has called the CDC to the school."

Canaan's hands nearly bent the steering wheel. He couldn't believe what he was hearing. "But without outward signs of an outbreak—"

"They're on their way," Preston said. "The school has been notified, and the staff on-site are handling the situation. I'd say the campus will be swarming with CDC and FBI agents within a couple of hours."

Canaan forced himself to focus on the road and remain calm—not an easy task. He'd known there was a problem, but this?

There would have to be a quarantine, of course. But a large majority of kids, teachers and dorm parents had already left for the weekend.

This was crazy! "Preston, are you sure they had the right blood samples? Maybe a mistake was made."

"They checked and rechecked."

Canaan thought about the outbreak of unidentified illness at another school, which he'd heard about just this morning. If this madness was true, then the danger multiplied many times over.

"Do you realize that it's possible, if Marburg is at the school, that you and I might have risked a lot of lives today?" Canaan continued to quake at the implications. "When you stopped to fill the van's tank, how many people did you see? I was at the university, for goodness' sake."

"Tell me what you found today that might help us narrow this down."

"Just more questions." Canaan forced back the fear. Panicking now would only complicate a horrible situation. "I can't even begin to connect today's information with the Marburg virus."

"It might help if you bounce the questions off me," Preston said. "I'm unbiased except for my *very good friendship* with Sheila. You could probably use my opinion, hard as it might be to admit it."

Ordinarily, Canaan would have responded to those little digs, but he was in shock, beyond any kind of reaction. Instead, he shared his concerns with Preston, along with the information he had discovered today in Flagstaff and Black Mountain.

"So you're doubting whether Kai is the culprit, due to his apparent conversion all those years ago," Preston said, and Canaan could hear the skepticism in his voice.

"That's right."

"You're willing to look for another suspect based on that information alone?"

"Judging by my experiences with Kai, in spite of his aggressive personality and gruffness, yes, I believe he had a true change of heart as a young man. I believe his constant diligence with the kids he mentors, and the fact that the children with whom he has had the closest bonds have remained true to their faith, attest to the good fruit of the spirit within him."

For a moment, Preston didn't reply, then he asked, "What do you think the witchcraft is all about?"

Even in the middle of a disaster, Canaan's evangelical radar picked up on Preston's discomfort with the subject of faith. "It's a Navajo belief that the motivation behind the witchcraft of a werewolf is greed for riches and power," he said.

"But wealth and power are the American dream," Preston said. "Didn't Johnny Jacobs establish his schools to make the American dream more attainable for the Navajo?"

The comparison disturbed Canaan. "I don't think my grandfather's desire to give the Navajo people the same opportunity as white people to operate in the world today was a bad thing."

"But often it seems there are more and more people seeking wealth and influence at the expense of others," Preston said. "It's one reason I left the world of finance."

"I've noticed that in my profession, as well," Canaan said, "even when individuals don't recognize avarice in themselves. I see no reason to work to death to stockpile riches, and I think my attitude comes from the Navajo influence in my life."

"I'm surprised at you, Canaan. I would have expected you to say Christianity was what influenced you the most."

Canaan grimaced. He was losing his touch. Preston was doing a good job of distracting him, and he appreciated it more than Preston would ever know.

"Here's the rub," Preston said. "If this Navajo werewolf is behaving true to form, then explain to me why you're investigating the backgrounds of staff members at all. Because I sure don't see any of them getting rich."

Canaan hesitated. "It's possible this wolf could be interested in another kind of payoff, easily interwoven with the practices of this wolf as I understand them."

"Like what?"

"Sexual child abuse." The very thought sickened Canaan. "Sheila suggested it to me earlier this week, and I refused to even consider the possibility."

"That doesn't seem to have a connection to anything happening at the school now," Preston said.

"There isn't necessarily a connection between the haunting of our children and this virus."

"But you've suspected a connection all along," Preston said. "I've come to believe this past week that you're a wise man. I think you were right. I've considered this today as I drove, and two ideas I believe are significant. For one, Sheila never mentioned hearing a rifle report last Friday just before she had her blowout, and she would have heard it. Her window would have been open, because her Jeep has no air-conditioning."

"You're thinking there was a silencer?"

"Exactly. An eleven-year-old wouldn't have a silencer on his rifle. So was it really a shepherd boy who did the shooting, or was something else going on?"

"For instance?" Canaan asked.

"I'm curious about what Sheila really saw out in the desert. Granted, the color of her vehicle would have blended into the desert background, so the stray bullet could have been accidental. But the lack of a rifle report bothers me."

"The boy admitted to the shooting," Canaan said.

"I think that, for a price, it might be easy to find someone willing to admit to something he didn't do, especially since he's too young to get into real trouble. But here's my second concern, which Dr. Sheridan suggested, and it's a doozie. Have you considered bioterrorism?"

Again, Canaan felt the shock run through him. "At Twin Mesas?" This could not be happening!

# ❧ *Chapter Forty-One* ❧

Preston pulled the phone away from his ear. Canaan was upset, he could tell. The love and pride the doctor felt for his grandfather's schools made him emotional.

"That was my response at first," Preston said. "Why would anyone want to attack one of the least populated areas in the country? But what if the attack isn't limited to Twin Mesas? You just happened to be suspicious of a recent death, so you had children's blood checked by the state lab. Dr. Sheridan couldn't believe the result of his first test, because, as he said, these kids would be dead, and they're not. What if the Marburg virus has been somehow altered?"

"Altered?"

"I don't know what you'd call it," Preston said. "I'm not a scientist. I know nothing about this stuff, but I sure do have an active imagination, and it's been driving me crazy for the past couple of hours."

"It's working on me pretty well, too."

"For instance," Preston said, "if Twin Mesas and one of its sister schools turned out to be the only places involved, what if this is a sort of double-blind study to see if this weapon of destruction can be effectively suspended, hibernated in a sense, possibly to detonate later? The schools would be ideal locations for testing, because the manifestations of Marburg, according to Dr. Sheridan, resemble hantavirus, which is endemic to this area, and therefore much less suspicious should there be an illness."

"Where did you learn so much about bioterrorism?"

"I got a crash course from Dr. Sheridan," Preston said. "So you think this is a possible scenario?"

"I hate to admit it, but it might be."

"I can't tell you how sorry I am to hear that," Preston said.

There was a long silence, then Canaan said, "Some might say our positions in this case are God ordained."

"Bioterrorism?" The cynic in Preston mocked the man's words, but another part of him almost wanted to believe. "God ordained?"

"He doesn't stop all the evil in the world, but He can place His people at the right place to fight it." Canaan said. "My so-called paranoia about the strange actions of the children, Sheila's arrival at the school, plus her recollection of some of what happened to her as a child, might all be guided by God to help us stop whatever is happening here."

"Now you sound like Sheila," Preston said.

"Your arrival with Blaze would also be God-given, as I've already stated. 'For all things work together for the good of those who love Him,'" he quoted. "I'm clinging to that right now."

Preston couldn't remember the last time he had actually sat still and listened to a minisermon directed his way without

protest. It would be so comforting to believe that a larger, be-
nevolent power was in control of this madness.

"My grandfather used to love to remind everyone that there
are no atheists in foxholes," he told Canaan.

"I've never been in a foxhole," Canaan said, "but I'm
grasping the concept today. I just have to keep reminding
myself that God has always proven faithful in everything.
Maybe we should just back off a moment and let Him guide."

Preston stared at the road before him, remembering that
Canaan shared a connection with Sheila that Preston did not.
It frustrated him. And yet…as Sheila had noted many times
in the past, he seemed to be protesting too much. He had been
more concerned about retaining his independence from God,
and showing others how independent he was, than actually
listening to Sheila's heart in this matter. If Kai honestly had
changed so completely after his encounter with Christ, considering the influence of Navajo witchcraft, then there was
definitely something—the same something he had always
glimpsed in Sheila, Canaan, Blaze and his family.

Sometimes it felt to Preston as if he was the only holdout
among his friends and relatives.

"Preston?"

"I'm here."

"How far are you from the school?"

"About forty-five minutes now. You?"

"The same," Canaan said.

"I'll race you," Preston told him and disconnected.

Preston tried Sheila's cell again, and was startled when a
deep male voice answered. A disgruntled, familiar male voice.

"You aren't Sheila," Preston said.

"Sure ain't," Blaze said. "Where are you, man? Everything's coming down hard, the CDC and FBI are on the way and the Navajo Tribal Police are already here, directing traffic. They think we really have the Marburg virus. What's up? Why didn't you warn me?"

"I did warn you it was a possibility. After Dr. Sheridan's last call, I had to reach Canaan first."

"And he ain't here, either. Where is he?"

"We're both on our way, Blaze. You need to sit tight. Just cooperate with everybody and help as much as you can. You know where the medical files are."

"I've got chaos here. The staff who are still here have been ordered to keep everyone else at the school and to call the others back as fast as possible. No one's allowed to leave, and we've got two sick people already—not sure if they're really sick, or if they're just scared."

"Where's Sheila?"

"She took off across campus before the whole ruckus started, and, of course, she left her cell phone behind in her purse. She never carries this thing on her. I'm gonna get her a special hook—"

"Why did she take off across campus?"

"Worried about a patient, why else?"

"Last time I spoke with her, she told me there weren't any patients."

"It was Betsy, in for her monthly shot. Sheila sent her home."

"What was wrong with her?"

"Just pain. I guess she's used to it, though. She's got rheumatoid arthritis, and she had a bad flare-up this week."

"A bad flare-up of pain? Blaze, that's one of the first symptoms of the Marburg virus."

"Well, I know that. I've done as much reading up on this thing as I could since I heard about it. But pain is also one of the first symptoms of arthritis and probably a thousand other diseases. That doesn't narrow it down much, and Betsy is arthritic."

"But Marburg has been confirmed."

"I hear you, so what should we do?"

"Sheila didn't take protective gear with her, did she?"

"She had that medical case with her. It's loaded with protective gear. Remember, this is plague country."

"But she doesn't know to use—"

"Even though she doesn't know yet that Marburg is confirmed, she's been alerted, and she's smart enough to use the gear. Have some faith in her, Preston."

"Isn't there anyone you could send after her?"

"Are you kidding? With the panic going on here? But you just reminded me of something else I need to worry about. This shot Betsy gets? It could make her especially vulnerable to the virus. The drug weakens the immune system."

"Did Sheila take Betsy's temperature when she was at the clinic?"

"Betsy wouldn't let her. Didn't want anything but her shot, so she could go lie down."

"I'm less than an hour away, and Canaan's on his way there. Hold things together until someone gets there to relieve you."

"I don't have much choice."

"Remember this is why you wanted to come to Arizona. You wanted the experience."

"I'm getting it. I don't think I want to take any more road trips with you. I've got to go. There's another patient coming in the door. She looks awful. You just hurry back."

Reluctantly, Preston disconnected. A couple of cars passed

him, exceeding eighty miles per hour. He knew, because he was doing eighty-two. He upped the cruise control to eighty-five, and found himself praying again.

It was getting to be a habit.

## ᴔ *Chapter Forty-Two* ᴔ

Sheila turned away from the dark windows of Betsy's apartment and walked past two buildings to the cafeteria. She'd have expected to smell something cooking, but no aromas hung in the air.

She found one of the cook's helpers, a young woman named Carla, rushing through the kitchen, slapping sandwiches together on the long worktable, shoving chips into bowls, chopping fruit. She barely acknowledged Sheila.

"Have you seen Betsy?" Sheila asked.

"No, and I haven't seen Steve, either. He said he'd cover for Betsy, but he's probably forgotten."

Sheila thanked her and turned to leave when Tanya Swift burst through the front door, followed by Jamey Hunt.

"April's run off, Sheila!" Tanya said. "I saw her running out into the desert this afternoon right after school, and Jamey says she hasn't come back."

"I think she's mad," Jamey said. "She got in trouble for playing those tricks on you, and she's been pouting all day."

"Well, she's a big girl, and she'll probably come back on her own," Sheila said.

"But she was running after somebody," Tanya said. "The person walked all bent over, too far away for me to recognize."

"Betsy walks all hunched over when she's hurting," Jamey said.

"But why would Betsy go walking into the desert when she's in that much pain?" Sheila asked. It didn't make sense.

Tanya nudged Jamey with her elbow. "You'd better tell her everything."

The boy shoved his hands into his pockets and looked down, his glossy black hair hanging into his dark brown eyes. "The wolf tried to get me last night, but I didn't let him."

Sheila stared at him in astonishment.

He squinted up at her. "He gave me something horrible to eat that made me sick, and he talked about serving some spirit that wasn't God. I showed him this necklace." He held up the gold-and-turquoise cross. "I think it scared him. I don't remember much after that, just being sick, and running as fast as I could back home."

"Who is the wolf?" Sheila asked. "Where did you meet with him?"

Jamey shrugged. "He's the wolf. He's himself. He came to me when I was sleeping."

"Like in a dream?" Sheila asked.

"Like for real. He was standing beside my bed and he woke me up. He talked with a growl, but he kept it quiet, and he had a wolf's head and fur and everything. He told me I was selected for the power ritual the next night. He told me to walk out into the desert, to follow the smoke. There was this tent, and the smoke came out the middle top, like a smoke hole in a hogan, only it wasn't a hogan."

"What did he try to do to you?" Sheila asked.

Jamey shrugged, grimacing. "Some kind of weird ritual to make me strong."

"So he was trying to drug you so you wouldn't remember," Sheila said.

"But I did remember…some of it, anyway. I told my brother about it. Steve was mad, and I think he was going to tell Betsy about it so he could get out of kitchen duty and go after the wolf himself."

Sheila swallowed hard. "If Steve told Betsy, then she would have gone after that wolf herself." The thought of hiking into the desert, where the object of Sheila's nightmares loomed, sent cold sweat sliding down her spine. Witchcraft, Betsy had said.

But Betsy shouldn't be out walking in the desert alone in her condition. What could she possibly have been thinking?

"So that's why Betsy didn't answer her phone or come to the door when I knocked," she told the kids. "Well, I know she's in pain, and I have pain meds in my pack, so there's no reason to return to the clinic."

"You're going with us to find them?" Tanya asked.

"No." Sheila led the way back out of the cafeteria. "You two go to the clinic and tell Blaze where I've gone. If he's free, tell him to come join me, but I want both of you to stay on campus. Just show me the way April went."

"It doesn't take two people to carry a message," Tanya said. "I'm going with you."

Jamey protested, and was overridden. His mission was to

take the message to Blaze, and send Blaze into the desert when he could get away.

Jamey took off at a run toward the clinic. For a moment, Sheila considered trying to drive her Jeep across the desert, but the trails were too narrow for a vehicle, and in spite of the four-wheel capabilities of the Jeep, she didn't like the prospect of soft sand. When she was a child, she remembered her father's car getting stuck all the way up to the fenders.

Tanya broke into a jog beside Sheila. "What if we find the wolf?"

"Greater is He that is in me than he that is in the world."

Sheila started to pray.

The cedar chips flare into flames quickly when I light them. I watch them burn as I chew another peyote button. It will draw the spirit closer, past the pain, past the fever that burns with increasing ferocity.

I pull on my skin, mold my face, streaking the colors so familiar in the ritual. I pull on the necklaces and bracelets of turquoise, coral, agate and silver. In spite of the pain, I leave nothing out.

As smoke spirals through the hole in the center of the hogan—the real hogan, where I keep all my supplies—I pull on the head, glad of the larger eye slits at the top of the snout. I become the wolf, sinking my thoughts, my whole being, into this spirit. I become the spirit as the power surges through me. I will be all powerful once again and I will be healed.

Though I have lost much blood, the wound is not my utmost worry, but the fever that has spiked in the past few hours. I've always been so careful with the vials, yet the fever, the fatigue…it is time to move from denial. I need the immunoglobulin.

A slight sound from outside—a whisper of a footstep—makes me jerk in surprise, and the wound burns in my gut. I feel the warm blood spilling again.

I pull the wolf skin more tightly around my shoulders and turn to watch the doorway.

A thin shadow darkens the ground outside. "H-hello?"

My breath catches. It's that brat, April. "What do you want?" My voice is the wolf's voice, low and harsh as a growl of anger. The spirit of the wolf is in me, and I am no longer myself.

Silence. As well she might be silent in the face of the wolf's anger. What right does she have to stalk me to my private hogan, my headquarters? She has no idea what this means.

I step from the shadows into the entryway, the wolf in full regalia. Her small, dark eyes widen at the sight of me. She tenses, like a startled rabbit. She looks down at my jewelry, then back up at my head, obviously terrified. Good.

"Did you follow me?" I demand.

Slowly she nods.

I raise my arm and allow her to study the jewels as they catch the dim light of the fire, then I step forward with the graceful glide of the wolf and lay my hand on her skinny shoulder. I could snap her neck with one quick jerk.

Her body shudders beneath my touch. She takes a deep breath and straightens her spine. "D-did you see my brother?"

I feel my whole body stiffen. "What do you mean?"

"He was looking for you."

"I am not your brother's babysitter."

"But he was going to talk to you."

My hand tightens on the small, bony shoulder until April winces and tries to jerk free.

I release her, my mind frozen with the effort to control a surge of panic. "Did he say why?"

"He said it was none of my business."

I stare down into the young, petulant face. I must be careful now, or this little one may have to be sacrificed, as well. But I am a master of mind control. I will make no more mistakes. I can make this child forget.

## ❧ Chapter Forty-Three ❧

Sheila recognized the lay of the land in the deepening dusk. The path grew more familiar with each step she took. Had she walked here in the daytime, she may not have recognized it, but in the dim light, much like the light of a full moon, she did. She recalled walking this trail to a hogan. How many times?

It seemed that when she experienced anew the things she had experienced as a child, the memory returned with sharp clarity. Where before the pain had been blunted by time, her mother's death now stung with a vivid, cutting edge.

She couldn't recall feeling fear as she walked along this path. All she remembered was a sense of eagerness, though she didn't know why. Not yet. How had she been made to forget the past so completely for so long?

Undiscovered truths continued to lurk in her subconscious. Knowledge was one thing, but authentic, experiential memory remained frustratingly elusive.

"Tanya," she said softly, "do you remember walking this path?"

"Steve used to take Jamey and April and me out here a long time ago, when he was on the track team. We don't come this way anymore." Tanya sniffed. "Smell that?"

Sheila stopped and sniffed the air. "Cedar smoke."

Tanya's steps slowed. "Sheila?" Her voice suddenly trembled.

"It's okay. I'm here." Sheila had seen Twin Mesas from this spot before. She glanced to the right of the trail, where footsteps led through a stand of piñon trees.

"They must have gone into Piñon Valley," Sheila said, pointing to the ground.

Tanya hesitated, then said softly, "It's haunted."

Sheila remembered it had always been considered so. Jamey had said nothing about coming here the night he met with the wolf. He was supposed to walk in the desert and follow the smoke.

"Tanya, I wish I'd brought my cell phone. If Blaze was coming, he'd be here by now. Will you go back and get it for me?"

Tanya crossed her arms in front of her. "It won't work here, anyway. No reception."

"Then I need you to find a place where you can get reception and make a call for me."

"This is the haunted valley, Sheila. This is where the wolf lives. You can't go down there alone!"

"Nobody knows for sure where the wolf lives, and no matter who's down in the valley, I'm following these tracks. If the wolf is down there, do you want to leave April and Betsy to its mercy? I need you to call for help. I'd feel a whole lot safer if I knew Preston or Canaan was coming to back me up."

Tanya hesitated. Sheila took that as acquiescence.

"Jamey's probably following us, knowing him," Tanya said at last. "I guess I could go back and see if—"

"Good girl. Get my cell phone, try to call Preston. His speed dial number is on my menu. Do you know how to find that?"

"Sure I do, but—"

"I need him here. I never dreamed Betsy would come this far, especially not with her arthritis, and I may need help getting her back to the school."

Tanya studied Sheila's expression closely, then glanced down into the hollow, where Sheila could see that flash flood waters from years past had carved sharp grooves and ditches, steep drops and overhangs into the sandy soil.

The more Sheila thought about Jamey's confession in the cafeteria, the more convinced she was that someone was using some form of mind control. Since the discovery of GHB in Tanya's blood, Sheila had begun to wonder if she, too, had been administered a drug to keep her from remembering all those years ago.

Tanya's eyes grew huge in the dusky light. "Sheila? What if… Did you think maybe…" She sighed, shaking her head.

"What, honey?"

"Well, you know the wolf could be anybody. Maybe someone from the school, maybe not. It might not even be a…man." She held Sheila's gaze, nibbling at her lower lip.

"You mean human?"

"I mean *man*."

Sheila felt anew the chill that had not left her since stepping foot onto the desert tonight. "You mean you think it could be Betsy."

Tanya's eyes filled with tears. Her chin wobbled, and she nodded.

Sheila wanted to cry, too. She wanted to escape this place and never return. But she couldn't escape the imprint the wolf had placed on her all those years ago. It was time to break that connection forever, and to make sure the wolf was stopped.

The bitterness of the peyote in my mouth is not nearly as bad as the agonizing throb in my gut, which has increased without mercy. It's so hard to will away the pain as I administer the injections to my young charge, and the injection of immunoglobulin into my own arm.

I reach for another syringe and brush aside some pots of paint—these paints have been so useful to me these past years. I can cease to be just an ordinary person when I wear my careful covering. I become the wolf to all who enter my tent…and now, once more, my hogan. I become the wolf to myself.

April looks toward the entrance. "I hear someone coming."

I turn sharply, then double over in pain. It is excruciating, and for a few seconds it is all I can do not to cry out, attacked on two sides, with injury and illness. Moving slowly, I creep to the hogan door and peer out. The breeze, more gentle in this hollow of the desert, rains soft kisses on my burning skin. As my eyes grow accustomed to the darkening of the sky, I catch a movement in the piñons.

I retreat into the shadows, drawing the skin cape more securely over my shoulders as I watch the approaching figure. It's Sheila. I see the paleness of her skin, the dark hair, that stance she always takes when she's considering something—arms crossed, legs braced.

Why didn't I hear her coming? How did this little drugged brat realize Sheila's presence before I did? How much power must Sheila command, when even the energy I received from Steve's dying blood did not prepare me for her arrival? His attack must have drained more from me than I realized.

I consider the sand painting, the curse I sent to Sheila. Did she manage to deflect it and turn it back on me?

Sheila stood in the shadows, ashamed of her sudden timidity. This was where it had all happened. She smelled the smoke drifting from the center of the hogan roof, thick enough to choke her. She saw the rectangle of firelight through the doorway—a west-facing doorway that was considered evil by the Navajo.

But there was no time to dwell on it now, or to try to remember. *Lord, You are my strength, my help. You brought me here, to this place, at this time, for a reason. Go with me now.*

"Betsy? April?" Sheila called, hearing the tremor in her voice. "Are you in there?"

A sudden cry reached her, soft and brief.

"April? Honey, is that you? Is Betsy in there?" She took a step toward that evil door.

A movement caught her attention from inside, away from the glow of the fire. A small, slender form stepped in front of the light, casting a shadow along the ground. A whisper emanated from somewhere in the hogan, and the small form stepped to the doorway. It was April.

"Honey, we need to get back to the school," Sheila said. "It's getting late." She had a flashlight in her medic kit, but if Betsy was in there, and she was sick…

April skittered back into the shadows. Sheila stared through that entryway and felt the barriers around more memories begin to crumble. This was the place of her nightmares.

She had to go into that hogan, not only to get April and, perhaps, Betsy out of there, but to find the answers she'd been seeking.

"Lord, be with me," she whispered as she walked to the hogan, paused at the entrance, and then entered the smoky, firelit dwelling.

There was a sudden movement to her right, and something sharp jabbed her in the right thigh. She cried out, stumbling away. And then she looked back.

The nightmare. Fangs bared and menacing in a gray face, a long snout, angry eyes, a coat of fur outlined in flames from the fire.

"Were you looking for someone?" came a guttural voice she knew only from her nightmares—her memories? It was unlike any other voice she had ever heard. She thought of Jamey's words when asked who the wolf was. The wolf, in Jamey's eyes, was simply the wolf.

Mesmerized by the form and voice, Sheila could only stare, slack-jawed. The tug at reality caught her with such intensity that it was as if she were again that little girl, weak and helpless, at the mercy of a terrifying power. Now she knew it was true. There was definitely a power here.

A demon?

"What are you doing here?" the harsh voice demanded.

Sheila swallowed. *God help me.* She wasn't alone. Never alone. "What are you doing with April?" Her voice trembled, but she was surprised she could speak at all.

"April is not the reason you are here."

The lines of the room began to waver. Sheila suddenly felt

as if her blood had thickened in her veins. She glanced toward the doorway. The straight edges of rectangle were no longer straight, but curved and curled like a slithering snake.

Was help on the way? Where was Tanya?

She returned her attention to the wolf. She knew this was only a human in animal skins. She could see the legs in buckskin, the human hands.

"You're not dealing with a child this time, wolf." Her voice sounded as if it were echoing through a long pipe. She closed her eyes and focused. The wolf had drugged her...some kind of hallucinatory drug. She had to think hard about what she was saying. "I'm taking April home. Where is Betsy?"

"That old woman?" There was scorn as well as puzzlement in the harsh voice. "What have we to do with her?"

Sheila glanced around the room. There was no one else, only April and the beast. Unless Tanya could have been right.

"April, let's get out of here," Sheila said. "I'll take you home."

April's heavy-lidded gaze traveled from the wolf to Sheila. She was most likely drugged, as the wolf had drugged other children. It was the screen of forgetfulness that allowed this animal to continue. April backed around the stone circle of the hearth until the flames licked and fluttered in front of her.

Sheila glared at the wolf. "Release the hold you have on her. She has to go home to her family."

"You don't tell the spirit of the wolf what to do."

The cold harshness of the wolf's voice echoed through Sheila's memory, plucking chords of darkness from the distant past. There really was a spirit of a monster beneath those dead skins. Someone else existed in that body, as well, but this could not be Betsy. Sheila's beloved old friend could not contain the hatred Sheila heard in this wolf's guttural voice. And a woman's voice could never be that deep…could it?

## ✍ Chapter Forty-Four ✍

The van sprayed gravel across the sidewalk as Preston swung in next to Sheila's Jeep and saw the darkened windows of her apartment. He leaped from the van and raced to the door.

"Sheila!" He pounded with his fist, tried the handle and for once found it locked. "Sheila!" He pounded again.

No answer. He'd called Blaze barely two minutes ago. The clinic had three patients, all with rising temperatures. Blaze was alone and busy. Sheila had taken off into the desert with Tanya, and they hadn't returned. That terrified Preston.

What terrified him even more—and impressed the daylights out of him—was that Blaze had taken fresh blood samples from the patients who had come to the clinic, and he had run those samples under the microscope. He had not diagnosed Marburg virus, which needed special equipment, but he had discovered plague. The Marburg virus and the plague— Two of the most deadly diseases on earth, both right here at the school.

What were the chances? None. The only way two of the world's most deadly diseases could show up at the same time and the same place, originating from opposite sides of the world, was if they were planted here. Bioterrorism.

Canaan, who had been fielding calls from the CDC and the FBI on his cell, was less than five minutes away. He would go directly to the clinic.

Wouldn't the CDC have a heyday when they discovered what was here? Canaan was agonizing over the possible spread across the Navajo reservation of the deadly disease because most of the children and staff had scattered to their homes. How many others would be exposed before everyone could be brought back to the school? And if Marburg and plague were both rampant on the reservation, where else might they have been planted? The country was barely prepared for one deadly bioweapon, much less two or more.

Preston jumped into his Jeep, praying in earnest as he drove into the desert, avoiding rocks and dodging arroyos that appeared suddenly in the deepening gloom. Faith—that elusive quality of heart and mind he had so often wished for and never been able to manufacture—continued to elude him. He felt himself teetering, with the rest of the world, on the edge of destruction, with no one to stop it. Still, he prayed.

Betsy battled her way to consciousness at the sound of knocking. If she lived through this, those knocking doors would haunt her dreams for years. If she lived through the pain.

Before she could gather the strength to answer the knock, the caller left.

Moments later, a key clattered in the lock. Betsy raised her head from the sofa pillow just as the door flew back and slammed against the wall. Blinding light filled the room.

A man gasped. Betsy squinted at the tall, broad-shouldered figure coming toward her. Canaan.

"Betsy!" He dropped to his knees beside the sofa. "This isn't the arthritis."

She shook her head.

"When did it hit?"

"Tuesday night, but I thought I just needed another shot."

"And so you put it off, as you always do." He reached into his pocket and pulled out a surgeon's mask. He placed it over his nose and mouth, pulled some vinyl gloves over his hands and a blue plastic gown over his arms and torso. He reached beneath her and picked her up into his arms.

"What do I have?"

"We'll find out as soon as we test your blood, but it could be bad."

"Am I going to die?"

His arms tightened around her as he carried her out the door. "We'll do everything we can to help you, Betsy."

She rested in Canaan's strong arms. She knew he would do all he could. Though she might not make it, she would still be fine.

Sheila moved with difficulty through the wavering atmosphere toward April on the far side of the hogan. She had to focus to stay on her feet; she couldn't think clearly.

Before she reached April, the wolf growled.

"What a valiant, self-sacrificing woman you are," the wolf mocked. "Like your mother."

The words made sense several seconds later. "My mother," she repeated.

She remembered that day when her mother had come looking for her and found her here. Mom had attacked the wolf in fury, screaming and punching. But even the strength of a mother's righteous anger was no match for the cunning wolf.

A whisper of movement drew Sheila out of the memory, but she didn't turn to look toward the source of the sound. Instead, she called to God in grief and agony, silently, unable to form the words in her mind, but knowing He heard her.

She focused totally on the strength she knew she had in Him. God's spirit lived in her. As she had told Preston, she believed she was here for a reason. Maybe this was it. Maybe it was not. But God was with her now, filling her as she prayed, turning the tide of evil with great power.

The wolf's shadow fell across hers on the hogan floor when she opened her eyes. She felt the warmth of another body close behind her.

"Do you think He will hear you?" The sandpaper coarseness of the voice softened to a caressing lilt.

She shut him out. *Blessed are You, Lord. My hope is in You, the Maker of heaven and earth, the sea, and everything in them. You remain faithful forever.*

"How foolish you are," came the voice behind her. "What does God have to do with you?"

Sheila turned, still praying silently. Something about the wolf's tone seemed to have lost its edge.

The wolf retreated a few inches, and though that monstrous silhouette grew in the firelight, an unearthly glow emanating from the bristling fur, Sheila was encouraged. He *had* retreated.

"Lord," she prayed aloud, "break the power of evil in this place. Protect—"

"Stop it!" Though still harsh, the voice seemed weaker, and laced with fear.

"Jesus, break the power of this Navajo werewolf that killed my mother with the very medicine that she needed to keep herself alive. Release the bondage this evil one holds over April."

The wolf turned, and for the first time, Sheila noticed its hunched shoulders. Much like Betsy's shoulders had been hunched in the clinic earlier. Perhaps, when under the influence of evil, this person even hunched over as a wolf would normally do, on all fours.

"Why did you kill her?" she whispered.

"Because she was *biligaana*." Cold, harsh, hate-filled.

"No," Sheila said, looking into the fire. The flame, a constant in all her nightmares, connected her memories in a pearled string of conflicting emotions—happiness over being singled out for special attention; confusion when the wolf began to hurt her with…needles?

Sheila looked back at the wolf. "You killed her because she found you holding a syringe to my arm." The shock of memory once again helped her focus and fight off some of the effects of whatever drug coursed through her system. "What were you injecting into me?"

"I injected nothing! I required a blood sacrifice." He said the words slowly…taunting her?

Again, the lines of the hogan wavered, and she fought for control. She remembered that once, a couple of years ago, when sleep had refused to come to her night after night following Ryan's death, she had resorted to a strong prescription sleep aid. During the weeks she'd taken that drug, she had found her body reflexively fighting to focus and stay awake, as if her subconscious knew something of the dreams that would bring so much darkness. Her mind had learned to focus well, in spite of the power of the drug. Now she relied on that practiced ability, maintaining control with great effort.

She gazed around the interior of the hogan. For the first time, she noticed that in place of the bare wooden beams of a traditional hogan, cabinets and shelves lined the walls.

It was much more modern, neater, than it had been all those years ago, but she had another memory—of vials and cases and syringes. Of alcohol swabs. Of pages and pages of notes…of notebooks and microscopes.

And in her mind, she continued to pray. *Dear Lord, break the power of evil in this wicked place. Show us the light of Your goodness. Your will be done, Your name be glorified.*

She became aware of the wolf's harsh breathing, growing less steady, more broken, filled with pauses. The breathing of someone in pain?

A quickening in the air teased the flames, sending smoke and sparks across the hearth. The evil that emanated from the dead animal skins seemed to dissipate into the air before reaching Sheila. Movement behind her brought her around to find the wolf removing the skins, pulling the cape of fur away to reveal painted flesh beneath…and…was that blood? She looked closer at the gleaming red splotch that mingled with other colors on a very human abdomen. Yes, blood. A male torso, painted with swirls of darkness and streaked with blood.

He tossed the cape into a dark corner and put his hands to his head. No, not his head, but the head of the wolf.

As he pulled up the head, she suddenly didn't want to know the identity of this vile being. She turned toward the doorway. She wanted out of this place, but she could not leave April, who still cowered at the far end of the hogan, watching with eyes of drugged stupor.

The head plopped to the floor behind her, and the wolf groaned, its guttural voice softening…the harsh groan changing to a moan. A very human sound, a different voice altogether.

"Sheila." A voice filled with anguish. Sorrow and defeat. A voice suddenly familiar.

She turned to him, and she saw his eyes. His short, black hair. His broad shoulders. The straight, white teeth bared in a grimace of pain.

No. It couldn't be.

# ⊹ Chapter Forty-Five ⊹

The headlights of the Jeep danced across the dark terrain, and Preston held fast to the steering wheel with both hands, evading boulders and anthills and an occasional heat-stunted tree as he searched for signs of life. His left front tire plunged hub-deep into a pit of soft sand. He steered hard right and allowed the four-wheel drive to pull him free.

That was when he saw the pale faces of two people in the distance, running toward him, arms waving. He broke free of the sand and gunned the motor. As he drew closer, he recognized Tanya Swift and Jamey Hunt. Sheila was not with them.

Preston slid to a stop as Tanya rushed to open the passenger door, yelling for Jamey to get into the backseat as she climbed into the front. "You came, Preston! We tried calling you on Sheila's cell phone, but the mesas block reception here. We have to get back to her!" She paused, panting for breath. "I'll show you. Hurry!"

\* \* \*

Tentacles of nausea clutched Sheila's stomach and her vision wavered, as if she had opened her eyes under water. One more piece of the puzzle wedged into place, and she cringed in agony. Her mother's killer grimaced, and she saw streams of blood trickling into the waistband of his pants.

"Doc?" *Please, Lord, no. It can't be Doc.*

Eyes as black as a cloudy night reflected the orange flames of the fire. Sculpted lines of darkness formed another wolf below the one he had discarded, but it was Doc, and he was badly wounded.

"Like a snake shedding his skin," he said, his voice hoarse from pain. The evil entity had controlled Doc while he was useful, but now that he was injured and unable to perform, the raw, cutting edge of hatred no longer reigned.

Sheila's prayers had been answered with swiftness and power.

Now Doc's expression was one of anguish that nearly matched her own.

"No," she whispered.

He breathed in through his nose, hard and fast, desperate for any relief the breathing technique could bring him.

"You killed my mother in front of me," she whispered, feeling the pain of this memory, like the thrust of a knife deep into her heart. "You're the monster in my dreams. Of all people, how could it be you?"

Doubled over, he stepped to a metal case beside the entrance. He pulled out a small cactus button. "Did you know peyote has analgesic properties?" He slipped the button into his mouth and chewed like a starving man.

Sheila tried to focus past the fact that this man—whom

she'd trusted and followed around like an adoring puppy when she was a child—was her mother's murderer.

She needed to know more. She needed to know everything. She gazed around the room again. "What is all this? Why were you drawing my blood?"

He shook his head. "None of this will matter in a few hours. You'll forget everything."

Not if she could help it. She would fight to retain these memories. Her sleeping pills had caused short-term amnesia, and she had learned to remain focused, to retain many memories. It could be done.

"You gave me GHB," she said.

He continued to chew his peyote, grimacing at the taste. She recalled the bitterness, herself. She remembered him placing a button of that awful cactus in her mouth. He had apparently fed countless children peyote laced with another drug that would cause amnesia. The GHB.

"You have such a need to know," he said softly. "So much like your mother, always seeking answers for everything."

"If I'm going to forget all about this, anyway, then why not tell me the truth? What are you doing here, and what are you doing to the children? Why did you infect them with Marburg virus?" It was a guess, because last she heard, it had only been a possibility.

Judging by Doc's expression, it was a good guess.

"You know nothing about it. You have no idea what we're doing here."

"Then *what* are you doing? Who else is working with you?"

"My employer is developing vaccines." He closed his eyes, leaning against the door frame. His voice sounded weary. "To save lives. Why explain it? The drug cocktail…you won't—"

"I need to know *now*." She heard the cold anger in her voice. "You owe me an explanation. You haven't saved any lives, you've killed." Her face felt numb, and she rubbed it hard. Had to stay focused.

He sighed. "In war, killing is necessary, and this is a war we're fighting."

"Against whom?" she demanded. "An isolated group of missionaries and schoolchildren?"

"The children are test subjects."

"And you're testing them with a deadly virus!"

"It can't hurt them," he snapped, his eyes opening at that gibe. "It's been attenuated. Weakened to protect the test subjects. Jaffrey shouldn't have contracted the virus. We don't test adults."

"What company would hire you?" she taunted angrily. "All I see is you terrorizing little kids with your elaborate wolf costume, luring them into the desert at night with promises of strength and then experimenting on their bodies, killing anyone, apparently, who gets in your way. Your amnesia drug doesn't work every time. Sometimes your victims remember."

For a moment, she thought he wouldn't respond. Then he said, "When my company hired me, I was a premed graduate with a phys ed major, also trained in phlebotomy. How I conducted my testing was up to me, and I had special training in mind control from one of my professors in college." His eyelids drooped, as if it was too much of an effort to keep them open. "I work for DeBraun Pharmaceuticals."

"That isn't possible." Sheila refused to believe that this killer was employed by one of the most progressive, successful pharmaceutical corporations in the world.

"It's been supporting Johnny Jacobs's schools for seven years now," he said.

"So you weren't an employee when you murdered my mother?" she spat.

"I was, but then federal regulations changed. Our double-blind studies would have been legitimate and voluntary, if the Feds had not shut down our operation soon after your mother's death. We would already be prepared for any attack against our country."

"Johnny would never have accepted donations from a corporation that would use the children as test subjects."

"He doesn't know who's behind the donations." Doc's words were clipped now, impatient. "He's so willing to keep his precious schools afloat that he'd accept help from the devil himself."

"Obviously, he has." Heat from the fire drew perspiration from every pore of Sheila's body; sweat slid down her back. She couldn't believe what she was hearing. How could a pharmaceutical company be so cavalier about the safety of children?

"So not only are you evil," she said, "you work for evil people whose hunger for power and wealth is endangering a whole population of people. The Dineh. Your own people."

"These tests could save millions of lives when the war hits us, and it will save the children here first. Bioterrorism will be the deadliest weapon on this earth, and our kids will already be inoculated against the worst terrors."

"And meanwhile, your employer will reap billions." She knew something about the way the system of drug research worked. First, a company had to apply for a patent, and only then could it begin studies. The patents were good for twenty years before the generic equivalent could be marketed, and it could take nearly all those years just to develop a viable drug. How much more convenient to get all the testing out of the way illegally, before applying for a patent. The money donated to the mission schools would be considered a pittance compared to the wealth that would be accumulated.

"How well your Navajo werewolf complements your employer's lust for wealth and power," she said, watching him.

His breath came in shallow gasps, and he, too, was sweating copiously, but he truly believed what he was saying.

"I was the one who saved Tanya's life Sunday," he told her. "Not Canaan or that E.R. doc, but me."

Sheila recalled the time he had spent alone with Tanya Sunday evening at the hospital. "How?"

"She was the first test subject to receive full-strength Marburg to test our vaccine, but the vaccine didn't work as well as we'd hoped." He paused to catch his breath. "I had to give her the immunoglobulin. It worked. And the vitamins the kids received so religiously? They served a vital purpose. I watched them closely. If any showed signs of illness, they received the replacement vitamins we engineered to carry immunoglobulin through their system."

Of course. The vitamins. Sheila felt sick at the violations performed against so many defenseless children. How would these inoculations affect them in the future?

The wolf had disguised himself so completely over the years that no one had known who was calling them out into the desert and using their bodies for experimentation. Everyone trusted Doc Cottonwood with their kids.

He opened his eyes.

Sheila gasped and stumbled away from him. Tears of blood coursed down his cheeks.

She looked away, and her gaze fell on April, who sat shivering in the spot where she had first run from Sheila. The child's black eyes reflected a deep, gut-wrenching horror.

Sheila found a blanket beneath a workbench and took it to her. "You need to stay here, but you don't need to watch this." She wrapped the unresisting girl in the blanket and turned her toward the wall. "I'll come back for you."

As she returned to the doorway, where Doc stood slumped against the wall, she fought to keep her mind focused. She wanted to grab April and run away from this place as fast as possible. Doc had killed Mom. He'd killed April's parents, and apparently others who might have exposed his activities.

Doc and his colleagues had wreaked havoc on this quiet, rural area, and she was so tempted to leave him alone to his fate.

"Where is some of the immunoglobulin you used on Tanya?" Sheila asked him.

He frowned, glanced toward the doorway, then up toward the roof of the hogan, as if he heard something.

Sheila heard it, too. Tanya and Jamey? No, there was an engine outside.

She knew the sound of that motor. It was Preston's Jeep.

## ✦ Chapter Forty-Six ✦

Preston stopped the Jeep at the edge of a deep arroyo. "You kids ran all this way?"

"We run in track," Tanya said. "I'll show you where she is."

Preston jumped from the Jeep. He and Jamey followed Tanya down the steep arroyo wall and into a small canyon overshadowed by the Twin Mesas.

"This is the haunted valley," Jamey said.

"It's where Sheila went," Tanya said. "It's where—"

A scream rent the air and echoed from the valley.

Tanya grabbed Preston's arm. "It's through these trees!"

He crashed through trees and stumbled over rocks behind Tanya until they came to a hut built into a dirt ledge.

"In there, Preston!"

He shot headlong through the entry, then stopped.

A man lay on the ground beside a smoking fire in the center

of the room, panting in short, ragged gasps. Sheila knelt over him. Blood was everywhere.

"Sheila!" Preston cried, then more gently, "Sheila?"

*Racing Deer is running…far from here…*

Doc felt the shock run through him, so painful that for a moment it blinded him. The blood that beat so hot and fast in his veins found the wound in his abdomen. He looked up at Sheila, but her face was fuzzy. The virus intensified the bleeding, and the wound was like a faucet, spilling his blood…his life…onto the dirt floor of the death hogan. The wolf had not protected him.

"Get out of here!" he growled at Sheila, but she refused to leave. He felt a wet cloth over his forehead, hands on his throat feeling for a pulse.

The pain shot through him once again, an icy-hot stab. He looked down to watch the blood stream down, shiny in the dimness of the hogan.

Smoke burned his eyes. Sheila said something he couldn't understand. He shook his head. The room spun around him. A whisper reached him from the farthest recess of the hogan. *"Racing Deer is running, racing, running…"*

He clutched the wound with both hands. What was happening?

He shook his head to dislodge the voice from his ears, but it continued to taunt him. *"Racing Deer is running, racing, running…"*

He closed his eyes. His hands grew numb. The numbness inched up his arm, spreading across his shoulders and down his other arm. The call continued, *"Racing Deer is running, racing, running…"*

It was a child. A boy named Racing Deer—that had been his name long ago, when he sat in the silent cave, singing to himself in the darkness, alone, afraid and hurting. Singing to ward off his terror of White Wolf.

*"Racing Deer is running, racing, running. Racing Deer is running, far from here."*

Doc knew that the curse he had sent out to Sheila had come back to him. But wasn't that the way he'd really wanted it? He wanted to be Racing Deer again. He wanted to be free, the way Racing Deer had been before he came into contact with the spirit of the wolf.

*"Racing Deer is running, racing, running…."*

His mind went numb until a new pain burst through his chest. Darkness blotted out the fire.

Voices danced in Doc's head, spirits circled him, merging with the air, clawing at the witching heart that had festered and grown within Racing Deer for so many long, lonely years.

*"Racing Deer is running, racing, running. Racing Deer is running far from here."*

The boy was coming for him at last. Now they would be free. Together, they would be free.

But the boy changed. His face darkened. He grew hair. He reached for him. Billy Doc Cottonwood tried to cry out, but the wolf grasped him, pulling him into final darkness.

Sheila allowed Preston to lead her from the dim hogan, aware of April's sobs and Tanya's comforting voice. Her senses gradually awakened to the sudden emptiness of the atmosphere, the dying fire, the dead body lying inside. Would she remember this? Or would she forget again and be haunted by whispers of it for years to come?

They stepped out into the moonlight, and Sheila took a deep, cleansing breath of cold, dry air.

Preston's arm tightened around her. "Are you okay?"

She looked up into his shadowed face and nodded. She felt the fresh kiss of wind against her face. Tears of pain and horror trickled down her cheeks, growing cold in the breeze.

"Let's get you back to the school," Preston said.

Sheila gazed once again at the tortured body of her mother's killer, who'd been destroyed by his own actions. Sheila felt no satisfaction in this knowledge, only a deep, heavy grief.

She gazed up into Preston's face, lit by the fire from inside, and she drew strength from his kind eyes.

As long as this world existed, evil would exist with it. The nightmare for the children had not ended with Doc's death, just as hers would not end. But she had endured that nightmare before. She wouldn't be alone.

"Sheila, I love you," Preston said softly. "No matter what happens, I love you. I'm not leaving your side."

She frowned. And then she realized the import of his words as she looked back toward Doc's body. She could be infected with the Marburg virus.

The drug had its way at last, and she felt Preston catch her as she fell.

Three hours after bringing Sheila in from the desert, Preston sat beside her cot in the cafeteria, where the CDC had set up a quarantine area. Masked people in moon suits tested and treated a growing number of schoolchildren, staff and families, who had been rounded up from distant parts of the reservation by the FBI.

A man could learn a lot if he became a fixture, sitting in one spot for three hours. For instance, through the simple art of eavesdropping, he had discovered that the dog, Moonlight, had not been shot by a shepherd boy, but by a research assistant who worked in a private laboratory owned by DeBraun Pharmaceuticals on the other side of Twin Mesas. The dog had been a research animal infected with plague organisms, and the CDC was now attempting to isolate not one, but two organisms, and perhaps a third. Three of the most deadly diseases known in the world had possibly been unleashed over these quiet, peaceful people. It had been discovered that Doc had been ill with plague because he handled the dead dog's body.

How many more patients would arrive, Preston didn't know. He was in his own protective gear, and he was here for as long as it would take.

Sheila's hand tightened in his. "Hey."

He looked down to find her awake at last, though her face was still pale, her eyes bloodshot.

"It's about time," he said. "You've snoozed half the night away. You could have warned me he drugged you. The agents combed the hogan and found an empty GHB vial."

She nodded.

"How are you feeling?" he asked.

"I'll be fine soon," she said. "GHB has a short half-life." She raised her head and looked around the cafeteria. "The CDC is here?"

"They've been here almost as long as you've been out. They've got some pretty impressive equipment, and good physicians. They've left orders for me to let them know as soon as you wake up." They were eager to debrief Sheila, but for the moment, Preston had her to himself. "Do you remember anything about the hogan?"

A shadow settled into her expression, drawing down the contours of her face. She looked into his eyes, as if hoping to find that her memories were nothing more than bad dreams. Then she looked away.

"Doc killed my mother." All the anguish she must have felt in the desert with that madman made itself known in that simple statement. "He was the wolf. I remember it, not because I remember everything, but because I can close my eyes and see Doc looking at me with the eyes of the wolf."

"I'm so sorry. He's dead."

He saw her surprise. "How?"

"We can talk about all of it later. When I found you, you were kneeling at his side, trying to save his life."

She closed her eyes, squeezing them shut, wincing as if she felt again the awful pain of her discovery. A tear slid from beneath her closed lid. "I would have wanted to kill him."

"But you didn't. I learned a lot from you today, and from Canaan. I learned how one quiet worship service in the name of Christ, in the middle of the darkest part of the Navajo reservation, touched Kai Begay's heart and changed him. He endured horrible abuse as a child at the hands of a white man, he was manipulated by a teacher in college, and yet he allowed the spirit to change him."

Her hand tightened and her eyes opened. She didn't say anything, but her expression changed, questioned, hoped.

"You were right," he said softly. "God does change things. Tonight you tried to save your mother's killer. And I wasn't even surprised, because I know the kind of person you are. You do good for others, despite what they do to you. God worked in Kai's life, and he worked in my parents' lives, my sister's."

Sheila tried to sit up, but Preston gently eased her back

down. "Don't get up and move around. The results of your blood tests are negative for Marburg for now, but it isn't definitive yet."

She frowned. "I remember blood. It was everywhere."

"Doc was bleeding from a knife wound from Steve Hunt."

"So Steve went after the wolf himself."

"And he received a flesh wound for his troubles. He's fine. Steve said Doc was acting really strange, batting at the air like someone hitting flies."

"The spirits, Preston," Sheila said softly. "They're real. Never underestimate the power of those evil spirits that can control and deceive a person. The only power that can conquer them is—"

"God," Preston said. He leaned closer to her. "*Our* God."

Sheila blinked at the significance of those two words.

"The evidence is irrefutable," he said. "For so many years, I've blamed God for allowing my family to suffer through the horror of Mom's schizophrenia, but as I look back, I can see the heritage of faith my parents gave me. I wanted God to change their lives and make everything better. He did something more important by changing their hearts."

"So you grasp the concept of God's grace intellectually now," she said.

"I grasp *Him* with everything I have—my mind, my heart, my soul. This is what I've longed for all this time, to see Him, know and grasp His Spirit for myself. It's like all the pieces of a puzzle have fallen into place, and my life is whole for the first—"

"Sheila Metcalf?" came a voice behind Preston. It was the FBI agent to interview her. The rest would have to wait until later.

## ⊰ *Epilogue* ⊱

The clinic buzzed with activity and the chatter of children. Sheila worked beside Preston, watching him record a child's vitals on a chart. Preston had been instrumental in helping the FBI research years of records to find activity of a certain anonymous donor—DeBraun Pharmaceuticals.

The chaos of this day was nothing compared to the chaos of the past two weeks, as the CDC, FBI and Navajo Tribal Police quarantined the complete lower half of the Navajo Reservation—not an easy undertaking in such a rugged, rural area. Homeland Security placed a high alert. News media from all over the globe converged at the borders of the quarantined area.

Not only had Doc been conducting research for Marburg, but the students of Johnny Jacobs's other schools had been used as unknowing test subjects for double-blind studies. DeBraun had been illegally developing inoculations for hemorrhagic viruses, for plague, for anthrax.

So far, one person had died from the plague. That person was Sheila's beloved Betsy Two Horses. Sheila, and the rest of the school, grieved her loss.

Preston finished with his patient and reached for Sheila's hand. "What a coincidence, we're synchronized, done at the same time for once. You ready for a break? You've been working a lot of hours."

She smiled at him. "So have you."

He didn't release her hand as they walked from the clinic. They passed Canaan and Blaze arguing good-naturedly about a patient file. Canaan's attention immediately went to Sheila and Preston's joined hands, and he raised an eyebrow.

Sheila caught his nod to Preston. The two men had spent quite a bit of time together as they shared what they knew with investigators. Sheila knew they discussed more than numbers and patients, because last Sunday Preston was baptized in the campus chapel. By Canaan York.

A sudden breeze from the desert teased strands of Sheila's hair and instantly dried the perspiration on her skin. Preston slowed his steps and raised her hand to his lips. Since that tragic night with Doc, Preston had been supportive, gentle and kind, but his and Sheila's time together had been limited. A national catastrophe did not allow for personal time. Sheila relished his touch.

"I know you still don't remember much about the night I found you at the hogan," Preston said. "But I told you something important then, and it's something that I need you to remember."

"That may never happen." She had tried so many times to recall the events that had transpired in the hogan that night, but neither she nor April had been much help to the federal authorities.

"You know how I've always admired your faith," Preston

said. "It was that faith, that strength of purpose I saw in you, that first began to draw me to God. It was Christ living in you through all the pain you endured with the death of your husband, the ugly revelations, the efforts you expended to forgive. Though you've frustrated me, I've always admired your refusal to settle for less than what God wanted in your life, specifically a man who also loved Him. I love Him now, because I've been watching your life. I owe you so much. I love you," he said. "That's what I told you that night two weeks ago. I'll be saying it again and again, because I waited so long that it hurts. I didn't want to—"

She threw her arms around his neck, and he caught her up against him. She felt the strength of his grasp, heard his unsteady breathing, smelled the clean scent of him and relished the moment. The barrier was down at last.

"I hate to break this to you," she said, "but that isn't news to me. A man doesn't just jump in his Jeep and drive halfway across the country for a woman he doesn't love. A man doesn't jump in his Jeep and race across a rough desert at night in search of a woman unless he loves her. I love you, too," she said. "But then, you know that."

He kissed her, and the power of his kiss, his touch, his obvious love, solidified a heart connection for her. She might be far from Hideaway, but she was home in Preston Black's arms. She always would be.

He released her slowly, reluctantly, and continued to linger in her personal space. He was welcome there. The man had the most beautiful gray-blue eyes she had ever seen. And those eyes held more love than she had ever experienced in her life.

"What do you say to a convoy as soon as we're released from

this place?" He kissed her cheek. "You and I can take your ratty old Jeep, and Blaze can take my—"

"Hey! Whose Jeep are you calling ratty?"

He laughed. He kissed her again. He drew her close, as if he couldn't bring himself to let her go. "Marry me, Sheila?"

She pulled away and stared up at him, mouth open, unable to contain her surprise.

"I've wanted to ask you that for months," he said. "Until recently I knew what the answer would be." He took her hands and kissed them. "Now I don't."

She did manage to contain a smile. "Obviously you haven't read any how-to manuals for proposing marriage. You don't insult a woman's only means of transportation, then in the next breath ask her to marry you. It just isn't done."

"Will you marry me if I promise you a new Jeep?"

She chuckled. "Most women prefer a ring."

"That would, of course, come with the Jeep," he said. Then all humor left his eyes. "Sheila, there's no other woman for me. I love you more than life itself." He frowned and gazed across the hot desert. "I think I've made that obvious." His attention returned to her, focused totally on her, and his eyes filled with adoration. "You've shown me the foundation of your soul, and you've shared Him with me. I want to share this with you for the rest of our lives."

She nodded. "So do I," she said, and watched the joy of her answer transform him.

"Hey, guys!"

Reluctantly, they turned to find Blaze gesturing to them.

"Come in here a minute! The CEO of DeBraun is about to be interviewed on national news."

Sheila and Preston reluctantly went in.

Canaan, Blaze, Kai and six federal agents were clustered in front of the small television screen in Canaan's office. The interview had already begun with the typical television hype, and Sheila and Preston slipped in the door and stood together.

"...charges being brought against your company for murder and terrorism—"

"That's ridiculous," the CEO said quietly. "Our company exists for the very purpose of protecting this country and others against the evil of the most obvious new threat of bioterrorism."

"Your company has unleashed a whole host of deadly diseases on the Navajo Reservation—"

"You don't understand our use of attenuated bacteria and viruses in a carefully controlled environment on a small test population, far enough removed from the general population that, with proper control, there would have been little risk of—"

"You're talking about children," the interviewer said. "You used children—"

"No one has died as a result of our tests."

"Tell that to the Bob Jaffrey family, and to the school at Twin Mesas, who lost a beloved member of the staff, Betty Two Horses."

"Investigation into those deaths has proved inconclusive at this point."

The man continued to excuse the actions of the company, as he explained the need to accelerate the timetable due to certain outside pressures.

"By outside pressures, do you mean competition from rival pharmaceutical companies also involved in research for these same vaccines?" the interviewer asked. "Aren't you just afraid another company will win the patent—and many billions of dollars?"

"What's wrong with making money while saving lives?" the CEO asked. "That's always been the American way."

Canaan switched off the television. "Sorry, folks, that's all this office can stomach today."

"Oh, Canaan," Preston said. "You're such a traditionalist."

Preston put his arm around Sheila as they returned to the busy clinic. "I love you," he said. "Have I told you that lately?"

She chuckled.

"And have I asked you to marry me? It's been on my to-do list."

Sheila paused as she watched him return to his work. "Thank you, Lord," she whispered as she followed Preston and picked up her stethoscope once more.

\* \* \* \* \*

## QUESTIONS FOR DISCUSSION

1. Do you feel Sheila is being unreasonable when she will not consider marriage to a man who does not share her faith? Have you ever experienced a situation like this?

2. Not only does Sheila have to face down specters from her childhood, but Preston does, as well, and they're both just getting started by the end of this book. How do you feel they should handle the lingering pain from their pasts? What kind of help should they seek from outside sources, if any?

3. Though Canaan York adores Sheila, he is told by Betsy that she doesn't belong in his world. What is she referring to, and why? Is she trying to protect Sheila or Canaan?

4. How difficult do you feel it would be for Canaan to not only observe Preston and Sheila's growing relationship, but to befriend Preston? Could you do the same thing?

5. How realistic is it for Sheila to attempt to save her mother's killer? Why do you think she did so?

6. Betsy Two Horses seems to have a confused concept of the power of the Holy Spirit. How many people do you know who also seem to have strange concepts about God? How often have you changed your mind about something you believed after reading scriptures?

7. Compare the twisted desires of the wolf with the desires of the company for whom he works. Which do you believe to be more corrupt?

8. What preparations have you made in case of future acts of bioterrorism in our country?

9. How would you feel if you were in Sheila's position, traveling halfway across the country to a different culture, risking your life to help others?

10. Do you feel Sheila chose the right man?

*Turn the page for a sneak preview of*
*Hannah Alexander's new historical novel*
Hideaway Home
*available in March*
*from the Love Inspired Historical line.*

*Monday morning, June 11, 1945*

Something was wrong. The news hadn't reached California yet, but Bertie Moennig knew something had happened. She couldn't pinpoint when she'd decided she wasn't jumping to conclusions, but her instincts had never failed her. She would have to wait and see.

It frustrated her no end, because she didn't like to wait for anything. Still in the midst of this wretched war, she'd grown accustomed to it.

Bertie paused in the noisy workroom of Hughes Aircraft to untie the blue bandana from her head. Her hairnet had broken this morning, too late for her to get a replacement, and there were strict regulations about keeping long hair restrained.

Now, half of hers had fallen down over her neck and shoulders, as if this plant wasn't already hot enough. Folks liked to chatter on and on about the wonderful weather in Southern California, but those folks must've never worked in a busy, noisy aircraft plant on a sunny day.

Another trickle of perspiration dripped along the side of Bertie's face, and she dabbed at it with her shoulder while fiddling with the bandana. She'd take a warm day out on the farm in the Missouri Ozarks over working a day in this plant.

Not that she disliked California. She loved it most of the time—the weather, the ocean, the mountains, the different kinds of folks from all over the country—but it could be a challenge for a country girl to get used to the crush of people and traffic, even after living here for eight months.

Back home in Hideaway, Missouri, Bertie would've ridden her bicycle the three miles to work, but Hughes Aircraft was on a busy highway south of Culver City. Riding a bicycle in Southern California would be suicide for her, even though she'd seen other people braving the traffic.

More cars passed by in fifteen minutes on the street in front of the apartment than she would see in a year back home. The crazy pace of Southern California had shocked her upon arrival, and not all that shock had—

"Hey, hillbilly!"

The barrel voice from behind made her wince. She looked around and up at the department supervisor, Franklin Parrish, and braced herself for yet another earful of complaining.

"Yessir?"

"Get back to work. And get that hair up," he snapped, looming too close, as he always did. He eyed the blond hair that fell around her shoulders, then his gaze wandered.

Even though he mocked her Ozark accent and figures of

speech, he made no secret of the fact he liked *her* figure well enough. She knew she wasn't the only one who had to suffer this kind of attention.

Quickly as she could, she tied her hair back on top of her head. "A man in your position should mind his manners, Mr. Parrish," she said quietly, wishing Edith Frost, her roommate, were here. She'd have an extra hairnet.

Franklin leaned closer to Bertie, his face flushed like that of a child who'd been caught snooping in his mother's purse. "And you'd better mind who you're talking to, hillbilly. I can turn you out of here by signing the bottom line on a little sheet of paper."

Bertie met his gaze boldly. He couldn't fire her without good reason, and she was determined not to give him one. After three hundred hours of instruction in St. Louis, she'd been sent here as a trained machinist at the company's expense. He would have to answer for his actions, and for wasting company money.

Still, she wished she'd had the good sense Edith had shown when she requested a transfer out of Franklin's department.

"You want these parts to pass inspection, don't you?" she asked. "We still have a war to win against the Japanese, and I aim to help win it." She smiled to take the bite out of her words, then hoped the smile didn't make her appear flirtatious. That was the last thing she needed with this man.

Franklin glowered. Bertie nipped on her tongue to keep it from getting her into deeper trouble.

Someday she'd go too far, but she didn't think that day had come yet. Her mother had tried to tell her years ago that a woman could get more accomplished with honey than with vinegar, but Bertie had found the two mixed well together.

That was especially true for a woman who'd found herself working in a man's world.

Besides, Mom had never depended strictly on honey to get what she wanted. Bertie knew that honey and cider vinegar were good medicine for several ailments, and Franklin was so cranky most of the time that he must surely have some ailment.

When Mom was still alive, Dad used to brag to the guys down at the coffee shop that his wife was full of more sass and vinegar than any plow mule in the county. Just recently, he'd accused Bertie of taking after her mother a little too much. It made Bertie proud, and it had given her courage when she needed it the most to know that she had some of the same strength of character as Marty Moennig.

Franklin turned away from her work table and strolled toward the next one. "Whose word will they listen to," he muttered over his shoulder as he left, "a silly female, or the man who's in charge?"

Bertie watched him leave, and she couldn't help pitying him a little as she returned her attention to the finishing job in front of her. *Best keep your mouth under control now, Bertie Moennig, if you know what's good for you.*

She felt a pang of homesickness. She missed her father, and couldn't stop worrying about him. She'd tried to place this dread in God's hands several times last night and this morning, but her mind kept grabbing it back again. *Where was he?*

She also missed Red Meyer like crazy, and thinking about him made the anxiety tighten her nerves even more. Though Red was off somewhere in Italy cleaning up after the surrender of the Germans last month, she knew she would feel closer to him if she were back home in Hideaway.

Of course, if Red were back in Hideaway, she'd be there, too.

So many memories…so much she missed. She wanted to be able to step out of the house and stroll around the victory garden in the backyard—had Dad even been able to plant a victory garden this year, all alone on the farm, with so much work to keep him busy?

She wanted to be able to ride her bike the quarter mile into town for a nice, long visit with Lilly Meyer, Red's mother. Bertie had always adored dear Lilly.

Still, Bertie knew she was useful here, serving in the war effort.

Fact was, news of Red hadn't come often enough to suit her lately. He'd stopped writing to her. Just like that, the letters had quit coming. She was pretty sure the Army hadn't suddenly stopped sending home the mail from their soldiers.

She glanced toward Franklin, who'd wandered over to harass Merilyn Hall at the next table. The man was the opposite of Red, which made her miss Red all the more.

Charles Frederick Meyer didn't like being called anything but Red. With a head of brick-colored hair and a blue gaze that looked straight into the soul, he was shy and respectful around women—particularly women he didn't know well.

In contrast, Franklin was brash and demeaning toward everyone he met—especially women. He'd been a machinist for ten years, and was proud of his skills. Bertie had learned from old-timers here at the plant that when the war started and women entered the workforce to help in the war effort, Franklin hadn't concealed his resentment, and had made their jobs tough for them every chance he got.

He glanced Bertie's way, and she started when she realized he'd caught her watching him. A slow smile creased his red-pocked face, and she cringed.

Not only did Franklin have a reputation for harassing women about their work, but he'd also been known to fire a couple of women who didn't respond well to his suggestive remarks and propositions. Sure, he'd always been able to give a reason for the dismissal—too slow at their jobs, talking too much—but he allowed the men to get away with much worse violations with barely a word.

As he slowly walked back toward her, Bertie braced herself. It looked as if she might be his next victim.

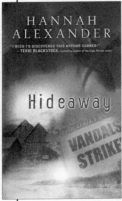

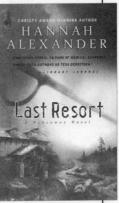

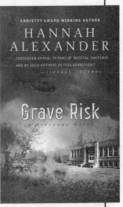

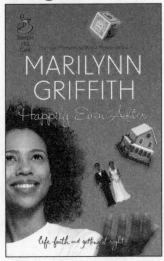